MW01140162

Focused on Murder

A Spirit Lake Mystery

Linda Townsdin

Copyright 2014 Linda Townsdin

This book is a work of fiction. Names, characters, places, brands, media, and incidents are either products of the author's imagination or used fictitiously. Any resemblance to actual events, locales, or persons, living or dead, is entirely coincidental.

All rights reserved. No part of this book may be reproduced, stored in a retrieval system, or transmitted in any form or by any means, electronic, mechanical, or otherwise, without expressed written permission from the author.

The author acknowledges the trademark status and trademark owners of various products referenced in this work of fiction, which have been used without permission. The publication/use of these trademarks is not authorized, associated with, or sponsored by the trademark owners.

Dedication

To Mom

Chapter 1

Perched on my usual stool at Little's Café, I pushed the half-eaten cinnamon roll toward my brother, and took the bait. "Why the smug look?"

Little set the plate under the counter, his head cocked like a snowy owl ready to swoop down on its prey. "I'm remembering when a certain person picked on her younger sibling for leaving teaching to move back home to Spirit Lake."

More was coming.

"A year later, here's the scoffer, a former big fish living in a big pond, now a small fish in a really small pond." He rubbed at a coffee ring, the barest hint of a smile tugging at his mouth.

I let him enjoy his moment. There was always payback. Little is thirty, four years younger than me, and his real name is Jan Johansson, Jr. He inherited our mother's petite frame, delicate features and good sense. I took after our six-foot-two, viperous old drunk of a father, now deceased thanks to me.

Sitting next to me, Little's partner Lars rattled the newspaper. "Hey, Britt, sweet picture you took of the Branson U hockey team getting trounced."

A fringe of pinkish hair stuck out from Lars' stocking cap. The former U of Minnesota English Prof now favored plaid flannel shirts and suspenders—circus clown meets Paul Bunyan.

Little raised an eyebrow at Lars. "It's the first week of January. I doubt she'll make it through an entire winter up here. Shall we make a wager?"

Lars' head bobbed. "Yah, Britt missed the real weather last year."

"Stop talking in front of me as if I'm not here." Baiting me was their favorite winter sport, especially when business was slow. Little's taunts carried an undertone, though. He knew I was restless. I'd moved back to Spirit Lake last summer, newly divorced from my philandering husband and newly fired from my job as a photojournalist at the *LA Times*. I'd come home to heal.

I wound my hair into a band at the back of my neck, and zipped into my ski jacket. "Mock me all you want, boys, I'm here to stay." Wrestling with stocking cap, wool scarf and insulated gloves, I pushed out the door amid a wave of regulars arriving for their morning gossip break, stamping snow and shedding coats. Lars lined up coffee cups on the counter and began pouring.

Soon the row of knotty pine booths along the windows facing the lake would fill. In case customers forgot they were in prime fishing country, glass-covered tabletops displayed maps of Minnesota's 10,000 lakes. Framed photos of fishermen with prize-winning bass lined the walls. Fishing never stopped here.

The aroma of fresh-baked cinnamon rolls, a Little's Café specialty, followed me out the door. Rock waited outside, tail wagging. I strapped on the sleek new Atlas Elektras I'd left propped against the side of the restaurant. Snowshoeing saved me. I used to be addicted to work, then vodka. These days, without much work to do at the *Star Tribune* northern bureau and alcohol taboo for me, I took the edge off with exercise.

"C'mon, Rock, winter in Northern Minnesota is not for the weak of spirit." I'd inherited the shaggy black and white spattered mutt as well as my cabin on the south side of town from an old friend. Gert took me in when I was a confused and angry teenager, guided me and loved me.

I ached with her loss, but felt her presence in my loyal companion. Rock and I crossed the street, passed eight-foot-high piles of snow cleared by plows after the last storm, and veered onto the Paul Bunyan Trail.

Fueled by caffeine and carbs, we left the trail and continued south past my cabin through the dense woods along Spirit Lake. My route skirted a mile of mostly impenetrable lakefront, and this was the first time I'd attempted to snowshoe in the area. Gert bought the land to ensure she wouldn't have neighbors encroaching, and it belonged to me now as well.

After an hour, I took a different route back, hoping it would be easier, but thick underbrush turned the trek into hard work. The sky dimmed to a leaden gray heavy with snow. Weak light might filter through, but we wouldn't see real sunshine for months.

The guys were right in their assessment of how I was handling winter, but the *LA Times* wouldn't take me back and Little wanted me to stay in Spirit Lake.

Daydreams of beaches and 80-degree temps entertained me until my left snowshoe jammed into a snow-covered log and sent me face first into a drift. My left ankle twinged when I stood, but it held my weight.

Rock barked at a brush pile next to the log. He scrabbled in the snow, his behind high in the air.

"What've you found, Rock?"

His bark changed to a high-pitched tone. I leaned in. "Watch it, whatever's in there might take a chunk out of your nose."

Rock backed out with a pink and dark red mitten dangling from his mouth. My radar went up. An odd place to find a mitten.

I knelt for a better look. "Drop it, boy."

It was a white mitten, blood-stained.

Adrenalin pumping, I grabbed my camera from its usual place in my zip pocket and parted the brush. A body, about five-six, and covered with several inches of snow lay in front of me. I gently blew the white powder away revealing a young woman's frozen face. Dark curls tumbled around it and long, black lashes rested against her white skin. Snow White.

Her dark gray boots tripped me, not a log. Dread seeped into my bones, colder than the sub-zero air. I'd witnessed death in urban back alleys and on a battlefield. A dead girl in the middle of the natural world surrounded by pristine whiteness and Christmas trees was an unexpected violation. The cinnamon roll started to come up. I swallowed, framed the shot and photographed her from every angle. Then I checked my cell phone for a signal.

Chapter 2

Sheriff Dave Wilcox rested on one knee next to the body and squinted into the brush. Even though Wilcox had gone soft around his middle, the wiry and wary investigator he'd been in his day lived just under the surface.

"Ah, shit, it's Isabel, Arnie Maelstrom's daughter." He tugged his cowboy hat forward.

"From Maelstrom's Resort?" I asked.

He nodded and lifted Isabel's head. I knew the back side of her skull was crushed. I'd already tampered with the scene by tripping over her, and couldn't resist checking for the red stain's origin.

He got to his feet, brushing snow from his knees. "I don't see how a fall could have done this."

So far Wilcox was treating me with respect. Our relationship took a nosedive after I solved a theft at the casino and Gert's murder last year. He'd called me reckless. Maybe, but I thought he was too cautious.

I continued to shoot photos of the scene, careful not to disturb anything else before the crime scene team arrived. It snowed last night, so no footprints to photograph and measure. The only footprints near Isabel's body were mine and Rock's, and a small creature's, now long gone.

Wilcox mumbled to himself. "Not much blood, so it seeped into the ground or she lost a lot before the killer brought her here."

The stained mitten would be bagged and taken with the body. Most likely, the creature whose tracks were near Isabel had nibbled on her fingers. The other mitten might have been carried away or dropped.

Wilcox frowned at me. "You just happened to have a camera on you?"

Maybe the lack of evidence frustrated him. "Like you, I'm always on duty." I almost always carried two cameras—one hanging from my neck, a lightweight backup and extra lenses in the zipped pockets in the lining of my down jacket. I'd left my best Nikon at the cabin. No way I'd take it out in this weather. Today I only carried the camera in my pocket.

Sheriff Wilcox worked in law enforcement in Denver twenty-five years before moving to Branson so his wife could be near her family, and he could ease into retirement. I expected he was out of the loop after spending the past five years in this quiet county.

Wilcox scouted the area for vehicle tracks. "I don't see any sign of her car. Somebody must have dumped her here."

I pointed to the frozen lake about twenty yards ahead through the trees. "Easiest way would be to drive across it." With twenty-six miles of shoreline, Spirit Lake was considered medium-sized for the state.

He hunched against the cold. "Probably too late on the tracks."

We migrated away from Isabel's still body to gaze across the lake. "I need information for the *Star Trib*," I said. Jason was covering a story forty miles away. The bureau staff was down to three, Jason, an intern, me and Cynthia, our reporter-editor. Our bureau covered fifteen counties and several Indian reservations, the entire North Central area of Minnesota. We kept busy, but that didn't mean we wouldn't be shut down if the economy and newspaper business continued on its current downward trajectory.

"Don't print anything until we notify the family."

"I know, Sheriff." I used my teeth to pull off my glove, located a pen and flipped open a pocket-sized notebook.

He sighed, "Isabel was twenty-one. She went to college up in Branson. A brother, Nathan, one year older, dropped out. Their older brother was killed in Iraq a couple of years ago.

There's a stepbrother who's a junior in high school. Her mother died when she was five and Arnie remarried the next year."

Maelstrom's Resort was located on the north shore of Spirit Lake almost directly across from where we were, although you couldn't see that far. My friend Ben and I worked at the resort to save money for college when the older Maelstroms owned it. The old couple died, and Arnie took over when he retired from the Army in the early '80s.

"Arnie was a war hero, right?"

"POW. Captured and tortured by the Viet Cong. He escaped and signed up for another tour. He's a hero around Spirit Lake. Now I'd appreciate it if you'd stay back until Thor comes."

On cue, a giant red-haired man followed by a teenager trudged toward us on my snowshoe path, carrying a stretcher and backpack. I could have sworn the guy's double was a regular on WrestleMania. He crushed the hand I offered.

"I'm Britt. You must be Thor."

"Nah, I'm Erik, here to help Thor with the body."

"Sorry."

"I get that all the time."

A petite young woman, not a teenager after all, stepped from behind him. "I'm Natalie Thorsen. People call me Thor."

One pink ear poked out from her wool cap. With flawless skin and symmetrical features, she could be at the top of the cheerleading pyramid, even with the multiple piercings. Four gold hoops followed the curve of her ear and a tiny gold spike stuck out from her eyebrow. A diamond stud glittered at the side of her nose.

Thor scanned the area.

I pointed. "Her body's right there."

She reddened and said, "I thought the new reporter might be with you."

"You know Jason?"

"I've seen him around, but we haven't met."

"He's in Cloud Lake on a story. He'll be checking with you when he gets back."

Thor took her backpack from Erik, nodded at Wilcox and proceeded to Isabel. I lifted my chin in Thor's direction. "How old is she, Erik? She looks like a high-school kid."

"Twenty-four. She's been at the sheriff's a couple years. Thor's serious about her work."

I raised an eyebrow. "More like she's serious about seeing Jason."

He crossed his massive arms. "Thor won't miss a detail. She does fingerprints and basics. They'll send the body to the crime lab in Minneapolis for the autopsy."

For the next hour, the baby-faced blond took photos, made notes, zipped the mitten into an evidence bag, and gathered what information she could. She tentatively put Isabel's time of death between seven and midnight the previous night. As Wilcox predicted, the wind blew away any trace of a vehicle on the lake or in the woods. The only tracks were recent ones from the badger, if that's what chewed on Isabel's fingers.

Thor finished and came back to speak with Wilcox. "I've done all I can here. We can head back."

"I believe he killed her somewhere else," said Wilcox.

Thor hoisted the backpack over her shoulders. "Probably didn't expect she'd be found. By spring her bones would have been carried off by animals."

Erik and Thor loaded Isabel's rigid body onto the stretcher and tramped back the way they came. Erik lifted a hand to say goodbye.

Wilcox pushed his cowboy hat back from his forehead, revealing a face creased from too much Colorado high-country air, and witnessing too many crimes against humanity.

"What do you think?" I asked.

"I don't know what to make of it yet. We get accidental shootings during hunting season, accidental drownings, drunks stab or shoot each other in bars, but few out and out murders. At least not until you arrived in Spirit Lake."

I did a double take. "You're saying I'm a murder magnet?"

He took another long look at the scene. "Send us your photos. It can't hurt to have yours and ours."

He shouldn't have insulted me before asking for my help but I let it go. Equal parts outrage at what happened to the young woman and curiosity played a familiar tune up and down my spine. This was real news, and I felt like a racehorse being let out of the gate.

Wilcox pulled his cowboy hat low over his eyes. "Make sure you give us your statement. You got that, Johansson?"

"Got it." Law enforcement always called the shots at a crime scene, but that didn't mean I liked it. When he first arrived, Sheriff Wilcox appeared younger than his fifty-five years. He headed back to his car stooped like an old man. I wouldn't want to be in his shoes right now. He had to tell her family.

I took a ten-minute steaming hot shower to thaw the ice in my veins. Rock curled up close to the antique wood stove between the kitchen and living room. Not as efficient as the new ones, I'd inherited the Franklin stove with the cabin and here it would stay. The two-bedroom log cabin was my second home as a kid, and Gert always said it would one day be mine.

Her nephew, Ben, inherited his family's resort on the other side of town and owned another lakefront home in Branson. He'd been happy for me to have Gert's cabin at first, but now he wished I'd never come back.

The threadbare sofa and nicked round oak table were the polar opposite of the butter soft black leather and sleek glass table in the L.A. condo I'd left when I moved back here, but I hadn't changed much of anything. This was my world now, and it was home.

I picked up my favorite framed picture—Ben and me with a string of fish between us, the lake breeze blowing his dark hair across one eye, my sun-bleached mane parted off-center and hooked behind my ears. We were thirteen, and competed for everything—who could catch the most or biggest fish or swim the farthest. A happy moment before life in Spirit Lake got complicated.

***

I stopped at Little's before going to the bureau office in Branson. Lunch smells mingled with coffee aroma, and the loud buzz of conversation meant everyone knew about Isabel. I found my brother in the kitchen working on an omelet, and asked him to tell me about her.

"At sixteen, she was crowned Spirit Lake Princess at the Fourth of July parade, and now every year she rides on Maelstrom's Resort float." He stopped, spatula mid-air. "I meant that in the past tense. Anyway, don't you remember her from last summer?"

I didn't remember ever having met Isabel. "Cynthia sent me to Pine Lake on a drowning on the Fourth."

Chloe brought in several more breakfast orders, so I said goodbye.

Lars filled my insulated cup with coffee for the drive to Branson, and I asked a few people about Isabel on my way out the door. The consensus was that Isabel was a sweet girl who couldn't have an enemy in the world, and no one from the area would have done this terrible thing.

I headed to Branson, thirty miles north of Spirit Lake and home of Branson University. The *Minneapolis Star Tribune's* northern bureau was in a brick building one block off the main drag. The bureau leased a few offices upstairs from Shoreline Realty, now consolidated into the bottom floor. We also leased the Realty's office equipment and inherited its décor.

Two posters hung on a wall across from my desk. One was an enlarged photo of the Realtor of the Month surrounded by tiny photos of the rest of the staff. Next to it hung a poster with an image of a huge ocean wave and the words TEAMWORK under it. Were the employees supposed to be motivated to work together or to compete for the coveted Realtor of the Month spot? I liked the wave picture, especially in winter.

Head tilted forward and bony shoulders drawn up, Cynthia looked up from her computer. "You found her on your property?"

My stomach quivered. "Tripped over her, actually. Wilcox thought she'd been killed somewhere else and dumped in my woods south of the cabin.

Cynthia pointed toward the door. "Jason's back from his assignment. I sent him over to the sheriff's."

I grabbed a better camera and went to find my young co-worker at the sheriff's office. The two-story building two blocks north of First Street, a shade of green never found in nature, housed the jail, water and parks departments, emergency management and the sheriff's office.

The lobby sizzled with energy. Deputies stood in clumps talking fast, and the phones rang steadily. Murder was a major deal here, especially the murder of a beautiful young local girl. I joined Jason in front of Wilcox's door.

His skinny reporter's notebook open, Jason asked, "Sheriff, can you tell us what happened?"

Wilcox sounded like a recording. "No media information until we get the autopsy report. Her body's on its way to Minneapolis."

Jason tried again. "When do you expect results?"

"Could be weeks." Wilcox disappeared into his office.

Jason shrugged at me. "I'm better at covering sports."

We headed back down the corridor. "Don't worry about it, Jason. We'll find out more information soon." At twenty-four, he was earning his chops at the tiny Branson bureau. He'd fit right in at an East Coast law firm with the navy V-neck sweater, button-down shirt and cords.

I needed to get a handle on the stereotyping. I'd already misjudged Thor this morning, but Jason didn't really seem to fit as a reporter. Ever curious, I asked, "No offense, Jason, but with the pathetic state of newspapers and your obvious apathy for the profession, why are you in this business?"

He shrugged. "My parents are journalists back east. They made it sound like fun. So far, I don't get the thrill." He stuffed his notebook into a jacket pocket. "I wanted to do graphic novels."

The door opened in front of us and a gust of cold air preceded two people. A jowly older man with a paunch, gray hair sticking out in all directions and eyes drowning in anguish marched to the front desk. The bereaved father, Arnie Maelstrom.

A young man with disheveled black curls and fair skin followed. The brother, Nathan, I assumed. He held his arms crossed in front of him, swaying as if ready to topple.

The clerk was speaking on his phone. Arnie's fist smacked the desk. "What's Wilcox doing to find my daughter's murderer?"

The clerk jumped back. "Sir, calm down."

I stepped up. "Mr. Maelstrom, I'm so sorry for your loss. We're with the *Star Tribune.* Can you tell us how long your daughter was missing?"

His head swung around, eyebrows drawn together as if trying to understand my question. "Isabel wasn't missing."

The young man spoke in a monotone. "We just thought she wasn't coming home this weekend."

"Do you mind?" I lifted my camera and clicked. Wilcox appeared and ushered them into his office. I took another quick photo of the three of them, the sheriff's arm around Arnie's shoulder. Arnie said to him, "How can you sit behind your damn desk at a time like this?"

Wilcox shot me a warning look and shut the door.

Jason looked puzzled. "Didn't the sheriff just talk to Arnie at the resort? Why's he here?"

"I'm guessing the family was in shock when he stopped to tell them about Isabel. Some grieve quietly and others get mad."

We were leaving when Thor and Erik passed us in the lobby. I said, "Thor, I'd like you to meet Jason." Her face flushed. "Jason, this is Thor. She's the forensic tech here. Be sure to get her number for follow up."

Jason gaped at the pink-cheeked cherub. "Hi."

Thor stuck her hand toward Jason, and said, "I like your stories."

He held on to her hand a second longer than necessary and snatched it back as if it caught fire. She fumbled in her pocket and handed him a card.

Adorable. The preppy and blond Goth. Beholding love in bloom raised my spirits even if my own love life was a disaster. Ben popped into my mind, and my spirits did a nosedive.

"Thor, can I have one of those cards, too? Wilcox asked me to send over my photos."

Her eyes clouded. "I guess mine aren't good enough." She handed me her card and disappeared into an office.

Jason babbled on our way out of the building. "I didn't know she did forensics. I've seen her with the sheriff a couple of times. Her name is Thor?"

What had I started?

At the bureau, Jason and I got busy on the Isabel story. I transferred photos to the system while he typed up the latest on the murder. It almost felt like a newsroom until Cynthia put down her phone and announced. "It's a local story, I doubt if Metro wants more than a paragraph for the regional section."

Jason and I exchanged frustrated glances across our cubicles. For a moment, I wished I worked for the local Branson paper. They'd do a huge headline and plaster it all over page one. Jason got busy cutting his story to the allotted couple of lines, and I finished the photo captions in case the *Strib*— newsroom shorthand for *Star Tribune*—wanted to use any of them.

Cynthia's phone rang. She answered, "Hello Sheriff, how can I help you?"

Jason and I craned our heads to hear the one-sided conversation through her open office door.

"Yes, Sheriff, I'll make sure they understand."

She hung up and stood in her doorway. "Wilcox says to stop interfering in his investigation. He'll talk to the media when he has information." She shut her door before I could argue.

I turned to Jason. "I found Isabel and that complicates things, but there has to be a way to stay connected to this story."

He thought for a moment. "We could do a profile."

I nodded, thinking out loud. "That could work. A young coed is murdered in a small town where there's hardly ever a crime. Who was she?" I doubted they would use it, but I couldn't come up with anything better.

We conferred, and stepped into Cynthia's office to pitch the idea. She was lukewarm until we said it would make a great sidebar when they caught the killer. Still, she looked more exhausted than convinced. "I don't have time to work on it." Frowning, she said, "Jason, you sure you're up to the task?"

Jason darted a look at me.

I said, "I'll help him."

He nodded to Cynthia.

She sighed. "You can work on it, but only when your daily assignments are finished."

That was all the go-ahead I needed. I grabbed my jacket, "I don't have anything scheduled, so I'll run out to Maelstrom's Resort for a look around, get some background shots."

She continued typing. "Arnie Maelstrom is an upstanding member of the community down there in Spirit Lake. Let the poor man grieve before badgering him with your questions." Her head came up. "And stay out of Wilcox's way."

"Why's everyone so afraid of stepping on toes around here?"

She went back to her computer.

It stung to be treated like a nuisance. I'd worked on a lot of crime stories, from L.A. gangs to white collar, although before getting fired my specialty was photographing what happened to the most vulnerable of the world—especially the children— during war, famine, natural disasters. I shared information I learned from talking to people I photographed with the writers, and sometimes I even got a tagline at the end of a story.

Our piece would run as a crime brief tomorrow, and the *Strib* would do another one when they found Isabel's killer. Finding her killer shouldn't be that hard to do. There weren't that many people around here.

On the way out of town, I pulled into the Forestry Service parking lot. I wanted to ask Ben what he thought about the murder, but hesitated. I couldn't take much more of his silent treatment.

We were best friends when we were kids, and he almost became my lover last year until I made a mess of it. Now he avoided me. A long, sad story I spent too much time thinking about. Wanting him was a habit I had a hard time giving up. I took a deep breath and got out of the car.

The freckled volunteer behind the front counter said Ben was working in the Boundary Waters Canoe Area Wilderness— a million acres of forest with more than a thousand lakes and streams bordering Minnesota and Canada. I once thought his job was tagging deer but learned he most often hunted humans, who used the national forests for all kinds of dirty deeds. Apparently, there was a lot I didn't know about forest rangers. I didn't know they were sworn officers or that they carried guns. I left a message for him to call but knew he wouldn't.

Chapter 3

I left the highway and picked up the Spirit Lake Loop to Maelstrom's Resort. Most of the land and lakeshore belonged to the Ojibwe, and like Maelstrom's, a number of lakeside resorts and summer homes were built on land leased from the Indians more than a hundred years earlier.

The twenty-six mile, two-lane road circling the lake was also my weekly route to a rehab and diabetes center run by the Spirit Lake Band of Ojibwe where I attended AA meetings. I'd become friends with a tribal elder, Edgar, an ancient blind guy with iron gray braids and an entourage of ghost ancestors. He encouraged the Band to make an exception and let me, a non-Indian attend AA meetings at the rehab center, although you'd be surprised at how many blond, blue-eyed people had Indian blood running through their gene pool in this area.

I'd replaced alcohol addiction with compulsive exercising. I whined at my brother and Lars a lot, too. Less painful than therapy, and it seemed to be working.

I took a few photos of the resort entrance before driving between rock pillars holding up the Maelstrom's Resort sign. The elegant entrance was new since I'd last been there as a teenager. I followed the meandering driveway and parked among cars and pickups near the lodge, where neighbors were gathering to support the family.

The resort looked nothing like the rundown grouping of lodge and cabins I remembered. Considering the tough economic times, I was surprised to see cabins freshly painted and others in the middle of construction. Arnie must have spent a fortune updating it.

Already getting dark at five in the afternoon, most of the cabins were barely visible. Many would be closed for the winter, with a few winterized cabins available for snowmobilers and ice fishermen.

In the shadow of a cabin across from the lodge, a teenager with stringy dishwater blond hair hanging in his eyes sneaked a cigarette. I waved and said hi. He stubbed out his cigarette and slouched toward me, his face almost invisible under his sweatshirt hood. A sparse growth of blondish wisps under his bottom lip curled around his pointed chin like a billy goat.

I introduced myself. "I'm taking photos for the Branson bureau of the *Star Tribune.* Are you a relative?"

"I'm Pauly, Isabel's stepbrother."

"I'm sorry to intrude at such a sad time. Any idea who could have done this to her?"

He shook his head, shivered and headed back to the house. "You coming in?"

"I'm just here to get a couple of exterior photos for background. Do you have a minute?"

He stamped his feet. "It's cold out here."

I edged closer. "Isabel's roommate must be totally freaked out by this."

He glanced toward the lodge, too polite to ignore me. "My mom said Amber was a wreck. When Isabel didn't come back to their apartment last night, Amber figured she and Brody were together."

"Brody was Isabel's boyfriend?"

"Yeah." He stepped away.

I followed. "Amber went home after the shock of this, right? Or did she stay at school?"

"She's with her mom in Cooper." Pauly darted a sly look at me. His head shrank back into his hoodie. "I've seen on TV how you guys try to trick people into telling you stuff they shouldn't."

"I didn't mean to snoop. It's awful, but major news and we need to cover it."

"I gotta help my dad." He hurried inside.

I learned that Isabel and her best friend Amber graduated from the consolidated high school in Cooper and roomed together at Branson U. Cooper was the larger town sixteen miles north of Spirit Lake. Give or take a few souls, Spirit Lake's population was five hundred, Cooper claimed a thousand. I passed it every day on my way to and from Branson, population a whopping fifteen thousand. Those were winter stats. In the summer, the entire county swelled with summer residents and tourists crowding the towns and lakes.

Fishermen's Café was Cooper's answer to Little's in Spirit Lake. People in town for an early dinner and to gossip about Isabel's murder were jammed into the overheated restaurant. Wedged between two women at the counter in an animated conversation with the waitress, it didn't take long to pick up the thread.

On my right, an elbow nicked my ribs. "Poor Amber, Doc Johnson needed to prescribe sedatives. She's afraid to go back to school."

I'd scooted over to make room for the other woman's ample behind perched next to me. She leaned over to talk to her friend and nearly unseated me.

"Mary told me she might have Amber finish out the semester at home. It's not much of a drive to Branson from here. You ask me, I don't know why these kids can't live at home."

A trim sixty with skills, the waitress brought my coffee and joined in, coffee pot in limbo. "Saves on rent and you know what they're doing at night."

Three heads bobbed.

Elbow lady said, "The Whitakers have had too much to deal with this year. Amber's dad takes off with his young secretary and now her best friend turns up dead."

Mentally thanking the trio, I extricated myself and took my ticket to the front. Still holding onto the coffee pot, the waitress rang up my bill. I told her to keep the change and asked to see the phone book jutting out from behind the register.

It showed one Whitaker.

The house was halfway up the hill to Cooper High School. Spirit Lake and several other small surrounding towns bused their kids to Cooper. My memories of the school remained vivid. Lots of kids hated their high school experience, but for me it was a place to escape. Basketball helped me forget my days at home running interference for my sensitive brother, and a mother who was no match for a tyrant of my father's magnitude. No one in Cooper knew about my home life, and that's the way I wanted to keep it, until the accident when I was sixteen that changed everything. When I'd done the unthinkable.

Slightly winded from the climb, I stood in front of a modest '60s era ranch house that could use a new roof and fresh paint. The walkway needed shoveling.

A middle-aged woman in stained sweats opened the door. I held out my hand. "Mary Whitaker?"

She shook my hand with a questioning smile.

I lifted the lanyard hanging from my neck to show my press tag. "I'm so sorry to bother you. The *Minneapolis Star Tribune* sent me and we were wondering if we could take a photo of Amber, since she was Isabel's best friend."

She stared at the camera and press tag, most likely torn between ingrained Minnesota hospitality and the unsettling fact that I was a stranger. "Amber's so upset. Sheriff Wilcox said he wouldn't disturb her until she's rested."

"Sure, I understand, but I won't take long."

Icy air blew unchecked into the house.

Her hands fluttered toward me. "Come in, you're half-frozen."

My job in L.A. would have been much easier with these temperatures.

Through the entryway, a figure in the next room reclined on a sofa with a blanket over her legs, and a box of tissues in her lap. I asked the obvious. "Is that Amber?"

Mary hesitated another moment. "Could you wait here just a sec?"

She talked to her daughter as I flexed my toes, willing them to thaw. Amber glanced at me in the entryway, and left the room. I thought that was that, but Mrs. Whitaker straightened magazines on the coffee table, folded the blanket and beckoned to me.

"Amber said she doesn't mind if you take her picture. She wants to put on some makeup first. Coffee?"

No one ever turns down a warm beverage here. I nodded and thanked her. In the time it took for my hands to be wrapped around the cup, Amber returned, her face still blotched from crying. She and Isabel must have turned heads when they were together—Isabel, the black-haired beauty, a contrast to Amber's pale hair and fair skin.

I introduced myself and said I'd like to take her picture for Isabel's profile. "I'm so sorry. I understand you were best friends."

She nodded. "We've been best friends since grade school."

"I won't take much of your time." I fitted the lens on my camera and asked her to sit on the sofa where the natural light worked best. She put on a brave smile.

I took a quick succession of shots from different angles. I asked, "Do you mind talking about Friday night?"

Mrs. Whitaker's hands fluttered again. "I thought you were just taking a picture."

Amber said, "It's okay, Mom." She swiped her nose with a tissue and took a shaky breath. "I thought she was with Brody Friday night. She went home to the resort a lot on weekends, only usually she told me." Mrs. Whitaker sat on the sofa and moved close to her daughter.

I asked, "What did you do Friday night, go on a date?"

"Some friends invited me to go to a club. I got home around eleven. Isabel wasn't back yet, so I figured she was still with Brody. I turned on "Grey's Anatomy." It's our favorite show. We watched it together all the time." Amber's mom put her arm around her distressed daughter.

"Were you concerned when Isabel wasn't there in the morning?"

24

She shook her head. "Sometimes she stayed at Brody's, only don't tell her dad. He would kill her."

Amber's hand flew to her mouth and she buried her head in her mother's chest.

Mrs. Whitaker said she thought that was enough questions for now. She said, "Amber slept in the next morning. She was still in bed when the deputy and I went to Branson to tell her what happened and bring her home." She patted Amber's knee and stood.

I zipped my jacket. I didn't want to cause her any more pain, but asked, "Amber, were Isabel and Brody pretty close?"

Amber sniffed. "She liked him, even when his jealousy made her crazy. I mean, we liked to do things just the two of us sometimes. But he expected her to blow me off to be with him. Guy stuff. They think they own you."

"Did they fight? Was he violent?"

"Not Brody. He's a great guy. Really. Great. He just complained that she should spend more time with him, but she can handle him." She hiccupped. "I meant 'could.' I can't believe she's dead."

Mrs. Whitaker said Amber needed to rest. I took a minute locating my gloves. "Did she mention anything unusual going on in her life?"

"No. I wouldn't have gone home weekends if I had a hot guy like Brody, though." Her face flushed pink.

Mrs. Whitaker led me to the door, her lips pursed.

Back on the highway headed south, my sympathy went out to Amber. If something happened to Marta, my own best friend back in L.A., the bottom would drop right out of my world. Marta and I worked together at the *Times*. She began as a reporter and moved into management early on. She was my boss until she fired me last year because of my drinking and long absences from work. A lot of bad stuff happened that year. I caught my husband, now ex, in the bathtub with an Asian woman when I unexpectedly showed up at our condo. He'd said he was going to be in Tokyo. I didn't get it at the time.

I was still sad about my failed marriage, but by the time we split up after five years of hardly seeing each other, it was clear we weren't much more than party buddies. What hurt was losing the fantasy I'd clung to.

My cell rang on the way to Little's for dinner. The bureau's ID came up on the screen. "Hey, Cynthia, what's up?"

She said, "You need to back off for a while. Wilcox is angry. You've talked to Isabel's brother and her friend before he did."

"It's not my fault he's slow."

"He doesn't have the manpower. He's got all the paperwork and media to deal with."

How could she defend him? "He should be grateful someone's doing his job."

She sighed. "He can shut us out altogether if he wants. Be patient."

The word patience did not exist in my vocabulary. Act first, think later—maybe. Another one of those character defects they talk about in AA. Personality traits I'd been proud of turned out to be what they wanted you to stop.

Another was single-mindedness, or what Little called obsessiveness. One look at Isabel's lovely face and the destroyed mess at the back of her head, and my code kicked in. Do Not Let the Bullies Win. That resolve caused me trouble since grade school. Maybe it came from being the new girl every time my father dragged us to another Navy base. I always had to fight the gang of girls sneering about my height. Little needed protection too. He'd had a tough childhood as a gay kid. Wherever we moved, I warned the bullies if they messed with him I would crack their heads. Unfortunately, our father was the biggest bully of all.

A dozen cars were parked outside Little's, and a red semi idled across the street, partially blocking the view of the lake. The large crowd was unusual for a Saturday evening in January, but not surprising, given the circumstances.

I spied my old friends in a booth across the room. Edgar, a tribal elder of the Spirit Lake Band of Ojibwe and his grandson Henry, chairman of the tribal council, waved me over.

Since Henry took up nearly his whole side, I slid in next to Edgar. "What brings you two to town?"

Edgar said, "Little's wild rice and chicken hotdish is my favorite. He always tells me when it's the special."

My brother made a mean hotdish, but I spent enough time with the old man last winter to pick up some of his habits, and Saturday evening at Little's was out of the ordinary. The ancient guy, nearly blind and suffering with diabetes, seldom left his home until spring except to go for treatments at the diabetes center on the reservation.

"I suppose you heard about Isabel Maelstrom," I said.

They nodded. "Bad business," said Edgar.

Lars came over with a plate for me, too. Always grateful when food appears in front of me, I said, "Thanks, Lars. I'm starving."

"Little says you should eat that salad, too."

He normally would have stayed to talk, but hustled to deal with all the extra customers. I hadn't eaten lunch, so the meal disappeared before I spoke again. "How are things at the casino, Henry?"

"Thanks for asking. Profits are back up, even with the economy in the tank. We're hoping for a good summer to recoup what we lost."

He was referring to a casino theft problem last year that Ben and I were involved in, to put it lightly.

Little and Lars stopped by for a quick chat during a lull, and when the three of us were alone again, Edgar spoke about his real reason for the trip to town.

He sipped his decaf coffee. "I haven't been sleeping well." The frail old man's long braids had thinned, and new lines crisscrossed his roadmap of a face.

Henry's almost black eyes were filled with worry. "He's having bad dreams." He nudged the table away to make room for his oversized body.

"Dreams about Isabel, the girl we found today?" I asked.

Edgar's head tilted back as if listening. "I hear crying on the reservation, but I don't know who's crying."

"Isabel wasn't found on reservation land," I said.

Edgar said, "Ray's looking into it, but he thinks my visions are the foolishness of an old man."

Ray Stevens, a tribal policeman, went by the book, whatever that was. I'd covered stories about crimes at the casinos in California and in Minnesota. Each tribe had its own set of laws and relationships with the local authorities. Local police and tribes didn't have to share information, even though many crimes crossed jurisdictions. I wasn't sure how it worked in Spirit Lake, but the problem of how to share critical justice data that involved traditional justice systems and tribal sovereignty was a big issue.

"I hoped to find Ben here," said Edgar. "He believes my dreams."

"If I see him, I'll ask him to call you." Ben would be better at dealing with Edgar's dream people. I was more skilled at finding out what happened to dead people.

Chapter 4

Sunday morning I grabbed the papers as they hit my doorstep. Jason's—very short—story, with my photos of the family and the resort ran in the *Strib* regional section, exactly where Cynthia said it would be. They used Isabel's high school grad photo. Her lips were parted in a look of pure delight. In the original photo she wore a filmy white top that set off her rose red lips and violet eyes, but all but her black curls and porcelain skin was lost in the black and white image printed in the paper.

The Branson daily ran an A-1 story on the murder. They used her high school photo, too, and an old one of Arnie in his Army uniform, pre-paunch and with military-short hair. The article said no one was in custody and quoted her boyfriend, Brody Wozniak, saying he hadn't seen Isabel since four in the afternoon on Friday. They didn't have any more information than we did, but my competitive nature wasn't pleased at the great play it got. Of course, the paper had only a fraction of the *Strib's* circulation.

Wilcox answered his cell, and after we got through the pleasantries of him warning me to stay out of his way and to check with him first before talking to anyone about Isabel, I asked, "What's the official cause of death?"

"Blow to the back of the head with a blunt instrument."

That confirmed what we already knew. "Was she raped?"

"No."

"So a random rapist-killer isn't preying on girls around the campus. Especially since she was found in Spirit Lake and not Branson, right?"

"I'm not speculating at this point." He hung up.

I watched the news while getting dressed. Most of Branson's TV stations played rebroadcasts of the Minneapolis stations. They showed Isabel's picture and reported the basics about her life and family.

In yesterday's broadcast, Wilcox spoke to a group inside the sheriff's building. "We have not found her car. We're looking for a 2012 silver Escalade." He repeated the license plate number a couple of times.

Arnie and Dee hadn't joined the sheriff at the press conference as parents of lost or murdered children sometimes do.

My stomach growled for Little's Sunday brunch, so Rock and I trekked the mile from the cabin to the restaurant. The temp was above zero. Where was my sunscreen?

My heart did a hesitant blip when I entered the café. Ben sat at the counter with a plate of eggs in front of him. As usual, several townspeople were gathered around him to say hello.

I hadn't seen him in weeks and watched him for a minute. Hawk nose, faint lines fanning out from the corner of his eyes. He spent most of the time outdoors. At six-two, Ben was four inches taller than me. He'd filled out since high school but was still lean. Years earlier, I'd taken a photo of him by the city dock squinting into the sun in a white t-shirt snug against the muscles in his arms and chest, the breeze ruffling his dark hair. The photo went everywhere with me. And that was before I fell in love with him.

The group moved on, and I ambled up to the counter, not wanting to appear too eager. He started to smile when he saw me, checked it and tilted his head instead. Still mad, then. Little and Ben were talking about Isabel. I slid onto the next stool and listened, ready to join in the conversation.

Brown ponytail swaying, Chloe leaned across the counter and handed Little a breakfast order. He took the ticket and headed for the kitchen. "Gotta whip up some pancakes for the folks by the window. Great to see you, Ben. It's been too long."

Chloe set a cup of coffee in front of me without my asking. I always wanted blueberry wild rice pancakes for breakfast, so she didn't ask about that either. Ben continued to eat his eggs. I fidgeted with my spoon, wanting to beg his forgiveness or say something charming. "Do you know Isabel's boyfriend, Brody Wozniak?" I asked, mentally slapping myself on the forehead. That's the best I could do?

I knew from covering college hockey in Branson that Brody was one of the star players. His family owned an outfitter business in Ely, one of the entrances to the Boundary Waters Canoe Area Wilderness where Ben sometimes tracked criminals.

He set his fork on the plate. "I'm friends with Brody's dad, Woz. He's been guiding twenty years up there." Ben glanced over at me. "Remember, you met him last year when we stopped in his outfitter store?"

I recalled the compact man with a full salt-and-pepper beard, deep-set eyes and a heavy brow who supplied us with maps and directions. "He wasn't big on small talk."

Ben darted another quick look at me. "What do you want with Brody? Wilcox questioned him."

I concentrated on stirring my coffee. "Wilcox won't give me any information."

"No, he wouldn't."

"It's just that Brody might have been the last person to see Isabel alive, and Amber said they had a stormy relationship. It makes me curious."

Ben lifted his fork again.

"Jason and I are doing a profile on Isabel for the paper."

Ben wouldn't be thrilled that I was on this story even though it wasn't his jurisdiction this time. Last year I disrupted his ordered life by forcing myself on him and his casino theft investigation. I knew I should leave him alone, but asked, "So what about Brody?" I stirred so hard my spoon got away from me. Coffee splashed onto the counter.

He put his fork down again. "He's a hothead, but what hockey player isn't? Helps his dad guide in the summer. Do you mind if I finish my eggs?"

I asked, "Want to take a ride up there to talk to Brody?"

He put money down and slid off the stool. "Not my business."

"You didn't finish your eggs."

"They're cold." He grabbed his jacket from the next stool.

I didn't often have a chance to be this close to him, and was scrambling for a way to prolong this moment. "Wait." I put my hand on his arm. "I forgot to tell you Edgar and Henry came to town last night. Edgar wanted to see you about a dream of girls crying on the reservation."

Ben's right eye squinted. "He asked you to tell me that?"

I nodded. "He didn't give any details. Henry said he keeps having the dream."

"I'll stop on my way to Branson."

"Mind if I tag along?"

"Not this time." A cross between hurt and anger flashed across his eyes as he left.

I sagged back onto my stool like a dog that's been told it can't go for a ride in the car. That was not the first time Ben took the wag out of my tail. Not that I didn't deserve it. When I returned to Spirit Lake last summer, after a fifteen-year absence, we'd become more than friends, although not quite lovers. Then I went back to my cheating husband, now my ex. I didn't stay with Richard for long, but it was enough to lose Ben's respect and his love. I'd rather he yelled at me than to continue to freeze me out this way. A moan escaped my lips.

Little set a smoothie and a stack of pancakes in front of me. "He'll come around. You put him through hell last year."

"Thanks for reminding me what a jerk I am."

"Was." He pointed, "Drink your smoothie."

"It's green, Little." He liked to sneak in healthy foods like kale and spinach along with my carbs. I gave him a bad time, but they usually tasted good.

For the next few minutes I stopped thinking about Ben and about Edgar's girls, dream and dead. Little's pancakes had that power.

When I was finished, Lars came by and added my empty plate to the pile in his hand. "What happened with your coffee?" He swiped at my splatters with his towel.

"My spoon was nervous. Thanks, Lars."

"Not a problem." He took the dishes into the kitchen.

You couldn't call Lars handsome, but his was the sweetest smile around. Little charmed with his food, Lars with his personality. Ben sort of adopted Little as a younger brother when we were kids, and he'd been Little and Lars's champion when they first opened the restaurant. At first, some of the locals didn't like the idea of a gay couple right in the middle of town, but everyone respected Ben, and one taste of Little's cooking was enough to blast through the prejudice.

I punched in a number on my cell. A gruff-sounding man answered the phone. "Wozniak's."

"Mr. Wozniak, this is Britt Johansson from the *Minneapolis Star Tribune*, and we're doing a profile about Isabel Maelstrom. I understand your son dated her, and we want to reach him for a quote."

"He's busy."

"Uh, Woz, Ben Winters said to tell you hello and that he thought you'd let me talk to Brody." The lie slipped out before I knew what happened.

"Hold on."

I tossed the lie in with the rest of the sins in my storehouse. No wonder Ben kept his distance.

Brody agreed to meet me at the hockey rink in Ely at three o'clock. He said he needed to get some practice in. He wasn't going back to school until Monday. I called Jason to ask if he wanted to join me.

"Really? I'll come if you want me to, but I sort of had plans."

"No need. I'm just going to take his picture, and I'll jot down a few notes if he says anything we can use."

"Great. Thanks." He sounded relieved.

Ely is several hours northeast of Spirit Lake, depending on the weather. The drive wound through the Mesabi Iron Range, passing through Grand Rapids and Hibbing, a city that claimed the largest open pit iron ore mine in the world, and Bob Dylan.

Most of the iron range towns produced notable hockey players, not poets or musicians of Dylan's stature.

I knew what Brody looked like from shooting Branson U hockey games. It didn't take long to find him at the rink. He was the guy in a Branson U jacket beating the hell out of a puck. Compact like his dad, his muscles strained against his jacket. I decided not to interrupt—better to let him get it out of his system. The team would win every game if Brody played with the same ferocity in Branson. I moved closer and shot him in action. Covering college sports events in my bureau job was more of a challenge than I'd expected. It's not easy to get that great dunk, flying tackle or puck smashing into the goalie. Sports photographers have mad skills.

The Zamboni started up, a signal to everyone to clear the rink, and Brody skated over. I met him at the bottom of the bleachers.

"I recognize you. You're that blond photographer who takes pictures at the games, the only female one." He skated in tight circles in front of me.

"I'm Britt. Can I buy you a hamburger?" Young guys were always hungry, and I hoped a full stomach would calm him down.

"No thanks. My mom is making her fried chicken."

He sat on a bench to change into his boots and we clumped up to the bleachers. He dropped to a seat, jiggling his legs like he was ready to bolt.

I sat slightly apart from him. "I'm so sorry about what you're going through. I know it's hard."

He rocked forward and back and stared at the exit door as if I held him prisoner.

"As I said, we're doing a profile about Isabel for the paper. Could you tell me about her?"

His brows drew together over deep-set eyes like his father's. "I thought you were just a photographer."

I let that go. "I'm helping the reporter out. He's out on assignment." I prompted. "Everyone says what a great person Isabel was."

The words exploded from him. "All the guys wanted to date her, but she loved me."

I pulled my notebook and pen from one of my zippered pockets. "Do you mind if I write down a few things while we talk? I'll need to give these to the reporter for our profile."

He kept talking as if he couldn't stop if he wanted to. "She was friendly to everybody. She probably got into a conversation with some random creep passing through town, and he grabbed her." He glared at the ice.

I wondered if that was exactly what happened. "Did you see her before she went home last weekend?"

"Sheriff Wilcox already asked me that question. We met at the student union after class on Friday, and she said she was going home. It ticked me off. She'd just been home the weekend before, and I thought we'd hang out."

I leaned in. "She often went home?"

He nodded. "Either she worked on resort stuff with her dad or she wanted to see her brother. I thought she spent too much time with her loser brother. She said they were best friends. I have two sisters, one older and one younger and I am not best friends with them. They're my *sisters.*"

He was getting heated up again. I put more space between us in case one of his powerful arms shot out to make a point and accidentally connected with me. "I heard Nathan's had a hard time since their older brother died in Iraq a couple of years ago."

He snorted. "A guy has to man up sometime, doesn't he? Instead Nathan drinks and gambles. He doesn't do any work at the resort, and their dad is always getting him out of messes. My dad wouldn't put up with that for a second. My dad and I guide in the BW every summer. It's how I help pay my way through school. Nathan had school paid for him, and he dropped out. Loser."

He glanced at his watch. "I hafta go."

I put away my notebook, and waited while he grabbed his gear. I kept pace with him on the way out to the parking lot. "So what did you do Friday night with no Isabel, a movie?" I asked.

"Me and a couple guys went to O'Reilly's and got hammered and then me and my roommate went back to the apartment around midnight." He looked at his watch again. "The sheriff's deputy already asked me this stuff."

"I won't keep you, but what time did you go to the sports bar?"

"Maybe nine or ten."

He angled away and hurried toward a black Chevy truck with giant tires, a Branson hockey team logo on the back window.

I called out to him. "No need to mention our conversation with Wilcox. Just between us, okay?"

"Yeah, as long as you don't tell my dad I went out drinking when I should have gone home to help him over the weekend. He didn't want me going out with Isabel, and he didn't like me out with the guys instead of helping him." He crunched across the parking lot, got into his truck and shot out of the parking lot.

I yelled into the wind. "Why didn't your dad like Isabel?"

Chapter 5

In the morning, I paid a visit to my favorite coven of news. An arc of elaborate script across the window proclaimed Bella's Beauty Shop, half of a lavender-trimmed duplex. Bella and her daughter, Violet, lived in the adjoining unit. The salon was on a side street two blocks north of Little's, tucked between a souvenir and antique shop, both closed for the season.

Violet waved her scissors above a woman with a cape covering her clothes. "Britt! We haven't seen you in a while. I'll be finished with Jen in a minute." Violet did the cutting and waxing and coloring now that Bella's hands trembled with Parkinson's.

She spoke from a rocking chair near the front window. "When are you going to let us cut your hair? All the ladies your age in town look stylish with the bi-level where it's shorter in back and longer on the sides." She picked up her knitting needles.

"You're right, Bella, I should cut it so I look like everyone else." I made a face at her.

She always brought out the snippy teenager in me. If Bella had her way, everyone in town would have short hair permed and sprayed into a helmet that could withstand a blizzard. Bella's hair hadn't changed in two decades, except to fade from brown to white. Mine hadn't changed either. I'd worn it long since I was ten.

"You always were a smart mouth." Bella stabbed the needle into the yarn, made a circle with her thumb and pulled the yarn through.

Violet lifted my hair and let it fall down my back. She said, "Don't listen to Mother. Your hair looks like honey poured right from the jar. It's pretty."

I mouthed, "Thank you," and she went back to Jen's cut.

Parkinson's kept Bella from working on hair with scissors and dyes, but it didn't stop her from working on people's heads to ferret out the gossip. The center of Spirit Lake's news her entire life, she placed her chair at an angle so she could hear everything in the shop, and still have a full view of the street. You could read the weekly *Cooper Gazette* from the bigger town sixteen miles north of Spirit Lake, or you could hear the real story from Bella.

Violet's lipstick, blush, fingernail polish—even the bow holding up her cascade of strawberry red hair—was pink. The last time I visited, she had platinum hair and Lady Gaga red lips and nails.

"Lovely nails, Violet." Anyone who could keep their nails perfectly shaped and colored deserved my respect. I'd given up that effort long ago.

Violet's face was like a cream-colored Lenox plate, her nose a mere blip on the shimmering surface. She beamed. "It's a new color sample of my fave products, Ocean Shell pink. Let me do yours?"

"You know manicures are wasted on these hands."

"That's from doing things like chopping wood." Her tiny pink mouth pouted. Both mother and daughter had pale blue eyes and rounded light brown brows, although a web of lines had settled into the folds on Bella's face.

Bella glanced up from her knitting, "Looks like you could use a brow wax, dear. A shame you don't have Little's eyebrows."

My brother's eyebrows sat like golden wings above his eyes. I'd always been jealous of them.

Her needles dug at the yarn. "At your age, you don't want to let yourself go. Violet hasn't been on a date in over a year, but I keep on her to be ready just in case."

Violet rolled her eyes. By my calculation, she was past forty. I perched on the corner of a lavender divan and opened an *O* magazine.

Bella took one last shot. "At least Little has put some meat on your bones. You were a skeleton last year. No wonder you couldn't hang onto Ben."

That one hurt. "That's mean, Bella."

She looked away from me, but it didn't take long for her to start fishing. "Sad about our Spirit Lake Princess."

Bella was a pro at gathering information. So was I.

"Her family must be devastated," I said.

"Arnie, for sure," said Bella. "He gave her whatever she wanted, and made no secret that the resort would be Isabel's someday. None of the other kids existed once she was born, especially after his wife died. Isabel looks just like her."

"Her stepmother must be just as sad." I said.

Bella sniffed. "Dee has Jesus for her strength."

"Isabel was a daddy's girl," said Violet. "Dee's all about Pauly, and Jesus of course."

"Is she Lutheran?" I asked.

"No, she belongs to that new church," said Violet. "It's only been here about ten years. Jesus Lives, just outside of town." She giggled. "I don't mean Jesus lives just outside of town. That's the name of the church. They're evangelicals."

"They have services over there non-stop seven days a week." Bella's lips pursed.

I watched Jen pat her new bi-level in the mirror. She said, "You won't see her at town events. She works like a dog at that resort and only leaves to go to church or the grocery."

After Jen left, I took my place in the chair, leaning in close to the mirror. Bella was right. "How about a brow wax, Violet?"

The plain white rectangular church sat on a knoll on the northern end of town. An unobtrusive white cross above the door the only indication it was a house of worship. I passed it every day on my way out of town and back without giving it much thought. The white Jesus Lives sign in front listed services morning and night seven days a week. Below that the sign said, Jesus Knows, in removable letters. Maybe I could get Dee to find out if Jesus knew who killed Isabel.

I took pictures of the church and sign and continued north toward Branson. The skin around my eyebrows stung, but a quick glance in the rearview mirror proved it was worth it. The furry creatures crawling across my forehead had been tamed into submission.

At the bureau, Jason set up an appointment to meet Dee that evening, and we got to work on Isabel's profile. We'd been at it a while when Cynthia motioned us into her office. She pushed her hair away from her face, revealing an inch of gray roots. She needed a trim, too. That wasn't like her.

"I have a call coming in, so this will be quick." She massaged her temples. "Isabel's profile is not our priority. Jason, you need to update several wire stories. Britt, you can photograph the catch of the month."

I inwardly groaned, but knew this was part of the job when she hired me. I bundled up to head out to Branson Lake.

Jason looked relieved. "At least I don't have to drive across the lake. I hate that." Groaning ice and the possibility of plunging into bottomless frigid water running under it terrified him, even if the slab of ice holding up the car was at least three-feet thick.

Gusts of snow blew in my face when I left the bureau. That catch better be a humongous fish.

Later that evening Jason and I met at Jesus Lives and went in together as evening services ended. A squat woman in a pastel blue down coat came toward us. She pointed to the camera hanging from a strap around my neck. "You must be from the paper. I'm Dee."

She led us to one of the church study rooms and gestured toward a grouping of hard metal chairs. I recognized Bella's helmet perm on Dee, who wore no makeup. A natural rosy pink circle dotted each cheek.

I sat in one of the chairs. "Dee, we're sorry to bother you at such a difficult time, but sometimes media attention uncovers new information. It could help the sheriff get this guy."

Jason sat next to Dee and took out his reporter's notebook. "Can you tell us about Isabel?"

Dee tugged at her sweater, crossed her arms over her thick middle and hunched forward in her chair, searching for words.

It wasn't unusual for people to appear nervous around the press. I tried a different subject. "I understand you married Arnie after your first husband died in Vietnam."

Dee raised her chin. "Paul was a God-fearing man." The dots on her cheeks grew brighter. "We all grew up in Spirit Lake. Arnie won't go to church with me, but he lets me go as much as I want, so I don't complain." Her smile wavered.

Jason didn't jump in, so I said, "I met your son, Pauly. He seemed concerned about Arnie. It sounds like they have a good relationship."

Her eyes narrowed. "He's favored his own kids over Pauly, especially Isabel. I guess it's to be expected."

I waited.

"After Paul died in Vietnam, Pauly needed a father. When I married Arnie, Pauly followed him everywhere, worshipped him." Her cheeks flamed. "I don't usually go on like this."

I sat back in my chair so she wouldn't feel crowded. "We won't put this into the profile we're doing."

She darted a look at Jason. "You wanted to talk about Isabel. Everyone liked her, although she wouldn't go to church with me either, and she teased me about being so pious. They all like to make fun of me." Her chin came up. "I pray a hundred times a day."

I did an impression of looking impressed and Dee relaxed slightly.

"I understand she often came home on weekends," I said.

The darting eyes again. Dee grasped the cross hanging from a long cord around her neck. "She loved the resort and always came up with projects to bring in more customers. Isabel was a business major."

"Do you have any idea who would have done this to her?" asked Jason.

"Some sick person hanging around the college, no doubt." She was still holding onto her cross.

"I'm sure the sheriff will figure it out," I said.

She sighed. "Would you like to pray with me?"

Jason looked at his watch. "Sorry, I've got to get back to Branson." He thanked her and hurried out.

I stood with my head bowed while Dee silently prayed. When she finished, I asked if I could take her picture. "We can go outside if your church has a rule about no photos inside."

"It's fine." With no prompting from me, she stood under a crucifix, crossed her hands in front, and lowered her head in a classic martyr pose. I shot from several angles, not happy with the florescent lighting.

After the stuffy meeting room, the icy blast outside was almost welcome. I asked, "Have you set a date for Isabel's funeral?"

Dee zipped her jacket up to her neck. Her short frame encased in down made her look like Humpty Dumpty dressed for winter. "They haven't released her body yet, so we're not sure when it will be."

Another surge of color flushed her cheeks. "Arnie insists on having it at the Lutheran church in Cooper." She spat out "Lutheran" as if she meant devil-worshiping heathens. "Jesus Lives isn't good enough." Her lips clamped together, biting off more words. She hurried to her car humming a familiar hymn, but the title escaped me.

I got into my SUV and pulled up next to Dee, still waiting for her car to warm up. I gestured to lower her window. "Were Pauly and Isabel close?"

She shivered. "He's four years younger, so not close like with Nathan."

"Nathan was a year older, right?"

She nodded. "They used to be practically inseparable, but not lately. They got into it again last weekend. It ended up with her crying. Nathan's supposed to be working on the resort since he dropped out of college, but all he does is drink and gamble. Pauly works harder than the other kids and gets no praise at all."

Typical mother protecting her offspring. "You didn't find out what they argued about?"

Her lips formed a thin line. "I don't believe in snooping."

In my experience, people who said things like that were usually guilty of it. "Who was home when you left for church on Friday evening?"

Dee ran the windshield wiper to clear the remaining ice. "Arnie had a VFW meeting and Nathan went to the casino. Pauly ran a resort errand. The sheriff knows all that. Bye now."

Her tires spun as she pulled out of the parking lot.

Dee's photo under the crucifix and a few lines could be used in the profile, but not much else. Either she blurted out personal information or didn't respond to a question at all. Stress caused people to act in unusual ways, but I wondered if Dee behaved oddly because of the circumstances or if it was her normal personality. I pulled out of the parking lot and drove home, looking forward to a quiet evening with Rock.

Ben's truck headed toward me on my way through Spirit Lake. His arm shot out the window signaling me to stop. A flutter of optimism lifted my spirits. I lowered my window and smiled. He didn't return it, so not a social interaction. My heart settled back into its normal tentative quiver when he was near me.

His words came out in a white huff. "What did you do to Brody? His dad is furious. You told him I sent you?"

"I just wanted him to let me talk to Brody. He doesn't know me and he likes you. I asked Brody a couple of questions for Isabel's profile, that's all."

He leveled the Ben Winters scowl on me, full throttle.

I lifted my hands in surrender. "I swear."

"He came home so disturbed after talking to you he drove right back to the college, and didn't even wait for dinner. His mother said he loves her fried chicken."

"He just lost his girlfriend. Wouldn't you be a wreck if someone killed the girl you loved?"

The accusing look subsided.

I wanted him to believe me. "If you'd seen the way he thrashed the puck around before we talked, you'd know it wasn't my fault."

"You don't want to get Woz mad at you."

"I'm not afraid of that jack pine savage." I asked, "Want coffee?"

"Thanks, but I have to get back to Branson. I drove down here to deal with another busted pipe in one of the cabins. I keep them open for the snowmobilers, and they always do something stupid that ends up costing more than I make."

It never hurt to try. When his dad passed away, Ben took over Winters' Resort on the northern edge of town. Now he lived in Branson near the Forestry office and hired people to run the resort. If not for burst pipes, I'd never see him in the winter.

"One last thing, Britt. Please don't go snowshoeing for a few days. We don't know what we're dealing with. Isabel was on your land." His window slid up. Snow sprayed from the back of his tires as he took off.

A hopeful smile plastered itself to my face the rest of the way to my cabin. He couldn't be too mad if he was worried about my safety.

Chapter 6

I strapped on the Electras and set out from my cabin with Rock running alongside. Ben was too cautious yesterday. No killer would be out at the crack of dawn, and I needed to think. I'd already done a hundred sit ups, squats and some pushups, but was still agitated.

I powered through the snow, my mind on the puzzle. People do horrible things in the name of love and money. If Brody was jealous of Nathan, wouldn't he have killed Nathan, not Isabel? Arnie willed the resort to Isabel. Nathan would be next in line, and people killed for much less. I needed to talk to Arnie and Nathan.

Ice crystals formed in my nostrils, and the dead quiet unnerved me. After half an hour, Rock and I retraced our path back home. No exploring alternate routes this time. Eyes seemed to be watching from behind every tree. Ben spooked me after all.

I dressed for the day in my usual black wool sweater, jeans and boots. Some days required thermal underwear. A big difference from L.A., where my wardrobe was black tank top, jeans and sandals. Black jacket for dress-up.

Cynthia emailed the day's assignments. I scrolled through them, prioritizing. The panel on local campaign spending could wait until later in the afternoon. Those gasbags could talk all day, and I only needed a couple of shots of the speakers. Just what the world needed, more photos of people at podiums or seated around a dais, but I wouldn't complain. I'd easily have time to talk to Arnie before going to Branson.

***

At Little's, I worked through a stack of wild rice and blueberry pancakes. In between taking care of customers, Little and Lars answered my questions about Arnie. They said he was friendly, belonged to the Spirit Lake Chamber of Commerce and Veteran's Club, and was Chairman of a Vietnam POW group in Minneapolis.

"He always volunteers for community events," said Little.

Lars pointed to a round table in the back. "He's a regular here in the winter when he's not busy at his place. Some of the resort owners get together in the afternoons for coffee. He gets along with everyone."

"Some are jealous his place does so well while they're struggling," said Little. "But everyone feels bad for him over this."

Lars poured coffee for a customer a few seats from me at the counter, and said, "He's not flashy, doesn't gamble, and he made the resort a grand place to leave to his daughter."

The customer nodded.

Father and daughter obviously had a special bond. Arnie could tell me more about her habits than anyone.

I waited in my black SUV. A six-foot pile of snow across the road from the resort made handy cover. I'd learned a few stalking tricks from the paparazzi during my *LA Times* years and knew people revealed more if they were unprepared. Little said Arnie usually stopped for coffee mid-morning after doing errands in Cooper early in the day.

I didn't have to wait long. Arnie left at nine, turning north at the highway. You couldn't miss the resort van. Both sides were covered with a giant Maelstrom's Resort logo flanked by pine tree graphics. The back graphic showed a grinning family waving from their canoe. "Maelstrom's Resort, a family tradition" was scrolled across the top.

Arnie parked in front of Cooper Hardware. After a minute, I followed him inside and pretended to be fascinated with furnace filters. He shuffled through the aisles as I trailed behind at a discreet distance.

I intercepted him in the plumbing aisle with an outstretched hand. "I'm Britt Johansson, doing a profile for the *Minneapolis Star Tribune* on Isabel. I work for the Branson Bureau. We met at the sheriff's office."

The buttons on his shirt didn't match up. His hair looked like he'd been running his hands through it. He'd missed several patches shaving. He shook my hand. "I remember. What can I do for you?"

"I'm aware it's a terrible time for you, but could we talk for a few minutes? Maybe our article will cause someone to come forward who might have an idea of what happened to your daughter."

An ache emanated from his gaze like heat waves. "I can't talk about it yet." He gripped a U-shaped piece of pipe.

Sub-zero for days, maybe his cabins had frozen pipes like Ben's. "Sure, I understand. Looks like you might be having problems with pipes bursting."

"It happens this time of year." He turned away.

"I've just moved back here. I'm Little's sister. Maybe you knew my dad, Jan? He served in Vietnam too, several years before you."

Arnie must have decided to be a good sport with the nosy photographer. He faced me again. "Sure, I remember your dad worked at the Post Office. Booze got to him, right?"

"Yes, it did."

More like it got to the whole family. Tall and skeletal, my dad lived on coffee loaded with sugar and blackberry brandy. He perched in our midst like a vulture, picked at our self-esteem, shredded our spirits, ripped at our hearts. Once, as a gawky thirteen-year-old, I mustered up enough courage to stand before him and ask why. He stared out the window until I left the room. An answer of sorts, I suppose.

Arnie said, "I'd hate to count all the guys who came out of that war with either a drug or alcohol problem. I don't touch it."

I ran my hands along a row of pipe fittings. "How long were you in?"

"Ten. Intended to make a full career of it but the folks died and I came back to take care of the resort."

"I heard your parents passed away. I'm sorry."

He tried once more to move on.

"The resort has never looked better," I said.

He stood straighter. "I've put my life into it." The color drained from his face. "I did it all for Isabel. At first I fixed it up to sell so Sybil, Isabel's mother and I could move to Minneapolis. Sybil was a French Canadian beauty who stood out like a rare flower among all these blond-haired blue-eyed Scandinavians. No offense."

"Isabel must have taken after her."

He nodded. "She was just like her mother, beautiful and smart. I met Sybil after I came home from Vietnam. I fell hard for that woman." He sniffed. "She died in a car accident that rough winter when Isabel was five."

"I'm so sorry." The poor man I'd accosted in the hardware store already lost his wife and a son and now a daughter. "What made you keep the resort after all?"

"I had the young ones to raise, and married Dee. Then Isabel became so fond of the place. At ten she said, 'Promise we'll always live here, Daddy.' " His eyes watered. "And I promised her. She was going to take over the resort in a few years when I retire." Arnie rolled the pipe between his hands. "Nathan's not interested. I have no one left."

That surprised me. "What about Pauly and Dee?"

"Yes, of course, they're a great comfort." He stared at the pipe in his hand as if he couldn't remember what to do with it, set it down and hurried up the aisle and out the door.

I followed him. "I heard you're the go-to guy around town if anything needs to be done for the community."

"I've taken every opportunity to promote Spirit Lake. This was my daughter's town, and I wanted it to be the best for her."

At his van, I asked if I could take his photo for our profile.

He turned, one hand on the van door. "Of course." His smile didn't reach his eyes.

I lifted my camera. "Does the sheriff have any leads yet? He's not letting the bureau in on his investigation."

Arnie's face twisted. "Wilcox hasn't left his fucking desk, but I'm going to find the sonofabitch who did this and rip him apart." The menace in his voice raised the hair on my neck, but I kept shooting. He yanked open the van door. "Now stop hounding me with your questions and pointing that in my face." He peeled out of the parking space, fishtailing on a patch of black ice.

I deserved that. I'd stalked him and goaded him to reveal his true feelings so I could get a good photo. And I'd learned something about him. Like most people, he lied. He'd said he didn't drink, but an unmistakable whiff of alcohol shot out of his mouth along with the anger. No wonder Dee shuddered when I asked how he was handling Isabel's death.

The exchange with Arnie left me feeling guilty and exhausted. My watch said noon so I headed to my assignment. Shooting campaign finance meeting photos would be a welcome break.

Cynthia phoned me as I was finishing up. The *Strib* newsroom editor in Minneapolis wanted me to shoot a breaking story about a meth bust in Cloud Lake—an hour northeast of Branson. I would have preferred to work on the profile, but an opportunity for our little bureau to prove its worth by getting a good story was the first priority. There was constant talk of closing the Branson bureau due to the economy and low readership. It wasn't like there were a lot of job opportunities up here. Isabel's profile would have to take a back seat for the moment.

Jason must have been watching for me to pull up to the bureau. He hurried out, jumped in and said, "There's no reason to stay here. Wilcox won't talk to me anyway."

When we arrived at the scene on the outskirts of town, men with FBI emblazoned on their jackets led an emaciated guy from a clapboard house. A news van was set up along the street. I grabbed my camera bag and hopped out, already framing my shots, thinking ahead to what I needed, doing what came naturally. Jason hustled off to ask his questions.

Within an hour, we were on the way back to the bureau. Jason was nearly bouncing in his seat. "That raid was the coolest thing I've ever covered."

I kept my eyes on the road. There'd been a slight warm up before a quick temperature drop. Patches of ice lurked, waiting to send our car careening across the highway. "What did you find out?"

He flipped through his reporter's notebook. "The guy's nickname is Snowy. How lame is that? Anyway, they're not saying a lot, but they expect him to rat out at least twenty guys who sell his stuff. Some, but not all, are from the reservations."

I'd gotten good shots of the building and Snowy being taken into custody, shaggy brown hair partially hiding his face, skinny arms and legs and a pot belly. They wouldn't let me in the front door, but one of the police officers assisting on the case said they found several bags of meth, guns and cash. They'd do forensics on his cell phone and find phone numbers for his dealers and contacts spread out across the region. An investigator left the house with Snowy's computer under his arm. Forensic techs would find even more information there. Technology helped investigators solve crimes, but in my experience, the bad guys were always a step ahead with the latest tricks.

A phone message awaited me at the bureau. Arnie said he wanted to make up for his rude departure at the hardware store and asked if we could meet for breakfast at Little's. He wouldn't have needed to do that. I'd caused the upset, but I jumped at another chance to talk to him and called back.

Dee answered the phone in a whisper. "He's in his office. He goes in there and cries. I hate to bother him when he's so upset."

"Please don't disturb him. Just tell him I'll meet him at Little's at 7:30 tomorrow."

Dee said she'd give him the message. Still whispering, she said, "He's so lost without Isabel. She always helped in the office."

It was past eight by the time I filed photos and wrote captions for the Cloud Lake story. I headed home with a snarling stomach, and aching shoulders from lugging camera equipment all day. I was getting soft.

Two miles from Spirit Lake, I rounded a bend and saw the sparkling lights of the Dreamcatcher Casino. My hands tightened on the steering wheel. The casino replaced the old Spirit Lake Tavern from my childhood, and the scene that changed my life when I was sixteen played out in front of me as it did every time I passed this spot at night.

Chapter 7

It was the night Tom called me from the tavern to get my father out of there. He'd gotten into a fight with a customer. My dad had the car so Ben dropped me off. He didn't want to leave me but I insisted. "Tom always helps me get him in the car."

I entered the dim bar. A neon beer sign with rippling blue water cast a weak light into the corner where my father sat worshiping at the temple of blackberry brandy with a coffee chaser. His hollow face swung toward me, red-veined bulging eyes trying to focus.

"What the hell you doing here?" He tossed off the rest of his drink.

"C'mon, Jan, Britt's taking you home." Tom hooked my dad's arm over his shoulder and I took the other side. We got him out the door and down the steps. It was so cold the snow squeaked under our boots.

With our help, he folded his long body into the passenger side, and sat tilted sideways glaring at me. I started the car, jumped back out and scraped ice off the windshield.

Back in the car, I let it warm up, our icy breaths fogging the windshield. His cigarette slid through his fingers and onto the seat. I grabbed it and threw it out the window. The engine was stiff, but I put the car in gear and headed toward Spirit Lake. The cold revived him. "You drive like an old lady. Give it some gas."

I spoke through clamped teeth. "The roads are bad."

He lurched toward me and grabbed at the wheel. "I'll drive."

The car swerved and I batted his hand away. "Are you trying to kill us?"

"You're just like your sissy brother and your cowering mess of a mother—afraid." He sounded like a schoolyard bully. "I thought I had one shipmate I could count on, but you're worthless just like them." He rubbed his hands together as if washing his hands of our whole sorry crew.

I stepped down on the gas, knowing it was dangerous. I wanted him out of the car.

His fist curled. "Hurry up. I have a surprise for Little. That's the last time he humiliates me in front of the whole town."

His tone scared me. My foot came off the accelerator. "What happened?" With a sinking feeling, I knew this would be bad.

His eyes mean, he said, "Sonofabitch at the bar said he saw Little and that Jensen kid holding hands at the creek. That makes me sick. I'm going home to teach him a lesson he'll never forget. Should have beat that out of him a long time ago."

He'd thrown Little into the kitchen wall two weeks earlier and dislocated his shoulder. I wouldn't let it happen again.

"No, you're not." I braked, the car slid to the side of the road and stopped. Nearly gagging at the sour smell of cigarettes and alcohol, I reached over my father, opened the passenger side door, brought up both feet and kicked him out of the car. He hit the ground with a grunt and rolled into the ditch.

My head exploding, I said, "I hope you die out there." I jammed my foot on the gas and shot forward. The passenger side door slammed shut as the car swerved and straightened.

In less than a mile, I hit black ice, hydroplaned sideways into a ditch and slammed into a stand of birch. My dad wandered drunk in the snowstorm until a car hit him. Everyone assumed he'd gotten out of the car by himself and that I was going for help. When they found us, it was already too late for him. I woke up a couple of days later in Branson hospital with head injuries. The passenger side took the impact, or I'd have died, too.

***

53

Shortly after Dad's death, Little went to live in Minneapolis with Mom while I stayed with Ben's Aunt Gert until graduating from high school. I left for L.A. and didn't return to Spirit Lake, even when Little and Lars moved back three years ago. The fact that Little really wanted me to come to his restaurant's grand opening and I hadn't still bothered him. He pointed out that I traveled all over the world at a moment's notice but couldn't come to see him. It wasn't Little I was avoiding, but Spirit Lake and the bad memories. When I was racing around the world with my camera, I could forget.

Last year I'd confessed to Little the reason I hadn't been back to Spirit Lake for so many years. He insisted that I would have gone back for our father if I hadn't crashed into a tree on the icy road. But I don't know if I would have, and I'll carry that black spot on my soul for eternity. I still wake in the middle of the night feeling his death grip on my arm. His eyes glitter, and he whispers in my ear. "Are you happy now?"

My goal since my return after getting fired from the *LA Times* was to undo some of the damage I'd done. Little and I were on better terms now, and I loved my brother, but until the day I found Isabel, I was going crazy from a lack of real purpose. You can only be nice to your brother so many hours in a day.

I shook away the old memory, and the tight band of anxiety around my chest loosened. I pulled into the Dreamcatcher parking lot and hunted for a space. You could mistake the casino for a contemporary church with its rock and cedar façade and peaked roof, but instead of a cross, a gigantic iron dreamcatcher sculpture faced the highway.

A full parking lot indicated that too many people had nothing better to do on a Tuesday night. My steps crackled like breaking glass as I made my way to the front door. Minus sixteen degrees with the wind chill.

Inside, it took me a few minutes to adjust to the change in atmosphere. After weeks of snow and gray skies, the flashing and rotating colors disoriented me. I'd been here a few times with Lars, usually on slow nights at the restaurant when Little asked me to get Lars out of his hair. Lars considered his visits to the casino therapy for cabin fever. He favored Queen of the Nile Poker with its pulsing purple and yellow jeweled scarabs. He even claimed a lucky slot.

My eyes adjusted to the noise and bright colors, and I found Henry in his office, his broad body bent toward a computer. As tribal chairman, Henry kept a close watch on the casino's balance sheet. He swiveled around in his chair when I tapped on the door.

"Britt, come in." He smiled and his eyes disappeared behind apple cheeks. Everything tickled Henry.

I stood just inside the doorway. "Want to have dinner with me?"

He patted his stomach. "Always."

We were soon seated at a plush booth in the quieter restaurant space. A basket of rolls and waters instantly appeared. The restaurant was famous for its fresh walleye in the summer, but we both ordered steaks. Henry sipped his water and I downed two rolls while we waited for dinner.

I asked, "Has Edgar mentioned his dream about crying girls?"

He nodded, a shadow crossing his eyes. "At his age it's not healthy to have trouble sleeping."

I told Henry what I'd learned about Isabel's family and friends so far. We stopped talking for a moment while the waiter brought our salads and refilled waters.

I took a few bites. "Good salad."

Henry said, "I think there's kale in it. No more iceberg wedge with blue cheese. We have to scramble to keep up with Little's. Your brother's café keeps stealing our clientele." His eyes disappeared in a smile again.

The waiter took our empty salad plates and said our dinners would be right out. I relaxed against the soft booth. It didn't take long for Isabel to pop into my thoughts.

"There has to be a thread leading to Isabel's murderer, Henry. I'm still looking for a chance to talk to Isabel's brother, Nathan. Have you seen him lately?"

"He's almost always here." Henry spoke into his cell phone. "Locate Nathan Maelstrom and call me back."

A moment later it rang. He listened and put the phone back in his pocket. "He's at the blackjack tables." Henry bit into a roll. "Behind the bar to your left."

I wanted to jump up and catch Nathan before he left. Henry saw my distraction. "Go ahead and relax and eat your dinner. He'll be here until we cut him off at the bar. Couple more hours."

I settled back down. "What's your opinion of him? His dad doesn't have much respect for him and Isabel's boyfriend called him a loser. Even his stepmother thinks he's lazy."

Henry shrugged. "He's a kid. He'll grow up."

Our steaks arrived sizzling and juicy along with medallions of sweet potato, and leeks. I dug in. "Not to insinuate anything, but don't you have some kind of a reciprocal deal with Maelstrom's?"

"Sure, we have relationships with several resorts. They shuttle people back and forth all summer, but Nathan never causes trouble and it's not our way to judge. He could use some healing though." Henry chuckled. "Let Edgar work him over."

I cut into my steak. "Right, he could sic his ghost ancestors on the kid."

Henry nodded. "Oh yeah."

Edgar was known for his entourage of what he called ghost ancestors. A few times, I'd noticed a wavering shadow near him and tried to capture it in a photo, but all I caught were blur spots.

After dinner, Henry went back to work and I wound my way through the tables. It didn't take me long to locate the young man. Curly, black hair like Isabel. Unshaven. He could be handsome if his skin wasn't so pasty under the sprouting beard. He wore jeans and a U of M sweatshirt.

Nathan held his cards in a haphazard fan. The man next to him kept his close to his face. I joined the table and played a few hands, observing Nathan and not saying much. The man with a tight grip on his cards busted and left. One by one the others left, and it was just us.

I introduced myself, and showed him my press tag. "Can I buy you a beer?"

He looked at me fully for the first time, and nodded. "Thanks."

We finished our hand and moved to the raised circular bar at the center of the casino. Nathan ordered another beer with a Jack Daniels chaser. I asked for a mock Mojito, hoping it would transport me to the tropics.

"I'm so sorry about Isabel," I said, and explained about the profile. "Do you mind if I take your picture and ask a couple of questions?"

"Go ahead." He lifted his beer in a toast to himself. "Nathan Maelstrom, fuck up. I gamble, and my father, upstanding member of the community, pays off my debts. He tries to ban me from the casino, but I go anyway and he always pays. He doesn't want to be embarrassed." A lopsided grin flashed and disappeared.

"Is that all there is to you?"

"More like all that's left." The bravado disappeared and he looked sad and lost.

I waited until he'd downed the shot of Jack Daniels to take his picture. His face slack from alcohol, he said, "My mother, brother and sister are dead. The Maelstroms are cursed."

I wasn't sure how to finesse my next question, so I just went for it. "Is it true you fought with Isabel last weekend?"

He gulped his beer. "I can't talk about it."

Maybe he couldn't talk about that, but I sensed he was dying to talk about something. "You fought about what? Brody?"

"I hate that hockey jock, but he's not what we fought about." He set his glass down sideways, sloshing it on the bar, a sign he'd had enough. I paid the bill and insisted on taking him home.

I helped him to my SUV, and glanced up at white flakes floating down. A few degrees rise in temperature signaled to the snow gods that it was their turn.

I drove around the lake toward the resort while Nathan talked without much prodding. A haunted looked played across his face. "I have to get away from here."

"Doesn't your dad need you?"

He snorted. "He hates me for not being just like Isabel. She was all he ever cared about. The only one who could make him grin like an idiot." He slouched down in the seat and closed his eyes. "Isabel affected everyone that way."

I drove with care on the icy winding road. Nathan seemed like a good kid, but troubled. I wanted to help him. Maybe I could get Edgar to suggest something. He was always helping lost souls, like me.

My hand went to my pocket for the familiar smooth agate with the wolf paw etched into it, a gift from Edgar last year when I couldn't decide whether to stay in Spirit Lake or return to L.A. He said, "You think of yourself as a lone wolf, but wolves need their packs to survive." He dropped the agate into my open palm. "This will help you remember."

I pulled into the Maelstrom's drive, parked close to the lodge entrance and left the car running. I opened the passenger side door, and the blast of cold air woke Nathan. He leaned on me as we navigated the steps to the lodge. He fumbled with the knob. "Shhh, don't want to wake Dee. She'll start praying and I'll never get to bed."

I nodded. "She's intense."

Nathan slurred. "I appreciate that she keeps the house, cooks and does resort work. It's the Onward Christian Soldiers she hums all day every day that drives me crazy." He laughed, but there was little humor in it.

"One last thing. Who gets the resort when Arnie dies, now that Isabel is gone, if you don't mind my asking?"

His head drooped. "I don't want it. As soon as the funeral's over, I'm going someplace warm like California." A hopeful look hovered on his face for a brief moment. "It's time to deal with it and move on."

The door closed behind him. Deal with what, Isabel's death? My eye caught a movement at the second story window near the upper deck, a shadow moved away, and the curtain fell back into place. Why didn't the person wave to show me the family was happy Nathan was home safe?

Chapter 8

Arnie didn't show at Little's at 7:30. I ate breakfast and headed to Branson. Normally, I would have called to find out why someone stood me up, but excused it because of his sad mental state, or Dee could have forgotten to give him the message. Not a big deal.

I passed through Cooper and had to brake for a familiar kid darting across the street. Hoodie up, he ducked into Eckhart's Drugs. I parked, grabbed my camera and followed him inside. Pauly was late for school.

I ordered a root beer float at the old-timey soda fountain. So what if it was sub-zero and I'd just eaten pancakes? In a few minutes, Pauly came from the back toward the front register with a package in his hand. He saw me and made a quick turn down a different aisle. His hands were empty when he came back into view. I sauntered over, slurping up root beer and ice cream. "Hey, Pauly, I'm Britt. Remember we talked in front of the resort?"

"How's it going?" His eyes did a full circuit around my head without making contact with my face. Typical teenager.

I set my drink down on the counter and reached for my camera. "My newspaper is working on a profile of Isabel. Would you have time for a quick interview and photo?"

"Sorry, I have to get to class." He hurried out the door.

His detour down the diaper aisle intrigued me, so I checked for out of place items. A package of cold medication tablets and a bottle of cough medicine were jammed next to pacifiers and baby lotion.

An older woman behind the cash register glanced up when I pointed out the window at Pauly. "Do you have trouble with shoplifters?"

The woman shook her head. "If that boy saw a twenty dollar bill on the floor he'd bring it to me. Some of the other high school kids get a thrill out of trying to get away with stealing, even the principal's daughter, but Pauly's no trouble. He's a decent student, too."

It wouldn't surprise me if she knew every student in school, what their parents did for a living, and even what they did behind closed doors. I put money on the counter. "Tragic what happened to his sister."

"Must have been some criminal up from the Cities." She shut the register with a bang.

I was slightly sick to my stomach on the drive to the bureau. Root beer floats tasted better in July. Cynthia kept me busy all afternoon freezing my ass off shooting the annual Polar Daze yahoos jumping into frigid Lake Branson. She said the *Strib* might use it in their regional section if they needed filler.

On my way home, I called Ben to whine. "Wilcox won't let his people talk to me. What's going on?"

He sighed. Poor guy. I was such a load.

"The case has taken a turn. Now tribal police are involved."

I sat up straighter. "Are you going to tell me why?"

"They found Isabel's car parked on Spirit Lake not too far from Gerald Jackson's house."

"I know Gerald's son, Tommy. He comes to meetings at the rehab and diabetes center, although not lately," I said.

"The kid's had his share of trouble with the tribal police and the sheriff. Dealing and using meth. He and his girlfriend were into it."

"Last I heard she took off with a guy from Cloud Lake," I said.

"Right, and Tommy got a fifth degree drug violation. She left him when he did thirty days at the tribal jail in Cloud Lake for probation violation. When he got out, going to the rehab center was part of his sentence."

"I'm going out to see the car for myself. Are you?" I asked.

"I'm tied up here."

"Will you at least tell me how to find the spot?"

"You take the north shore loop and turn off at the first road you see."

Ben was never much for long explanations, but at this point, any communication with him was better than none. "I don't remember that road."

"It's not marked and hardly anyone uses it. The Jacksons' place is the only one out that way. It's about three miles from the highway, but you keep going past that to the lake access about a quarter mile. You'll see the sheriff's and Ray's cars. Take a flashlight."

"I'm almost at the turnoff. Thanks, Ben."

"You did not hear it from me."

I found the road and continued on until I passed the Jacksons' driveway. At the road's end, the sheriff's car, tribal police car, Thor's van, and a tow truck were backed up to the lake.

I grabbed my flashlight and followed the path toward Wilcox and tribal officer Ray Stevens standing near Isabel's car. Thor's dim outline moved back and forth, checking for evidence.

Not your usual college student's vehicle, a silver Escalade covered with snow sat on the ice, tucked up against the shore about thirty yards from the lake access. They'd tow the car into town to go over the inside for prints and other evidence. Blood, maybe.

As I shot the scene from all angles, the flash broadcasting my presence, Wilcox stomped toward me. "What are you doing here?"

"My job. Thanks for keeping me in the loop." The cold was giving me a headache, so I pulled my stocking cap down until it nearly covered my eyes, and asked, "Who found the car?"

"Jake Anderson saw it on the way to his fish house across the way." He pointed to the middle of the lake, but I couldn't see much of anything in the dark.

The kid I'd seen at AA meetings sat slumped forward in the back of the sheriff's car. I bent down to the window. "Hey, Tommy."

He shook his head when he saw me. "Man, this is so fucked. I didn't know her car was there."

"Mind if I take your picture?"

He shrugged. "Tell Wilcox I'm freezing my ass off. At least someone could turn on the heat if I have to sit here."

I got a few shots of Tommy shivering in an unzipped jacket over a black T-shirt covered with skulls and a band's name in Old English. His long hair was tied at the back of his neck. He didn't seem to be high.

He raised his chin. "Call my brother, would you?" He gave me the number.

"Where's your dad?"

Tommy stared ahead. "He hasn't been around much this winter."

Tommy's mother died when he was twelve. He lived with his dad, but whatever money the dad made, he gambled away. It wasn't surprising that Tommy got into trouble. He'd been unsupervised most of his teen years. The kid was twenty-two now.

Ray Stevens stepped in front of me with his arms crossed. "No more pictures or conversation."

I let the camera fall from its strap and dug in my pocket for gloves. "Whatever you say, officer." Weren't they used to reporters and photographers around here?

"It's sergeant now."

Stevens was forty, medium build, fit and wore his hair military short. His face had some scarring as if he'd suffered from acne or chicken pox as a kid. He spoke in a low, menacing voice. I wouldn't want to mess with him.

"Congrats on the promotion," I said. "You and Wilcox working this together?"

Ray glowered. "Not exactly."

Wilcox came up and the two stood across from me, their arms crossed over their chests. At least their hands weren't on their guns. I told them to expect Jason to call for a statement.

They scowled in unison. Usually battling over jurisdiction, the two were a united front against media coverage.

Wilcox said, "There's no story yet, Johansson. Tommy hasn't been charged with anything. We just need to ask him a few questions."

"Why the handcuffs? Did you find him with the car?"

"No, but his house is the only one out here. We went over there to ask if he saw anything."

"He lives near where you found her car so you're taking him in? How come you didn't take me in? I live near where I found Isabel."

The sheriff leveled me with a look. "The kid has a history of trouble. He wasn't cooperating."

I involuntarily stepped back. Wilcox scared me a little. "Seems pretty weak for putting the kid in handcuffs."

Wilcox glanced at Ray. "That was Ray's call."

Ray got in his car and busied himself with turning on the heater. "He was acting suspicious."

"Suspicious how?" I asked.

Wilcox yanked his cowboy hat over his forehead, a sign he'd lost patience with me. "Tommy's hiding something, and we didn't want to give him a chance to get rid of evidence. We're getting a warrant. "

Wilcox stalked away and Ray drove off. I wouldn't get any more information from them. I waved goodbye to Tommy, but he stared through me. Tommy had a reputation at the rehab center for his short fuse. One time a guy called him a liar, and Tommy came right out of his seat at him. It took three people to subdue him and he wasn't allowed back to meetings for a month. Tommy could tell stories that made everyone laugh, too, but nobody talked about that.

I didn't get a signal on my cell until nearly in Spirit Lake. Daniel, Tommy's brother from a different father, said he'd get to the sheriff's right away. Tommy talked about how he couldn't live up to his successful older brother in the rehab meetings, but I'd never met Daniel.

I called Jason and filled him in on what happened. "Tell Cynthia I'll send my photos to the bureau when I get home."

"Cynthia's gone home. Is Thor still out there? Maybe I should come out to talk to the sheriff."

"They're leaving for Branson soon. You'll have better luck catching up with her there."

"I'll wait at the jail then." Jason's new-found enthusiasm for reporting was adorable.

The dinner crowd had thinned at Little's. Rock snoozed in the book alcove, but perked up when he saw me. He wagged his back end so hard his whole body wiggled and his lip drew back in a dog grin. I wished I could get that kind of enthusiasm from Ben.

At my usual place at the counter, I took my camera from around my neck and set it next to me. I'd never leave it in the SUV in this cold.

I polished off Little's dinner special of pot roast and vegetables while telling the guys about Isabel's car. I asked, "Is the brand new luxury car hers or her dad's?"

Little said, "Arnie bought it for her. He talked about it in here. His little girl would be safe driving back and forth to college on those icy roads." Little shook his head. "Sad."

I got up from the stool and helped myself to a chocolate chip cookie from a tray. "They hauled Tommy Jackson in. They found her car on the lake near his place."

"Really?" Little dropped down onto the stool next to me. "He's been in trouble before. I heard he got mixed up with meth using and dealing. He went to jail, I know that."

Lars faced us from behind the counter where he could keep an eye on customers who might need coffee refills. "Now he does maintenance at the casino, bow hunts and harvests wild rice."

"I hope he didn't have anything to do with this, but you never know, with drugs," said Little.

"Thanks for the background, guys. You saved me a trip to Bella's."

Little's mouth curled. "Bella could tell you his girlfriend's name, everything about his family background, even how much time he did and where."

Chloe filled salts along the counter, which reminded me that I wanted to ask her about Pauly. They must be about the same grade in school. "Hey, Chloe, what grade are you in?"

"Junior. One more year to go and I am out of here." Her ponytail swished.

"Do you know Pauly Maelstrom?"

Her eyes rolled up. "Everyone knows everyone here."

"What's he like?

She continued her task of filling and wiping the salt and peppers. "He's weird. No one pays much attention to him."

"How weird?" I asked.

Chloe tossed her ponytail again. "He's just not one of the popular kids. You have to be on the hockey team or a cheerleader to be included in that crowd. He works on the resort all the time, so he doesn't do sports and school activities."

Chloe moved away to fill condiments at another table. "I can relate," she added.

She'd worked at Little's for a couple of years, saving up for college. I sat back down on my stool.

Little frowned at me. "Back off, would you? I have to make a living in this town. Not everyone is a sinister killer."

Lars asked, "Why are you checking Pauly out?"

"I saw him earlier today in the Cooper drugstore, maybe pilfering."

"I've never heard that about him." Lars shot Little a "your sister is goofy" look.

I looked out at the darkness. I might be goofy, but someone out there was a sinister killer.

I was about to leave when Arnie Maelstrom came into the restaurant. He waved and returned hellos to the locals across the room, making his way toward me. He'd shaved, properly buttoned his shirt and combed his hair, but his eyes were bloodshot and puffy. He said, "I saw your car outside and wanted to tell you I'm sorry about not showing up this morning. We lost a snowmobiler and I spent the morning finding him."

"Not a problem. Do you have a few minutes now?" I asked.

He smiled. "Of course."

I grabbed my camera and we moved to a booth. Arnie passed a rolled-up bundle across the table to me. I shook it out and held up the Maelstrom's Resort T-shirt, with its familiar logo in black script flanked by two green pine trees.

"Thanks, Arnie." I warmed to him. He didn't have to do that. The poor man had a lot on his mind.

Lars came by with coffee. "Want pie?"

We both declined and he moved on.

I said, "I suppose you heard they found Isabel's car out by Tommy's and he's been taken in for questioning."

He nodded. "I'm glad they got him, but it doesn't bring her back, does it?"

My respect for him grew. I'd expected him to be angry even if Tommy was only a suspect.

Arnie sipped his coffee. "I wanted to meet so I could tell you I'm sorry I lost it yesterday at the hardware. You're just doing your job. I'll even speak to Wilcox about working with you on your profile to make it up to you."

"No need to apologize. I'm sorry for being so insensitive. I'd appreciate a word to Wilcox, though."

"Done."

"About the profile, we'd like to mention your POW experience. Would it be okay if Jason called you later, or could I ask a couple of questions?"

"I don't mind talking about it. There were plenty of other guys who went through more than I did. You're there to serve your country, and you do your best."

"I heard you were tortured."

He rolled up his shirt sleeve. An elaborate dragon tattoo ran from shoulder to wrist, artfully rendered in black, yellow ochre and reddish orange. Something about the dragon's fiery tongue repelled me. I looked closer. The tattoo covered an angry red scar that ran the length of Arnie's arm, ending in grotesque tongue that appeared to reach out at me.

Arnie watched me recoil at the image. He used his finger to trace the scar's path. "The VC carved it into my arm, slowly working their way to the veins in my wrist unless I gave them the info they wanted. I wanted the tattoo to hide the scar, only it didn't work. It looks even worse."

"Could I get a picture of that? I've never seen anything like it."

"Go ahead."

I took a succession of shots from different angles. "Did you give them what they wanted?"

He bristled. "I gave them fake information and figured out a way to escape. Once they found out my intel was false, I'd have been a dead man."

He rolled his sleeve back down.

No wonder people in town respected Arnie. He'd been through a lot for his country. "Little said you're active with the veterans here in Spirit Lake."

"It helps to be with people who've been there. I belong to a group of ex-POWs in Minneapolis, too."

We talked about the Vietnam War for a while—my dad had been in that war too—and then I asked if we could talk about Isabel for our profile. Arnie nodded so I jumped in. "Was there a special reason Isabel came home so often from school?"

His eyes filled. "My daughter loved the resort and liked to spend time with her family." He blew his nose with a napkin. "Lately, we were working up plans for a restaurant nightclub overlooking the lake. Isabel said a summer nightspot would draw young folks."

The conversation was already too hard for him. "I'm sorry, Arnie. We don't have to talk about it."

He nodded and slid out of the booth, shrugging into his coat. "I should be getting back."

I looked around. We were the last two customers in the restaurant. I stood, said goodbye to the guys, and left with Arnie.

Arnie's van was parked near my SUV. I asked, "How's Nathan doing today?"

"I haven't seen him, why do you ask?"

"I gave him a ride home from the casino last night."

"You did? His car wasn't in the drive, but I figured he went with a girl he sees from Pine Lake."

Maybe Nathan slept all day. "Please say hi for me when you get home. He's a nice kid." Something flickered behind Arnie's eyes. My photographer's eye saw a lie, but Arnie got into his van and left before I could discover what it was.

Chapter 9

Tacking back and forth through the fresh snow where they'd found Isabel's car last night revealed nothing so far, and I regretted my early morning trek through the woods. The sheriff's people combed over the area yesterday, and now all tracks were filled in from last night's snow. If she'd been killed in this area, finding a weapon would be nearly impossible.

Dense brush made it difficult to move, but I kept at it until my snowshoe crunched over a fallen branch, setting off a series of crackles. Corresponding shivers traveled up my spine and raised the hair on my neck. Tense since entering the woods, I'd told myself not to worry, Tommy was still in custody.

Avoiding the next branch, I bumped into a tree and got an avalanche down my neck. I wiped the snow away, now chilled to the bone. I'd had enough.

Rock stayed close to my heels on the way back to the SUV, and that made me more edgy. He usually bounded ahead. I wove through the trees, anxious to get back to the car.

Rock's nose lifted to sniff the air. His sharp bark split the quiet and he took off at a run. I snapped around to see what excited him. A blur whizzed toward me, grazed my head and spun me to the ground.

Dazed, I ran my hand over the curve of my ear and felt a hole in my stocking cap. Blood dripped from my finger. An arrow stuck out of a birch tree a few feet behind me. I screamed, "Rock! Come back!"

In the distance, a human shape hovered too far away to identify. What hunter wouldn't help someone they'd accidentally hit? I rose to my knees, lifted my camera, zoomed and clicked as the shape vanished into the trees. Rock took off after him, and I called him back again. I couldn't live with myself if someone hurt Rock.

He came back to me, still barking. I checked my camera. The photo was blurred and no wonder, my hands were still shaking.

When my strength returned, I yanked the arrow out of the tree. Rock whined and circled, itching to chase. I called to him. "C'mon boy, we're getting out of here."

I made it to the car on wobbly legs and set the arrow on the back seat. Needing visual proof that my ear was still attached to my head, I checked the rearview mirror and breathed a sigh of relief. The arrow scraped the skin above it.

With the heat on full blast, I grabbed a handful of napkins out of the console—left over from my usual drive-through lunches—and stuffed them under my cap to staunch the blood flow.

Half-way home, the pain set in. At the cabin, I cleaned the wound, wincing at the sting, and washed the red stain from my hair. I tried to calm down, reminding myself I'd had close calls before. One look at the wall above my sofa told the story of a photographer who frequently got too close to the action.

All I'd brought from my condo in Brentwood was my framed photos. Articles were written about them in photography magazines, and many won awards. The bombed-out buildings in Iraq, the mothers trying to put the pieces of their babies back together. I'd experienced a lot in twelve years at the *Times*. My ex, Richard, said my photos didn't belong in a home. True, they didn't harmonize with the cabin's inherited patchwork quilts and hand-loomed rugs. Yet the odd combo fit me.

I'd almost been killed by bullets, grenades and fire storms, and today an arrow nearly ended my life. The trembling began again when I pulled on a fresh stocking cap to hide the bandage. The arrow was obviously intentional, but I wouldn't mention it right away. The sheriff didn't need additional excuses to keep me away from the story, and if Little found out, he would have a fit. I'd swear Thor to secrecy the next time I saw her and ask if she could get some prints from the arrow.

***

Jason called as I checked emails in my compact home office between the laundry room and garage. I'd inherited Gert's desktop computer and printer along with a hacker kid from the Twin Cities. I contacted Sebastian once when I needed tech help of the dubious kind, hoping his mom wouldn't answer the phone.

Jason had new information. "Tommy's fingerprints were all over the passenger side of Isabel's car and on the door handle. They found hair samples that haven't been identified yet. An eyewitness saw her pick him up on the outskirts of Cooper Friday evening on her way home from Branson. They released him last night into his brother's custody, but Wilcox got a warrant and I'm not sure if he found any evidence in Tommy's house. They won't tell me."

"Wait, did you say Tommy's not in jail?" My hand went to my head.

"He's out, but as I said, that might not be for long. It's not looking good for him."

Another call came in while I spoke to Jason, but I ignored it and finished the conversation.

With a heavy feeling in my stomach, I thought about what Lars said yesterday—Tommy was a bow hunter.

The blinking light on my phone reminded me a message was waiting. I hit play.

"Hey, Britt, this is Henry. If you're not busy, Edgar would like you to visit him today. He gets lonely in his new house. No need to call ahead."

An hour later I set out to visit Edgar after a quick stop at Little's. Once again, I navigated the Spirit Lake Loop's north shore, veering off where the road headed into the center of reservation land. From the air, the reservation would look like a fish's tail. A sign pointed to the right. Edgar Turner 1 mi. I crested the hill and slid down the ice-slick road, braking carefully. Last summer, I'd been to Edgar's when Little and I asked for his help with the rehab and diabetes center, and nearly slid into the lake coming down that hill.

Edgar recently moved into a new cedar home facing the lake after decades in a spare one-bedroom house with a tarpaper lean-to next to it. Lights shone from all the windows of the new house, and welcoming smoke trailed from the chimney. I rang the bell and prepared to wait for Edgar to make his slow way, but two giggling girls flung open the door and told me to come in. Henry's daughters, Emily and Olivia, eight and nine years old, each took one of my hands and led me to Edgar, sitting across from a stone fireplace, a red and black blanket draped across his knees.

The sisters took seats on the sofa next to their great-grandfather to resume the task of braiding his hair. He appeared dignified, even with the sparkly bows Emily added to the ends of his braids, just like hers. Edgar said it was okay for me to take their picture. When they finished braiding, Olivia asked if they could play Skylanders, their new favorite video game.

I picked up a ferocious finned creature from the coffee table. Emily said, "That's Zap. He's my favorite action figure."

"Girls, please bring us some coffee before you play." Edgar spoke to me. "It's their turn to grandfather-sit today. All twenty-four of my great-grandchildren like to take turns helping me."

I handed Zap to Emily. Edgar's old face creased into a grin. "I always have new electronic games for them, but first they have to sit with me and learn our Ojibwe language."

Little once told me Edgar's story. As a young boy, the U.S. government took him from his family to a boarding school, along with most of the reservation kids. They tried to force him to forget his culture. He'd since spent a lifetime making sure no one took his heritage from anyone in his family, ever again.

I offered Edgar the bag of cookies I'd brought from Little's, and he told the girls they could each have one. The girls brought our coffee and left to play their game in the other room. Edgar and I sipped our coffee and talked about Isabel. I told him about the family members I'd spoken with. Edgar knew everybody in Spirit Lake.

"What do you know about the Maelstroms?" I asked.

"Arnie's dad was an ornery fellow, and Arnie was a sulky kid. I don't know, maybe the Army helped him grow up," Edgar said, and shivered.

"Want me to throw another log on the fire?" I asked.

"Yes, thank you."

I took a log from a birch bark basket next to the fireplace and built up the fire, still waiting for Edgar to get to the subject of why he wanted to see me. More was on the old man's mind than a chat.

I sat on the chair across from him, and asked, "Are you still dreaming about the crying girls?"

Edgar's frame looked shrunken in his faded denim shirt and jeans. He rubbed watery eyes. "They won't let me sleep."

A twinge of guilt made me defensive. "I've been trying to find out who killed Isabel or I would have helped you. I guess Ben's too busy on his project right now, too."

Ben was the one with the Ojibwe grandmother. Maybe she passed on some of that mysticism, and he could figure out Edgar's dream.

Edgar said, "I think you two are working on different sections of the elephant."

I leaned toward him. "I need more, Edgar."

The old man's thin shoulders sagged. "I've told you all I know, but I fear time is running out."

"Time is running out for the crying girls in your dream?" I rose from my seat and touched his arm. "I wish I knew how to help."

His bony hand clamped around my wrist. "I asked you to come here for another reason, Britt. I heard Tommy Jackson's in trouble." He let go and gazed toward the fireplace. Ethereal flickers hovered above it. Did a damp log cause a puff of smoke or was this Edgar's ghostly entourage?

I sat back down, looking into the fireplace, wondering if I'd see them again. I first saw them, wearing traditional clothing, blankets covering their shoulders, hovering in the background last summer when I took a picture of the old man standing between his houses. The picture showed only a white spot behind Edgar. They appeared again, watching from the edge of the woods at the reopening of the rehab and diabetes center. The last time was in my hospital room when Edgar encouraged me to go into rehab. I'd been driving under the influence and crashed my car on the Spirit Lake Loop. That was the catalyst for my getting sober and realizing that Spirit Lake was the best place for me to heal. Edgar insisted the ghost ancestors were a benevolent presence, but they gave me the willies.

I tore my gaze from the fireplace, and said, "Tommy's a suspect in Isabel's murder and Wilcox might or might not have incriminating evidence—that's all I know so far. What's the story on his dad anyway?"

Edgar faced me, and sighed. "Gerald's my nephew. He used to work at the casino, but they let him go about three years ago. A shame, he was one of the best dealers, real popular with folks. But he stole chips."

"I heard he has a gambling problem," I said.

"I hope he's changed his ways. He went to work at the casino over at Mille Lacs, but I don't know if he's still there."

"Tommy was a dealer too, in drugs." I touched the spot above my ear. Had Tommy shot me with an arrow?

Edgar leaned forward. "Tommy wanted to learn the skills to be a dealer at the casino but they couldn't chance it. He needed to prove he was reliable, not like his father, and look what happened. Now they think my great-nephew is a murderer."

I asked, "But you don't think so, do you?"

He stared into the fireplace again. "I don't know. You should talk to him."

I'd do anything for Edgar. He and Little were the reason I'd gone to rehab. "I'll try, but he probably won't have much to say to me."

"Take him some smokes."

"Sure, I can do that." Edgar must be related to everyone in Spirit Lake.

Edgar's head drooped. I said goodbye and let myself out into the cold to the sound of giggling and shouting from the game room. Heads bouncing, Olivia and Emily didn't look up when I passed them.

My SUV powered up Edgar's hill fishtailing until the tires gripped its slippery surface. I flew down the other side like a NASCAR driver gone berserk. After swerving too close to a pine looming in my path, I slowed and made it to Branson in one piece. If someone wanted me dead, the job would be done for him if I continued to drive like a crazy woman. Unanswered questions did that to me.

I wasn't sure I wanted to go to Tommy's, not knowing if he shot the arrow at me, but I'd stop at his house after work. Cynthia expected me at the Branson U hockey game and a few good photos tonight might appease her impatience with my Isabel obsession.

Jason waved to me from the press seats. For the next two hours, I shot the game from my position across from the goalie, shooting absentmindedly. Brody's head didn't appear to be in the game either. The guy he guarded taunted him with trash talk, and soon they were in a clinch attempting to tear each other's heads off. The crowd loved it, but the second time Brody got into it, he smacked the ref who tried to break it up. The ref kicked him out of the game.

After waiting half an hour at the team exit door, I accidentally ran into Brody on the way to his truck. I didn't have a specific reason to talk to him, just a need to keep asking everyone close to Isabel questions until something made sense.

He tried to duck away. "Wilcox said I'm not supposed to talk to you."

I intercepted him. "I'm not supposed to talk to you either. Do you always do what you're told? I don't."

"I sucked out there tonight." He kicked at the snow under his boots. "Last game of the quarter." His chin dropped to his chest.

"I'm sorry you lost. You heading to Ely over winter break?"

He nodded. "My dad has a project he wants me to help on."

"You have a close relationship with your dad?"

"He taught me everything." Brody almost smiled. "Except hockey. He can't skate."

"Like what else did he teach you?"

"All the guiding, tracking, hunting stuff. Plus, he taught me to fly."

"Your dad's a pilot?"

"He flew in the Air Force. We have an awesome plane you put floats on for water landings. We drop off supplies to the people we guide for and stuff."

As we went our separate ways, I called out, "If Wilcox asks, you haven't seen me."

I met Jason back at the bureau, uploaded my photos and wrote the captions while he pounded out a story. Cynthia had gone home for the night.

I got ready to leave, and remembered to ask Jason if he'd checked the sheriff's to see if they got anything at Tommy's place.

He hit speed dial. "I'll check now."

After he hung up, Jason said, "Tommy's back in custody. Wilcox found $5,000 in cash at his house, but no drugs."

I cruised past the sheriff's office shortly after ten. His car wasn't in the lot so I made an illegal U-turn and pulled in.

I strode up to the young blond-haired desk officer. "Hey, Kyle, I'm here to see Tommy."

Kyle checked his sheet. "You're not listed, Britt."

"What? The desk officer this morning didn't write it down? I made an appointment." Why did I feel so much guiltier lying in Spirit Lake than L.A.?

He frowned. "It's way past visiting hours."

I pointed at the camera hanging from a strap around my neck along with my press credentials. "We scheduled a photo. I'm late because I covered the hockey game."

"Too bad they lost their last game," he said. "I heard Wozniak got the ref."

I scanned through my shots and showed Kyle one of Brody clocking the ref.

Kyle half-laughed. "Man, he really nailed him."

Guys get such a kick out of watching each other in combat. Kyle thanked me for showing him as if I'd given him a gift. I knew he would. "Look at your appointment schedule again, Kyle. It must be there." I tapped my foot, stared at my watch, and tried to appear formidable, but was careful not to overdo it and ruin our moment.

Kyle said, "Ten minutes. You'll have to take your photos through the bars. I won't let you in there. He's already killed one woman."

I raised one eyebrow. "You've tried and convicted the guy? Is that what you learned at the academy?"

His cheeks flamed. He led me down a corridor and unlocked it to reveal a block of ten cells, five on each side. Luckily, Tommy's cell was one of the first ones so I didn't have to walk past all of them. It smelled like a combination of antiseptic and lingering food odors. I heard snoring, and low murmuring. There were no windows. I'd been in jails before and this one wasn't that intense, but still not a fun place to hang out.

Tommy lay on a cot, staring at the ceiling. He scowled when I said hello.

Kyle reminded me I had ten minutes, and left. I jumped when the door clanged shut behind him. Why do they always have to clang?

Still on his back with his hands behind his head, Tommy asked, "You got a cigarette?"

I pushed the pack through the bars. The cot squeaked when he got up.

We faced each other with the bars between us. About my height, a rawhide string held Tommy's hair back, and a flannel shirt hung loose from his wide shoulders. He took the pack and matches from me without saying thank you.

"My brother said not to talk to anyone unless he's here." He paced and smoked. "I need to get out of this place."

"Edgar said you didn't tell Wilcox everything about Isabel. I won't use anything you say in the paper. My word."

He shook his head.

"If you didn't do it, it's in your best interest if the real killer is found, don't you agree?"

He blew out a stream of smoke. "Edgar sent you?"

"All he said was I should talk to you."

"That Edgar." The corners of Tommy's mouth turned up.

I took it as my cue and moved closer to the bars. "How did you happen to get a ride with Isabel?"

"I go to the Triangle bar in Cooper most Fridays. I knew if she saw me on the road on her way home from Branson, she'd give me a ride. We knew each other from Cooper High."

"Where was your car?"

"It's been, ah, non-operational all winter. I hitch into town and back when I need to go."

"And Isabel picked you up in Cooper and took you home."

"It was on her way. She went home after class on Fridays. Kind of a regular thing."

"You didn't lose your temper with her and accidentally…?"

He scowled. "I didn't touch her."

"Maybe you were high?"

His lips flattened. "I don't do meth anymore."

I showed my palms. "Sorry, just asking."

"I'm not talking to you anymore."

I pretended not to hear that. "Did she always drive you all the way to your place, or drop you at your turnoff?"

He stretched his rangy body and sat on the squeaking cot again. "She usually took me all the way unless the snow was too deep for a car to get through, even the sweet ride she drove."

"Your house is the only one out there, right?" I asked.

He nodded. "The road doesn't get plowed much."

"I wonder why you didn't fix up your car with that $5, 000 Wilcox found at your place. You know, instead of hitching everywhere."

The cot squeaked and I stepped back when he came close to the bars. "I already told the sheriff that was money I was saving from my job to buy a new car."

I touched the sore spot above my ear. Not that I expected him to confess, but I wanted to watch his face when I asked. "You didn't happen to be out hunting this morning, did you? Lars said you were a bow hunter."

He looked at the floor, the hallway and ceiling. "No, I wasn't out hunting. Didn't I say I'm done answering your questions?"

"Okay, I'm leaving." I raised my camera. "Will you let me take your picture?"

Tommy's angular face was close to the cell bars, his cot a shadow in the background. His left hand gripped the bar above his head. He held the cigarette to his mouth with his right hand, blew out a protective cloud of smoke, and said, "There aren't enough pictures of Indians behind bars already?"

His anger felt like another presence joining us in the space. I was grateful for the steel bars separating us, and said, "There are no Tommy Jackson pictures out there."

"Go ahead, then." He stared straight into the camera and expelled another plume of smoke. "Here's a smoke signal for you."

My camera was still clicking when a door slammed and Kyle stalked toward us. "I called the sheriff, and he said to get you out of here. Now."

I didn't mind leaving. Tommy was too intense even for my so-called nerves of steel. Kyle led me away, his ears red from the chewing out. The wrath of Wilcox would come down on me next.

Chapter 10

I sat across from the sheriff's desk, trying not to feel like a criminal under his hard stare. A night's sleep hadn't cooled his anger at my unauthorized visit to Tommy. I didn't even try to outstare him. Instead, I took an inventory of his desk. It held the usual computer and printer, phone, in and out box and yellow pads crammed with illegible writing, at least from my upside down vantage point. One photo angled slightly toward me showed a smiling woman standing in front of the Maroon Bells mountain peaks in Colorado.

"Beautiful photo. Is that your wife?" I asked.

He slanted the photo away from me.

I went on the defensive. "I took a pack of cigarettes to Tommy. I'd been out to see Edgar and he wanted me to do that. I was there two minutes, that's all. What's the harm?"

Wilcox said, "Forget about Tommy. We let him go this morning."

"He's not a suspect?"

Wilcox thundered. "I didn't say that, and he's not why you're here. What I want to know is what made you think you had the right to follow Nathan Maelstrom to the casino and question him?"

The Nathan question caught me off guard. That was days ago. I stuttered. "We're doing a profile. Cynthia told you about it. I ate dinner with Henry at the casino, and he mentioned Nathan was at the blackjack tables. After dinner I wandered over to say hello." I opened my eyes wide like a basketball player called on a foul.

Wilcox jabbed a finger at me. "The way I think it happened, you got him drunk and pumped him for information about Isabel. A valet watched you put him in your car, and that's the last anyone saw of him."

I looked away. True, I'd bought him drinks, but the part about being the last anyone saw of him confused me. "I took him home."

"As I said, no one's seen him since Tuesday night."

"How did you find out he was missing?"

"He wasn't at the resort when we went out there to ask him a couple of questions about Isabel. Arnie said he thought he went to a girlfriend's place."

"I saw Arnie the next day and told him I dropped Nathan off." I leaned across the desk. "Why are you questioning me? If it were me, I'd want to know why the family didn't tell you sooner that he was missing."

Wilcox said, "Arnie said Nathan sometimes stayed with her for a few days. We checked, but she said she hadn't seen him in weeks."

I paced in front of the sheriff's desk. "That doesn't make sense. I helped him up the steps and into the lodge."

"They insist he didn't come home." His index finger stabbed the table.

I stabbed my finger on the table, too. "Somebody watched from one of the windows upstairs so someone saw him."

"Who?"

I dropped back into my chair. "The person stepped back from the window. I couldn't see who it was."

Wilcox crossed his arms. "Why would they do that?"

"It's not exactly a happy family from what I've gathered."

"How happy would your family be if a sister or daughter were murdered?"

Good point. "Maybe he decided to leave town. He said he had nothing left here, and might take off to a warmer climate. I thought he meant after Isabel's funeral."

Wilcox flipped on the recorder. "Tell me what you talked about. Every word."

***

Forty minutes later, chastened, I promised not to talk to the Maelstroms for the rest of the day. I should have told him about the arrow, but he'd know I'd gone back to look for evidence his people might have missed in the dark. If Wilcox got too mad, he'd call Cynthia and she'd kill the profile.

I passed the Forestry Service building on my way to the bureau. Ben didn't spend much time indoors, so I was pleased to see his truck. I swung into the lot.

He sat behind his desk staring out the window overlooking Branson Lake. He swiveled to face me when I came in, his expression impassive.

This time I took care not to bump his hat sitting on the edge of the desk. I'd once made the mistake of mocking the flat-brimmed forest service hat. It turned out he loved it.

"What do you need?" He reached for the hat and set it on a bookcase. In another episode of bad behavior I'd sent it sailing across the room when he told me he'd gotten engaged to the art history professor he'd been seeing. I'm not proud of that. Controlling my temper is an area I'm working on.

"Were you aware Nathan is missing?" I asked.

He nodded. "I talked to Wilcox a couple of hours ago."

"Did you rat me out about talking to Nathan Tuesday night? Maybe Henry told you what I did?"

"No." His lip twitched.

"So what do they think?" I dropped into the chair across from his desk.

"They think he didn't go home."

"I helped him up the steps and into the front door. I'm getting tired of people not listening to me."

Ben squinted when deep in thought. "Maybe Nathan left after you'd gone."

I leaned forward in my chair. "Were any cars missing at the resort? We left his at the casino."

He shook his head. "His car is at the sheriff's now. Do you think he could have hitchhiked?"

"No, he could hardly stand up, and it was snowing. Where would he go in the middle of the night?" It occurred to me that as drunk as he was, he could have decided to go for a walk. I asked, "Have they checked on the side of the roads? Maybe he's in a ditch." He'd be frozen solid now. I thought of Isabel's body lying in the woods, and shivered.

"The sheriff's people are looking."

"What does Arnie say?"

He looked toward the door, a not-so-subtle hint. "He still thinks Nathan took off on his own and is sleeping it off someplace. Wilcox is checking on it."

I could tell he wanted me to leave, but asked, "What about Pauly and Dee?"

"They say they didn't see him after he left for the casino around eight Tuesday evening."

"Someone watched from upstairs and saw me bring him home. The curtains twitched." That came out more strident than I intended.

"Maybe wind blew the curtain." He stood up from behind his desk.

I huffed, but he cut me off. "I'm not saying I don't believe you, but it's your word against Arnie, Dee and Pauly."

Not only did I discover the dead Isabel on my land, I was possibly the last one to see another member of the Maelstrom family, who disappeared. "Nathan talked about leaving. Maybe he woke up in the night and decided to go to California. I guess he could have called someone to drive him to the airport in Branson, or even Minneapolis. Have they checked flights?"

"The sheriff will figure it out." That was Ben's way of telling me to back off.

I got up to leave. "Did you know Wilcox let Tommy go this morning?"

He nodded. "They didn't have enough to hold him. The story about getting rides from Isabel checked out. But something's fishy with that kid. What's he doing with $5,000?" He came around his desk, seeing me to the door.

I gave it one more shot. "Want to get lunch?"

"Another time, thanks. Wilcox asked me to get another search group going."

I didn't expect him to have lunch with me. Even though every rejection stung, I hoped he would wear down in time, at least enough so we could be friends again. "Does he think Nathan's disappearance might have to do with Isabel's murder?"

"He's not saying." He opened the door and stood aside. "I've got to get out there looking for Nathan."

I passed in front of him on my way out. He said, "Wait," and leaned in close, warmth in his eyes.

If I was poetic, I'd compare looking into his hazel eyes to pebbles at the bottom of a clear stream, dappled with sunlight. But poetry was not my thing.

"What's the white stuff sticking out by your ear?" He swiped at my neck and looked at his fingers. "Blood?"

His look contained only the concern you'd have for anyone with a cut. I sighed, tugged the cap down and tucked in the bandage. "A rabbit darted in front of my snowshoe. I tripped and fell into a bush."

An arched brow. "You've been tripping a lot lately."

"It's just a scratch." I should have told him about the arrow, but he'd tell Wilcox and Little and Lars, and the four of them would gang up on me. I made a promise to myself to tell Wilcox about it later.

"Be careful, Britt."

He was softening toward me. I went for my opening. "Ben, can't we start over? I promise I've changed."

His face shut down again. He stepped away. The moment disappeared, and I wanted to grab it back. "You'll never forgive me for messing up your relationship with Ellie, will you?"

Ellie, with the intelligent brown eyes, a quiet girl-next-door type, who didn't cause all the drama. Everyone said they were the perfect couple until hurricane Britt came along and blew everything apart just before their wedding. Ellie left her tenured position at Branson U to start over in Oregon. I would go to Eugene and bring her back to him if he'd stop hating me.

His head bent toward me, his lips brushed my ear, his voice a low rumble. "What I'll never forgive you for is messing up my relationship with you."

He gave me a little push and I stumbled out. The door shut behind me.

***

I inched along behind a line of cars at a McDonald's drive-through. When the tinny voice asked for my order, I said, "never mind," and drove back to the office. A burger and fries wouldn't even begin to take the hurt away.

My feet dragged me up the steps to the bureau office. I slouched over my computer and stared at the wave. The poster reminded me of the ocean, and that reminded me of getting fired from the *Times* and my failed marriage to Richard. He was a self-absorbed, philandering jerk, and his last act caused me to ruin my last chance with Ben.

Jason returned from lunch and did a double-take. "You look like you just lost your best friend."

I winced. "That's pretty much it."

My cell rang and the caller ID said Ben. Maybe he wanted to say he was sorry. I hit answer, hating the bubble of hope in my chest.

Chapter 11

Ben wasn't calling to say he was sorry. "I have news."

I could tell from his tone the news wouldn't be good.

"They found Nathan. He apparently hanged himself at the resort. Time of death was sometime during the night on Tuesday. He's frozen so Thor's still figuring it out."

"Oh, no." I sat down on the nearest chair. "He said he wanted to get away."

"Permanently?"

I replayed our conversation in my mind. "I didn't get that impression. Nathan was mixed up and depressed, but I thought he meant he wanted to get away from Spirit Lake."

"Wilcox will want to talk to you again. You were the last person to see him alive."

That didn't sound good. "You're sure about that?"

"Alleged. Look, I've got to go. Wilcox is talking to the family and I want to be there."

Jason said he'd drive his own car and meet me at Maelstrom's.

I parked at the lodge and trudged to the remote cabin where the sheriff's car, Ben's forest service truck, police cars, ambulance and Thor's van were parked haphazardly beside piles of banked snow. Yellow crime scene tape surrounded the area. This scene was getting to be too familiar.

Arnie looked like he'd been trampled by a stampeding herd of buffalo. Dee and Pauly were not visible. I found Wilcox by the cabin. "Is this a crime scene or a suicide?"

He closed his cell. "As far as we know, it's a suicide."

"Note?"

He shook his head.

I edged toward the door. "Mind if I look inside?"

"Yes, I do mind. Thor's in there."

"How about if I stand at the door and shoot a couple of pictures?"

Wilcox recoiled from me as if I was a ghoul. "He's been cut down."

Now I was offended. "I figured. I'm not being grotesque, just getting a sense of what happened."

He held up two fingers. "Two minutes."

"Last week you wanted my crime scene photos." I needed to break that habit of always going for the last word. Wilcox yanked at his cowboy hat, and I got out of there before he changed his mind.

I ducked under the tape at the cabin door. Thor's green-tinged face stopped me. "You can't come in until I'm done with the prints."

"I'll stand in the doorway." The icy cold cabin wasn't one of the winterized ones kept open for snowmobilers. That explained why they didn't find him right away. I surveyed the scene, framed my shots and started shooting.

An overturned four-legged stool. Another stool was next to an island between the kitchen and living room. Four high-backed chairs were tucked up close to a round dining or game table beside the fireplace. A rope like the kind used to tie a boat to a dock hung from a beam. They'd moved Nathan's body already. I saw no evidence of another presence or a struggle. He must have left the lodge and made his way over to this remote cabin after I left.

My body reacted like I'd slammed into a hard surface. I never got used to death in any of its forms, no matter how typical the scene. Most of the time, I didn't know the victim, but I'd just talked with Nathan days ago. Someone should have helped him before it came to this.

He didn't sound like someone about to end his life, more like someone about to change his life. Maybe I misread him. The alternative was that someone killed him. Why? Did it have to do with Isabel's murder? Did he discover information that led to her killer? Or did he kill her in a rage, and take his own life in remorse?

Thor methodically examined every inch of the interior. Her peaches and cream skin remained the color of green tea. She swallowed. "I went to high school with him. It's hard to believe he did this."

I thought so, too. "Are you checking footprints?" I asked.

"Of course."

"The stool?"

Thor stopped searching the floor and put her hands on her hips, her voice slightly tremulous. "I know how to do my job."

"I'm sure you do. It would be a good idea to check the stool for impressions such as what might come off a boot, and do all sides of it and the top. Maybe there's a smudge where he kicked it, or if it was yanked away."

I wasn't painting a cheery picture. Thor winced. "What are you thinking?"

"It wouldn't hurt to treat it like a homicide just in case."

"The sheriff said it was routine. Everything points to suicide. Plus, I don't take orders from you." Thor went back to work on the prints and doing her own photos.

I ignored her last comment. "If it's not too late with everyone who's been trampling the scene, I'd check prints on the floor and compare them to Nathan's."

"Anything else?" She crossed her arms.

Thor acted like I did at that age. Cocky and defiantly aware of how limited my knowledge really was. I considered myself an alumnus of the school of fake it till you make it.

"What's that smell?" I hadn't needed to ask. I knew vomit when I smelled it.

She pointed to a stain on the wood floor. "Someone upchucked over there. They didn't do much of a job cleaning it up."

"DNA?"

She nodded. "We'll send a sample of it, but it takes a while."

I doubted Nathan would clean up his own vomit if he planned to hang himself.

Snow blew sideways into my face on my way to the SUV. I sat inside and waited for Jason with the heater on high. The car was starting to warm up when the passenger door opened and Ben jumped in, startling me. He rubbed his hands together. "Damn, my fingers won't bend."

How could he act like he hadn't just told me he'd never forgive me? I put the hurt out of my mind. This was about Nathan. I asked, "Have they found tracks leading to the cabin?"

"No tracks. Four inches of snow since last night, plus the wind."

"Did you see him?" I'd already imagined Nathan dangling from a rope. I'd seen a few hangings and they weren't easy to forget.

Ben nodded. "Poor kid must have struggled a long time. People think it's like in the movies, and believe they kick the chair and they're dead. But if they don't know how to do the knot or the noose isn't on right, it's a brutal way to die."

"How long?" I swallowed.

He sighed. "Could have been six or seven minutes."

The image of Nathan struggling for so long caused my stomach to revolt. I took a deep breath. "What about people staying at the resort?"

Rubbing his hands together and blowing on them, he said, "Two groups of snowmobilers from St. Paul were in a cabin on the south side of the resort. They were out on the sleds all day and a couple of them were at the casino that night. They left there by ten so they could get an early start the next morning. No one saw or heard a thing."

Ben got a call from Wilcox that the search of Nathan's bedroom was underway. I watched him walk toward the lodge with his hands in his pockets. Wilcox would welcome Ben's input. Their mutual respect for each other made me jealous.

I saw Jason winding through the cars toward me. I pointed to Wilcox on the other side of the driveway talking on his cell. Jason nodded, and headed over to get comments from the sheriff.

Arnie walked toward a side door to the lodge and met Dee coming out with a tray of cups, an insulated coffee pot and doughnuts. I shut off the blasting heater and slid the window down to hear what they were saying. I heard the cups rattling from several yards away. Arnie took the tray from her, and said, "Let me get that. You go on back inside where it's warm." She scuttled back into the house.

I intercepted him on his way to the officers standing outside the cabin. "Arnie, I'm so sorry about Nathan."

His spine stiff, he jerked the tray toward me. "Coffee?"

I shook my head. "No, thanks. I just wanted to offer my condolences. I talked to Nathan only a couple of days ago."

His big head swayed as if too heavy to hold up. "Isabel's death was just too much for Nathan to handle." He moved past me like a robot and set the tray on the hood of the sheriff's car. Several deputies helped themselves. As they talked, clouds of frost hung in the air like conversation balloons. Arnie filled a cup for himself and stood with the group.

I went into the lodge by the main entryway. Dee stooped over a lacquered oak coffee table the size of a dining table, gathering empty plates. New-looking sofas and chairs were arranged into a lounge area on the main floor. When I worked for the elder Maelstrom's years earlier, a few beat-up couches and nicked end tables sat around the room in a slapdash arrangement.

She jumped when I said hello behind her. "Oh, I didn't see you."

"I'm sorry if I startled you. Could I warm up in here?" A stone fireplace filled one wall, fire blazing.

She held the cross hanging from her neck. "Of course. Let me get you coffee."

The poor woman's hands trembled. I gathered several empty glasses and followed her to the kitchen. The Maelstroms' kitchen faced the lake in back, and the family quarters were upstairs.

"Dee, why don't you sit down, and I'll bring you coffee?"

The bright spots on her cheeks stood out even pinker against her drawn face. She filled the cup and handed it to me. "It's better if I keep busy."

Warmth spread through my stiff fingers. "I'm so sorry about Nathan. Your family has suffered so much tragedy."

"I'm going to church when Sheriff Wilcox is finished here. I have to pray for Nathan's soul." She loaded cups into the dishwasher and hummed an agitated rendition of "Onward Christian Soldiers."

"Dee, did you happen to see me drop off Nathan Tuesday night?" I glanced toward the ceiling. "From the upstairs window?"

She didn't look up from her task. "I sleep in the back bedroom facing the lake."

"Did it occur to you he might be thinking of suicide?"

"The sheriff asked me that, too. Nathan never talked about it. He slept all day and went to the casino at night, unless Isabel came home from college." She rinsed a cup and a sad note crept into her voice. "As a kid, he was so happy, always out on the lake. People change, I guess."

I picked up a towel, took the cup from her, and dried it. The kitchen door opened and Arnie came in with the tray of empty cups. He set it on the counter with a clatter, and put his arm around his wife's plump shoulder, "You should go up to your room and rest."

She fled from the kitchen. Arnie turned to me. "No need to help with the cleanup. I'll get Pauly in here later."

"Where is Pauly? I haven't seen him."

"He doesn't want to come out of his room. Hard on a kid, what happened."

"I understand." I put down the towel.

Arnie stared out the window. "Even as a baby Nathan was over-sensitive." He rubbed his unshaven face. "Look, if you don't mind, I'd rather you didn't talk to us about this anymore. It upsets my wife and we've been over it all with the sheriff. Can't you people get your information from him?" The muscles in his right eye jumped. "I'm just protecting what's left of my family."

"I'm sorry, I didn't mean to intrude." I splashed out the coffee and rinsed my cup at the sink. "I just came in for a second to warm up."

He took the cup from me and stared out the window again. "This resort is all I have left of Isabel now."

Jason caught up with me as I headed to my car. He said, "I'll meet you later in Branson. Maybe Thor will have more info if I stay here a while."

Still feeling chastened by Arnie's plea, I nodded. "Since you two are so tight, see if she'll call as soon as she gets the print results."

Jason ducked, but I saw the blush. He said, "I'll ask her. She admires you. She told me to Google you if I wanted to be impressed."

That surprised me. Thor was so touchy whenever I offered any suggestions. Marta, my best friend and editor back in LA told me I needed to be more tactful.

When I backed out of the resort driveway, I noticed the arrow from yesterday's incident in my backseat. Strands of my hair still stuck to it. Thor would be too busy now to check fingerprints. I cranked the heat to high and headed to Branson, deep in thought. Isabel and Tommy were connected through the rides home, but was there any other connection? And what connected Nathan?

Dinnertime was long over by the time Jason, Cynthia and I wrapped up Nathan's story. For the bureau, it would be a couple of photos and another few paragraphs in the *Strib's* regional section. The local paper got the tip from their police scanner, so they were onto the story shortly after I left Maelstrom's.

Nathan's death took my appetite away, but I needed to talk to someone. Little, Lars and Rock represented an oasis of normalcy that drew me in for comfort at times like this.

The closed sign hung in the door, but a light meant someone was still roaming around in the restaurant. I rapped on the window, and Little's head popped out of the book alcove.

He led me back to the corner where he unpacked and sorted a new shipment of books. He called the alcove his Food for Thought bookstore. My brother's second love after food was books. Listening to him talk about a new title he'd received on Ojibwe history soothed me after the scene at Maelstrom's Resort.

He stopped talking about the new books mid-sentence. "Have you eaten today?"

I shook my head. "Wilcox demanded to see me early this morning so I missed breakfast. We were out at Maelstrom's at noon, and I worked through dinner at the bureau. I'm not hungry, though."

"Why don't you go out to the garage and say hi to Lars? I'm almost finished here, and I'll fix you a light dinner. You need to eat."

The garage was only a few degrees warmer than outdoors. Leaning over the roaring snowmobile engine, Lars didn't hear my hello through the thick wool cap covering his ears. Rock licked my hand. I called to Lars again with no response, so Rock bumped Lars in the back of his leg with his nose. Lars' head popped up, wrench in hand.

"Hey! Britt, how's it going?" He shut off the engine.

I pointed to the snowmobile. "Want to let me take it for a ride?"

"Jayzus, no."

Last winter I'd caused his favorite snowmobile to end up at the bottom of Spirit Lake. He wouldn't let me near this replacement and I knew it.

"Joking."

"You're on crack if you think I'll let you on this baby." He patted the new raspberry red Ski-Doo, "In fact, you're standing too close. Back away from the sled."

I'd started it, but didn't have the heart to banter with Lars tonight. "I've just come from Maelstrom's."

His orange-fringed head dropped forward. "How much can one family take? Maybe the place really is cursed."

"Cursed?"

"Edgar told Little part of the resort was built on an Ojibwe burial ground. People are superstitious. It almost went bankrupt before Arnie took it over. His first wife died young, his oldest son died in Iraq, Isabel and now Nathan."

Little often sat with Edgar and listened to stories, so it wasn't surprising he knew about old burial grounds in the area. Lars' recounting of the Maelstrom deaths raised the hairs on my neck. "I doubt if it's more than misfortune, Lars. In Nathan's case, if it was a suicide, it could have been prevented."

Lars put his tools away. "If someone wants to kill himself, it's not so easy to stop."

All my pent up frustration over the Maelstroms poured out. "Nathan was depressed. Couldn't they have sent him to a therapist?" I paced from one end of the garage to the other. "People up here talk for hours about fishing, weather, hunting, knitting, gardens, more weather, yet no one ever talks about problems in their families. Instead they hold on to the hurt and bitterness until they're old and senile and don't care what they say. But it's too late. They're locked up in nursing homes with uncaring caregivers who shove their wheelchairs off into corners and let them moan at the walls."

"Jayzus, Britt, you're lumping an entire region into one stereotype." My rants never fazed Lars.

I threw myself into a chair by the barrel stove. "It's taking much too long for the sheriff to figure out what happened to Isabel, and now Nathan. I'm not convinced it was a suicide."

Lars covered his snowmobile, shut the lights and pulled me up from the chair. "Let's see what Little's cooking."

Little believed in the healing properties of comfort food.

Lars went into the kitchen to tell Little we were there. I sat, elbow on the counter, my chin cupped in my hand, propping my head up. Like magic, a steaming and fragrant vegetable pot pie appeared in front of me, the crust flaky and golden.

Twenty minutes later, I'd licked the last bite off my fork and was mellow as an old tabby sitting in a sunny windowsill. My brother the alchemist. "Great dinner, guys. Thank you."

Little stood behind the counter directly in front of me, his brows drawn together. Lars moved next to Little and crossed his arms. A united front.

"What have I done wrong this time?" I asked.

Little spoke first. "We want you to back off and let Wilcox figure out what happened."

They'd tamed me with food for a reason.

Lars crossed his beefy forearms. "If what you say about Nathan turns out to be true, there's a crazy killer out there."

I got up from the stool and faced them, ready for combat. "It's news. I photograph news events for the paper. It's what I do."

Little said, "It's dangerous," drawing the word out syllable by syllable.

No longer a sunning tabby, I hissed. "Don't worry about me. I can take care of myself. I'm not stupid."

Identical skeptical expressions on their faces stopped me.

I sat back down. "Okay, maybe I did some stupid things last year, but the new me is careful, and sober."

Little threw down his towel. "I knew this would be a waste of time. All you think about is yourself." He stomped into the kitchen.

Lars wiped the back counter.

I grabbed my jacket and stalked out the door. Lars caught up to me on my way back to the garage to get Rock. "Don't you get it, Britt?"

"Get what? All Little does is needle me about being reckless or leaving town. I'm tired of it." I opened the garage door and Rock ran out.

Frost plumed from Lars' mouth. "He expects you'll take off again. Ben, too. They worry about you."

"I don't have time to hold everybody's hands. They should get over it." I started toward my SUV, feeling like a martyr.

"It wouldn't hurt you to hold some hands. The damage you've done isn't undone so easily." He shivered and dashed back into the restaurant. Ten-below-zero in shirt sleeves, not the best outdoor attire for a long argument.

Lars was right, as usual. But as far as I knew, I wasn't going anywhere, and I could take care of myself. I wished I knew how to do this better.

At home, I re-bandaged the scrape near my ear, strapped on a helmet, set a stool in the middle of the room and placed pillows and sofa cushions around it in strategic positions. This stool was not as tall and only had three legs, but it would do for my experiment. I stepped up on it and attempted to kick it out from under myself. I tried hopping and kicking it with one foot and then with the other. The first time I almost landed on the woodstove between the kitchen and living room. The second time I just missed the coffee table. A giant Alice in the tiny house.

I stood on the stool a third time, looked up to the beams and realized it didn't make sense to do this without a noose. Before carrying that thought any farther, common sense kicked in and I got back down. I'd learned what I wanted to know anyway. No need to hang myself to prove it.

Nathan's life had been wasted and I didn't know why. I yanked my jacket and boots on, trudged to the woodpile on the east side of the cabin and grabbed the axe. Even though a stack of wood already filled the space behind the stove, and it was pitch dark and bone-aching cold, the physical exercise and rhythm of chopping helped me think.

I set a chunk of wood on the chopping block, lifted the axe over my shoulder and put my weight into the downward motion, splitting it perfectly. The pieces fell to the ground, and I set another on the block and did it again.

Two members of the Maelstrom family were dead within a few days of each other. Did Nathan kill his sister in some freak accident as a result of a fight about Brody? Would the guilt cause him to commit suicide? Arnie said Nathan was over-sensitive and he'd admitted he was depressed. I sensed the tension at Maelstrom's Resort. Of course, two family members just died. Dee's son behaved oddly with his furtive glances and silly goatee, but with a mother like Dee, no wonder. Where did Brody enter the story? Hot temper. Jealous, even of Isabel's brother.

My mind ran circles around itself. I brought the axe down hard, not paying attention to my stroke and it tipped. The side of the axe smashed sideways onto the wood, jarring every bone in my body. I stared at the mark. It matched the indentation at the back of Isabel's head. I lost my vegetable pot pie.

Chapter 12

An internal Morse code tapped its message of pain through every nerve ending in my body. The hot bath last night didn't mitigate the abuse from repeatedly throwing myself off a stool. Sometimes even I thought I was an idiot. A brisk snowshoe trek before work would loosen my aching limbs, but I hesitated. Today was an anniversary of sorts. One week ago I'd vaulted over Isabel's dead body.

I called Cynthia to check whether she needed me to come in. Working on a Saturday wouldn't have been unusual on a story this big.

Her voice was barely audible. "No need for you to come in. I'll call if something comes up."

The long day yesterday must have really tired her out. She wasn't that old, you'd think the woman would have more stamina. Jason emailed that he'd checked, and Wilcox wasn't giving them any new information about Nathan's death. My next call was to Thor to tell her my theory that Isabel could have been murdered with an axe. Thor usually listened to me, even if begrudgingly.

She said, "No axe with brain residue in evidence so far but I'll pass it along."

I thought of Wilcox. "Don't say it came from me."

Little's was hopping with snowmobilers "up north" from the Cities for the weekend. I sat at my usual place at the counter pretending the guys weren't still mad. In a few minutes Chloe set a plate with scrambled eggs and toast in front of me. She must have been distracted because she always brought me pancakes.

"I didn't order eggs. These for someone else?"

Chloe tilted her head toward the kitchen and arched her eyebrow. I got it. Withholding my favorite pancakes was punishment, but Little wouldn't let me pay for meals, so I couldn't complain. I dug in.

Lars came from the kitchen with a green smoothie and set it in front of me. "Little said you should drink this."

Maybe he wasn't so mad after all if he wanted to keep me healthy. The eggs were so light and fluffy I might have to expand my list of favorites. On the way out I grabbed a couple of blueberry muffins from the bakery case and poured a large coffee to go.

Lars watched me with his mouth hanging open. "You can't still be hungry after that breakfast?"

I hurried out the door to avoid more questions. "This is for later."

Rock jumped into the SUV and we pulled away. He'd be helpful for the mission. He weighed only forty-five pounds, but his bark was ferocious.

Another five inches of snow covered Tommy's road, filling up the trail made by the law enforcement traffic earlier in the week. In fact, the sky looked ready to dump another load of the white stuff. The SUV powered through without too much trouble until I reached Tommy's drive. Rather than risk getting stuck with no way to make a hasty retreat if necessary, I parked the car facing toward the road and honked a few times. People didn't like to be surprised by visitors around here. They might be likely to blast you with a shotgun.

Grabbing the coffee and muffins, I slogged through a quarter mile of snow from the SUV to his house. Rock bounced through it with no trouble.

If Tommy shot the arrow that nearly de-eared me, I'd be stupid to confront him, but I needed to ask him a couple more questions about Isabel. I called out his name a few times. No lights were on in the house. No smoke rose from the chimney. I knocked.

Rock sniffed at the porch. Footprints, partially filled with snow, headed toward the road. I encouraged Rock to check them out. "Good dog."

I followed Rock to the SUV. He kept going toward the highway, so I called him back and drove the two miles to the intersection. Nose down, he had the scent again and followed the prints south for a few yards. He stopped at a grouping of footprints by the roadside, and looked back at me. The end of the trail. I caught up and imagined the scenario. Someone stood at that spot, stamped his feet while waiting for a ride. Several long strides headed south, and the footprints disappeared. He'd run toward a vehicle and hopped in. If it was Tommy, he was in the wind.

I drove to the Dreamcatcher, a couple of miles north. I couldn't tell how old those tracks were, and maybe Tommy went to work at the casino this morning. Lars loved to tell me I was always getting ahead of my skis.

Not even noon, and Saturday gamblers crowded around the tables and slots. The highlight of their week, no doubt, and who could blame them? There wasn't much else to do around here.

I wound my way through the slots and tables to find Henry sitting at his usual place in front of his computer monitor, peering at columns of numbers. He swiveled to say hello when I tapped on the open office door.

"Hey, Britt, have a seat." He indicated a chair across from his desk. "Terrible news about Nathan."

I handed Henry the bag of muffins, Tommy's loss. "Little made them fresh this morning."

He thanked me and bit into one.

I talked while he chewed and made appreciative noises. "Everyone thinks I was the last one to see Nathan alive, but I have no idea what happened after he went into the house. I don't even think the sheriff believes me about that."

Henry's usual twinkle was missing today. "We feel bad here. The staff liked him and no one thought he'd kill himself.

We would have let Arnie know if we'd suspected anything like that."

I leaned forward in my seat. "I know you would have. I didn't get that sense from him from our conversation either. I'm even wondering if he committed suicide."

Henry's eyes widened. "You think it's another murder like Isabel?"

"I don't know. Everyone's waiting on forensics. By the way, is Tommy working today?"

Henry got up from behind his desk. "He was scheduled but didn't show up. Let's walk over and ask if the maintenance team have heard from him."

We left his office and made our way through the slots and tables toward a door at the back. I asked, "Does Tommy miss a lot of work?"

"He's been pretty reliable up until a week or so ago."

"You mean when they found Isabel's car?"

"No, before that. I think it was something to do with his dad."

"His dad was in town?" Tommy's dad was rarely around. I wondered why he showed up now.

Henry worked his way toward a back area. "Gerald's banned from this casino. He called over a week ago and left a message for Tommy to call him back. I don't know if he did or not. His dad got addicted to the gambling, and pretty much abandoned Tommy."

Someone stepped in front of me, so I waited until they moved to the side to continue our conversation. "Edgar said his dad went to work at the Mille Lacs casino after you fired him. Is he still there?"

"He might be." Henry let a cocktail waitress slip by us with a tray of drinks.

"I'm surprised they hired him after he stole from you."

"We were too. It's not like they didn't know. I'm sure they watch him pretty close."

We reached a door that said Staff Only. Henry poked his head in and called to one of the maintenance guys. "Any word from Tommy, yet?"

He hadn't heard anything and asked us to wait while he checked with the employee who'd taken Tommy's shift. He returned and said no one had been in touch with Tommy.

I thanked Henry. "I know you're busy. I'll let you get back to work."

We retraced our steps back to Henry's office. "Don't mention it. How come you're looking for Tommy? I'd stay away from him if I were you, especially now. The kid has a temper."

"I just wanted to ask him something. It's not important. By the way, anything new on Edgar's crying girl dream?"

Henry said, "People think it's just an old man's rambling."

"Let me know if there's any way I can help." It felt like an empty gesture. I didn't know how to help Edgar.

He went back to his desk and sat, the chair creaking under his weight. "Be careful, and thanks for the muffins. Little's are the best."

With no afternoon plans or assignment from Cynthia, I left Rock at the cabin and took off for Mille Lacs, fifty miles south of Spirit Lake.

Mille Lacs boasted the largest casino in the area and a hotel with close to five hundred rooms.   Early afternoon, and this casino was also already full of Saturday revelers. Busloads from the Cities and locals from all around flocked to the excitement and possibility of big winnings. It took me a minute to adjust to the dimly lit space with neon bouncing around. The noise level hit my head like an assault. I asked one of the roaming men with casino nametags if I could speak to the manager.

"She's in a meeting. Can I help you with something?"

I showed him my press badge.

He looked me over. "It says "photographer." Did you get authorization for photos?"

I'd brought only a small camera, zipped into an inner pocket of my jacket. "I'm not here to take pictures. I'm looking for someone."

He guided me to an alcove with a table and couple of chairs and asked me to wait. I peered into the crowd trying to pick out

Tommy. In a few minutes, a slender Ojibwe woman in her fifties wearing a pantsuit and starched white shirt came over and shook my hand. Her only accessory was a long necklace with an intricate beaded pendant in turquoise, orange and white. She introduced herself, indicated the chair, and asked what she could do for the *Star Tribune*.

I sat across from her. "I'm here on personal business. I'm looking for Gerald Jackson. I understand he's a dealer here."

Her lips pursed. "Not since about a week and a half ago when he stopped showing up for his shift."

"Has he been in some kind of trouble?"

"Not that we know about. He's a good dealer, showed up on time and did his job, no funny business for nearly two years now."

"Were you aware of his history at the Dreamcatcher?"

Her lips tightened again. "His cousin works here and vouched for him. I was outvoted on hiring him, but he hasn't done anything illegal. He's usually here gambling on his days off, but, as I said, we haven't heard from him. That's cause for termination."

One of the name-tagged guys whispered in her ear. She nodded and said to me, "If there's nothing else, I need to attend to something."

"Just one more thing." I showed her my photo of Tommy behind bars and asked if she'd seen him.

She shook her head. "I'm usually in the office so I don't see who comes and goes unless there's a problem. Check with the bartenders. Most people usually end up there."

I made my way to the bar, checking the area for Tommy. Three bartenders worked the horseshoe-shaped bar, all busy filling orders for cocktail waitresses and a throng at the counter. A bus must have just disgorged a gang of about forty seniors. They headed straight for the bar, shrieking like teenagers. Good for them. The casino must be a lot more fun than watching reruns and soaps.

When one of the bartenders glanced up, I motioned him over and showed him Tommy's photo. I said, "Have you seen him? He might have been here yesterday or even this morning."

He shook his head, and his long braid swished behind him. I handed him five bucks. "Are you sure?"

He looked amused. "This isn't a TV cop show. You don't have to bribe me. I honestly haven't seen the guy."

He pointed to a bartender with close-cropped hair and rimless glasses on the opposite side of the bar. "Ask Kevin. He was here all day yesterday."

I left the five on the bar anyway, mostly out of embarrassment, and signaled the bartender who'd been pointed out to me. The dress code seemed to be black T-shirts with the casino logo, and black jeans. He looked closely at the photo. "It's hard to tell with the smoke hiding part of his face but he looks like a guy last night asking about one of the dealers."

"Gerald Jackson?"

"Right, but I haven't seen Gerald for a while so I couldn't help him."

"I don't suppose you know where Gerald lives?"

"Sorry. Even if I did, it's against casino policy to give anyone phones or addresses of employees." He glanced up at a monitor above him. "Seriously, if they even thought I gave anyone personal employee info I could get fired, so if you don't mind?"

I thanked him and left him a five too. Now I knew Tommy was here looking for his dad, and Gerald was missing.

I sat at a poker machine and watched a blackjack game at a table nearby. The bartenders couldn't talk to me and that probably meant dealers couldn't either, but there was no casino rule about customers chatting with each other.

I stepped up to the blackjack table and played silently for a while fighting the creepy feeling that someone behind the monitors watched my every move. I lost twenty in no time.

I spoke to the group. "I'd hoped Gerald would be dealing today. I've had some luck at his table." I craned my neck around as if looking. "Anybody know who I'm talking about?"

The dealer's eyebrows raised a fraction. One guy asked what he looked like.

I had no idea what Gerald looked like. "Ojibwe, about fifty," I said, knowing that described many of the people in the casino, including staff. The dealers were both male and female, American Indian and other ethnicities, and I doubted if any of them would tell me about Gerald. Heads shook, and everyone kept playing.

On my third table, an old guy holding his cards in a sloppy fan looked up as I did my spiel. "Gerald? Sure, great guy. Heck of a dealer." He glanced at our dealer, who barely suppressed a yawn, and said, "No offense, you're a damn good dealer too."

The dealer's lips stretched into a minimal smile for a fraction of a second. "Thanks Al. You ready for another card?"

The game went on for a few more hands and when the old guy busted for the last time, he said, "Well, hell."

He wobbled away from the table, and I kept my eye on his progress through the casino. He sat at a slot, still not ready to give it up. When my hand was finished—and that time I actually won back a few bucks and considered it good luck—I ambled over to sit next to him.

"Hi, Al, my name is Britt. We were playing together a few minutes ago."

He glanced over from his slot. "Oh yeah, you busted too?"

"I'm finished for the day. How about you?"

He patted his pockets and looked at the slot with regret. "I'm done. You were looking for Gerald, right?"

We made our way through the crowd toward the front door. "I'm actually looking for his son, Tommy." I pulled out the photo. "Have you seen him?"

He squinted at it and shook his head. "Gerald's a friend, though. After he gets off work we gamble together, but he's no better at it just because he's a dealer." Al cackled. "He loses more than I do."

"He hasn't been around lately?"

"He got in trouble with some loan sharks." His head wagged back and forth. "He tried to borrow money from me, but I'm always broke. Now I have to wait for my next Social Security check. I'll sit and watch TV for the rest of the month and eat beans but it's worth it. Sometimes I actually win." His defeated sigh made me wonder if that was true.

I pointed toward the restaurant. "Want to have a sandwich with me before we go? My treat."

He said he needed to get home.

Outside in the parking lot, Al shivered in his tattered coat.

"I don't suppose you know where Gerald lives, do you?" I asked, slowing my steps to match the old guy's.

"Sure I do, sometimes I drop him off at his motel since he sold his car. It's on my way home."

I walked with him to a 1990 Ford pickup. He got in and waited for it to warm up. I raised my voice so he could hear me. "What did you mean about a loan shark? Do you have a name you could give me?"

He rolled down the window. "Sorry lady. I need both legs."

"Do you mind showing me that motel you mentioned?"

He nodded and gestured for me to follow.

I hurried over to the SUV and trailed him out of the parking lot. Loan sharking was a problem I would have expected in Las Vegas, but it was obviously naïve of me to be surprised they'd be doing business in northern Minnesota as well. About two miles from the casino, Al made a right turn and drove into one of several motels along a strip I'd passed on the way in. I pulled up beside him and thanked him.

He waved toward the end of a double row of rooms, all ground floor. "His is the room right around the corner. I've had a couple of beers with him in there before."

"Thanks for your help, Al. If I see Gerald I'll tell him you asked about him." I handed him a twenty. "I hate to think of you eating beans every night."

He thanked me and I watched him drive off. The truck made a left, heading back toward the casino.

The Winning Hand motel needed a paint job. Several lights were blown on a neon vacancy sign. A few rattletrap cars were parked in front of two rows of ten units, one behind the other. I went to room eleven and knocked, waited and banged harder. No one answered.

A bell jingled when I opened the office door. A stained plastic chair sat in one corner next to a rack of tattered brochures touting the local attractions. My nose wrinkled. On a side table a pot of scorched coffee sat on a burner with a few paper cups, packets of sugar and creamer strewn around it.

Behind the counter, a guy in a faded Vikings sweatshirt sat on a dingy brown couch. "Help you?" He didn't look away from the TV.

I shouted to be heard over the sports announcer. "I'm looking for someone who lives here. Gerald Jackson, room eleven. He didn't answer my knock."

The guy took his time getting to the counter but didn't turn down the television and his eyes never left it. "He must not be home then."

I showed him Tommy's photo. "Have you seen this guy? He might have been here looking for Gerald?"

He glanced at it. "If you don't want a room, I need to get back to the game."

I pulled out my press badge. "The guy in the picture is a meth dealer, and I know he came here. I don't suppose you want the police checking all the rooms for illegal substances or prostitution, right?"

His eyes widened. "You can't do that."

"Talk to me a minute, and I'll get out of your hair. Otherwise, I'm going to badger you until you've missed your entire Saturday sports lineup and then I'll get the cops here." I liked messing with this jerk.

His gaze moved up and to the side as if doing some deep thinking. At least his eyes weren't fastened on the TV anymore.

"I don't know where Gerald is. He hasn't paid his rent in a month and I'm about to clean out the room and toss his stuff in the dumpster. I would of done it sooner but with so many units empty, I figured what's the rush?" He poked a finger at Tommy's photo. "I didn't see that guy and I don't know anything about any drugs. If he was here to see Gerald, he wouldn't have. Gerald's gone."

"I need to look in his room."

He crossed his arms. "That's not happening."

I looked the scrawny desk clerk up and down. I could take him if he got physical. I pulled out my phone. "I'm calling the cops right now."

He glanced one last time at the TV, grabbed a master set of keys and stomped across the parking lot to Gerald's room. "There's nothing to see. Make it quick."

Two pairs of black slacks and two white shirts hung in the open closet. A casino nametag sat on the night stand next to a digital clock. The bed was rumpled and a chair overturned. There was a television stand but no TV. A razor, deodorant and a toothbrush were scattered on the bathroom sink, and there was blood. More than a shaving cut, less than a mortal wound.

I got my camera out of the inner zip pocket of my jacket. "Did you know about the blood?"

"It's not the first time Gerald's been roughed up. He always owes the loan sharks." He fidgeted with the keys.

I moved around the room, taking photos of the sink, bed, and the clerk.

He twisted the bottom of his Vikings shirt into a knot. "Why you taking my picture?"

I asked, "What loan sharks? Give me a name."

"Are you crazy? Those guys are bad dudes." He pulled the curtain aside and glanced out the window as if they might be watching.

I pocketed my camera. "That why you didn't call the police?"

The guy let out a frustrated growl. "Gerald usually comes back after a few days. I didn't want my motel shut down."

Anything related to the casinos was tribal business. I didn't know any tribal police in Mille Lacs and they wouldn't appreciate a Branson photographer getting involved in their issues. Gerald Jackson's problems were not my business, but I didn't want the motel manager to touch Gerald's room in case Tommy was involved. Not sure if it was the right move, I called Sgt. Ray Stevens in Spirit Lake and told him the situation.

Ray asked, "What's the motel manager's name?"

108

I spoke to the guy. "The sergeant wants to know your name."

Sweat beaded on his forehead. "Mel Schneider."

I told Ray the name.

"Put Mr. Schneider on the phone." Ray didn't care for small talk.

Mel shot me a baleful look and took the phone. He listened for a minute. "No sir, Sergeant, I won't touch anything in the room, and I won't let anyone go in there until the tribal police get here."

He handed the phone back to me with a look that said I'd totally ruined his day. I said, "Ray, I need to get back to Spirit Lake. I don't have to stay, do I?"

He said, "I'm calling the Mille Lacs tribal police to look into it. You can go, but I want to talk to you when you get back."

I told Ray about Tommy. "He wasn't at his house today, and Henry said he didn't go to work."

"Why didn't you tell me right away? I told him to stay in town. I'm heading out there now."

I drove back to Spirit Lake in low spirits. Tommy was hiding something, but I'd wasted precious time getting distracted by his family problems, and still no closer to finding out what happened to Isabel or Nathan.

Ray called me as I pulled into my driveway to tell me he found Tommy at home and he'd insisted he never left. He hadn't gone to work at the casino because he thought he worked the night shift. He and Henry straightened that out, and Ray gave Tommy a ride to work. Tommy insisted that if someone said they saw him at the Mille Lacs' casino, they were lying or had the wrong guy. Now even Ray sounded skeptical about my story.

Chapter 13

Cynthia called me at home Sunday morning, more subdued than usual. "I need you and Jason in my office at two o'clock."

"What's this about?" I assumed she wanted to go over the material running in the regional section. Maybe she wanted a follow-up right away.

She sighed. "Just be here."

I was getting used to Cynthia sounding like she'd rather be anywhere than at the bureau. The meeting wasn't until afternoon, so that gave me time to check in with Ben on the Maelstrom's.

"Sorry, I don't have time to talk right now. I'm getting ready to go to Minneapolis."

I expected the brush off, but asked, "What's going on down there?"

"Nothing related to the Maelstroms or Jacksons." I detected sarcasm.

"You heard about my trip to Mille Lacs already?" I wasn't surprised. Everyone but me seemed to be in the loop.

"Ray filled me in, but I've really got to go now."

"Sure, I understand." I didn't really. How could I win Ben back if he refused to see me? I consoled myself by fantasizing that I'd ask him to dinner when he got back from Minneapolis, we'd talk about what we were working on and he'd remember how good it could be between us. I'd even wear something more tantalizing than my pilled black sweater. One look in the mirror reminded me why he wasn't interested.

Maybe it was time for another visit to Bella and Violet. Bella could tell me why Ben was going to Minneapolis, and

Violet could fix my blotchy skin. My wishful thinking that he'd go anywhere with me or even tell me about his case was pathetic, but I couldn't stop hoping.

"OMG! Someone needs a facial." When not working, Violet spent the time texting, posting on Facebook, Pinterest or Tweeting. She'd eventually stopped trying to get me to follow her makeup blog.

I dropped into Violet's chair. "My face hurts."

She shook out a plastic cape and fastened it behind me. "You're wind-burned and your lips are chapped." She pushed and pulled at my skin. "Have you even opened that jar of moisturizer?"

Bella came in from the back of the shop trailing a skein of yellow yarn. "I'm making you a scarf. The one you wear is blah."

Bella was making me scarves again? After I'd brushed out the beehive of curls she'd created on my head for Junior Prom she'd stopped knitting them for me. "No consideration," she'd vented to the whole town. "I worked on that head of hair two solid hours."

She plopped her old bones down in her rocking chair. After a quick scan out the window, Bella's needles clicked. "It's been so long since you've been in, we thought you'd run off again."

Was there a conspiracy? What about my brow wax less than a week ago? "The scarf looks beautiful, Bella. I can't wait to wear it."

Violet pummeled and splashed and exhumed my face with soothing balms. She pointed to the scrape above my ear. "I see you've hurt yourself."

"A branch caught me." The arrow story would have been all over town before I left Bella's if I'd told the truth.

She peered closer. "Some branch."

"Hey Bella," I said. "Do you know anything about some big project Ben's on?" A glop of lavender-scented goo fell into my mouth, the perils of talking while Violet got creative on my face.

"It's usually illegal drugs, weapons, or humans coming across the Canadian border." Bella worked the yellow yarn. "Forget Mexico. You want to get something illegal into the U.S., go through Canada. Soft border, especially through the BW. They fly or go by boat. In the winter they drive across the lakes through reservation land."

"So what's Ben doing in Minneapolis?" I should have guessed he was involved in border problems.

"My sources say they're about to bust a smuggling ring. They have to move the contraband, so it's the Cities or Chicago." Bella rooted into the basket of yarn at her feet. "You want me to add purple to this yellow? Give it some pop?"

"Sure, sounds good. Thanks, Bella." Who needed Wikipedia with Bella in the neighborhood? Violet offered a choice of either a eucalyptus or citrus wrap.

"You pick, Violet." I figured she was the expert.

In less than an hour, my skin warm and rosy, I left the shop. The cold hit my open pores like daggers as I ducked into my SUV and headed to Branson.

Bella's information about Ben dealing with smuggling in the Boundary Waters and Minneapolis added another dimension to my list of possible scenarios and suspects. Brody and his dad were guides in the BW. Could they be smuggling? Maybe Isabel learned Brody was smuggling, confronted him, and he reacted with violence. She told Nathan and Brody silenced him too. Ben probably didn't want me pursuing them because it might be dangerous, so he downplayed their possible involvement. Wilcox would laugh at me if I said any of that out loud. Lars would say I was getting ahead of my skis again.

Instead of going to the bureau, I parked in the forest service lot. Ben's truck wasn't there, but someone might drop a hint about his project.

I asked the freckled young volunteer handing out maps at the counter if she'd seen him. "He just left. You might be able to catch him at home, if you hurry."

I'd never been to his new house. "Can you tell me how to get there?"

She pointed to the location on a laminated area map on the counter. "It's on Branson Lake."

A tree-lined private road ended at a cedar home overlooking the lake. Its peaked roof and large windows looked similar to Edgar's new home. I'd expected Ben would live in a cabin like the ones at his resort in Spirit Lake.

I hurried up the walk before changing my mind, but hesitated with my finger on the doorbell. He wouldn't be happy about my dropping in. I pushed the bell. Add stalker to my list of transgressions.

Ben filled the doorway. "What brings you here?"

"Could we please talk about Isabel?"

He pointed to a packed bag by the door. "I told you I'm leaving for Minneapolis on an investigation."

"A minute?"

He stepped aside. "One minute."

My mouth went slack when I took in the interior. Rough open-beamed ceiling, gleaming wood floors, and a rock fireplace and a huge television mounted above the mantle. I crossed to stand in front of a wall of windows letting in light from the lake, my boots sinking into a thick tan rug. A dark brown sofa faced the fireplace, the leather melting under my fingers.

An overstuffed swivel chair in a muted blue-green chevron designed fabric sat opposite a recliner. I dropped into the seat without being invited, swiveled to the lake and back to the fireplace. Just right for this Goldilocks.

Contemporary art filled the walls. In one corner stood a maple sculpture shaped like a woman's torso with metal antlers and a heart cutout near the center. I said, "No buzz saw art for you, I see."

Thunder rolled across his face. "That's all you can say?"

I cringed. Wrong timing on the humor. "What I mean is, your place is beautiful. It's warm and welcoming and the art work is amazing."

He left his post by the door, and came nearer to me. Pride and modesty played across his face. "I buy a few pieces when the art instructors at Branson U have exhibits."

I swiveled in the chair. "This is a great chair. Sky and lake colors. It's lovely."

He glared at me, arms crossed. "I pictured you sitting in it when I bought that chair."

A huge lump filled my throat. Another reminder of what I'd lost. I pointed to a spiral staircase leading to an upstairs loft. "Want to give me a tour?" I pictured a cozy bed with windows overlooking the lake, the two of us finally together. We'd almost made love in a tent last summer, until he remembered he was engaged to Ellie.

He went back to his sentry position at the door, and said, "Another time. I do have to go."

I got the unsubtle hint and got up. "What investigation are you working on? Maybe smuggling through the Boundary Waters?"

He was silent for a beat. "I can't talk about it."

"C'mon, Ben."

He spoke in a fast monotone. "I'm meeting an informant in Minneapolis. He's giving up the kingpin in an outfit using the BW for an entry point into the U.S. The area is my responsibility as a ranger."

"I know. You protect it and the people who use it."

His jaw pulsed. "Don't mock me."

"You're not the only one who's trying to do their job. I'm covering a murder. Can't you help me out?" I could feel the heat behind my eyes. Why wouldn't he listen to reason?

Ben said, "What you mean is you want me to get information from Wilcox, relay it to you so you can go off on your own and put yourself and others in danger." He looked at his watch. "I'll stay out this time."

I stood with my hands on my hips, legs apart. "We used to be friends and discussed things."

"We'll talk later." He tried to usher me out the door.

I hung back. "Are we friends or not?"

He didn't look at me. "Maybe someday. I'm not ready yet."

"I've changed. You might even still love me, you just don't know it yet." What was meant to be imploring came out as a demand, and too late to take it back.

He opened the door. "Stop pushing, Britt. It won't work this time."

As I moved past him to leave, he said, "And I do not love you."

I zombie-walked to my car.

I sat at my desk at the bureau with no memory of the journey. Jason's mouth moved, but I didn't comprehend what he said. Like a record stuck in a groove, "I do not love you" played over and over in my head, and finally penetrated my heart. I'd been fooling myself all along, and I couldn't take the spirit-crushing pain of keeping hope alive any longer.

I sucked back the hurt. I'd have to go forward on my own. No more groveling to someone who didn't want me. After all, I'd been a successful photojournalist without Ben's help, or his love. I thought I wanted a real relationship and not the arrangement Richard and I briefly called a marriage, but I didn't know how to do it. I doubted I could learn at thirty-four. Every word I'd said to Ben came out wrong.

Jason perched on the corner of my desk, still talking. He looked like a chastised puppy dog.

I asked, "What's wrong?"

"Weren't you listening? Thor's not speaking to me, and she shoots me these murderous looks. I thought she liked me."

"She has to concentrate on this case. Give her some time. Plus, there are bound to be issues when you mix your mythological creatures."

"What?"

"Thor, Norse myth. Jason and the Argonauts, Greek. A joke?"

He stomped back to his desk. "This isn't funny. I asked you if you'd talk to her."

"I'm not the person to give advice on personal issues."

He put his head down and whaled away at his keyboard until I couldn't take it anymore.

"Okay, I'll talk to her." Me, a relationship counselor—what a laugh. I grabbed my bag and jacket. "I'm going to see if Wilcox has new information, and I'll check to see if Thor's gotten the reports back on Nathan's forensics. If Cynthia asks, I'll be back in half an hour for the meeting."

He lifted forlorn eyes to mine. "I just need to know if she's mad at me."

Jason and I were both gluttons for punishment.

Wilcox's door was shut. His deputy said someone was with him. Down the hall, Thor typed at her computer.

I stood in her doorway. "Busy?"

She flexed her fingers. "Filling out reports. C'mon in, but I don't have results on Nathan yet."

Sans stocking cap, Thor's hair spiked up on her head like a gosling. If she was going for one of those edgy looks, it didn't work. Instead, she looked even more wholesome.

"I'm waiting for Wilcox. Just thought I'd check."

Thor ducked her head, and said, "Sorry I've been rude. I'm touchy about not being taken seriously, and I overcompensate for being little and cute." She spat out the words. "You probably never had that problem."

I leaned back against the door frame and crossed one ankle over the other. "Thanks."

Her entire head blushed. Pink scalp radiated through the spiky hairdo. "I mean you're tall and have those eyebrows."

I touched my eyebrows.

"I just meant you look intimidating, and you have experience. You're so good people have to take you seriously, Britt."

"I wasn't always. I got good, just like you will."

She scowled, deepening the dimple in her right cheek. "I'm working on it."

I studied her stapler like I'd never seen one before. "Jason thinks you're mad at him."

"Jason said that?" Thor's eyes popped open, transporting me to a field of cornflowers. No wonder Jason was lovesick.

116

I said, "He likes you." I mentally rolled my eyes. So high school.

"I like him too. I just don't have time for guys. I need to go to where the real action is, like you did."

The last thing I wanted was to promote giving up a dream. This conversation was way out of my depth.

Thor looked serious. "I mean you're like, thirty, right? You've been around a long time. You never even let marriage slow you down. I read your bio online. You went to Afghanistan, Iraq, Somalia, and all over the U.S. I don't want to get stuck here."

"Don't use me as an example of a balanced and joyful life. My marriage didn't last and I drank too much." I didn't add, and lost a job I loved.

"How did you get all those awards and the Pulitzer on that series about the children of war?"

I flopped into a chair across from her. "Honestly? I'm not smart, I'm not that tough or even a brilliant photographer. What I have is a knack for catching the moment of truth. I've been looking through a camera lens for twelve years, focusing on that moment."

She leaned toward me, and asked, "How do you know when it's the right shot?"

I shrugged. How do you explain something that only comes naturally with experience? "It's a recognition thing. It's like, there you are. I knew you were there."

Thor whispered. "I feel the same way when I discover a vital piece of forensic information. I want to make a difference too."

Her wide-eyed expression bordered on adoration, and that made me uncomfortable. I thought about my father. It was really all about atonement. "Stopping the bullies motivates me, but I take pictures. The ones who live it every day are the heroes. "

Thor's head snapped back as if I'd slapped her. I hadn't meant to be so harsh. "I have to go. Just let Jason down easy."

I checked Wilcox's door before going back to the bureau. Still shut.

***

Back at the bureau, Jason followed me to my desk. "What did she say?"

"She's been busy on the Maelstrom's."

"That's all?"

Cynthia poked her head out of her door and signaled us, saving me from a tough conversation. She pointed a finger at me. "You're late."

I could read faces and didn't like what I saw. We trooped in and sat in the two chairs opposite her desk. She stood behind it, leaning forward, her hands on the desk. "We're pulling the Isabel profile."

I sprang out of my chair. "You've got to be kidding."

Cynthia shrank into her oversize jacket. "You were supposed to be working on a profile of Isabel, not attempting to find her murderer and interrogating the family. You blew it and you know it."

"We've put a ton of work into this project. A murderer is loose out there." I knew better than to argue with editors, and yet I never stopped trying.

"It's the sheriff's job to investigate, not yours. We have a backlog of stories. We need to cover Branson U sports better. People expect it." She snapped at Jason. "And Thor can handle forensics without you hanging around her all day."

Jason scrunched lower into his seat.

I sat down, crossed my arms, and took a deep breath. "This is the hottest story since the casino scandal and you want me to cover college hockey?"

Cynthia ran her hand over her face as if to wipe me out of her line of vision. "Wilcox is furious. He said you've been impeding his investigation and upsetting the Spirit Lake townspeople."

"Not true." In my mind, I'd been doing more investigating than Wilcox, and those townspeople I'd upset could be the guilty ones.

"This is not LA. It's a small community. Everyone has to get along. We're not doing the profile. The sheriff will contact Jason when he has news about Isabel." Cynthia leaned back into her chair. "Subject closed. Jason, I emailed you a list of stories to update for the website. Britt, wait here a sec."

Jason shambled out, and Cynthia closed the door. She stared at her computer, her face worn. I wondered if she'd fire me for insubordination.

She said, "Minneapolis is short on photographers this week. You might need to go down there on short notice. We're working out the details, so keep in contact."

I slammed the door, rattling the posters on the walls.

Wilcox glanced up from his phone when I barged in. "I'll get back to you. I have a situation to deal with." He put the phone down. "You get the word, Johansson?"

"Are you afraid I might solve these murders while you're trying not to hurt people's feelings?"

He reared out of his chair. "You're telling everyone Nathan was murdered. On what evidence?"

I stepped back. "Thor's checking out a few things."

His fist slammed the desk. "Thor doesn't work for you."

Fist slamming didn't intimidate me. I fired back. "Just let me do my job. I'll stay out of your way."

He leaned in. "Like having Tommy's lawyer waiting at the jail when we got there?"

"He asked me to call his brother." I shrugged. "Daniel happens to be a lawyer. Plus, you didn't have a motive."

Wilcox's face turned the color of a rusted tailpipe. "If I see or hear of you annoying the Maelstroms, or stirring up trouble in Mille Lacs again, I'll throw your ass in jail for impeding an investigation. Now get out."

I stuck my index finger inches from his face. "You're making a huge mistake, Wilcox. Remember Gert's murder? Who nailed that one? Not you."

At the cabin, with my feet resting on the Franklin stove's warm platform, I sipped chamomile tea. Little said it would relax me.

True, since moving to Spirit Lake, I'd gotten my life back on track with help from family and friends. But I was bored, and just when a project came along that used my skills and talents, Cynthia and Wilcox yanked it away. I wasn't great at relationships, but my instincts as a photojournalist were solid. Maybe I'd stirred something up that would lead to Isabel and Nathan's killer, but now there was no chance of that happening unless Wilcox stepped up.

With Rock's comforting presence at my side and my feet warming at the stove, perspective returned. Marta put her reputation on the line when she got me the job at the *Strib*. I couldn't let her down this time. If I had to back off to keep from messing up my life again, I would. No one said I had to like it, though.

What really hurt was Ben telling me he didn't love me. I looked at the freezer where I used to keep my vodka, picked up my cup of tea and hurled it against the refrigerator. I buried my face in Rock's fur.

Chapter 14

Cynthia's weary voice on the other end of the line ruined my day before I was even out of bed Monday morning.

"The photo editor wants to borrow you to work on that story in the Twin Cities. Several busts of massage parlor fronts for prostitution are happening over the next two days. As I said yesterday, they're short on photographers."

Last night I'd resolved to not make waves. My hand tightened on the phone and I gritted my teeth. "Sure. No problem."

She didn't speak for a second, and then said, "Great. You need to head down there right away."

I sensed relief. Perhaps she expected more histrionics. I felt like such a grownup. "On my way."

I got ready, packed a bag and called Little. "Okay if Rock stays with you for a while?"

"I knew it. You're leaving again."

"I have an assignment in the Cities for a couple of days."

"Right. Bring Rock whenever." He hung up.

He didn't believe me. What was wrong with everybody?

I arrived at the *Strib* building in Minneapolis by noon. Disgruntled at being exiled, yet curious about the assignment, I waded into the usual newsroom pandemonium to the photo department. Reporters were on the phone and talking over each other, hustling back and forth, tapping at their computers or laptops, standing together gossiping.

This wasn't the first time I'd been called to an assignment in the Twin Cities, but I didn't recognize anyone I knew. The pod of photographer's cubicles at the back of the newsroom was empty. The photo editor spoke on the phone in his office. He was new to me, too. He got off the phone and reached over his desk to shake my hand, his shirt buttons working hard to keep from popping open. "I'm Bill Knox. Perfect timing, we've got a murder."

I sat on the edge of the chair he pointed at. "I thought I was shooting massage parlor busts?"

"It got complicated." He explained they'd discovered a dead man that morning at one of the places slated to be in the sting. The story changed from a routine bust to a homicide investigation. My interest level jumped several notches.

"Sorry for the rush, but you'll need to get over there right away." That ratcheted up the assignment. I shouldered my camera bag and hurried out.

The strip mall was on the outskirts of Coon Rapids, a bedroom community of Minneapolis. Similar to every other strip mall without a chain grocery store as an anchor, it consisted of a group of ragtag shops at the edge of the neighborhood where people tried to make a meager living. A gas and convenience shop at one corner could be accessed from north-south and east-west streets. The place was probably robbed weekly.

The massage parlor was tucked between a dental office with a sign that said Affordable White Smiles, and a cleaners. A simple sign above the massage parlor said Massage and Herbal Remedies. Police, ambulance and Federal Immigration and Customs vehicles filled the parking lot. Crime scene tape roped off the area in front of the massage parlor. A young police officer asked a group of gawkers to step away. They reluctantly dispersed into their shops and went about their business.

I headed toward the massage parlor entrance, and the young officer stepped in front of me. I pointed to the press credentials hanging around my neck. He glanced at them. "What's a Branson photographer doing so far from home?"

I explained about being on loan for the weekend and lifted my chin toward the crime scene. "What happened?"

"We've got a Vietnamese guy named Huy Hoang, who's been tortured and ended up with his throat cut. The girls who work there were locked in their quarters in back. We're waiting for a translator."

"When was he killed?"

He shook his head. "CSI's still in there, but it looks like he's been dead for days."

"How'd you get the tip?"

"Some guy walking to the donut shop complained about the smell coming from the massage parlor. Body was right inside the door, and some blood leaked out."

An older sergeant appeared, lips closed tight under a trim mustache. He pointed at me and asked the officer. "Who's this?"

I showed my credentials again. My camera hung from a thick strap around my neck, and my equipment bag was slung over my shoulder.

He read my name. "I knew I hadn't seen you before." The Sergeant spoke to the young officer. "Haven't I told you not to talk to the press?"

"I didn't say a word." The officer darted a look at me and went back to guard the crime scene.

"I'm on loan from the Branson bureau." I said to the sergeant.

"I'm Drake. Branson, huh? You with Winters on the border thing?"

I stared uncomprehending for a second before recovering. "I'm familiar with it. Could I take a look at the scene?"

"Not while they're working in there. Winters can fill you in."

I looked around, but didn't see Ben. "Sergeant, I heard the guy was tortured. So more than a robbery gone wrong?"

"Off the record, it's different. It looks like a professional hit that got personal. Took off a couple of fingers to get whatever he wanted. The death was overkill like your typical crime of passion. Bunch of hacking knife wounds." He pointed to my camera. "That's holdback. We don't want that in the news."

Sergeant Drake left me and joined the other officer. He didn't follow his own advice, or maybe he just liked to be the one to talk to the press. I wished Wilcox acted more like him.

Ben was on his way to Minneapolis, but hadn't mentioned the details of his project, and Cynthia would have filled me in if she'd known about Ben's connection. I was nervous about him thinking I was getting into his business, but this was really a coincidence.

I switched out my lenses, hitched my bag over my shoulder and got to work taking photos of the massage parlor sign, crime scene tape swaying in the wind, officers milling around stamping their feet. Moving a short distance away for a corner shot, I backed into someone, turned, and said, "Excuse me."

Ben and I locked eyes. He looked more surprised than annoyed for a change. "What are you doing here?"

A part of me wanted to hurt him for hurting me, and I enjoyed the confused look on his face. "Cynthia sent me. I'm on loan to the mother ship for a couple of days."

We faced each other in the middle of the parking lot. "I'm asking why you are here at this scene."

"I'm supposed to cover a trafficking sting. Maybe you'd like to fill me in."

His lips tightened. "I don't have time."

"I know you've been in the BW a lot, and now you're here. Is there a connection?"

"I'm part of the team. I've been working the border connection in the BW." He pointed at the massage parlor. "We were hitting this one later today. Huy, the dead guy in there, ran it. He was supposed to give up the head of the entire operation in exchange for leniency."

"I'm sorry. It looks like your kingpin beat you to it."

His shoulders drooped. "Months of work just went down the drain. We shut down the massage parlors that are fronts for the sex trade, they pop up somewhere else. It means nothing if we don't get the guy bringing them in."

"I'm really sorry. Are you back to square one?"

He snapped. "Just stay away from this. The last thing I need is for you to get in the way. Aren't you covering Isabel's murder?"

It was my turn to snap back. "I'm off the story."

I'm sure he wanted details, but he didn't ask. He said, "This operation is postponed now that we've got a murder to deal with. You should go back to Spirit Lake."

"Last I checked you weren't my employer. By the way, Edgar made a vague comment about the Maelstrom deaths and the case you're working on. Is there a connection?"

He looked at me like I'd lost my mind. "You can't think those two kids were involved in the sex trade?"

"Maybe the kids found out about someone who's connected. How well do you know Woz and Brody? They've got the plane and the access. He crosses the Canadian border when he's guiding. Who's to say he doesn't have a side business?"

"Impossible. I've known Woz for years." He stopped and faced me. "For what it's worth, I'm sorry for Saturday. I was a jerk."

"Not a problem." What he called being a jerk, I called being gutted like a deer. I think both of us were relieved when the sergeant motioned Ben over. This wasn't the time or place to have that conversation.

The parking lot filled with television station vans, call letters bright against the leaden sky—KARE, KSTP, WCCO. The aborted sting and gruesome murder attracted all the press.

A guy with credentials hanging from his neck and a reporter's notebook waved at me, and introduced himself as Lee Chang from the *Strib*.

"We heard they were sending you down. What's someone like you been doing up north with the jack pine savages?"

I wasn't in the mood to get into my story. "I'm going back to deal with my photos and write captions, unless you have other ideas."

He said no, that the city desk sent him because he spoke a little Chinese, and might get something from the girls, but the police wouldn't let him in with them. My phone interrupted me, so I excused myself and took the call.

Cynthia heard about the sting being called off, and wanted me to report for work as usual in Branson on Monday. I stomped toward my car with the phone in my ear. She ended the conversation with another reminder not to work on the Maelstrom deaths. I tossed the phone into the passenger seat. Shooting hockey and town meetings were all I had to look forward to now.

At the paper, I told Bill the photo editor the story. Bill rubbed at a grease stain on his white shirt. A crumpled KFC bag and large diet Coke littered the top of his desk. "You ever want to transfer down here, call me. We could use a pro like you full time."

Nearby, a photographer's head popped up from behind his computer. Bill's comment probably didn't make his day.

"Thanks, Bill, I appreciate your offer. I'll keep it in mind." If Cynthia continued to be such a wimp, I would consider it. Who needed to work for a bunch of small timers protecting their own asses?

I finished up my captions, and gathered my camera bag, ready to hit the road for Spirit Lake. One of the photographers wanted to talk equipment, but I wasn't interested. I'd owned a collection of about forty cameras at one time, but left them at the L.A. condo. Early on, I'd been an equipment junkie, wanting every new gadget, but for years now, I'd relied on my eye and three favorites.

No lights were on at Little's when I arrived back in Spirit Lake. They closed early most Monday evenings. The guys were probably watching TV in their residence at the back, but I didn't feel like getting into a long conversation. I'd pick up Rock in the morning.

I saw a familiar figure on my way through town and did a double-take. Tommy was leaving Olafson's bar with a brown paper bag under his arm, his head ducked against the wind.

I'd spent some time in Olafson's last year before I quit drinking. Booths lined one wall, a long saloon bar ran down the middle, and tables were scattered on the other side. In the front area, a window like a bank teller's sold booze by the bottle or case. I watched as Tommy tucked the bag inside his parka.

I honked and lowered the car window. "Hey Tommy, what brings you to Spirit Lake?"

"Daniel told me to stay away from the bar in Cooper." He didn't look at me. "And I didn't want Ray watching every move I make so I hitched down here."

"I'll take you home."

Tommy slid in the passenger side, keeping his head down.

I glanced over. "I suppose Ray told you someone in Mille Lacs said they saw you at the casino."

He shrugged. "It wasn't me."

"Have you heard from your dad lately?" I drove through town, all but deserted this evening.

"We don't talk."

So far this conversation was like trying to talk to Ben. "At least Wilcox let you go."

"He still thinks I killed her. My brother convinced the judge I wouldn't run off or go on a killing spree." He bared his teeth at me. I pretended it didn't unnerve me.

"I didn't think they would hold you without a motive."

"The sheriff's out to get me. My fingerprints were in the car but so were about half the town and a bunch of her school friends. It's bullshit, but it's not like they're going after a Branson U frat boy when there's someone like me to blame."

I wasn't a fan of the sheriff, but knew him to be fair. "They'll keep looking for evidence. Be patient."

His voice wobbled. "Do they have any other suspects?"

"I don't know what's going on with the investigation. Cynthia took me off the story and Wilcox won't tell me anything."

His sigh mirrored my own frustration. I left town and merged onto the highway. "Your brother is trying to help you, so why don't you do what he asks and stay away from the drinking?" A stupid thing to say.

"Last I checked, alcohol isn't against the law. Anyway, what difference does it make? If they're putting me behind bars for the rest of my life, why not drink myself to death first and at least go out feeling good?" He slipped the bottle from inside his jacket, taking quick sips. We neared his turnoff and he tucked the bottle back into his jacket. "I can walk from here."

"It's two miles to your place and ten below. This is a four-wheel-drive." Tire tracks had already opened up the road. I said, "Looks like someone else drove through here."

The car tracks swerved into a turn-out area about a mile before Tommy's driveway. I pointed. "I thought you said no one used this road. Who would be stopping there?"

He mumbled. "Probably hunters?"

I said, "Maybe that's who clipped me with an arrow last week. Unless you did it."

"I didn't do anything." He rocked forward and back. "My head feels like it's going to fucking explode." He took another drink from his bottle.

I made it to the driveway of his house but I'd have needed a plow attached to the front of my vehicle to get any closer. I hoped he'd get out quickly. The smell of bourbon got to me. I seldom needed to fight the demons anymore, but feeling depressed over Ben and frustrated in my job were not helping my willpower, especially when the stuff was right under my nose.

Tommy seemed overwrought, and I wasn't sure how to deal with that, especially since he was drinking. He opened the door and I got my first good look at him under the interior light. The right side of his face was bruised and swollen. I touched his arm. "Whoa, what happened to your face?"

He chewed on a fingernail. "I got in a fight."

"Was that fight in Mille Lacs?"

"I told you I didn't go down there." He looked around as if someone might be watching, hopped out, hurried down a narrow path to his front door and disappeared inside his house. I waited for a few more minutes, but no lights came on.

If I hadn't given my word that I'd back off the story, I'd come back tomorrow with binoculars, and I'd wear a helmet.

Chapter 15

Now that I was off the Isabel profile, and no early assignments from Cynthia, I joined the morning coffee drinkers at Little's. A magnet was pulling me off the stool toward Tommy's, but I stayed put.

When he saw me from the kitchen doorway, Little's eyebrows lifted. "I thought you'd be gone longer, if not forever."

"Maybe someone overreacted? I got back too late last night to pick up Rock."

He came through the swinging doors. "How was Minneapolis?"

Unable to keep the bitterness from my voice, I said, "The bust was a bust."

He pivoted. "C'mon, I'm working on my lunch menu." I followed him into the kitchen and watched him add spices to his soup pot. He asked, "So you're back on Isabel's murder?"

The aroma of homemade vegetable soup almost made me feel better. "Cynthia took me off the story. Apparently, Wilcox is her real boss."

He brightened. "Really?" I leveled him with a death stare, and he went back to stirring his soup. "You want some breakfast?"

"Thanks, maybe later. I want to snowshoe for a while. Where's Rock?"

Little pointed his hot pad toward the back. "In the garage. Lars' snowmobile has a glitch. I'm jealous, whenever it's slow in here he runs to his Ski-do."

I wiggled my eyebrows at Little. "She is pretty, and I hear she's fast."

"If he's not out there, he mentioned needing a part." Little went back to his cooking.

"See you at Isabel's funeral this afternoon." I grabbed an apple on the way out.

Lars and Rock were not in the garage, but the potbellied stove was still warm. I was debating whether to wait for Rock when my phone rang. The display showed the *LA Times* prefix. My spirits lifted.

"Hey Mart, I was just thinking about you. You'd be proud of me. They took me off the Isabel story and I didn't throw a fit and get myself fired."

Marta made a sound between a snort and a cackle that sounded like she needed sinus surgery. "That's real growth for you."

"So what's up?" Marta's big-framed glasses would be pushed up on her head, holding her chin-length hair away from her face. The newsroom sounds on the other end of the line, phones ringing, people tapping keyboards, the buzz of conversation were part of my circulatory system. I'd absorbed its energy in Minneapolis, and now it zapped me from 2,000 miles away. I missed that scene, especially today.

"Interesting you should mention getting taken off your local story because I'm calling to make a much better offer."

"Shoot." I dropped into a chair, stretching my boots toward the heat, senses on alert.

Marta's usually vibrant voice dropped so much I could barely hear her. "You're doing so well in Spirit Lake, better than you've been for years. Maybe this isn't a good idea."

Marta did not usually dither. "What's wrong? Spill it, friend."

"It wasn't even my idea. The photo editor approached me and he'd already gotten management's approval."

"Marta!"

"All hell is breaking loose on just about every part of the globe."

"We do get the news up here." I wanted to strangle the phone.

"They want to hire you back. They've let people go with the crap economy, and now they don't have enough talented photographers left on the payroll to cover everything."

I shot to my feet. "The *Times* wants me back?" The shame of getting fired drained away. What if I wasn't a total loser after all?

Marta hurried to add, "I'm just saying you're healthy and sober and not in the same state as that jerk Richard, to be sucked back into his so-called charms."

My jaw clenched. "You think I'm that fragile?"

"I'm worried it's too soon." A whoosh of air came across the phone line. I pictured her blowing her bangs off her forehead, a habit when stressed.

I wasn't used to hesitancy from Marta. As city editor, she barked out assignments, no second-guessing. "It's been a year, Marta. You don't think I could handle L.A. or working war zones, after having done it for twelve years? And done it well, I might add." Whatever hackles were, mine were rising.

"Yes, you've got the awards, but at what price, Britt?"

I got it. Friend Marta was at odds with Editor Marta. I said, "Richard's in England anyway, no doubt with his latest twenty-something."

Young, ambitious MBAs thought he was a great mentor and the ticket to rise in the business climate he'd mastered years ago. I'd caught the last one with him in our Jacuzzi. My hair band held her shiny black hair off her neck in an adorable pony tail. My lemongrass bath bubbles cascaded across her shoulder and down her breast like a homecoming corsage.

"He'd come back if he knew you were here." I heard the concern in her tone.

"So are you offering me a job or not?" The silence lasted so long I wondered if she'd changed her mind.

"Yes, the *Times* is offering you a job."

Her trepidation didn't inspire confidence. "I'll get back to you." I hit the end button.

An icy draft crept through the garage. My hand touched the tender spot near my ear, and I stuck my head through the doorway into the adjoining area where the guys parked their cars. Rock came toward me, tail wagging.

"How'd you get in here, buddy? Didn't I get that door shut?" I ruffled his fur and he danced around, our usual greeting. Rock followed me back to the stove and watched me pace in front of it.

Did Marta have to remind me of past foolish decisions? Her concern irritated me. Was I hiding out in Spirit Lake, or taking care of myself? My fingers sought Edgar's wolf agate in my pocket, and my thumb stroked the smooth stone's familiar groove. It always calmed me.

What about my talents and ambition? If I didn't make my move now, would I ever have the nerve? Or would I become like Wilcox or Cynthia, unwilling to rock the boat, opting for the safety and quiet of a simple life? What did I want? Ben, only he didn't want me. Little thought he needed me, but he had Lars. I wanted to do what I did best, cover major news like a photojournalist. This was a chance to redeem myself and not be remembered as that former star photographer who washed out. That said, I knew the real reason was something I couldn't name. That nameless drive compelled me forward, almost without regard for my own free will. I started to call Marta back, but put the phone away. Snowshoeing with Rock would help clear my mind before the funeral.

I stood at the bottom of the Lutheran church steps in Cooper, framed the scene and took photos as friends and family in somber clothing, heads bowed, passed through the entryway.

Cynthia's instructions were to take photos, period. "No intrusive questions, Britt. Your photos probably won't be used until they find her killer and we do a wrap-up, if then."

Inside, Isabel's enlarged high school graduation photo leaned against an easel surrounded by roses. Mourners stopped to write in an open booklet on a table. A basket held tasseled bookmarks with Isabel's birth and death dates and a passage from Revelations about the old order of things having passed.

Wooden beams crisscrossed the peaked ceiling of the spare Scandinavian design interior. Stained glass depicting scenes from the Bible cast colored shafts of light from the weak afternoon sun as three musicians played gentle hymns behind the pulpit.

Today, in the peaceful place of worship, agitation stirred below the surface. How could this have happened in this close-knit and quiet community of law-abiding Swedes, Norwegians, Germans and Ojibwe?

Once again the Snow White image came to me as I gazed down at the raven-haired beauty in her white velvet-lined casket. Arnie spared no expense to send her into the next world in the finest carriage money could buy: Black steel with silver hardware shaped like tiaras, her name embroidered inside the lid. After mourners filed past the open casket, the funeral director closed it and covered it with a cascade of red roses. Isabel would rest in a vault until spring, the ground too frozen to bury her.

The sweet scent of roses followed me to my seat. Ben sat next to Little and Lars. They didn't say hello when I slid in beside Ben. What had I done now? I whispered to Ben, "How's the investigation in Minneapolis progressing?

"No new leads."

"What have you heard from Wilcox?"

A muscle jumped in his jaw.

"Please don't shut me out of this, too."

He whispered between clenched teeth. "Brody doesn't have an alibi for the time of death. He could have gotten to Spirit Lake and back in the hours between when they were seen arguing in the student union and when he met friends for drinks, but so far they don't have evidence to connect him."

"That's it?"

"They've interviewed students and everyone who knew her on campus. No motive, no evidence."

"So Tommy still looks the best."

He nodded.

"I won't tell Wilcox you gave me information."

He shifted position and moved farther away. "Suit yourself."

Conversations hushed as the pastor began Isabel's eulogy. "We are here to say a sad and fond farewell to a sweet young woman loved by all who knew her."

I scanned the pews, half listening. What did I expect to find? A furtive glance? A guilty face? A fearful twitch seemed to have everyone in its grip.

Brody sat with friends. Where were his parents? Amber and her mother sat several pews away. Amber darted looks at Brody but he didn't appear to notice. His deep-set eyes were hollow and red-rimmed. Sheriff Wilcox and his wife were there. Townspeople from Cooper and Spirit Lake and a group of college friends filled the church. Dee and Pauly sat in the front row with Arnie. They'd have to have another funeral when Nathan's body was released.

After the eulogy, a DVD of photos of Isabel and her family and friends set to her favorite music played on a large screen. Images flashed before us of Isabel as a baby, as a toddler and a teenager, playing in the water, kayaking with Nathan. Isabel sitting on Arnie's lap with her arm around his neck, a besotted look on his face. Isabel waving from a float made of tissue flowers for the Fourth of July parade. Isabel tossing her hat at graduation, grinning because her whole life was ahead of her. There wasn't a dry eye in the church, including mine.

Several people shared tender memories at different stages of her life. Wispy Amber tottered up the few steps in a black skirt and heels. Tremulous, she tried to speak but gave in to tears. Her mother helped her back to her seat.

The pastor stepped back to the pulpit to say a few last words. He began, "Isabel's death touches us all."

A commotion in the front pew drowned him out. Everyone craned to see Arnie jump to his feet and charge the pulpit. The pastor stepped back, confusion and concern on his face.

Arnie glared and gripped the sides as if he would hurl it at the crowd. "No, it touches ME." He slapped his chest. "Isabel was MY beautiful child. Everything I did was for her. I wanted

Isabel to have the perfect childhood. I wanted every day to be a joy for her, and just like her mother, she was taken from me."

Arnie's outburst caused people to gasp and draw back. Some cried.

"Now all I have to remember her is the resort she loved." He sagged against the pulpit, spent. The pastor pried Arnie's fingers away and coaxed him down the steps to his seat. Arnie bent forward, his head in his hands. Dee clutched the cross at her neck. She didn't put out a comforting hand to her husband. Pauly scooted down in his seat.

The pastor ended the service with a nervous prayer, one eye on Arnie.

Downstairs, two long lines of people shuffled forward to fill plates with food prepared by the church ladies in a cavernous community room. A subdued buzz of conversation swirled around. Mingled aromas of baked beans, corn bread, meat and cheese hot dishes, and the ever-present coffee filled the room.

Dee filled a plate at a table loaded with platters and bowls and slow cookers. I offered condolences and commented on the video and all of the beautiful touches. "Did you do all that, Dee?"

Her gaze dropped. "I went through all the photos, but a church committee did most of the work. Arnie wanted it to be special."

"I'm surprised both funerals weren't held at the same time."

Dee put a spoonful of potatoes on the plate. "Arnie wanted it to be just for Isabel."

I touched her arm. "How are you holding up?"

She glanced at Arnie. "I don't know how we're going to go on at the resort. He's so devastated."

Arnie sat at one of the tables, staring forward. No one dared approach him. They didn't know this Arnie. Their familiar friend was submerged in grief. He took a flask from his coat pocket and brought it to his lips.

Dee straightened her shoulders. "I need to get his food to him." She moved through the tables in a calf-length black skirt, sturdy black shoes and a wool coat, her rosy cheeks oddly out of place. Pauly followed close behind, so quiet I hardly noticed him.

Before they could join him, Arnie lurched to his feet, his folding chair crashed to the ground and a vase of flowers wobbled. "Screw this," he said, and stalked out.

Dee stood with the filled plate in her hand for a moment before she dropped into one of the chairs. Bella hobbled over and sat next to her, patting her hand. Everyone took a moment to regroup before hushed conversations again filled the silent hall.

I caught a movement at a table in the corner. Amber left her mother's side and went into the bathroom. Cynthia said to stay out of it and I agreed not to ask questions. However, the other Britt was in charge of my actions at the moment. I followed her into the bathroom, checked under the stalls and locked the door so no one would disturb us. When she came out of the stall, I asked, "How are you, Amber?"

Her face scrunched up. "I messed up. My speech was all prepared, but it was too hard." She dabbed under her eyes. "My mascara's all over the place."

She took the tissue I offered, blew her nose, and still looking in the mirror, said, "Everyone thought Isabel was so great. Even when people talked to me, they were looking at her, just like today up on the screen."

I pumped foam into my hands and ran water over them. "It couldn't have been easy being her best friend."

Amber nodded. "She was so lucky. A dad who loved her so much he changed his mind about selling the resort, just for her. And my dad, he takes off with his secretary, who isn't even much older than me and leaves Mom and me with a broken down house and not enough money to pay the bills. I guess this makes me an awful person, only why should everything work out so great for her?" Her lip caught between her teeth. "Oh, god, I guess it didn't after all." Amber bit her bottom lip. "I'm an awful friend."

Tossing my paper towel into a bin, I said, "I'm still trying to figure out why she went home so much on the weekends."

Amber blinked. "I mean, most of us would rather hang out but she and her dad were working on starting up a nightclub next summer at the resort. She was going to run it."

"Did she behave differently that week?"

Her brows pulled together in a frown. "Yeah, she was way intense. Not like you get during finals, though."

Someone banged on the bathroom door. I unlocked it and several women swooshed in, enveloped Amber in their arms, and shot outraged glances at me. I left her to the ministrations of the ladies.

Ben stood at the back of the reception hall, drinking coffee. I filled a cup from a giant silver urn and stood next to him. Two old friends sipping coffee. Maybe he'd never love me again, but I'd never give up on our friendship. I said, "Big turnout."

He nodded and continued watching the crowd.

Thinking fast for a topic he might respond to, I asked, "Have you helped Edgar with his dream?"

"They can't start knocking on doors all over the reservation to check if any girls are being mistreated on the basis of a dream. People are keeping their eyes and ears open." He set his cup on a table. "Why are you pretending to care about this community?"

That comment was like a punch in the gut. I wanted to ask what he meant, but he'd already gone. I scanned the room for a friendly face and waved at Bella and Violet, but they acted like they didn't see me. Were they snubbing me? Several others darted quick glances at me and whispered to each other. I filled a plate and set it down next to the guys. Little jumped up. "I have to open up the restaurant."

I raised an eyebrow at Lars. "What's gotten into him?"

Lars gathered their plates, dumped them in a bin and followed Little. They were halfway to the restaurant by the time I caught up, panting. "What's going on?"

Little kept walking, arms pumping. "You said you were staying. Were you just going to disappear again?"

It wasn't hard to keep up with him. His legs were shorter than mine. "I haven't decided anything. Marta just called with an offer."

They kept walking.

"Wait. How did you find out? You eavesdrop on my private conversations?"

Lars' face reddened. "I came back into the garage this morning and heard you on the phone."

Now I understood how Rock suddenly appeared. "So you ran to tell Little? Backstabber."

His head ducked. "I should have made my presence known, but I wanted to keep him from being too upset. I wanted to be the one to break the news."

Frosty gusts shot from my mouth. "I can talk to my own brother. It was none of your business."

"Little *is* my business." Lars could be formidable with his barrel chest and long arms flailing. "You're too abrupt and you two would have another falling out. I wanted to prepare him, and orchestrate a better outcome."

If I wasn't so upset, I'd laugh at the way Lars could switch from saying "Jayzus" before every sentence to forming the phrase, "orchestrate a better outcome." He tried to fit in as a local, but he would always be a professor.

Little spoke through gritted teeth. "Since when are you the manager of my life, Lars?"

Lars whirled around so fast I slammed into him. "Handle your own relationship for a change and see how far it gets you. Look what happened before I came into the picture. You and Britt hadn't seen each other in years. You two don't need a mediator—you need a referee." He jabbed a finger at Little. "Don't expect me to pick up all the pieces and put you back together again if this is all the thanks I get."

He peeled off in the other direction, leaving us with our mouths open, chastened. I asked Little, "How does everyone in town know about my conversation with Marta?"

He looked at his feet. "I got kind of loud when Lars first came into the restaurant and told me what you said in the garage. Everyone knew about it at the funeral."

It was too cold to stand still, so we hustled toward the restaurant. "Great, now even Bella and Violet are mad at me."

"Not to mention how hard it hit Ben."

"He'd be thrilled to have several continents between us."

"You're so clueless." He sighed, and went into the restaurant with his shoulders hunched forward.

I called after him. "I'm probably not going."

He closed the door without looking back.

Lars was right. I was hopeless at relationships. I even messed up other people's. Now Little and Lars were fighting. Everyone cared about Little and Lars and if they were upset, it rippled through the whole town. I yanked open the SUV door and drove to Branson. Cynthia expected my funeral photos for tomorrow's paper. That, I knew I could get right.

I was back in Spirit Lake by dinnertime. My stomach growled but I kept going past the restaurant. Little and Lars had a better chance of working out the mess I'd caused without me hanging around.

Headlights glowed in my rearview mirror as I neared my cabin. My heartbeat quickened, and I touched the wound above my ear. Then I recognized the familiar green forest service truck bumping down the road behind my car. Maybe Ben wanted to add to his list of grievances against me.

We got out of our vehicles and faced each other, wary, like prize fighters before a match. "I've been looking for you," he said.

The thunder on his face told me he was ready to have it out. I'd nagged him to get his anger out in the open, but staring it in the face made me want to get back in the car, throw it into reverse and tear out of there.

I asked, "Why did you follow me through town? Everyone's avoiding me like I'm contagious."

He spoke when he was ready, as usual. "Just like that you're taking off for L.A. Now Little's ranting at everyone in the kitchen while Lars tries to keep things calm. Nice work."

I threw up my hands. "I haven't decided." I knew better, but asked anyway. "What about you, how do you feel about it?"

Arms crossed, he said, "I hate to see your brother like this."

I moved closer to him. "Be honest. You don't want me to go, and yet you won't even try to work out what happened last year."

His hand shot out and circled my neck. Our faces were so close Ben's breath swirled around mine in the cold air.

"Are you going to strangle me?" I almost wanted him to. It would put me out of my misery.

He let go, and with his lips clamped together, pointed to the deck outside my bedroom. The infamous wooden swing sat there, covered with snow. He jabbed his finger at it. "That's why it's over between us."

Ben hadn't been the same since that awful night last summer. Richard came to Spirit Lake to talk me into going back to him. I hadn't had anything to drink in months, but Richard made his special Midsummer Night's Eve cocktail, and charmed me into going out to one of the big resort nightclubs. We'd danced and had too much to drink, and ended up falling asleep on the porch swing.

In the morning, Rock barked and woke me when a truck pulled into the driveway. Richard and I were still tangled in the blanket on the swing, glasses and bottles and the pitcher of punch were strewn on the deck, Richard's tousled sandy was head in my lap. At least there'd been no sex that I remembered.

Ben's boots crunching in the gravel felt like someone pounding rocks into my skull. Wincing at the sun in my eyes, I'd squinted up at him standing in front of me. "This isn't what it looks like. We didn't, we just fell asleep here...."

He yanked Richard away from me, held him up with one hand and pulled his fist back to smash it into his face.

Still so drunk he hung limp in Ben's grip, Richard said, "Whoa, dude, what's the problem?"

Ben dropped Richard on the porch, and said, "You asshole."

He didn't speak as he stomped to his truck, but I'd heard his thoughts loud and clear. He never wanted to see me again.

Now he stared at the swing, pain in his eyes, and for the first time I really understood how much I'd hurt him. My voice faltered. "I'm so sorry."

"You went back to L.A. with him."

I could only see Ben's outline in the moonless sky. I moved closer, imploring. "I told you it wasn't what it looked like."

His jaw tightened. "You promised not to drink, he showed up and got you drunk again. The same thing will happen if you go back to L.A. now."

That's what this was about.

Steam blew out his nostrils. "Why are you trying so hard to get me to love you again, anyway? Why now? Because you could have had me in high school, you could have had me last year."

I'd thought about his question and knew the answer but didn't know how to say it. "I was confused, and afraid."

"Afraid of being with me?"

He was getting angry again. I knew that wouldn't come out right. "I was afraid I couldn't live up to your standards. You're the reliable one. People know they can count on you, Mr. Integrity. You wouldn't even know how to tell a lie."

"That's bullshit, Britt."

"Okay, then why did you fall in love with me? You never said anything in high school, so that comment wasn't fair. But last spring you said you loved me. Why then?"

He took my hand. "You were willing to die to save my life last spring. When we were flying across the channel on that beat up snowmobile with the ice breaking up behind us, your determination was what kept us from going in. And in my hospital room, I knew you loved me when I heard you praying to God that if I lived you'd never touch another drink."

I looked at the swing and shame washed over me. "I did, though."

With a long, low sigh, he said, "You're passionate, and unpredictable." His thumb pushed the hair behind my ears, and lingered. He leaned forward, kissed me lightly on the lips and stepped away.

"And it's too hard to love you right now." He got into his truck.

What I'd wanted was for him to strip me naked right there and make mad love until we melted the snow down to the ground. For a moment it almost seemed possible. "You're a coward," I said.

He spoke through the open window. "Would you give up doing the work you love to stay here?"

I wanted to say yes, but the words didn't form. My face was hot even though we stood in minus seven-degrees.

I watched his truck until the tail lights disappeared. He'd never trust me. Why should he? I didn't even know what I really wanted.

I fed the stove enough wood to heat three times the space, my movements thick and clumsy. My psyche contained a graveyard of shameful memories. Looking back at my life path was dangerous, negotiating all those twists and turns, getting lost in a maze of why's and why me's. Better to go forward. Everyone in town was mad at me and it wasn't fair. I didn't even get a chance to think about Marta's offer free of everyone else's opinion. Small towns sucked.

Chapter 16

With my feet propped on the oak dining table and laptop balanced on my knees, I scrolled through *LA Times* stories on the latest developments in Syria. The photos taken by my former colleagues made me jealous. I belonged there, where all I had to deal with was getting the perfect shot, and not getting shot myself. The phone rang and I slapped the laptop cover closed, even though no one could see me.

"It's Thor. I have results on Nathan's boot prints at the cabin. Wilcox told me not to talk to you about the case, but I owed you this one."

A familiar thrum of excitement moved through my system. "What did you find?"

"I'm in my lab if you want to check it out. Wilcox isn't here."

"I'll be there in thirty minutes."

In addition to her office near Wilcox's, Thor worked in a windowless lab downstairs, outfitted with forensic equipment. Not the latest and best, but what the department could afford. My nose wrinkled when I entered. The place smelled like my high school chemistry lab.

Table tops and open lockers held containers of collected materials, camera, evidence bags, portable lights, and all the kits—fingerprint, tire and shoe impression, blood sample, rape, gunshot residue and chemicals. File cabinets lined one wall, no doubt filled with information on past cases to supplement computer files.

Thor wore camo pants and a long-sleeved black T-shirt with a profanity printed on it, and rings on every finger. I wanted to take her photo, but she was all business. She pointed to the stool on her work table. "I found Nathan's boot print on the top of it, but none on the floor or the steps and no scuffs from his boot on the stool where he might have kicked it. There was a partial from another boot on the lower part of the stool where he couldn't have kicked it himself. So how did he get up on the stool without walking into the cabin?"

I nodded at the stool. "I'd say someone carried him."

She said, "His fingerprints weren't on it, so how did he get himself up there without leaving fingerprints?"

"Someone put him there." I'd thought that's what happened.

Thor said, "They were wiped or Dee must be a super-thorough cabin cleaner because it was completely clean of fingerprints."

I smiled at her. "Good work."

Thor flushed. "Once I eliminated all the law enforcement footprints, it was obvious that someone swept the floor before they left. Oh, and still no results on the vomit."

"Thanks, but why not tell me this over the phone?"

Thor studied the floor. "Is it true you're going back to the *LA Times*?"

I leaned against the door frame. "Gossip gets out of hand up here in the winter, doesn't it?"

"Are you?"

I shrugged. Everyone wanted to know the answer to that, including me.

Thor's eyes sparkled. "I'd go. It's so boring here, and I heard you got taken off Isabel. It must piss you off. It would me."

Thor's excitement about the glamorous life of an international photographer reminded me why I couldn't wait to get back to American soil after every assignment. The moral dilemma haunted me—try to help people, or get the picture? Did showing the world the horror make a difference or did it just sell papers?

Thor said, "I wish I could be detached like you. It was hard at that cabin. Nathan was a friend."

Detached? A part of me died every time I saw a child hurt. I'd made it my mission to document the suffering of children in war-torn countries, but my impotence at the injustices left me so frustrated I drank so I could sleep at night. My doctor said my drinking was self-medicating to help with the PTSD.

"You get used to it," I lied. I kept that pain locked up or I'd never be able to do the work. Over the years, I'd learned to put everything aside but the job. When the job was over, the feelings could have their way with me, in private.

Thor stretched. "I'm done here. Wanna get some pizza and beers?"

College kids and families crowded the booths and tables at Luigi's, a Branson favorite for forty years. Waiters and waitresses dodged back and forth with pizzas and pitchers of beer. Loud and lively, the place smelled divine. I was glad Thor talked me into coming. She ordered a veggie with no cheese on a thin whole wheat crust, and I ordered a combo with extra everything.

Thor sipped her Hefeweizen and badgered me to talk about my work for the *Times*, but I changed the subject to Nathan. "What do you think lured Nathan out of the lodge after I dropped him off?"

She picked a wad of spinach from her pizza and popped it in her mouth. "No idea. That's the sheriff's area. I just collect and analyze evidence."

I took another slice. "It was a bold move to murder him at the resort, unless the killer was confident it would be considered a suicide."

Thor washed down her mouthful of spinach with a gulp of beer. "How did you figure out the stool?" She caught the waiter's attention and ordered another one.

"I wondered why Nathan wouldn't have used one of the high-backed chairs. It's much easier to kick the back of a chair than a stool. And how could he have kicked the stool so hard it landed across the room?"

145

In my experiment, I'd struggled to get the stool to fall over, and my neck wasn't in a noose. I didn't tell Thor about the test. I crooked a finger at her mouth. "A chunk of spinach is wrapped around your right front tooth."

She worked it off with her tongue. "Want another Hef?"

I pointed at my water. "Someone your size, I bet your alcohol level is already hovering at the limit." At thirty-four I was an old lady who passed judgment on the younger generation.

She said, "It's Nathan and Isabel. I sort of want to block it out right now."

I knew from experience that was a risky path. Thor was in no hurry to leave, so we talked about Jason while she ordered her third beer. She admitted she really liked him, but was afraid of the commitment. She said, "Jason says he wishes he could be as much of a badass as you. Like at that FBI bust in Cloud Lake. He said you owned that scene. The other photographers just got out of your way."

Thor's comment embarrassed me a little. I hadn't realized Jason was watching me that day. "I didn't start out wanting to be tough. We moved so much when I was a kid, and I needed to protect my brother." I sipped my water. "War photography is still a male world, so I had to be aggressive at the *Times* to keep up in that environment, and to stay alive. It's true, I'm physically strong. I work hard at that." I flexed my right arm, and grinned. "And now I kind of like the badass reputation."

Looking as tough as a baby chick, Thor lifted her beer. "To badass women."

In the parking lot, I steered her, wobbling, to my SUV. No way was she driving home. She glanced into my back seat when she got out of the car at her apartment. "Where's your bow?"

I looked back to see what she was talking about. She pointed at the arrow.

"Someone shot that thing at me a week ago. I meant to ask you to check it for fingerprints, but got distracted."

Her beery eyes widened. "Someone shot at you and you didn't report it?"

"I didn't want Wilcox to have another excuse to keep me away."

She pulled a set of latex gloves from her pocket and slipped them on. Always prepared. The kid really did remind me of me, except for the tiny and cute part.

She held the arrow away from her body. "I'll check it tomorrow and get back to you."

"Thanks, but please don't mention it to Wilcox. In fact, don't mention to anyone that we talked about your evidence from Nathan's death either."

I didn't want to get Thor in trouble for talking to me. I couldn't do anything with the information anyway, now that I was benched. Wilcox would use Thor's information and figure this out. Except he thought he already had his killer.

Everything looked different in the morning. Last night I'd printed photos of everyone connected to Isabel and spread them out on the oak table. Photos didn't lie. Townspeople described Arnie as a great father and community leader, but Dee hinted that he wasn't so great. Pious Dee, head lowered in prayer, yet not so gentle and compassionate when she talked about her son. Pauly's skimpy goatee curling under his chin and apologetic smile couldn't hide the fury under his downcast eyes. Girls got excited about guys like Brody with his heavy brow and brooding way, but jealous and possessive could be an explosive combo.

I remembered Brody's dad, Woz, from Ben's and my trip to the BW last summer, his face hidden by a heavy, dark beard. Ben said he was just rough around the edges, but no one suspected the people they saw every day.

Isabel's best friend was jealous and she had a crush on Brody. Could she have been an accomplice? Was she sad over losing a friend, or filled with remorse?

Tommy, a defiant and scared meth dealer with a secret.

Anger masked fear, and I understood it. It caused me to go over the line a few times. Right now, I feared losing my reason to get up in the morning. I needed challenges, and my mission to not let the bullies win trumped everything.

Now there were two murders, and I needed to know why. There was a time when I would have agonized longer over this decision to do the opposite of what everyone wanted. Knowing I chose once again to put my family, friends and boss second troubled me, but didn't change my mind. I intended to have it out with Cynthia.

I yanked open the door and took the steps three at a time to the bureau office. As usual, she wasn't in. Was my editor checking out, phoning it in? When Marta got me the job, she described Cynthia as a tough old bird and a respected editor. The one who went after the hard stories, who hung on like a bulldog, let no one intimidate her. That hadn't been my experience with the woman, especially lately.

Jason sat in his cubicle drinking from a large Caribou Coffee to-go cup.

"It's past nine. Where is she this time?" I asked.

Instead of his usual button-down shirt and V-neck sweater, he wore a stained Branson U sweatshirt. His face bristled with unshaven whiskers. I assumed he was still tortured by the sting of Thor's disinterest. I could relate.

He didn't look up. "She went for a walk by the lake."

I left the building and followed a path the short distance to Branson Lake. We'd experienced a warm spell the past two days. Ten above and everyone was outside basking. Perched on the edge of a snow-covered bench, Cynthia gazed across the ice. She brushed a mitten under her eyes when I approached. I hadn't expected that. "Is everything okay?"

She looked away from me. "I'll be back inside in a few minutes, Britt. Can't it wait?"

"This will only take a second. We found out Nathan was murdered too, and I need to keep looking into Isabel and Nathan's deaths for my own personal satisfaction. I'd like to take a few comp days."

She laughed, only it wasn't a happy sound. "Great. I no longer have control over my own staff. Do what you want. I don't care."

"You know what? I'm tired of working for someone who lets everyone tell her what to do. You should fire me."

Her upper lip twisted. "It doesn't surprise me a hotshot like you wouldn't last long here. Who offered you a job?"

"What happened to you, Cynthia? Small town-itis? Marta said you used to be the best." I wanted to shake some reaction from her, and I got it.

She rose from the bench and poked a finger at my chest. "Who do you think you are? Maybe you once got the awards, but you're a has-been too, fired from the *Times* for drinking, unreliable. You didn't think I knew? I brought you on as a favor to Marta."

My chin lifted. "The *Times* wants me back." I didn't intend to bring that up but she goaded me.

She sat back down, already defeated. "Don't you think I've seen how little respect you have for me? Yes, I'm the editor of a Podunk bureau and I no longer have the energy to fight the sheriff or even corporate. I do what I have to do to get through the day."

I looked at Cynthia, really looked at her, and saw what had been there all along, and I'd missed it. Where were my powers of observation? No one changed that much, that quickly. I perched next to her, feeling ashamed for my taunting and insults. "Cynthia, you're sick, aren't you?"

She spoke with effort. "I'm not sick."

Looking down at my hands, I said, "The weight loss, your hair, dark circles, fatigue, disappearing without telling us?"

She sighed. "My clothes don't fit anymore and I don't even care. There's no time or energy to deal with my hair. I know I look like a buzzard."

"Is it cancer?" I whispered.

"It's my husband, Alex. He has ALS, Lou Gehrig's disease. We're in the last stages. He can't do anything for himself anymore."

"Oh god, Cynthia, I'm sorry. Why didn't you tell us? You should take time off."

"Can't risk it. I need this job for the medical insurance. No one can find out. They're looking for an excuse to shut down

149

this bureau." Tears dribbled down her face. "We've been married twenty-two years. There's no respite from the hopelessness and grief, and it's all falling apart. I'm up with him all night. I can't afford day and night help."

She apologized for crying, and kept crying. I helped her to my car. "I'm taking you home."

She said they'd been saving for a condo in Maui where they planned to retire. That was just too sad to comprehend. By the time we pulled up in front of her house, her emotional breakdown was over. Cynthia took a few deep breaths and brushed her hair back from her face, now red and puffy. "Sorry, I guess that was all bottled up."

"I'm the one who's sorry. I wish you'd told me sooner so we could have helped you through some of it." Wrapped up in the murders and my own dramas, I didn't see her distress. I'd make it up to her.

The caregiver told Cynthia her husband had a better day. She took off her coat and went to his room while I made her a cup of tea and fumbled around the kitchen finding things to make her a sandwich.

When Cynthia returned she said Alex rested quietly. She sipped the tea and nibbled at a corner of the chicken sandwich. I convinced her that Jason and I could handle the calls for the rest of the day. She eventually agreed but made me promise to forward any calls from the *Strib* editor if he called. She said she would try to get some sleep before her daytime help left.

Before leaving, with shame hammering at me, I tried again to express my regret. "I'm so sorry for making your life harder."

A glimmer of her old fire flashed. "You're sorry, but you still want to go after the double murders. I won't stand in your way. Let Wilcox roar. Document whatever you find and we'll write it."

"Thanks, Cynthia. About the *Times*—I haven't decided yet."

"Do what you have to do." Her tired smile mocked me. "We'll manage."

***

Jason sank low in his chair as I told him. He said, "All I do is complain about the cold when Cynthia wants me to cover a story and she's been going through this. I'm a jerk."

"If it's a jerk contest, I win hands down. We have to help her." I swiveled my chair until my head swam, trying to figure out what to do.

Jason said, "I can deflect her calls so she can stay home longer."

"Me, too. Although, if it's her boss, we'll need to tell her right away so she can return the call. They can't find out she has a problem."

We vowed to take some of Cynthia's load, and find her night help at home. Maybe Little could cook up a week's worth of meals for me to take to her. She didn't have to go through this alone. She'd tried to tough it out and it exhausted her.

"Maybe he'll get better and everything will go back to normal," Jason said.

I knew that wouldn't happen. "There's no cure for ALS."

Jason and I decided the best thing we could do for Cynthia was to get to work.

We spent the morning catching up, filing regional stories, and in general, acting like grownups rather than the spoiled brats we'd become.

He went out to pick up lunch for us, and I realized I'd forgotten to tell him Thor's findings. When he returned, I grabbed my sandwich from the bag, and filled him in. "I'm still going after the story. I even have Cynthia's unofficial approval."

"Wow, two murders." Jason got serious. "If you're back on it, so am I."

I stood next to Jason's desk, talking between bites. "Here's what I don't get, Jason. If Isabel and Nathan's murders are connected, why were they so different?"

He swiveled in his chair. "I see what you mean. It's only a fluke that you found Isabel."

"Right, even if the coyotes didn't get her, by spring she would have sunk into that marsh and never have been found."

Jason's eyes lit up. "It was supposed to look like Nathan committed suicide at the resort, nowhere near where she was dumped. They wanted him to be discovered as a suicide." Jason dug into the bag for his sandwich and concentrated on eating.

I stared out the window at the light snow falling, feathering the trees with white. "Nathan and Brody didn't like each other. Brody didn't like for Isabel to spend so much time at the resort. If they fought and it got rough and he accidentally killed her, he'd want to hide the body. If Nathan suspected, he'd have to be gotten rid of, but it would have to look like suicide to keep Wilcox from investigating that angle."

Jason joined me. "But how would he have gotten into the lodge, taken Nathan to that remote cabin, and hanged him without help or anyone hearing?"

We looked at each other, and shook our heads.

Brody seemed to be the only connection between the two deaths, even though a tenuous link. I sat back down at my computer and scrolled through virtual tours of kayak and canoe trips on Wozniak's website. Grinning people held up strings of fish at campsites. Idyllic scenes rotated on the screen of waterfowl, deer and moose, kids swimming in clear lakes and couples paddling near waterfalls. For the serious camper or hunter, Wozniak's services included flying them into the BW with supplies and picking them up several days later.

On the surface, the Wozniaks appeared to run a wholesome business and helped people stay in touch with the wonders of nature. They provided outdoor family fun and adventure, but looks could deceive.

Chapter 17

Jason assured me he could handle the office, and I drove to Ely for the second time in a week. Getting my questions answered was a long shot, but I had to try.

On the three-hour drive, thoughts about the L.A. job and the murders ping ponged across my brain nonstop. It was a relief to arrive at my destination.

Wozniak's was tucked back along a recently plowed road. A simple sign above the log building said Wozniak Outfitters. Some outfitters rented out cabins, but Wozniak's offered only a few camper hookups—a business for people who took the outdoors seriously.

A blue and white plane taxied across the lake behind the store and lifted into the air. I'd just missed Woz. Where was he going? No one would want to camp out in twenty-below-zero temperatures.

Lights were on inside and smoke rose from a chimney. A bell tinkled when I opened the door, and a middle-aged woman behind a knotty-pine counter looked up. "Help you?"

I thought fast. "My boyfriend and I were thinking about doing a BW backpacking trip. I wanted to ask about the option of being flown to a remote site, and picked up a week later. We saw the cool plane on your website and got the idea."

The woman stopped marking prices on the items spread out on the counter, and smiled. "It's a De Havilland Beaver. It has a powerful radial engine, carries a lot of weight and has excellent range."

"You know planes."

"In the summer we put on floats. At the moment, it's converted to a tail wheel landing gear with Tundra Tires for off-airport landings."

"You really know planes."

She threw her head back and laughed. "Too much information?"

I instantly liked her.

"Our whole family flies. It's a kick." Her head tilted. "We don't schedule during the winter though."

That meant Woz wasn't guiding when he took off in the plane, and the woman before me must be Mrs. Wozniak. She seemed too open and friendly to be married to the dark-bearded, taciturn man I'd met last summer with Ben. "Sorry. I meant a trip for this coming summer."

She handed me a brochure with rates and explained how it worked. "We'll even help you plan your trip and work with you on the routing, so contact us when you and your boyfriend decide."

"If you don't mind my asking, why do you stay open all winter if there's no business?"

She tossed a thick braid over her shoulder. "My husband is outdoors most of the time and the kids are away at school. It keeps me occupied, and sometimes people come in for supplies."

The shelves and tables were stocked with fishing and camping gear, snowshoeing and hunting equipment. A sign said to ask for permits and maps. Background murmurs from a television mounted on a wall above the fireplace filled the silence.

She extended her hand. "My name is Jenna Wozniak. Need any supplies?"

As suits are to Wall Street, Jenna wore the traditional Northwoods uniform—flannel-lined denim shirt over a turtleneck tucked into jeans, a moose head carved into her silver belt buckle.

I introduced myself and pointed to an emergency backpack with a first-aid kit displayed on a table. "I could stock up on supplies to keep in my SUV, just in case."

"Up here, everyone should have that." Jenna showed me a choice of packs and offered suggestions about what to fill it with. Water bottles, energy bars, and a thermal blanket went into the pack. I set it on the counter, searching for a tactful way to ask why her husband didn't like Isabel and where he just went in the blue plane.

Jenna gestured toward a coffee maker, cups and a plate of cookies on a table by the fireplace. "Would you like to join me in a cup of coffee? We don't get many visitors this time of year." She pointed to the knotty-pine wall behind the counter. "And I'm tired of talking to these guys." A giant walleye forever arched in its final struggle stared down at us. Deer, bear and moose heads grimaced with outrage, and some just looked annoyed.

"I'd love coffee. Are those chocolate chip?"

She patted her plump stomach. "I bake when I'm bored."

Jenna poured coffee for us and gestured toward worn chairs by the fireplace. "So, what's going on in the outside world?"

The woman was so direct, and I couldn't continue the lie while eating her cookies. "That's actually the real reason I'm here. I'd hoped to talk to Woz about Isabel."

"You're not planning a BW trip?" Jenna's eyes narrowed above the rim of her cup.

I held out my credentials. "I'm sorry for not telling you right away, but the sheriff thinks he already has Isabel's killer and I don't agree. Since Woz isn't here, do you mind helping me out with some background on her?"

Jenna considered a moment, and shrugged. "We'd like to know who did this too. Brody is miserable. He was silly over her."

I said, "I've talked with Brody a couple of times. He said he and Nathan didn't get along so well."

"He didn't mention that to me, but Brody didn't like Isabel spending so much time at the resort. He wanted her to spend time with him."

"Her murder has to be hard for him," I said, recalling how upset he was at the skating rink.

A mother's compassion swept across her face. "Isabel was his first love." She tossed a log on the fire, sending up a small fireworks display, and sat across from me. Direct eyes on mine, she said, "We can talk, but I still don't appreciate the lying."

"I'm sorry, and I actually would like to backpack into the BW." I smiled, but she didn't return it. "One thing puzzles me—Brody mentioned his dad wasn't crazy about his relationship with Isabel, but everyone else says how much they liked her."

"It wasn't about Isabel. Woz doesn't like Arnie, and he didn't want Brody involved with that family."

That surprised me. "Arnie was a war hero and everyone in town says he's a wonderful guy."

Jenna leaned in. "It's a sore subject around here. Woz's younger brother was in Arnie's platoon, and nearly everyone was killed or injured in one tragic skirmish. Woz's brother was one of the soldiers who died, and Arnie came out a hero."

"Woz blames him for that? But they captured and tortured Arnie."

"Nothing went right for their squadron after Arnie escaped from the Viet Cong. The VC was always one step ahead of U.S. forces in the area."

According to my knowledge of that war, the VC was always one step ahead everywhere. Most likely Woz needed to blame someone, but killing Arnie's offspring for revenge seemed like a stretch. Jenna didn't appear to have anything to hide, but she might not know. Spouses hid all kinds of secrets from each other. My ex came to mind.

I surveyed the empty store. "If there's no tourist business, where was Woz going in his plane just before I came in?"

Jenna's glance darted toward the window overlooking the frozen lake. "Why are you asking?"

"Curious." I licked chocolate from my fingers, unable to look at her.

"He has a regular poker game with some old friends across the lake." She pushed the plate of cookies toward me, and stood. "Please, have one for the road."

"Thanks." I put the cookie in my pocket and lifted my camera. "Would you let me take your picture?"

She stiffened. "What for?"

I shrugged. "It's what I do. Publicity for your business can't hurt, right?"

Jenna stood behind the counter with a ten-point buck looming above her. The buck looked proud, curious, confident—admirable qualities and look where it got him. The camera clicked.

At the door, I thanked her for her time and the coffee, feeling like a dinner guest who's overstayed her welcome.

She held up my emergency pack. "Don't forget this."

I'd been home less than an hour when my phone rang. A gravelly voice, said, "This is Woz. My wife said you've been over here meddling in our business again."

I tried to explain but he interrupted. "From now on, leave Brody and Jenna alone. If you've got questions, talk to me." He hung up.

I'd rattled his cage and that made me even more suspicious. Woz hated Arnie and maybe he even had a vendetta against his kids. He took off in his plane at odd times. His wife said business was slow, no hunting or guiding trips planned, so where did he go? Jenna and I settled in for a cozy chat until I asked where Woz had gone just minutes before, and then she couldn't wait to get me out the door

I needed help but didn't dare mention my visit to the Wozniaks to the sheriff. Ben was hunting down the miserable scum who ran an international trafficking ring. We hadn't talked since the night we'd nearly frozen to death in front of my cabin discussing why it wouldn't work between us.

That left Sebastian, the seventeen-year-old hacker from St. Paul. I hesitated at contributing to the illegal activities of a minor, but opened my laptop and typed in his email address. Always connected, he fired back an instant greeting.

- Hey, Britt.

Sebastian did most of his work when the regular world slept. I first saw him at Gert's funeral, a rail-thin teenager with

157

dyed black hair and a trench coat. He'd slunk up to the lectern and gulped out his gratitude to Gert for saving him from freezing to death in a fish house on Spirit Lake where he'd been hiding out. He'd run away from his parents in Minneapolis after getting in trouble for a hacking prank that cost his parents a lot of money. While in her care, Sebastian helped Gert hack into the casino's financial records to find who was stealing from it. When the thief killed her, Sebastian helped me hack into the murderer's personal computer, and Wilcox was able to nail the guy. I typed,

-Do you have a minute to check out a couple of things for me?

How could he stop hacking if unprincipled people like me kept the teenager on the wrong side of the law? We'd never met openly, relying on phone and email to communicate, although I couldn't follow his technical terms. Sebastian knew he was the smartest guy in the room. He replied,

-Sure, I'm just doing a school project. It's not due till tomorrow. What you after?

He pretended to be a rock star with his ear plugs and tattoos, but Sebastian always responded to my requests for help. As he put it, he liked keeping his coding skills up. I dodged another pang of guilt by telling myself it was for a worthy cause, and asked if he could get into Wozniak Outfitters emails and financial records.

-A guy named Wozniak owns a million dollar plane. For a small-time guide business in Ely, Minnesota, it's a red flag. I hate to take up your time if there's nothing, but I'm stuck.

He responded instantly.

- Always good to look at the money. That's all you need?

I typed,

- I know it's pretty vague, but do your homework first, okay?

He shot back.

- Good one.

My cell pinged at three in the morning with message.

- Wozniak Outfitters appears legit but he uses way more airplane fuel than a seasonal guide business and it doesn't match his guide schedule. I cross-referenced.

Either Woz spent a lot of time playing poker across the lake, or he was into something else. What, if anything, did it have to do with Isabel or Nathan?

Chapter 18

I'd intended to spend the day at the bureau covering for Cynthia, but a message from Thor changed everything.

"Tommy's prints were on that arrow."

Jason's reassurance that he could handle the office and would call if he ran into problems was all I needed. I packed high-powered binocs and a camera with a powerful lens for the day's work ahead. Back-up camera, driver's license, credit card, cell phone and press credentials went into zip pockets inside my down jacket. Rock would have been good company, but I dropped him off at Little's garage. No use torturing him with a long afternoon and evening of waiting.

When I left the restaurant, Little handed me a thermos of vegetable soup, a giant insulated coffee, an egg salad sandwich, and a baggie of veggies. No cookie. He was still miffed. To keep him from worrying, I'd told him I'd be gone all day on an assignment for Cynthia.

My tires crunched through hard-packed snow on the way out of town. I called Ray to find out what he'd learned about Tommy's dad. I didn't tell him about the arrow or my intention to watch Tommy's place.

Ray said, "The Mille Lacs tribal police haven't found any trace of Gerald. I hate to say it, but those loan sharks could have killed him and dumped him someplace where he'll never be found."

"What's the point of that?" I asked. "Once he's dead, he's never paying."

"It's all about appearances. They have to keep people scared. The tribal police down there are working with the casino to figure out who Gerald owed money to, but he owed everybody. They said he's disappeared before, and they couldn't put a lot of time into looking for him on a rumor. I can't either." I could hear Ray's frustration. Ray had a big territory to police.

"Tommy comes and goes as he wants, but what if he really is dangerous? Can't you keep a closer eye on him?"

"We should, but we don't have the resources."

I believed that. "What about Wilcox? What's he doing?"

"Tommy's a person of interest, but they don't have a motive or any evidence directly linking him to Isabel's death, or Nathan's either."

So far, Ray patiently answered my questions, so I kept asking. "What about the $5,000 Wilcox found at his house?"

I might have overstepped. His next response sounded like it came from Wilcox. "Tommy's probably back to dealing but with no meth, there's no case yet."

The prospect of watching Tommy's place on my own made me uneasy. "Someone should be watching him."

Ray's voice rose. "I'm heading out to deal with a domestic abuse right now and my team is spread out all over the reservation on different calls. I'll get to it when I can."

I rounded the curve toward the Spirit Lake Loop. "Thanks for the info, Ray." He ended the call. I should have said, "Thanks for the lack of information."

My chest tight, but still more curious than scared, I left the highway onto Tommy's road. I'd suspected all along that Tommy shot the arrow at me, but if he seriously wanted to harm me, he'd had ample opportunity. I'd driven him out on that desolate road where he lived, and he knew I lived by myself in the woods. He could have gotten to me any number of easy ways and didn't. Maybe he mistook me for someone else that morning. Or maybe he thought I was stalking him and came after me.

I should have told Ray about the arrow, but he'd be more likely to take it seriously if I had something concrete to report, like Tommy making a drug deal. Unhappy to find only one lane open, I checked my phone for a signal. Nothing. Even if I needed Wilcox or Ray, I couldn't reach them.

The narrow road flanked by walls of drifts made me claustrophobic. Across the road from Tommy's driveway, I used my four-wheel drive to back the SUV behind one of the drifts. I'd be facing toward town in case I needed to move out fast.

Reasonably hidden, I trained my binocs on the house.

No one came or left all day, but I sensed that someone was in there. I ate my sandwich and soup, intermittently warming up the SUV when my extremities turned to ice bricks. After squatting to pee in the snow for the second time from too much coffee, I came close to aborting the vigil. The caffeine didn't help my nerves either. I fiddled with my phone, my cameras, tapped my feet, and even ate the carrots Little packed.

All contrasts went out of the surroundings at dusk, turning the world a dirty gray. My resolve diminished along with the visibility. What if Tommy watched me? I flinched once again at the memory of an arrow whizzing by. He could have me in his sights. I examined the woods and saw a glint of silver in the distance. With shaky hands, I raised the binocs and found it—a metal band around a tree.

I almost missed Tommy when he appeared at the back of the house moving fast toward the lake. Chunks of firewood stuck out of his backpack. I left the SUV and followed at a safe distance. He wasn't carrying a bow, but what about a gun or a knife?

I didn't even consider confronting him. A camera was my weapon. It brought down fraudsters, child predators and murderers, but at this moment, something more protective than a camera might have helped with my jitters.

Hunched into his parka, Tommy broke from the woods and moved diagonally across the ice. I didn't dare follow but kept him in view through my binoculars. He opened the door to a fish house less than a quarter mile from shore. A steady plume of smoke trickled from the chimney. Fish houses on Minnesota lakes can be as big as a mobile home. I estimated this one could sleep four in bunk beds.

After half an hour, Tommy headed back to his house with an empty backpack. He hadn't been named in the recent Cloud Lake bust Jason and I covered, but that didn't mean he wasn't dealing. I watched Tommy's place and the fish house for another fifteen minutes, but Tommy stayed put, and no one else left or entered.

It wasn't a big stretch to figure out that Tommy could be doing his drug deals from the fish house, but my money was on someone else being inside. Not my business, but I wanted to see for myself if it was who I thought it was. Before losing my nerve, I sprinted across the ice.

My knock echoed in the quiet. "Hello? I'm a friend of Tommy's." Billows of white frost came out with my words. "Can I talk to you a minute?" The door remained closed. I peeked in a window the size of a five by seven photograph and jumped back. A brown eye stared back at me. The eye disappeared and the door opened.

The man had a trim haircut, thin mustache and deep grooves like apostrophe marks from the sides of his nose to his chin. I put out my hand. "Gerald?"

He peered into the darkness, blinking hard.

I stamped my feet. "Can I come in? It's freezing out here."

He nodded, I stepped in and he quickly closed the door behind me. The space was comfortable, even with the cold blast I'd let in.

He pointed at a chair. "Why are you here?"

That was a good question. I said I'd been looking for Tommy in Mille Lacs and run into Al, who told me about the loan sharks. "How come those guys didn't kill you?"

Gerald looked away. "Tommy gave them $5,000. I have another week to come up with the rest."

So that's what Tommy was doing with the money. "How much is the rest?"

"I owe another five. Tommy's helping me get it together."

I wanted to shake him. "You're hiding here while your son risks going back to jail for dealing drugs to pay your gambling debts?"

Gerald jumped up from his chair. "Tommy's not dealing. He said a friend gave him the money. I only let you in because I thought you might be the friend."

Tommy had a friend with $5,000 to loan? Not sure if Tommy inherited his bad temper from his dad, I tried to be less combative. "It wasn't me." I leaned forward in my chair. "What's his friend's name?"

"He didn't tell me." Gerald poked at a log in the stove. "I'm going to pay him back once I get back on my feet."

"What are the names of the guys who are after you?" If I could get that information to Ray, maybe the sergeant could run the loan sharks out of town.

He stared into the dark fish hole. Frigid water swirled three feet beneath us. "It wouldn't be safe for you to know that. In fact, you shouldn't even be near me."

Tommy hiding his dad in the fish house made sense in case any big guys with bats showed up at the house looking for him. But, judging from Tommy's bruised face, they'd already paid a visit. I pointed to a spear with seven barbed tines, leaning against a bunk. "Not much protection."

He opened the door. "You should go now."

I didn't use a flashlight on my jog back to the car. Tommy might think I was one of the loan sharks and shoot me, or he might just shoot me anyway.

Gerald's story didn't ring true. Tommy must be dealing. I'd call Ray as soon as I got cell service, or home, whichever occurred first. Ray needed to know about the arrow, too.

Midway to the highway, I turned on my car lights. They illuminated fresh car tracks in the same pull-out area I'd noticed before. It snowed nearly every day and these looked like they'd been made today, maybe even while I watched Tommy's house. He'd said the car tracks might have been hunters, but what were they hunting in the dark?

Curiosity propelled me from the safety of my SUV. A quick look and I'd get out of there. I shielded my flashlight with a glove, training the thin beam on a smudge of footprints leading into the woods. It looked like whoever it was came back using the same path.

I rubbed the agate in my pocket for courage, and followed the tracks to a hunting shack about a half mile from the road. My nose quivered. A thin trickle of chimney smoke curled up from the dark shack. I pocketed my flashlight and crept closer.

The rough-hewn logs were so old the building leaned sideways, and the trees stretched toward it like they were propping each other up. The roof sloped higher in front than back, built that way so heavy snow would slide off. The weathered wood and rotten tilt of the building looked like a strong wind could blow it over, but a brand new padlock secured the door.

I heard a sound from inside and put my ear to a boarded up window. High-pitched female voices spoke rapidly in another language. I stumbled back, startled. When my pulse dropped to near normal, I leaned in and listened again. Vietnamese, I guessed. I checked my phone. Still no bars. I needed Wilcox and Ray but I'd have to deal with this alone. Thinking it might be my only opportunity, I took a picture of the shack. The flash illuminated everything for a split second, and the voices stopped. I knocked, even though they couldn't open the locked door. "Hello. Who's in there?"

Silence. They probably didn't speak English. "Do you need help? My name is Britt."

A rustle, whispers and a faint response. "Yes, help please."

"Hold on. I'll break the lock." A rusty axe partially covered with snow lay not far from an upright log.

I smashed the axe down hard, but instead of the lock breaking, part of the door split apart and the metal dangled from broken wood. I stepped inside a dark room barely warmer than outdoors.

The inhabitants stared at me in horror. Silhouetted in the dark doorway, I must have seemed like a crazed Amazon coming for them with an axe. I set it outside and left the door open to let in light from the sliver of moon.

A group of Vietnamese girls huddled in a broken down hunting shack in the middle of the Spirit Lake reservation was the last thing I expected. I gaped at them until I realized how terrified they were and snapped out of my shock. I pointed to my flashlight. "I'm turning this on. Don't be afraid." I offered an encouraging smile and took care not to shine it directly on them.

A child of about nine lay on the floor, struggling to breathe. A teenaged girl with tangled waist-length black hair stood in front of her, arms up, ready to do battle. Two more girls clutched each other against the back wall. Tears streamed down their faces.

A shiver ran up my spine. I'd found Edgar's crying girls.

Chapter 19

I raised my camera. The small rectangle framed four human beings—about to be added to the statistics along with hundreds of thousands of other children. I took three quick pictures. The flash ricocheted off the walls, and the girls flinched.

I'm sorry!" I regretted flashing bright lights into their eyes, but my photojournalist's instinct took over before my brain kicked in. Now they were like skittish cats, afraid to come near me.

I hesitated, unsure of what to do next. My job was to document—others stepped in and took action. Usually, I was with police or military, authorities whose job it was to handle the situation. My role was clear. Get the photos, maybe ask a few questions, and go. But with no phone service, I couldn't call the sheriff, Ben or Ray to come out here and deal with this. If I left to get help, the girls could be gone when we returned.

I needed to take the girls to the sheriff's office quickly, so Wilcox could come to the shack and catch whoever locked them in.

The girls hadn't moved. I could really only see the whites of their eyes in the dark shack. I needed to get them to safety, but they were terrified and wouldn't come with me if they didn't trust me. I dropped down to one knee. "Do you speak English?"

The girl shielding the sick child stepped forward. "A little. My name Ly." She pointed to the floor. "Hanh my sister."

"How old are you girls?"

"Hanh eleven. Binh fourteen like me."

Under her fringe of bangs and rosebud lips, Binh appeared younger. A ragged scar ran from the corner of her lip to her chin. She ducked away from my scrutiny.

"Quan found Binh on streets of Ho Chi Minh City with Kim." Ly said.

I assumed Quan was the trafficker.

Ly pointed at a girl with a round face and compact, sturdy body. "Kim oldest, fifteen."

Kim crossed her arms, more angry than afraid now. "Quan said I get to America and work at massage parlor. Get new clothes, nice house, not this."

Ly said, "Quan trick us."

"Are you and Hanh from there too? Do you have family?"

Ly spoke haltingly. "We work uncle's rice farm. Our father and mother die. Uncle sell to Quan."

"When did you get here?"

"A week. Quan took us in plane. Then man take us here across lake of ice."

Kim kicked at a small pile of trash. "Candy bars and chips only food. Always dark. One blanket each. Not enough firewood."

A rickety stove sat in one corner. Several blankets lay next to it. One chair was the only furniture. "Where is he taking you?" I asked.

Ly said, "Two men. First say take to Huy in Minneapolis, but now say Trung in Robbins."

"Who are they?" I asked.

The girls all shook their heads. "Wear masks. Don't say names."

Her mouth drawn down in worry, Ly bent over Hanh. "My sister sick." The child's chest rose and fell with effort. Her tiny body shivered under the blanket.

"I'll take you to a doctor. You'll have to walk with me a little way to my car." I pointed to Hanh. "I'll carry her."

"I carry." Ly wrapped the blanket around the girl and gathered her into her arms. I lifted my camera and clicked. This wasn't just one more photo, this was the one.

167

On the wall, I saw the shadow of an axe looming behind me. Ly cried out. I ducked, but not in time, and the blow sent me to the ground. The camera flew from my hands and a light show of stars filled my vision.

I tried to rise. A boot slammed my face into the floor. I tried again, and the boot rammed me in the side. Everything went black.

When I came to I couldn't move or see. Pain radiated from my face and chest in waves. My arms were tied behind me, and a rope secured me to the chair. Each ankle was tied to a chair leg. My stocking cap was pulled down over my face. I heard shuffling footsteps and a gust of cold air. That meant they were leaving.

I shouted, "Stay together. I'll follow you."

A fist smashed into my right eye and I cried out. He stuck a strip of tape across my mouth and whispered in my ear, his breath a foul stink.

"That's funny, coming from a dead woman." The door hinges creaked and they were gone.

The man's menacing whisper didn't sound familiar. There'd been no need to tape my mouth. Only the wolves would hear my screams. Something wet trickled down my face, dampening my stocking cap. Blood, I assumed. I bounced the chair along the floor until it hit a wall, and rubbed the side of my head that wasn't throbbing against it until the cap came off. I could see out of my left eye, and didn't want to think about what happened to the right one. Pieces of my smashed phone were strewn across the floor. The camera nowhere in sight.

How scared the girls must be after what they'd been through. Ly said at first they were supposed to go to Huy in Minneapolis. I might have stumbled on Ben's ring, unless there were a lot of traffickers in Minneapolis named Huy. He'd been tortured before his throat was cut. I guess I was lucky.

What else had Ly thought she heard? Trung? Robbins? I'd heard of a Robbinsdale suburb. I rocked back and forth to keep from freezing. Keeping my body parts moving until someone found me was my only hope, even though the sharp pains in my rib cage hurt worse than anything I could remember. Was Tommy the guy with the boot?

Little would worry when I missed dinner and didn't come for Rock. He or Lars would call or check the cabin, and start looking for me. They'd tell Wilcox and Ben, but no one knew to look here. They might even believe I left for L.A. without saying goodbye. If only I'd told Little where I was going.

I prayed to all the gods and goddesses and saints and saviors I'd ever heard of and threw in a few angels as well. I tried to conjure up Edgar's ghost ancestors. *Okay, Edgar, if your ancestors happen to be wandering in the ether, could you please tell Ben and Wilcox where I am?*

My chin dropped to my chest, and my head snapped back up. Waiting to die was not an option. A rusted stove sat on spindly iron legs. I bumped the chair forward and worked myself so close to it my knees knocked against it. I felt the barest hint of warmth.

If I could set the shack on fire, someone might see the blaze and find me. Once the fire got going, I'd roll out the door. At least the heat would keep me alive for a few more hours. Worst case scenario, I'd burn to death instead of slowly freezing, a toss-up in horrible outcomes.

In a burst of crazy adrenalin I threw myself against the stove, knocking it and me to the floor. The door fell open when it hit the ground, scattering a few glowing embers. The crash loosened the duct tape from one side of my mouth, and I let out a scream of pain.

On my side, I gently blew on the embers, praying they'd be hungry for the rotting wood floor. They glowed brighter and a wild surge of hope coursed through me.

Minutes later they fizzled, and my hope died as the last weak plume of acrid smoke dispersed into the air. On my side, attached to the chair, head resting on the floor, I allowed myself a brief pang of self-pity.

When it passed, I gathered up another burst of energy and flopped around like a landed fish. Determined to break the rickety chair apart, I strained until one chair leg and then the other detached from the seat and fell to the floor. I stood, half squatting. The bottom of the seat was still tied to my back end.

Waddling in an awkward crouch, I slammed the back of the chair into the wall until the seat dropped to the floor, and I could stand erect. The chair back remained attached and my hands were secured to it behind me, but I didn't care. I was mobile. My legs were strong from snowshoeing all winter. They would power me out of the woods. I kicked open the door, stepped into the night and headed to the highway. The duct tape, one end still attached to my face, whipped against my chin and finally stuck in my hair.

My SUV was where I left it and the keys were in it, but I couldn't drive it with my hands tied behind my back. I kicked at a snowdrift and almost cried from the sharp pain in my ribs, but didn't want my one good eye to freeze shut. With no time to waste, I took my first step of the long walk to the highway, and stopped, dead still.

I heard them before I saw the pack. Three gray and one black wolf stood on a ridge watching, gaunt bodies at attention, ears forward and alert. A shiver ran down my spine. I couldn't fight them off with my arms tied behind me. Outrunning them would be impossible.

The highway was two miles away. Tommy's place was half that. I'd have to try to get to Tommy's. If he helped the guy take the girls, he'd be near Minneapolis by now and I could break into his house. I bent forward into the wind. I might have a chance if I stayed on my feet.

Even if Tommy saw me leave his place earlier and followed me to the shack, how did he get the girls away with no car? Where were the accomplices? Trafficking would explain how Tommy came into $5,000 to pay his dad's loan sharks. I glanced back.

The wolves were still behind me. Were they letting me tire myself out so they wouldn't have to work so hard? I trudged on, trying to convince myself being torn limb from limb and eaten by a pack of starving wolves was preferable to freezing to death. My options were improving.

I saw the dark outline of Tommy's place another quarter mile ahead. So far yet to go. I sank to one knee, all my strength gone. The pack moved closer. The faces of the girls floated in front of me. What would happen to them if I died out here? I struggled back to a standing position and dragged one foot in front of the other.

They were silent now and so close I could hear them panting. The larger black one, at least a hundred pounds of muscle, took the lead. The others spread out to the side to surround me. Once they got me on the ground, they'd go for my throat. Panting for breath, I lurched forward.

Something shook me. Did a wolf have me in its jaws? I wanted to be left alone, drifting. I wanted to sleep.

"Britt. You have to wake up."

My eye squinted open, and I was vaguely aware of Tommy standing over me with a washcloth, eyebrows drawn together. He dipped the cloth into a bowl of warm water and dabbed at my face. He set the bowl down, the water dark pink from my wounds, and patted my face with a soft, dry cloth. I lay under a blanket on a couch, shivering. Tommy handed me a mug of coffee, but my hands were too numb to hold it.

He paced in front of the fireplace. "Your face is busted up. You need the doctor."

I remembered seeing Tommy's house, then nothing. "How did you find me?"

"Someone was kicking the shit out of the front door and I looked out and there's this wild-haired thing with spokes coming out its back. It's got a bloody face and purple eye and a silver tongue hanging out of its mouth. I think, in the middle of the night it's the Windigo coming to eat me. Then it just fell over."

Still agitated, Tommy said, "I wasn't going to open the door, but I figured it must be human, otherwise those wolves wouldn't be after it."

Through the haze of pain, I realized it couldn't have been him at the shack. "I'm really glad you opened your door, Tommy."

171

He put the cup to my lips, but I couldn't drink it with a split lip. Tommy went to the kitchen, fished around in a drawer and came back with a straw. I thanked him and drank.

"What happened to you out there?" He darted a look at the door as if worried something might burst in.

I tried to get up, the room tilted, and I fell back against the pillow. Tommy went into the kitchen again, the microwave beeped, and he brought me a steaming cup of chicken noodle soup. The broth revived me even more than the coffee.

He asked again. "Where did you come from? Who beat you up?"

"I don't know. At first I thought you did it."

He drew back. "Why me?"

I raised up on an elbow, ignoring the rib pain. "Didn't you shoot at me with an arrow?"

He didn't look at me. "That wasn't me."

"Someone tied me up in an old hunting shack." I pointed in the direction.

His face scrunched up. "Why?"

I could tell Tommy wanted to ask more questions, but I stopped him. "You need to call the sheriff right away. We have to get help."

He shrugged. "I lost my cell phone."

"No land line?"

He shook his head.

"And your car isn't working either, right?" I sat up and set the blanket aside.

"No."

Knowing it wasn't a good idea to goad someone known for hair-trigger emotions, I couldn't stop myself. "And yet you had money to give your father."

He turned his back to me. "That's not your business."

My brain cleared slightly, and I could feel strength returning to my body. I needed to go after the girls. "Will you help me back to my car?" A bit wobbly, I stood. At least my jacket was on and I wouldn't have to lift my arms to get into it.

Tommy watched me. "You're in no shape to walk."

I zipped the jacket and took a few tenuous steps toward the door.

Tommy pulled on his boots and grabbed his parka. "I'll help you, but wait till I get my rifle."

"Good idea. The wolves weren't happy to miss dinner," I said.

His upper lip curled. "If they'd wanted to eat you, you wouldn't be here now. And we don't shoot wolves."

Little once explained a part of the Ojibwe creation story to me as told to him by Edgar. He'd said wolves and the Ojibwe were brothers. I still thought they would have torn me to shreds, but touched the agate in my pocket.

The pack was gone when we stepped into the night. I filled Tommy in on everything on the way to the SUV.

His eyes widened. "No shit? There were girls in that shack?"

"Yes, one was only eleven and really sick. They took them to Minneapolis to sell as sex slaves." The thought of losing them spurred me to walk faster.

Tommy's mouth hung open. "I don't believe it."

"Are you sure you didn't see anything going on? You never noticed a trail that led right to it from that spot where I asked about the car tracks?"

"I remember seeing a hunting shack out there, but it's falling down. No one uses it."

"Someone used it." Whoever left me in that shack expected me to die, and they probably thought Tommy would be the suspect again. Otherwise, they would have tried to hide my car.

We made it to the SUV with no wolf attacks and Tommy jumped in the passenger side. "Give me a ride back to my place?" he asked.

Favoring my right side, I eased into the driver's seat and pulled forward. "Sorry, I need you to tell Wilcox what happened. If I go in, they'll keep me answering questions and make me go to the hospital. It will be too late for those girls."

"They won't believe me. They'll arrest me again." He tried to jump out but the car was already rolling.

"You have to do this, Tommy. Tell them about the shack and that I'm looking for a trafficker named Trung in the Cities, maybe Robbinsdale. That's where they're taking the girls. He's connected to that murdered massage parlor guy, Huy. As soon as you tell him, Wilcox can get the police down there on it."

Tommy sulked the rest of the way to Branson. I stopped in front of the sheriff's building and told him to hurry. "I'll call Wilcox from my cabin to let him know I sent you."

He got out of the car. "I'm trying to convince them I didn't kill Isabel, and you expect me to walk right in there with this weird story? Wilcox will slap me back behind bars."

"I promise I'll call him, but I can't lose the trail. I have to go now. Thanks, Tommy. You saved my life."

"Why does everything happen to me?" He kicked the snow.

I floored it out of Branson. He'd go in. He wouldn't let me down.

Chapter 20

After dropping Tommy off at the sheriff's, I drove home to my cabin to grab another camera and my laptop. My cell was in pieces at the shack. I used my land line to call the sheriff's office, and left a quick message telling him Tommy had information from me, and where I was headed. Wilcox wouldn't be in the office this early, and waiting for him was another thing that would have slowed me down. Even if he didn't believe Tommy's story, he'd go out to the shack, find plenty the evidence, and help should be on its way. I didn't intend to confront anyone. I just wanted to find the girls.

In and out of the cabin in three minutes, I sped down Highway 371 for the four-hour drive to Minneapolis. I tried to compensate for my blind side and lack of peripheral vision on my right side, by rotating my head. It was exhausting and not that helpful. After about an hour, I got the hang of it. Luckily, I was the only one on the highway so only a danger to myself.

With my laptop powered up, I messaged Sebastian with one hand on the wheel.

-Need address for a Trung in Robbinsdale. Sex trafficker.

My hacker friend thrived on impossible requests. My battery was low and I needed it to connect with Sebastian, so I left only a short message for Wilcox in case he missed my phone call.

-Listen to Tommy. Will call from Mpls.

I fired off one more quick message telling Little I was okay and not to worry about me before shutting down the laptop. As I drove, the bass drum banging at the back of my neck kept me awake. I fought dizziness and nausea and tried not to think about my sightless eye.

I made it to the Twin Cities by mid-morning. The laptop battery was low, so I'd waited until near the city to check for a response from Sebastian. He'd sent a brief email.

-First off, there's a zillion Trungs in the area, but here's your guy, Hoa Duc Trung.

He'd typed in an address.

-He actually advertises on the Internet. I wouldn't go near him if I were you. He's an evil dude.

I didn't intend to go near him. I'd locate him and alert the police. I checked for a message from Wilcox, but he hadn't responded yet.

The house sat in the middle of a quiet cul de sac in Robbinsdale, north of the city. Cars were tucked into garages in this older neighborhood dotted with mature evergreens. Diligent snow blowers and shovelers kept driveways clear. Two bundled up little girls built a snowman in a front yard. Their mother stood nearby talking into her cell phone. I pulled up across the street and took a few photos of the ordinary ranch-style house at the address Sebastian sent. I'd call 9-1-1 once I was sure.

In half an hour of watching from my car, no one entered or left, and no curtains stirred. I didn't dare ring the doorbell. It could cause them to leave before the authorities arrived. I caught a glimpse of a woman standing at a picture window staring at me. I'd parked directly in front of her house.

The door opened a crack when I rang her doorbell. I held up my credentials. "I work for the paper. Do you have a minute?"

A seventy-year-old in pink Uggs, jeans and a hot pink sweatshirt opened the door. She frowned up at me. "What happened to your eye?"

I tried to pull my hair forward to cover it. "I slipped on the ice."

"My name's Roxy. I've been getting the paper for thirty years. Yet you people are always calling to get me to subscribe. Right hand doesn't know what the left is doing."

I pointed to the camera hanging from my neck. "I'm Britt Johansson, a photographer. I'm not here to get you to subscribe."

"It came half an hour late today. Tell them to get it here when they're supposed to. I like to do the crossword with my morning coffee." A pencil stuck out of a cloud of white hair in a knot on top of her head.

I forced myself not to roll my eyes. "I'll let them know." It's the first thing people ask when they find out you work at a newspaper. I'd given up telling people to call the circulation department.

She ushered me in. "You're letting in the cold air." Her topknot inclined toward Trung's. "I see you're watching that house."

"I am. Have you noticed anything strange about it?"

"The whole neighborhood's strange. Worked in Corrections for the state for thirty years, so I don't miss much. Come to the kitchen and I'll get you a cup of coffee."

"I'd love one, but I need to stand here by the window to keep an eye on that place."

She called over her shoulder. "Don't rob me while I'm in the kitchen."

I stifled a laugh. Roxy didn't look too concerned about me robbing her. In a few minutes she came back with two mugs. I sipped my coffee, and detected no movement across the street. Roxy stood beside me at the window.

"It looks like a decent neighborhood, Roxy. I saw a couple of cute kids with their mom down the street."

She sniffed. "She takes them to the park she's on her phone, brings them back she's on her phone, lets them play in the front yard she's on her phone. She should pay closer attention." Roxy pointed to a house on the corner. "Registered sex offender."

I'd been watching out the window, but that got my attention. "A guess?"

"Bona fide fact. I checked him out online. I watch him through my binoculars watching them. He knows I do. He must have an ankle bracelet. He never goes to the park."

"What else?"

She re-positioned the pencil in her topknot. "Across the street there's a woman who hits her husband. I think the poor bastard likes it. He brings her flowers after. Directly behind me

177

a couple of friendly young guys have a greenhouse in the back yard. On a breezy day I get loopy. They told me it's medicinal marijuana. Where do they think this is, California?"

"How old are you, Roxy, if you don't mind my asking?"

"Seventy-nine. Shovel my own walkway and chop my own wood."

I lifted my camera. "Mind if I take your picture?"

"Let me put my lipstick on."

She disappeared for a minute and returned wearing lipstick the same color as her Uggs and sweatshirt. I asked her to stand next to her picture window, and took photos of her as we watched. "Nothing interesting across the street, though?" I asked.

"Oh, it's interesting. A navy blue SUV with tinted windows comes and goes during the day. An Asian guy drives it. He wears a fedora. They're back in style I guess. And dark glasses, even in winter. Thinks he's Mr. Cool. Early this morning a light-colored van pulled into the garage. About the time my paper was "supposed" to be there. It left within half an hour. Why the interest? Drugs?"

I nearly dropped my camera. "Could I please use your phone? I have to make a couple of calls."

"I thought everyone used the smart phones."

I pointed to my eye. "Mine got broken when this happened to me."

"You need to get a nicer boyfriend."

She brought me a phone. "I have three of these. Living room, bedroom and one in the kitchen. Plus my iPhone. Keep a Sig Sauer 9 mm in a canister in my kitchen. You can't be too careful at my age."

Nothing surprised me about Roxy at this point. I called the Minneapolis police, gave the dispatcher my name and told them I worked for the *Star Tribune*. I told them a man named Hoa Duc Trung was trafficking Asian girls and gave them the address. I said it had to do with the case the department was working on with Immigration, BCE and the Forestry Service out of the Branson area. I suggested they call Ben Winters and gave them his number, and I told them to contact Sheriff Dave

Wilcox in Branson, and that it could be connected to the man named Huy who'd had his throat cut in Coon Rapids last week. Ly said his name in the shack. It could be a different Huy, but I doubted it.

They put me on hold.

An officer eventually came back on the line and said Sheriff Wilcox didn't know what they were talking about, but they'd check out Trung's house. He told me to wait until an officer arrived.

I called Ben, and we talked at cross purposes until I figured out that Tommy hadn't done what I asked. I said, "Tommy was supposed to talk to Wilcox hours ago."

"I'm standing right here in the sheriff's office. Tommy hasn't been here. Where are you? Wilcox said you sent a message that didn't make much sense."

A piece of dark blue fabric flew out a window at the side of Trung's house. "I don't have time to explain. Find Tommy. Call Minneapolis PD and tell them to get to this address fast. It's probably connected to your trafficking ring. I have to go."

I tossed the phone to Roxy, thanked her and raced out, camera focused on the high-set bathroom window. A head with long, black hair popped out. My camera clicked. Next came shoulders, and the young woman catapulted out, landing on a cushion of snow. She gasped, jumped up, grabbed the blue jacket and flew down the street, hair whipping behind her like a black flag.

I hurried toward her, yelling for her to stop, but it hurt too much to run. I got back to my car and took off after her, nearly broadsiding a motorcycle as I slid through a yellow light. I caught up to her near an intersection a block away and shouted from my window, "Ly, it's me—Britt. I'm going to help you."

She bolted through the bushes, but I stayed with her. She eventually saw me and leaned over, hands on her knees, her mouth open, dragging in air. "You alive?"

"Please get in and tell me what happened."

She jumped in, her body shaking with ragged sobs. "He sell Hanh to ship. I have to find."

"Where, Ly?"

She struggled with the word, but it sounded enough like Duluth to get me going in that direction. Duluth was an international port, ideal for trafficking.

"We'll find her."

Roxy could fill in the officers. I had no time to get caught up in red tape. If I took Ly back, who knew what would happen to her once they got her in the system? They'd try to do the right thing, but would it help her unite with her sister? Did I have the right to make that decision? No, but I decided anyway.

"Where are Kim and Binh?"

Ly's face crumpled again. "I leave. Find Hanh."

I put my hand on her shoulder. "I called the police before you jumped out the window. They'll make Trung tell them where she is."

Once Ben rounded up Tommy and he told Wilcox everything, the hunt would begin. I hoped it would be in time. Girls sold to ship's crews might not be returned until months later, if ever. I pulled the laptop onto my right knee and got back online with Sebastian, knowing it would take a miracle.

-Can you help me with trafficking or prostitution locations near the Duluth port?

He answered immediately.

-Sorry, physics quiz. I can get on it when I get home.

I replied.

-Thanks. Low battery. Shutting down till Duluth.

Ly stared out the window. Her face and clothes were filthy, she was too thin, and completely exhausted. I pulled to the side of the road. "We have to drive for a couple of hours to get to Duluth. By that time, I should have an address where we can look for Hanh and call the authorities."

I opened the door. "I'm getting a pack from the trunk with food and water."

I couldn't tell if she understood everything I said but she nodded. After we shared the energy bars and water, Ly asked how I got away.

"First, tell me why they took Hanh and left you with Trung."

Looking for words, she spoke haltingly, and sometimes pantomimed. "When we stop, Trung say didn't want sick girl.

The man who brought us said Hanh and I virgins, but not charging much for Hanh. Trung said not keep Hanh, she half dead and what he do with dead body." Ly stopped talking. She stared at the cars whizzing by on the highway.

"If it's too hard, we don't need to talk about it, but it might help us find Hanh."

She squared her shoulders. "I have to find her."

"The masked man took Hanh with him, right?"

Ly nodded. "Two men. One toss Hanh in back of van and slam door. I try get to her. Trung put hand on my mouth and shove into house. Garage door open and close. Hanh gone." She took a shaky breath. "Masked man tell Trung get me ready, buyer come for me soon."

I slowed as mini-explosions detonated in my skull and my vision blurred. With luck, the Minneapolis PD would get Trung and save Kim and Binh. The sheriff would put out a bulletin on a light-colored van, but there were probably thousands in the area.

Ly stared into the windshield. "Please go faster."

The pain subsided and I accelerated again. "Tell me about your sister."

Ly's chin dropped to her chest. "Hanh make us laugh. She tell funny stories, even worst times. I responsible for sister."

"What happened to your parents, Ly?"

"Three years ago, father step on mine leftover from war. Legs blown off. He die from infection. Mother too sick work. She die, too, and uncle sell us to Quan."

Her sad eyes searched mine. "Now lose sister too."

"We'll find Hanh." I sounded assured, but didn't feel confident. I hated the defeat on her face after such bravery and valiant effort.

Ly's bottom lip caught in her teeth. "Your face bad. I try to warn at shack but happen fast."

"You couldn't have stopped him, and I got away just like you did."

She nodded.

"Do you remember more about Trung?"

Once Ly began, the story rushed out. Sometimes she used Vietnamese words and lost me, but I put most of it together. Ly wouldn't do what Trung told her to do at first. He said he would beat her for defying him, but she had to be ready for the man coming to get her. He shoved them all down the stairs and shut the door.

The three girls waited in an empty seating area. They watched a show on the television until Trung came back. He flipped a lock on the side of a large framed mirror that opened on hinges like a door, and prodded them one by one through the small space. I wondered if the task force found the secret room.

Five girls stared at them from mattresses on the floor. There were no windows. The girls' belongings were stuffed into plastic bins in one corner. Ly said, "A Chinese girl call us stinky. They hold nose and laugh. Binh get on dirty mattress and go to sleep, not speak."

I hated to ask painful questions, but Ly seemed to be doing okay. "How did you get away?"

"Trung make me go with him. Kim try to come and Trung slap her. Silver hair clip man at shack gave her fell on carpet. Trung take it. Kim pretend to be tough, but she scared. Upstairs, Trung show me bathroom, tell me clean self. He give me red halter top, short skirt and high heels."

Ly's face scrunched up. "Door not lock. Wide man in hallway smoking."

"So you climbed out the window."

"I turn on shower, put towel stand in tub. I step up and push out screen to squeeze through."

Her head fell back against the seat, tired from the strain of trying to make herself understood in an unfamiliar language.

"That's good information, Ly. The sheriff will get those guys." We rode in silence for a while. I wasn't feeling optimistic. Even if the police got to Trung's before they disappeared, the chances of finding Hanh diminished every second. My good eye prickled, wanting to close. I'd have to keep talking or fall asleep.

"When you got to the U.S., this guy Quan was the only one who came to the shack?"

"No, he go away in plane. Men who come to shack always wear mask when bring food and firewood. Don't talk."

"Two men?"

She said, "Just one most time. We stay close to stove. Hanh cough, get weak." Ly brushed at her eyes.

"You don't have to tell me more if you don't want to."

"It's okay. Man took Kim to van. He give silver hair clips but never touch Kim."

"Did you see anything else unusual?"

"One time we hear shouting outside but it go away."

I perked up, "This is very important, Ly. Please tell me everything you saw and heard."

"Too dark to see. Shouting, then quiet. We wait, afraid. No one come back. No wood or food. Very cold."

My stomach churned with anger at what they'd gone through. "You were all brave girls. I'm sorry you suffered so much."

"Locked up like animals. We think we die."

Chapter 21

We entered the Twin Ports area of Duluth, Minnesota and Superior, Wisconsin. On the western part of Lake Superior, it's the largest freshwater port in the world. The aerial lift bridge dropped after a freighter moved through, an impressive sight.

Selling girls onto ships was another part of the sex trafficking epidemic. The *LA Times* did a big spread on it a few years ago. I hadn't been the photographer, but I'd read the pieces. Two million children worldwide and more than 100,000 in the U.S., and those statistics had likely grown exponentially by now.

I opened the laptop. No contact yet from Sebastian. His parents monitored his computer activities these days. I doubted he could help with this one anyway. We needed a miracle.

We started our search for the beige van at a run-down section of taverns and strip joints near the port. After a frustrating thirty minutes of checking back alleys and side streets, Ly gasped, and said, "There!"

I took a quick turn around the block. The van was parked close to an alley behind The Shipwreck Bar. An orange truck was backed up to the bar's back door.

I parked on a cross street close enough so we could watch the alley from a side mirror. It took some convincing, but Ly promised to stay locked inside the SUV and wait for me to check out the van and bar.

I peeked around the side of the building. The van looked empty. I took a picture of the license plate number. There were no windows in the back. I put my face to the passenger side window but couldn't see the back area. I hurried to Ly, gave her my card with the van license plate number on it, and both Ben's and the sheriff's numbers.

"If the van leaves while I'm in the bar, watch the direction it goes. If I don't come back in half an hour, find a police officer."

She swallowed hard, and nodded.

Ben wouldn't like what I was doing and Wilcox would call my behavior reckless. I agreed, but every minute spent getting the authorities up to speed was a minute lost if we wanted to find Hanh. I took photos of the bar storefront, and tucked the camera in my pocket before going inside.

Loud music battled with a hockey game on mounted TVs above the bar and tables. Sweat, whiskey and stale beer assaulted my nostrils. This was a bar for rough men who loaded and unloaded cargo or spent weeks aboard freighters or fishing vessels.

With a combination of boozed up men too long at sea, probably more than a few fights would break out. That accounted for the guy with the thick neck standing by the door with huge biceps crossed. Used-up women of indeterminate ages sauntered through the tables or sat at the bar. No one would look twice at a woman with a split lip, bruised jaw and swollen eye in this environment, but a five-foot-ten woman got a few stares. I plowed through the crowd as if I belonged there.

I didn't know who I was looking for, but he knew me. With luck he wouldn't try to kill me with all these people watching. I hoped he'd show himself. I worked my way through the dim interior. A man sitting on a stool at the bar leered as I passed, reached out and grabbed hold of my hair. He yanked my head back and grinned with tobacco-stained teeth. "Hey, honey, you look like you could use a beer."

My elbow caught him just under the nose. He yelped and let go to grab it. No crunch at impact, so it wasn't broken. His buddy cracked up as I sailed forward and the crowd closed behind me. I didn't want to make a scene, but I'd reacted before thinking. My instincts said it wasn't the guy at the shack.

I checked out the back hallway. Bathrooms were on the left, two closed doors were on the opposite side and at the end, a door with an exit sign above it led to the alley. I put my ear against one door and heard nothing. At the next one, someone with a nasal twang spoke.

"The cap'n likes 'em young, but I can't keep her here. We can't move her out to the ship until dark. Bring her back then."

The response wasn't clear enough to hear the words.

Nasal spoke again. "Take it or leave it."

The other guy argued some more, and the doorknob turned. I ducked into the women's bathroom, waited a second, then opened it a crack to see who left the room, but the hall was empty.

A skinny woman with thick black eyeliner stared into the mirror above the sink, her nose nearly touching it. Mid-day and her eyes were dilated. That explained her difficulty focusing. Her pink phone sat on the dirty sink. I washed and dried my hands and threw my paper towel over her phone. She wobbled on stilettos into one of the stalls, forgetting the phone. I swiped it, checked the hall and ducked into a storage closet. I dialed 9-1-1, gave my name and location and told the dispatcher an eleven-year-old Vietnamese girl was about to be sold as a sex slave on a freighter and to send help fast. I told him the van's license plate number and hung up. No time to answer questions.

My next call to Ben's cell phone went to voice mail. Wilcox wasn't in, so I attempted to leave a message with the deputy who answered. I gave him the van's license number. He asked, "Why are you calling the sheriff about a problem in Duluth?"

"Tell him Britt called and give him the information. Don't forget Shipwreck Bar. Do it."

I peeked out of the closet. The passageway was clear, so I stepped out. The woman teetered out of the bathroom, slightly more alert than when she went in. "Hey, my phone!" she said.

I handed it to her. "Sorry, I just borrowed it for a second. I had to call my old man to come get me."

"He do that to you?" The woman grimaced.

"He hates it when I backtalk." I touched the eye and winced for real.

"You're better off keeping your mouth shut, honey." She tottered into the bar.

Half my height with long arms and a bulbous red-veined schnoz, Nasal emerged from the room, pocketing a set of keys. I stumbled into him, laughed too loud, and flopped on him again. "Whoops. Hey, babe, wanna buy me a drink?"

He shoved me away. "Hell no. You look like shit even for his place. Get out of my way before I give you another swelled up eye to match the one you got." He pushed me again and stalked into the bar.

During my act of misdirection, I'd easily snatched the ring of keys from his bulging jacket pocket, and was inside the office on my third try. Stacks of boxes filled one end of the room. Across from the boxes, Hanh sat on the floor tied to a desk, her body sagging against it, shaggy hair nearly covering her face. I set the keys on the desk, got down on one knee and took several quick pictures, catching the low light slanting across Hanh's tied hands. I stood and moved back for a wider view of the scene, then pocketed my camera. I intended to document everything for the police, and use the photos to show the world the stark reality of how these children were treated.

I knelt next to Hanh and whispered, "Remember me? I'm a friend of Ly's. She's waiting for us outside. I'm taking you to her." Glazed eyes stared uncomprehending at me. I didn't dare take the tape off her mouth in case she screamed.

I scrabbled through the desk drawer for a box cutter or knife to cut her ropes. The doorknob jiggled and I slid behind a stack of boxes, squatted low and sneaked a quick glance. The guy I stole the keys from came in with a ferret-faced man.

Voice like a razor, Ferret-face said, "This room is supposed to be locked."

"I thought I did. I lost my keys. Maybe they're in here somewheres."

I saw his shadow move toward the stack where I crouched and held my breath.

"They're on the desk right in front of your face. Load her into a box and get her aboard."

The shadow receded. "Where do I put her?"

"The usual place, you idiot. Captain Pratt's quarters. They're through loading the coal, and it's leaving first thing in the morning. I can't believe you let him leave her here in the middle of the day. It's your ass if something happens."

Ferret-face left, and I watched Nasal untie Hanh from the desk and retie her hands before he pushed her into an open container. Hanh didn't put up a fight. He closed the container, shoved a dolly under it and backed out the door, locking it behind him.

I unfolded from behind the stack of boxes and wasted a minute wiggling the doorknob, shoving my sore body against the door and finally raised my boot and kicked hard enough to smash through. I ran out the back door. The orange truck was already gone.

At the car I told Ly that Hanh was in the orange truck. "Did you see it?"

She pointed. "That way. Hurry!"

I took off, my chest tight. No screaming sirens or police cars with flashing lights passed us heading toward The Shipwreck Bar as we sped toward the port. Maybe they dismissed my call as a prank, as I'd feared.

At least twenty docks lined up along the fifty miles of waterfront in the harbor, including cargo terminal, fueling depot, tug/barge services, and a shipyard with two dry docks. It would be impossible to find one orange truck and one little girl in the vast maze. I stepped on the gas.

Facts learned in high school scrolled across my mind like the information running across the bottom of a television screen. The port area was a hub for cargo like coal, grain and heavy equipment. I'd heard Ferret-face say they'd loaded coal, but how that information could help, I didn't know.

Ly too, saw the hopeless task in front of us. "What we do?"

I heard the tension in my own voice. "If we see the orange truck, we're going to watch where it goes, find a police officer or someone with a phone and call for help." The police didn't come to The Shipwreck Bar when I gave them an exact address, so no point in calling them now. We would find Hanh and then get help.

***

Ly's gaze swept back and forth as we drove through the dock areas, our necks craning to see down the rows of crates.

I was nearly ready to admit defeat when Ly shrieked. She'd spotted the orange truck leaving one of the loading areas. After the truck turned a corner, I moved forward and parked the SUV behind a row of cargo crates.

"C'mon, Ly, let's take a look at that freighter."

We crept forward and peeked around a crate. Ferret-face said the ship would leave in the morning. I hoped it meant a skeleton crew would be on board. In the fading light and the angle from where we stood, I couldn't see the ship's full name, but could make out what looked like a first, middle initial and longer last name. A guard stood at the top of the gangway.

I whispered to Ly, "We know where she is. We have to find a police officer now." I nudged her back toward the car.

Ly stood firm. "I go get Hanh."

"See that guard? We can't get past him. The same thing could happen to you as Hanh and they'd probably dump me overboard. Let's go." I tugged at her arm, but she still wouldn't move. I'd seen her feet and shoulders set like that at the shack when she thought I might harm her sister.

"Okay, here's what we'll do," I pointed to the guard. "We wait until dark. Maybe he'll leave and I can get on board and find her."

She shook her head.

I understood her urgency. The longer Hanh was left on this ship, the more likely something horrible would happen to her. But Ly didn't have gloves or hat or even a warm jacket to be standing out here in the freezing cold.

"You have to stay in the car. Once I signal that I'm going onto the ship, wait half an hour." I told Ly to do the same thing we'd talked about at The Shipwreck. She shivered and reluctantly agreed. On our way back to the car, we rehearsed how she would explain where we were if Plan A didn't work.

I found a flashlight in my glove box and put it in her trembling hands, trying for a confident smile. Her eyes held little hope. She locked the door behind me.

Believing our task to be futile, I went back to watch the guard. The chance of Ly finding either a police officer or kind person in this eerie and forbidding location was unlikely. My chances of getting on board would be slightly better at night.

I watched and waited. A chill wind whipped through the canyons of crates, invading my clothes, skin and internal organs as if I were a skeleton. The guard at the top of the gangway stamped his feet and hunched against the cold but didn't move away from his station.

I wondered why no police sirens were racing to the port after getting the message that a young girl was being taken onto a ship. My game plan was to find the girls, alert the authorities and wait for them to catch the bad guys. But no one answered my calls for help.

Finding the girls was a shock. I'd been looking into Isabel and Nathan's murders. Now it seemed like that happened on another planet. Everything went sideways when I'd discovered that hunting shack.

I was ready to go back to warm up when the guard checked his watch, talked into a phone, and hurried away. Maybe he headed for an early dinner.

I dashed back to the SUV to give Ly a thumbs up, hurried back, raced across the dock and up the gangway. In the deepening twilight, I ran in a crouch along the catwalk and made it to the deckhouse. With luck, no one would man the crow's nest until morning.

I'd heard Ferret-face say Hanh would be delivered to Captain Pratt. At least they made that easy for me. It didn't take long for me to spot a sign above a door that said, "Captain." No sound came from inside. I tried the knob, surprised to find it unlocked and stepped into the dim room. A single light shone from a wall lamp.

The captain's quarters was weather-beaten with dirty furnishings, beer bottles were strewn on a table along with a chewed half-smoked stogie in an ashtray. The box that held Hanh lay on its side in a corner, empty. The remnants of a rope were on the floor, a drawer of utensils open in the galley. The tape covering her mouth was in a ball next to the rope. She'd escaped, but where? I took a photo and I willed myself to think. What would I do if I were a terrified eleven-year-old?

Find a hiding place. Hanh would be disoriented. She'd crawl into the first small space she found and try to disappear.

The lifeboats were secured next to the deckhouse. That's where I'd hide. I edged toward them, watching for the guard and calling softly. "Hanh, I'm going to take you to Ly." Whistling wind blew my words back in my face. I moved further along the secured lifeboats and kept calling to Hanh. A returning whisper so faint I wondered if it was the wind playing tricks floated back to me.

"Ly?"

It took a moment for my eye to locate where the tiny sound came from. A shadow in the corner of the lifeboat moved. The frightened girl was curled into a ball in the corner, her quivering hands held a knife in front of her. I set the flash, focused my camera and took the picture. She blinked and crawled from her hiding place. "Ly?" she whispered.

I pointed away from the ship, and reassured her that Ly waited for her, and we had to go so they wouldn't find us. Hanh looked ready to cry. She didn't understand.

I made a running motion. "Go fast, okay?"

She nodded but stood frozen to the ground. I knelt beside her and gathered her into my arms, whispering that everything would be okay now. She twined her thin arms around my neck and squirmed so close to me it was as if she intended to burrow under my skin. My fingers smoothed dark hair from her flushed face. I knew with certainty I would kill to protect her. I lifted her, and she wrapped her legs around my waist. We hurried along the dark, unlit catwalk and made it past the place where the guard had been and almost to the gangway, when someone called out.

"Hey!" Heavy feet thudded after us.

"Hold tight." With Hanh's head tucked into my chest, I barreled down the gangway, ten yards ahead of our pursuer. I lost him when we ducked behind the row of crates, and sprinted to the SUV.

Ly unlocked the door, I tossed Hanh into the back, jumped behind the wheel and floored it out of there. Ly's legs flew past me as she catapulted into the back seat with Hanh. Hearing their sobs brought tears to my one good eye, and I dashed them away. I needed to see to get out of the port area maze before someone stopped us.

We made it into the mainstream of rush-hour traffic, and I pulled onto the shoulder to wait for my knees to stop knocking. When my vital signs normalized and the adrenalin dissipated, the pain in my ribs and throbbing at the back of my neck returned full force. I hadn't felt it when we ran from the ship.

When it subsided to a manageable level, I pulled back into traffic and asked Hanh, still in Ly's arms. "Were you asleep in the room where the man put you in the box?"

Ly helped with the words, and when Hanh responded, Ly said, "Man gave Hanh white pill. Make sleep. "

"How did you get out of the captain's quarters?"

Ly translated again. "Hanh not so sleepy after a while. She tip over in box and push out. Find knife. "

I spoke into the rearview mirror at Ly. "Your little sister is a smart girl."

I handed out water and energy bars for all of us from the emergency bag, mentally thanking Jenna for the suggestion. Hanh fell asleep before she finished hers. I cranked the heat up, Ly tucked the thermal blanket around Hanh, and they both slept.

Giant flakes melted when they hit the windshield as I drove into the night. I wanted to get away from Duluth before stopping to call Wilcox and Ben. What happened wasn't what I'd planned, but I found two of the girls, and surely by now the Minneapolis police located Kim and Binh.

We soon left commuter traffic behind. The wind picked up, the temperature dropped and the gentle flakes turned into ice picks. I glanced in the rear view mirror again. Hanh's breathing seemed less labored than before, or was that wishful thinking?

A red light flashed on the fuel gauge. My gas tank and stomach were empty, and the girls needed a hot meal. I left the highway and pulled into a gas station on the outskirts of the city. I asked the clerk for directions to the closest Asian restaurant. He directed me to a Vietnamese restaurant down the road.

Passing the usual burger and pizza joints, I found it, parked and ushered the groggy girls inside. Hanh perked up as the aroma of broth and vegetables hit her nostrils. An inlaid black lacquer screen with images of peasants and oxen separated the entry and seating areas. A square man stood behind the counter scrutinizing our ragtag trio, Ly leaning against me, Hanh hanging onto Ly.

He pointed at the door. "No sick people in here."

I stood my ground. After what we'd been through, he'd need a crowbar to get us out of here.

Chapter 22

The man who'd refused to seat us pointed at my face. I glanced in the mirror next to the framed newspaper and magazine articles proclaiming Vo's Restaurant the best Vietnamese food in the area. The right side of my face was black and blue, one eye swollen shut, split-lip caked with dried blood, and dirty matted hair hung down my back. My image blurred. I felt a twinge of fear that my brain was broken.

A slender woman came from the kitchen and spoke rapidly in Vietnamese to the man. He pointed at my face again. I told the woman our names. "These girls were brought from Vietnam for sex trafficking. I'm a journalist. I'm trying to help them." I unzipped my jacket and showed the *Star Tribune* credential hanging from my neck. "We won't stay long. We're hungry and I need to use your phone."

The woman tapped her lip with a forefinger and summed it up, "Little girl is sick and you are hurt." Her gaze took in my arm pressed tight against the sore rib. It hurt worse since the mad dash down the gangplank with Hanh plastered to me.

The husband crossed his arms over his broad chest and lifted his chin. "We don't want trouble."

The woman let out a high-pitched stream of Vietnamese words at him, causing the people sitting at a table near us to stop eating, chopsticks in midair. She continued berating him as he hurried to the kitchen.

When he'd escaped, she bowed. "We are Mr. and Mrs. Vo." Fine lines appeared at the corner of her eyes when she smiled. "We would be pleased to serve you. Follow me."

Shooting angry glances at the kitchen where her husband cowered from her stinging tongue, Mrs. Vo led us to a booth in the back. Ly trailed behind and stopped at a shrine in an alcove. She stood for a few moments looking at the fat Buddha, inhaling the incense, touching the flowers and plate of pears. Her cheeks were moist when she joined us.

Mrs. Vo pointed toward the back. "The bathroom is through there. You wash up."

The three of us went together. I wasn't letting the girls out of my sight. We used the toilet, and I attempted to clean my face with paper towels, but didn't see much of an improvement. The girls were too tired to even try.

Mrs. Vo indicated a booth for us in a back room that must have been for large parties. Booths and tables were set for eight to ten. Mrs. Vo didn't want to scare her other customers, or maybe she was being considerate. We waited for our food in silence.

In a few minutes, Mrs. Vo set a steaming teapot on the table. It smelled like old socks. She slid in next to Hanh and held the tea to Hanh's lips. Hanh's nose crinkled and she pulled back. Mrs. Vo encouraged in soothing tones until Hanh tasted. By the time she'd finished it all, Hanh breathed easier. We'd all been holding our breaths during the process.

A few minutes later, his mouth set in a thin line, Mr. Vo brought us soup with thick noodles, and chicken and vegetables with pots of rice. He waited a few feet away from the booth, watching as if curious.

Ginger, lemon grass, cilantro and chili scents filled my nostrils. Hanh's face erupted in a gigantic smile that landed directly on Mr. Vo. His face softened as if she'd given him a big hug. Hanh bent low over her bowl, a flurry of food and chopsticks flying.

We three sipped the steaming broth and slurped noodles with abandon for the next few minutes. Mrs. Vo sat close to Hanh, and quietly questioned Ly in Vietnamese. Ly answered between mouthfuls of food, the worry in her eyes lifting. I didn't know what they were saying, but Mrs. Vo looked alternately angry and pained at what she heard. When finished

195

eating, Ly bowed to Mrs. Vo and thanked her. "It taste like home." Mrs. Vo returned the bow.

At the end of the meal, I asked to use the phone. Mrs.Vo pointed to the front desk. I took a deep breath. Not an easy call to make.

I preferred shouting to Ben's low growl. "You were told to wait in Minneapolis."

"If I had, who would have found Ly?"

"You have one of the girls?"

I leaned against the lacquer divider, almost unable to hold myself up any longer. "I have two of them. Ly and her sister, Hanh. They took Hanh to Duluth and sold her to a ship's crew."

The anger left his voice. "We got your message about The Shipwreck Bar. Duluth PD is all over it now. How did you find her in Duluth?"

My rib throbbed. I couldn't find a comfortable position. "Ly heard them mention it. I wasn't sure of the exact location, but looked for the seediest area near the docks. Did anyone trace the license plate on that beige van?"

"The plate was stolen. They've contacted the highway patrol, sheriff, PD, Bureau of Criminal Apprehension, border patrol, rangers, everyone's on the lookout, but they've probably stolen a different one by now."

I moved away from the wall and bent slightly forward to ease the pressure. "You have to get those guys. Ly said there were two, but they always wore masks."

Ben said, "We'll get them. How did you find Hanh at the docks?"

I described the freighter's location, and mentioned Captain Pratt. "Finding Hanh was luck and timing. I wasn't that far behind them at each step. I'd hoped for assistance from the Duluth authorities, but that didn't happen."

He groaned. "The Duluth-Superior port is a law enforcement nightmare with all their jurisdiction issues. ICE is hamstrung as well, but I won't depress you with the details."

"Tell me. I want to know."

He snorted. "Maritime law prohibits local and state law enforcement officers from boarding ships, so if you hadn't gotten Hanh off the ship when you did, even if they knew about her, the Duluth PD couldn't have acted."

"No wonder the bad guys are winning."

"No kidding."

Our conversation was like the old days, easy, comfortable, warm. I was afraid to ask. "You got Trung and the other girls, right? There should have been seven including Binh and Kim.

I heard him exhale. "Not yet. Trung and the girls were gone by the time the officers arrived."

"Oh, no." I glanced into the banquet room where the girls were still eating and chatting with Mrs. Vo. I didn't want to tell Ly about her friends.

"Roxy saw Trung's car leave shortly after Ly ran away with you chasing her. She got part of the license plate so we'll find them."

"Everyone should have a neighbor like Roxy. What happened with Tommy?"

"We found him hanging around in front of the sheriff's. He didn't want to talk to Wilcox until his brother arrived, and Daniel was out of town."

I'd worried about Tommy bailing on me. He was so afraid of Wilcox, I wondered if he did have something to do with Isabel's death. He didn't have to be involved in trafficking to be guilty of committing a crime.

Ben said, "Hold on. Wilcox wants to talk to you."

"I don't want to talk to him."

Wilcox was already on the line. "Too late, Johansson." He launched into a tirade. "I've got pandemonium going on here. Tommy showed us the shack. Tribal police and our deputies were out there. We found blood inside, a banged up chair, stove on its side, evidence of people staying there. We got your camera with the photos of the girls. I thought I told you to stay away from this."

"And yet, my evidence is all you have, right?"

Somber, Wilcox said, "We've already sent the photos all over the region. We'll get those other girls."

The conviction in his voice mirrored my own feelings. "I know you will, Sheriff."

Ben was back, sounding worried. "Tommy said you were beat up. Shouldn't you see a doctor?"

"I'm leaving as soon as Ly and Hanh finish their dinner. I'm only about three hours away. I can make it home."

"Be careful, Britt. A storm's on the way. We'll be waiting for you at Branson Hospital."

The girls finished eating and were nearly asleep in the booth. I gathered them up, fished my credit card out of one of the inner zip pockets of my jacket and handed it to Mr. Vo.

He wouldn't take it.

Mr. Vo put a protective arm around Hanh. Mrs. Vo drew Ly's arm through hers. I asked if I could take a picture. They could have been a family.

Mr. and Mrs. Vo must have thought so, too. They offered to keep the girls with them until they felt better. I explained that the sheriff needed Ly to help them with information to catch the bad guys. I left my card with them and the sheriff's number so they could keep in contact with the girls.

Mr. Vo studied my eye. "Needs herbs."

I thanked him and said his delicious soup revived me. I hated to drag the girls away, but we needed to get ahead of that storm.

Once again, they both fell asleep in the back seat almost immediately.

I'd been driving for two hours when the storm caught up to us, battering the SUV and making it hard to stay on the road. I'd thought I could beat it. It was another hour to Branson, and I wasn't sure I could make it. My eye wanted nothing more than to close, each blink like sandpaper scraping across it. But if I did, we'd end up in a ditch. I grabbed my water bottle and splashed my eye. The action brought a moment's relief and woke me.

I wouldn't let us die of exposure after getting this far. Knowing that Little and Lars and Ben would be waiting kept me going for the next stretch, until finally, nearly at the end of my endurance and using blind faith to navigate, I pulled into the hospital emergency entrance at one a.m. The three-hour drive turned into four with the storm.

Ben burst out of the hospital door before I put the SUV in park. His eyes registered shock as he helped me from the SUV and into a waiting wheelchair. "For the love of God, why didn't you tell me you were in this condition?"

Someone loaded the girls into wheelchairs. I said, "Hanh's the one who needs help. Make sure they're in the same room."

We were whisked inside and I let my eye close.

Morning light slanted through the blinds. My trembling fingers traced around the bandage. I fought down rising panic. Was I now a one-eyed photographer?

Through my good eye, I focused on Little talking with Edgar near the window. The old guy's gnarled hand rested on the cane propped next to his chair. Little said to Edgar, "Britt's awake." Edgar used his cane to boost himself from the chair and came to my bedside. "I'm glad you found those crying girls."

"Me too, Edgar." I sensed what it must be like for Edgar, who was almost blind. According to his grandson, Henry, Edgar could still make out shapes, but few details.

"Do you still carry the wolf agate?" Edgar asked me.

"Yes, it's always in my jean's pocket. It didn't help me much at the shack, though. A pack of wolves nearly ate me."

The old man said, "They were your incentive." He smiled at Little. "Thank you for bringing me to see Britt. I know you have to get back to your restaurant."

Little told me he'd be back after he dropped Edgar off at his house, and the two left the hospital room.

Next, Ben came to my bedside and there was no mistaking the relief in his eyes. I grabbed his hand. "Be honest. Did I lose my eye?"

A gentle squeeze. "Dr. Fromm says you'll be able to see, but you have to be patient."

I nearly choked on the lump in my throat. Wilcox, cowboy hat in hand, stood next to Ray near the door. How long had all these people been in my room waiting for me to wake up? I felt like I'd been caught half-dressed.

I looked down at my faded blue hospital gown and pulled the covers up under my armpits. An IV dripped into a vein on my left arm.

Wilcox moved closer, cowboy hat in hand. "Why didn't you tell us what you were doing? You withheld information."

"I tried, Sheriff." My actions were extreme and maybe foolish, but I knew if I'd stopped at the sheriff's and waited for them to check my story, the girls would all be lost.

Ben put his hand on the sheriff's arm. "Later."

Wilcox sputtered. "Who was your contact? How did you find out about the trafficking?"

Ben loomed, dwarfing Wilcox. The sheriff slapped his cowboy hat against his leg. "I need you to tell me exactly what happened from start to finish. Soon."

The door swished shut behind him.

"Thanks, Ben." My words sounded far away.

"You rest. Wilcox can wait." He smoothed the hair away from my face, and I leaned into his touch. I attempted to ask if he wanted to go to lunch, but my words dissolved and I drifted off.

A fist smashed into my eye. I screamed and woke. It took a minute to realize it was a dream. My eye throbbed, probably bringing on the dream.

Worry lines creased the space between Little's brows. "Are you hurting? You were calling out."

"Every time I fall asleep, a boot comes at me, or a fist." I pushed the button for more pain killer and checked around the room. Everyone was gone except Little. I thanked him for being there, and said, "Don't you have a restaurant to run? I hope you didn't leave Lars in the kitchen. You'll lose all your customers."

"You're better." He patted my foot.

I asked, "The girls?"

"They're fine. Ben can tell you about them. I should get back to my kitchen." He made a face. "You're right about Lars."

"Go. I'm good."

Little patted my foot again, "I'll ask Lars to bring you some decent food later."

He left and Ben came back in the room. Afraid to read too much into his caring behavior, I asked, "How's Hanh?"

"She has pneumonia, but is doing better. Ly's with her."

A giant boulder rolled off my chest. "What will happen to them?"

He said, "Mr. and Mrs. Vo want to keep them. We'll look into it."

"That's great news." I steeled myself for the answer to my next question. "What about the other girls?"

"Trung's nowhere to be found, but we aren't giving up."

The bile rose in my chest. "They'd better get those guys."

He squeezed my hand and said he needed to go. They were all working nonstop to find the girls. I drifted off again until the aroma of Little's chicken soup wafted under my nose, waking me. A covered dish sat on the stand next to my bed. I was trying to move it close enough to eat the contents without my ribs screaming when Jason came in with Thor. Were they holding hands?

"The nurse said we could stay a minute if it's okay with you." Thor stuffed her striped stocking cap in her pocket, and the platinum spikes of hair sprang to life. She'd added one neon blue stripe.

I checked the window. Time had slipped its moorings. I must have slept most of the day. "I'm glad you stopped by. Jason, my camera's in my jacket in the closet. Check the inside pocket. The photos aren't great quality, but they'll help you tell the story."

Jason stared at my face. "Are you blind in that eye?"

Thor's elbow connected with Jason's right rib. He said, "Sorry. I'll get that camera." He ducked into the closet.

Thor said, "We got the autopsy report on Nathan. They found tape residue around his mouth. There's no question it was murder."

Cynthia appeared behind them, her eyes still ringed with dark circles. "Hi Britt. I thought you'd want to know, the *Strib* wants the trafficking story for page one. We've talked to

Wilcox, and Ben filled us in on how it connects to the aborted sting last week in Minneapolis. When you're better, we'll add your information."

I was tired, but Cynthia lived with the reality of her beloved husband dying and she showed up for work as much as she could. "Of course. I'll go to the bureau as soon as the doctor cuts me loose."

Doctor Fromm came in with Nurse Connie, who ushered everyone out. The doctor knew me from the time I wrapped my car around a tree back when I was drinking. Nurse Cranky had not approved of my blood-alcohol level. They both wore round, rimless glasses and often communicated by reading each other's minds. I believed them to be aliens, the extraterrestrial kind. Fromm checked the chart and mumbled something to her in their coded language as she took my vitals for the thousandth time.

I pointed to my eye. "When will I be able to see out of it? How come I keep falling asleep? I need to get home. I want my dog." Whining felt good.

"The bandage might not come off for a week, maybe two." Fromm put the chart back.

Panic made my voice shrill. "Why so long?" I tried to rise, but eased back when a sharp pain jabbed my ribs.

Dr. Fromm spoke slowly. "Your eye needed surgery." He gave me the medical version of what he'd done, but it terrified me so I stopped listening until he said, "We're sedating you to keep you quiet long enough to heal. In our experience, you don't follow orders. If I let you go, you'll do the opposite of the recommended bed rest."

"I want to go home." I'd turned into a two-year-old.

He rapped his knuckle on the chart. "You have a cracked rib and a concussion. They tell me you drove for two days like that."

Nurse Cranky, aka Connie, tsk'ed. Sturdy, compact, judgmental, she was my favorite nurse.

Fromm peered at me over the top of his glasses. "We're interested in how you received your injuries. We're aware of the blunt force trauma to the lower back of your head, boot in the ribs, punch in the face causing eye, lip and jaw trauma, and the abrasions on your hand, arms and ankles from being bound." He studied me. "We're wondering about the infected wound on your scalp above your ear? It's older than the others. And what caused those other old bruises?"

Rather than bring up the arrow, or admit to the self-inflicted damage from my three-legged stool test, I said nothing.

Cranky tucked the blanket tighter and replaced the bag that dripped liquid into me.

I asked, "Is it morphine, I hope?"

Another tsk. "We're rehydrating you."

"I'll be leaving this evening, doc. Thanks for patching me up." Even as I said it, I knew better. I could hardly move.

He put the chart back. "There's no way you're going to be released until tomorrow."

He and Cranky telepathically signaled each other and levitated from the room.

In the morning, Dr. Fromm examined my eye, and Nurse Cranky replaced the bandage with another, thicker one. I was still afraid they weren't telling me the truth. A hateful inner voice convinced me that I would never again see out of that eye. I held a mirror to my face, and stared at the bulbous white bandage above a green and purple bruise ending at my jawline. And an entire family of blackbirds could be nesting in my matted tangle of hair and I'd never have known it.

With perfect timing, Violet sailed in with a basket loaded with grooming items. "Oh, your poor face. You'll have to come in and have a healing facial, once you've, you know, healed."

I set the mirror aside, glad for the distraction.

She plumped down on the bed sending my ribs into spasms, and chose a few items from her basket. "First, let's see if we can get those snarls out of your hair."

Violet brushed, starting at the ends and working up to my scalp, her touch so gentle I hardly felt any tugging. She wound my hair into a loose braid, and turned her attention to massaging lotion into the un-traumatized half of my face, neck and shoulders.

"That feel better?" she asked.

I nodded, not trusting myself to speak. Her ministrations were a hundred times better than the painkillers Nurse Connie doled out.

"I have a cut in half an hour, so I'd better go." She arranged the brush and lotions in the basket as if they were magic elixirs. "I'm leaving this for you. Don't forget to do the night cream."

My good eye teared up. "Thanks, Violet. It smells like spring." I didn't want her to leave.

She smiled. "It's vanilla and lavender. Restful." At the door, she turned and said, "Mother's arthritis in her hip is acting up so she couldn't come with me. She said if you come by as soon as you leave the hospital, your waxing is free."

I said, "She wants all the details, right?"

"OMG, she's *dying* to hear everything."

In the afternoon quiet, the inner voices tore into me. How could I leave? These people in Spirit Lake took care of me. They cared about what I ate and keeping my face moisturized. Marta loved me, but when in work mode at the *Times*, I was just a resource.

That evening, Little came in followed by a graceful girl with shiny blue-black hair. I hardly recognized Ly from the ragged and dirty child I'd first met. Her haunted face was transformed to gentle sweetness. "Thank you so much for finding my sister."

"I heard she's going to be fine. I'm so glad."

"I like your dog. He sleep at my feet."

Little saw my confusion and explained. "Lars and I insisted she stay with us last night until Mr. and Mrs. Vo could come."

Ly nodded. "Little make Pho. I have hot bath, wash hair, sleep in soft bed." She opened her arms to show off her new jeans and sweater and offered a shy smile. "You kind people. Maybe America okay."

"You look lovely, Ly." It pleased me that Ly, whose life was difficult even before Quan snatched her, was experiencing a few comforts.

Her face clouded. "No Binh and Kim."

"They'll find them." I hadn't gotten much more than a quick impression of them at the shack, but Binh seemed more mentally fragile than the others. At least she and Kim, a survivor, were together.

"You find us. Now maybe you find them?" Her words appeared innocent, but I detected a challenge behind them, and admired her for it.

Before I could make a promise I didn't know how to keep, the door whooshed open and Dr. Fromm came in followed by Nurse Cranky, who escorted Little and Ly from the room.

I sat up straighter. "Doctor, can I go home now?"

He examined my eye again. "I'll release you, but come back in tomorrow for me to check it."

I put on the clothes Little brought from the cabin. He wheeled me out of the hospital room, although my legs came through the ordeal unscathed compared to every other inch of me.

Little had already met Hanh and said she wanted to see me. He pushed the chair into her room a few doors down from mine. Her face broke into a grin when she saw me. "Britt!"

Hanh had taken up lodging in my heart, and I smiled back at her. She was still pale, but full of life, jabbering in Vietnamese and English, her joyful personality shining through, just as Ly described her on our drive. After a while, Connie let us know that Hanh needed to rest. She had to stay in the hospital one more night.

I hugged her, careful not to pull on the needle taped to her arm. The same feeling of yearning tugged at me as when she first threw herself into my arms. Would I ever have a child to love?

As we left, Nurse Connie asked Hanh if she'd like to look at a picture book she'd brought from the hospital library. Hanh nodded and was happily distracted when we left.

Little navigated the wheelchair down the hall, into the elevator and out to his waiting car. It wasn't lost on me that even though my brother was often justifiably mad at me, he always had my back.

Little, Ly and I went to Spirit Lake, and I steeled myself for another confrontation with Wilcox.

Chapter 23

The triple threat—Ben, Ray and Wilcox—waited in a booth at Little's Café. I took a few deep breaths to gather energy. I knew Wilcox would grill me over what I'd done wrong by taking off on my own.

He moved his cowboy hat resting on the seat between us, and I slid in next to him. Across from us, Ray and Ben looked like they weren't enjoying this anymore than I was.

Wilcox said, "Let's eat dinner and talk about the case after."

We all agreed.

My jaw was still too sore to chew, so I spooned up cream of asparagus soup while sending covetous glances at their steaks. After the meal, Lars brought coffee, cleared plates and the sheriff started his recorder.

I recited every detail from the moment I parked near Tommy's and discovered his dad in the fish house. Ray said, "We checked Tommy's place and the fish house. Gerald's gone."

Wilcox wanted to know how I discovered the girls. He was skeptical about how I'd gotten an address for Trung. I said I'd heard a street name mentioned at the shack and did an Internet search. He couldn't make me give up the name of a source, although he could slap me in jail for obstruction of justice. He didn't push it, though.

Ben ran a hand over the stubble on his face. "Off the record, this guy Quan could be the kingpin we've been after and likely the guy who murdered Huy Huong. The two in the van are still unknown. "

I asked about the men involved at the harbor. Wilcox said they'd disappeared along with the elusive Captain Pratt. "The Shipwreck Bar's been closed down. If they try to re-surface in the area, they'll be caught."

The change in Wilcox puzzled me. "How come you're so civil, Sheriff? I expected you to be furious."

His face flushed. "My wife says I'm jealous of you. You remind me I'm old, lost some of that fire. Maybe she's right." He grabbed his hat and pulled it low over his forehead. "Nothing happens here in a year, and now I've got two kids dead and a sex trafficking ring going on in a ten-mile radius. Maybe I am losing my touch. This thing has me baffled, and if there's a connection between them I sure as hell don't see it."

After Wilcox was gone, Ben said, "You can close your mouth now."

"Mrs. Wilcox sounds like someone I'd like to meet. What was that all about?" I wondered if the painkillers were still making me fuzzy.

Ray said, "We've all been blindsided by this trafficking ring happening in our county. They even used the rez. We all look bad."

He left, saying he had to deal with Tommy, and Ben stayed behind. He looked at his watch. He'd been so protective of me at the hospital, and so gentle, but now I sensed he was distancing himself again. I wanted to keep him with me a little while longer.

I asked, "What about Isabel and Nathan? Could there be a connection with the trafficking?"

"I'm beginning to believe anything's possible. That case is getting colder by the day." He shrugged into his jacket. "Lars and Little have been taking good care of Ly. You should stay here tonight and let them fuss over you, too. It's obvious you're in pain."

He hesitated as if he had more to say. I waited. Maybe *he'd* like to make a fuss over me. But he left without another word. Did I look too pathetically eager?

Little and Lars tried to talk me into staying the night but I wanted my own bed. Rock would keep Ly company at Little's for another night. Lars drove me home, and built a fire in the Franklin stove.

He set a cup of tea on the nightstand with my pills next to it. "I don't mean to give you a hard time. You did a courageous thing finding those girls, but Jayzus Britt, your brother was worried sick. Could you maybe take it easy for a while?"

"Don't worry. I intend to take it easy for a long, long while." I crawled under my blessed electric blanket and several layers of quilts, washed down a pain pill with a sip of tea, and fell asleep listening to the comforting creaks and groans of my own space, my home.

An early morning phone call from Cynthia woke me. It took a moment to comprehend her excited words.

"Believe it or not, Wilcox called me. They found one of the other girls. I already sent Jason over to the sheriff's."

I hung up and punched in Wilcox's number. "It's Britt. Who did you find?"

"Binh and Kim were dumped at a truck stop south of Minneapolis on I-35 this morning. A couple of truckers found them and called 9-1-1."

"That's great news." A load slid from my shoulders.

"Not so fast. Before the highway patrol got there, one of the girls disappeared. Binh, the one they were able to hang onto is here, and the truckers are on their way if you want to get photos. I mean, if you can, with the one eye and all."

Wilcox invited me to take photos? I told him I'd be there in twenty minutes.

"If you're here in twenty minutes I'll give you a speeding ticket."

That was more like the Wilcox I knew.

I made it to Branson in twenty-six minutes. A fire-engine red, eighteen-wheel Kenworth rig took up half the parking lot, clashing with the anemic green two-story sheriff's building.

Inside, I found Binh in a small conference room sitting at a table next to an Asian woman. When Binh saw me, her rosebud lips formed an O, she jumped from her chair, grabbed my arm, and talked fast in Vietnamese.

I didn't understand what she said, but nodded and sat in the chair next to hers. The middle-aged woman said her name was Ms. Fulton, translator and victim advocate. She said Binh knew some English, but we spoke too fast for her to follow. Binh said she was surprised I was alive and asked about finding Kim. I said we hoped to find her soon.

A cup of tea and empty carton of food sat on the table in front of Binh, and she appeared more solid than when I last saw her. Losing Kim must have shaken her from her near-dream state. I asked if she would tell me how she got mixed up with Quan.

Ms. Fulton interpreted as Binh spoke. "We lived in Ho Chi Minh City. My stepfather came to live with my mother and me when I was nine. He beat me many times." She touched her lip near her thickest scar. "When I healed enough, my mother helped me escape."

"How long were you on your own?"

"About six months. After that, Kim found me. She took care of me like a sister. When Quan found us, we thought our lives would be better." She covered her face with her hands.

A deputy stuck his head in the door and said Wilcox wanted me to join him with the truckers.

Binh's tearful voice rang out behind me. "Please find Kim!"

In the conference room, I slid into a chair next to Jason, who was scribbling into his reporter's notebook. Two women, identical twins, sat across from us, bouncing with excitement. Wilcox, at the end of the table, introduced Kaeli and Karli Sorenson, owners of the eighteen-wheeler. Late twenties, athletic, they looked like they could take care of themselves on the road. Karli wore a John Deere ball cap, and Kaeli, a multi-colored wool laplander cap with chin ties dangling. Without the different caps, I couldn't tell the blue-eyed blonds apart.

A young deputy offered coffee and doughnuts and hovered over the twins until Wilcox scowled. The deputy retreated and Wilcox turned on the recorder. At his prompting, Karli, in the ball cap, said, "We're just pulling in at the truck stop on I-35 when a dark SUV pulls up with tinted windows and an Asian guy in shades and a fedora gets out and slides open the back door. It's packed full of Asian girls. He pulls two of them out, leaves them in the parking lot, jumps back in and takes off. Crazy, right?"

"We appreciate that you got the license plate number. Great work. It matches the car we were already looking for." Wilcox wasn't frowning, a rare sight.

The twins rolled their eyes at each other. Kaeli spoke. "We belong to TAT, Truckers Against Trafficking. With all the assholes on the road these days, it's like we're singlehandedly doing the highway patrol's job."

Wilcox said, "Now, wait a minute." I cut him off and asked, "How did you get the girls to go with you?"

Karli turned her ball cap backward, and leaned toward us. "They were freaked out but they settled down when we took them inside the truck stop and ordered food and tea. One of them spoke a little English. The other one kept saying the name Ly, so we thought it was her name."

"A couple of starving kittens." Kaeli frowned. "We were so mad that guy took off with all those other poor girls, I wanted to go after them myself."

Karli said, "We seriously would have, but we wanted to take care of those two. So we called 9-1-1 and they said to stay with them, HP was on its way."

Kaeli jumped in again, hat tassels swinging. "We're in the truck stop eating and this sleazy guy at the next table is staring at them. Those girls were lucky we found them. Believe me, we run into the sickos."

Wilcox and I agreed.

Karli stood up. "So the short one, Kim, said she wanted to go to the bathroom. When we realized it was taking too long, I checked the bathroom and she was gone."

My head swiveled from one to the other as they interrupted and finished each other's sentences.

"He must have grabbed her at the back door by the bathrooms." Kaeli's eyes widened. "That sleazebag who was staring at them was gone, so we put two and two together."

Karli said, "The patrolman shows up and we tell him one of them disappeared so he helps us hunt for her. No one in the restaurant saw anything." She pointed in the direction of the room where Binh sat talking with the interpreter. "And she's hysterical and screaming and I held on to her so she wouldn't run off and end up getting taken too! Then a whole convoy of patrol cars show up and surround the place."

They shook their heads in unison. "Too late, though."

Wilcox stopped recording. "You're good citizens, Kaeli and Karli. Patrols all over the state are looking for Kim."

"Yah, we better go." said Karli, "We're already late on our route and we have our own rig. If we don't deliver, we don't get jobs." She settled her ball cap on her head, bill forward this time. Kaeli followed her twin to the door, cap tassels bouncing. "We'll put the word out among the truckers."

They gave Jason their cell phone numbers in case he needed more information for his story. I asked for one too, handed them my card and asked them to call if they found out anything about Kim.

Jason left first to head back to the bureau, and Kaeli pumped me for information. "He's cute. I like that V-neck sweater. Does he have a girlfriend?"

I nodded. "He kind of does."

The deputy with the doughnuts disappeared into one of the offices. I guess he gave up on getting to know the truckers. A TV van and a reporter for the *Branson Gazette* showed up as the twins and I left the building. I'd take my photos before the rest of the media figured out what was going on.

As we crossed the parking lot, Karli pointed to my face. "Did you get in an accident?"

I told them an abbreviated story about what happened and pointed to my camera. "Could I take a photo of you and your truck?"

The girls stood with hands at their sides, dwarfed by the giant semi. I admired their truck and continued to shoot, hoping the photos would turn out with my one-eye disadvantage. "How did you get into trucking?"

Karli threw her arm around her sister's shoulder, their faces filled with pride. "When our dad retired, he trained us and gave us his truck."

I moved to catch the fading sunlight, shooting as they talked. Kaeli climbed up to the driver's seat. "When we worked at Honeywell we sat in cubicles all day staring at computer screens."

Karli grinned. "No more business outfits now. We get to be our own bosses. Way better."

My camera clicked. "It looks like a tough job to me."

Kaeli pulled the door shut on the passenger side. "Parking is hard and we hate the paperwork. And driving in winter can be scary. We love the "Ice Road Truckers" show, though."

"People honk at us to go faster but dad taught us safety's the most important priority for a trucker. You could hurt someone with this monster." Karli patted the side of the truck.

"What do you haul?"

"We'll take anything but hazardous waste." The massive truck roared to life.

Karli called out. "Check out our blog. Twin Truckers. We post great photos, like when we snowboard up in Idaho."

They blasted the horn, nearly blowing me off the pavement, laughing their heads off. I hoped it wasn't the last time I'd see them. They were so full of life and energy, it was contagious.

Back inside, I leaned against the sheriff's doorway and waited for him to put the phone down. He said, "I thought you left."

I sat on the edge of one of the chairs across from his desk. "How come you called the papers and TV? It's not like you to invite the press to do a story."

"Kaeli Sorenson was right—we need all the help we can get. I want to get the word out, and it takes lots of eyes on the streets and roadways. We're dealing with an epidemic." He opened a file, a discouraged slope to his shoulders. "There's no getting ahead of it."

His passion on the subject made me think there might be other times I'd been too hard on him. "One more question. Were you able to find out where the girls were between leaving Trung's and when they were dropped?"

"We asked Binh with the translator's help, but she didn't know. I'm guessing Trung figured out Minnesota was too hot for him, so he headed south on I-35 to Chicago."

Mr. and Mrs. Vo hurried in as I left the sheriff's. We shook hands, and I said, "I understand you want to help Hanh and Ly."

Mrs. Vo nodded. "We have no children. They could go to college and have a good life with us."

Mr. Vo crossed his arms in front of him, nodding. "First, lots of red tape, paperwork." The man was a teddy bear after all. They told me they belonged to an organization that helped Vietnamese people, and they would see to it Binh, and Kim once she was found, were placed with families and taken care of. I followed them back inside to meet Binh and take their picture.

Wilcox said he would take Binh to the hospital in a few minutes. Mr. and Mrs. Vo would follow. After the harrowing whirlwind of the past week I wanted to keep the girls close to me, but I knew they were in good hands with the concerned couple looking out for them. They deserved a break. Ly, the lionhearted; Hanh, with her mop of hair and big grin; Binh, stronger than even she knew; and Kim, the little toughie.

I wondered if I would get to take a picture of Kim, safe with her friends in Spirit Lake.

Cynthia and Jason were grateful for the extra hand at the bureau. I wrote captions for the photos they'd retrieved from my camera at the shack a lifetime ago, and more captions for the pics from my backup camera. I was so relieved my one-eyed photos from the past few days were okay, I wanted to cry. That was happening a lot. I didn't know what to make of it.

In between working on the project, Jason talked nonstop about Thor. I could relate to being obsessed with someone who didn't reciprocate, but being reminded of my own pathetic self annoyed me. Ben was off tracking leads to Quan and hadn't even said goodbye.

I snapped. "Give it a rest, Jason. No woman wants a needy man." And to myself, I added, and no man wants a needy woman.

His fingers struck the keys like hammers. I wished I'd kept my mouth shut. His chatter was better than the typing tantrum.

By early afternoon, I drooped over my computer, barely able to stay awake. Cynthia insisted I go home and I insisted she go. Jason told us both to go, he could handle it.

Dr. Fromm's office called. He wanted to check my eye and I said I'd be there in half an hour. Maybe Fromm would give me more magic pain killers to help me sleep. Before heading to Fromm's, I drove out to Branson mall for a new phone, and for once it wasn't snowing. The sky was the color of skim milk, what passed for sunshine in this part of the country.

I'd felt naked without my smart phone. With the new phone synched up, missed text messages and emails started pinging. I scrolled through the calls in the mall parking lot. Marta wanted to know what was wrong with my phone and had I made a decision about L.A. Management was impatient. Old calls from Little and Ben and Wilcox. One new message was from Karli. "We found the sleazy guy from the truck stop but no Kim."

I hit call back. It went to voice mail. I tried Wilcox. "They got the guy already?"

"How did you find that out? It just happened ten minutes ago."

"I asked the twins to keep me informed."

Wilcox said, "Karli and Kaeli drove through a weigh station down in Iowa. They saw a trucker who looked like the guy watching Kim at the truck stop and demanded to search his truck. He resisted, so they got the station guy and a couple of other truckers to help them. The truck came up empty, but Kaeli recognized a silver barrette on the floor of the sleep compartment from the one in Kim's hair."

"That's right, she wore two silver barrettes." I couldn't believe the amazing luck.

"The guy told them he heard CB chatter about a trucker who abducted an Asian girl, so he dumped her on the outskirts of Des Moines and took off. The highway patrol has him in custody and they're waiting for the FBI. He insists he didn't touch her, of course, but trafficking, kidnapping, crossing state lines, he's in trouble."

The poor, scared kid could be anywhere. "What are you doing to find Kim?"

"I've sent her picture to everyone down there. They've got a Missing Child alert out." He sighed. "Now, we wait."

The whole scenario was too much coincidence for this skeptic. I called Karli again and this time she answered. "Hey, Britt. We got that guy."

"I heard. You just happened to be in Des Moines and before that you just happened to be at that truck stop where the girls were dropped?"

Her voice hard, she said, "What we're doing is important. We don't like to blab it all over. TAT is everything to us."

"It was no accident that you were at that truck stop where you found Kim and Binh?"

"We had a load to deliver in that county, and yes, we watch that truck stop. It's a known trafficking spot."

"And that guy you went after?"

"We put out the word to look for a guy with his description, but we were headed south already."

I shivered, started the car and set the heat on high. "How did you get him to confess he took Kim?"

"You don't want to hear about that."

I couldn't keep a certain amount of awe out of my voice. "You're vigilantes."

Kaeli came on the phone, her voice wary. "Please don't tell the sheriff."

"I won't, but I'd like to hear the real story."

"Our little sister Mia ran off when she got mad at our dad for being too strict. A trafficker got her at a park in Minneapolis where she was hanging out with some kids. They found her in Chicago a year later." Her voice trembled, "Dead. Mia was thirteen."

Karli's voice again, firm and resolved. "We are licensed truckers. We just report what we see. That's all."

"I understand. Thank you for telling me. I'm so sorry about your sister." I sat stunned in my car when my phone rang, startling me. The sheriff's ID popped up.

"Meet me at the hospital—now."

He'd already hung up so I didn't have time to ask why.

Chapter 24

Wilcox and I pulled into Branson Hospital at the same time. Together, we burst through the doors and down the maze of corridors toward Hanh's room.

Slightly ahead of me, he talked over his shoulder. "They found Kim at a KFC in Des Moines, and she wants Binh."

"Kentucky Fried Chicken?" I hurried after him, panting and holding my arm against my side.

He said, "I sent her photo to every law enforcement agency in Minnesota and adjacent states. Des Moines highway patrol matched it up with a report about an Asian girl who locked herself in a KFC bathroom, and refused to come out. She said she wanted Binh, and you." Slightly out of breath, he stopped before we opened the door to Binh and Hanh's room, looked at me, and said, "You must have made an impression."

I shrugged. "I promised I would find them."

He pushed his cowboy hat off his forehead. "It never occurred to you it would be near impossible to follow through on your promise?"

I looked him in the eye. "Only every minute of every day since those guys took them, and left me to die."

He reached for the door, but I stopped him. "Wait, don't those public bathrooms have locks on the outside in case they have to go in after someone? Why not just get her out?"

His eyes rolled. "You couldn't make this stuff up. The employees couldn't find a key and couldn't reach their manager, so they called the fire department to break down the door. They were about to do it when the highway patrol arrived and told them to wait for us."

"No one thought of a locksmith?" I asked.

"I guess not. Clueless bunch of kids. One of them was trying to pry it off with a screwdriver."

I looked at the time on my phone. "Kim's been locked in there several hours already." Wilcox opened the hospital room door, ready to charge in, but I put a hand on his arm. "Slow down, Sheriff. Don't scare them."

"Right." He took off his hat and smoothed his hair.

Ly and Binh sat next to Hanh's bed. Their smiles warmed my heart. Maybe they wouldn't be afraid of every stranger if enough decent people crossed their paths from now on.

Wilcox told them we'd found Kim. The girls crowded close to him while he explained what happened, and that he wanted Binh and me to come with him. Ly translated for Binh. She grabbed my hand, ready to go.

Wilcox spoke to someone at the nurse's station, and hustled us to his car. He hit the gas before we were buckled, and spun out of the parking lot. "We're flying down," he told me.

We held on as he shot through Branson with lights flashing and siren screaming. "Maybe we should wait for the plane," I said. He whipped around corners, tore through intersections, and sped down the highway to the airport.

The pilot had the engines running. We hustled aboard and in less than two hours arrived at the Des Moines airport. A highway patrol officer took us to a KFC on the outskirts of the city.

Inside, a couple of firefighters and two police officers, male and female, waited near the bathroom hallway. A line of people at the counter appeared mildly interested in the drama, but most faced forward, looking at their smart phones.

Wilcox tapped on the bathroom door. I urged Binh closer. She spoke in Vietnamese and when she stopped, I called to Kim. "It's Britt from the shack. We'll take you to Ly and Hanh."

Another fast exchange between Binh and Kim in their language, and the handle jiggled and opened. Kim stood in the doorway blinking at the crowd of people watching her. Binh threw her arms around her with another outburst in Vietnamese. They hugged, crying and laughing. My camera clicked.

Kim turned to me. Her body trembled, but her chin was up. She said, "You took long time."

I lowered my camera, kneeled to be closer, and said, "I know. And you've been so brave."

I stood up, and walking backward with my camera clicking, urged them toward me. Binh took Kim's hand, and the two walked through a gauntlet of uniforms—firefighters with their axes, police officer, Wilcox and the local sheriff.

Wilcox came forward and pointed to a small round table. "Let's get the young lady something to eat." I seated the girls and went to the counter for food while Wilcox talked with the law enforcement brigade still waiting. In a few minutes, they all left, except for one officer who would take us back to the plane.

With Binh sitting across from her talking nonstop, Kim wolfed down several pieces of roasted chicken, and a large iced tea. Wilcox and I sat at a table next to them with our coffee. I said, "Sheriff, I admire your restraint in not bombarding Kim with questions right away. I'm definitely seeing a kinder side of you with these girls."

His head tilted as if trying to figure me out. "I could say the same about you."

The moment turned awkward, and we both got busy checking our phones. He said, "I want to wait for the interpreter/advocate back at the office and get Kim's story recorded, but there is something I'd like to know. He leaned toward the girls' table. "Why did you pick KFC, Kim?"

She gulped her tea. "We have KFC and Burger King in Vietnam. I didn't see Burger King."

As we were leaving, a young employee with a dimple in his left cheek came over to the table and shyly handed Kim a stack of KFC coupons. "I'm sorry if we scared you."

I sat across from the girls on the plane. Kim pointed at my eye, and winced. "I watch that mask man in shack kick you."

I nodded. "He got me pretty good." Kim knew more English than the others so I didn't wait for the interpreter. "How did the trucker get to you?"

She said, "I go to bathroom and man with gloves grab me and put his hand on my mouth. I try to bite, but glove too thick. He lock me in little room in truck. I scream, but truck too loud."

I hesitated, and then asked, "Did he make you have sex?"

The question didn't seem to upset her. She shook her head. "He said saving me for later, but after we drive long time he stop and push me out. I run until I find KFC."

I reached across the aisle and tucked her hair behind one ear. "No more bad guys now."

Dark smudges bruised the area under her eyes. "My mother was prostitute in brothel. She get sick and they throw her on street. I take her place and support her until she die, then run away and Quan find me." She looked at me, disillusion in her eyes. "I think America a chance for better life. Not like this."

"A chance for a better life" were Binh's exact words, too. I took Kim's small, square hand in mine. "It will get better now."

We didn't need an interpreter to tell us what the girls were saying in Hanh's hospital room. When their laughter and loud chatter subsided, Binh helped Kim shower and wash her hair. Nurse Cranky, who had a soft side for everyone except me, even let us stay while she checked all the girls' vitals and hooked Kim up to the nutrients that would help her recover more quickly. Dr. Fromm examined her, and said, "You should be able to leave the hospital tomorrow afternoon. You're a tough young lady."

In her oversized blue hospital gown, her dark head with its unruly hair resting against the white pillow, Kim looked more tired and vulnerable than tough. She'd earned the right to let down her guard now and enjoy a moment of peace with her friends.

Hanh would be released as well. Mr. and Mrs. Vo said they would be back for all the girls the following day. A background check by the sheriff's office revealed they were upstanding citizens, and active in their Vietnamese community organization. I'd thought so, but understood the need to check them out.

When Kim and Hanh slept, I took Binh and Ly to Little's for the night. At first, Binh hadn't wanted to be separated from Kim, but she agreed after Ly coaxed her.

Little fed them and Lars and I settled them in the guest bedroom. Ly asked me to leave Rock again. After they'd closed down the restaurant for the night, Little, Lars and I sat in their living room and talked about the girls and their sad past.

"Mr. and Mrs. Vo are about to change that for them," said Lars, leaning back into the cushions.

Resting his stockinged feet on the coffee table, Little nodded. "They might never forget their hardships, but with love and care they can heal in time."

I told Little and Lars all about Kaeli and Karli.

Lars said, "You know they come in here all the time, right?"

Little noticed my confused stare. "They park that red semi across the street. It irritates some of the customers because they can't see the lake when it's parked there, and their airbrakes scare the old folks."

"We love those twins, said Lars. "They've been coming in since I put the sign out on the highway two years ago."

I dimly remembered seeing a red semi in front of Little's, but lots of people came and went from Little's that I didn't know. It pleased me that they knew the twins and liked them as much as I did.

Before going home to my cabin, I checked on Binh and Ly, asleep with their arms around each other. Rock was curled at the bottom of the bed. His reassuring presence watched over me many times in the past as well. I scratched Rock's ears and went home.

Gratified that everything worked out so well with the girls, I still wanted to contact one more person. I tossed a few chunks of wood in the stove, called Edgar, and set his mind at ease.

"Now we can all get a good night's sleep, especially those children," he said. "Thank you, Britt. I know it's too late to save

Isabel and Nathan, but have you heard if Wilcox has figured out who killed them?"

I didn't have anything to offer. Those poor kids had been all but forgotten in the wake of the trafficking ring.

Hoping a hot bath would help me sleep, I peeled off my eye bandage so it wouldn't get wet. The fearful Windigo image that scared Tommy stared back at me from the mirror. The bruise that ran from my eye to my jaw had turned green, a slit was visible beneath the bulbous swelling and an inch long vertical scar ran from my eye into my eyebrow. In fact, I had half an eyebrow now. At least it would mean less work for Violet. I hoped my eye wasn't permanently closed. I twisted the top off a bottle of bath bubbles she'd given me and poured it in. Steaming hot water percolated around my body like a good witch's brew, drawing out aches and pains. It didn't relax me, though. Edgar reminded me that there was still work to be done.

In the morning, I pulled my laptop onto my lap and checked out the Maelstrom Resort website. I hoped to see something that didn't fit. The twin truckers finding the girls was no coincidence, and I didn't think Isabel's and Nathan's murders were a coincidence either, or the connection with Tommy.

The website showed the resort as a summer wonderland. Kids played on the giant inflatable trampoline on the lake, and grinning, sunburned families waved from pontoons. A pyramid of jewel-toned kayaks was stacked on the shore, and a fleet of slick speedboats lined the dock. The resort even offered boat shuttle service to and from the casino. A banner ran across the top of the site: "Coming Soon! Isabel's nightclub! Watch this space for updates."

The website described the cabins as having all the amenities of a five-star hotel. The blanket of winter hid all the expensive boats and kayaks and updated cabins when I'd visited the resort. The cabin where Nathan was hung must have been one of the older ones, not yet renovated.

I hadn't focused on how up-scale the resort was now and wondered why Maelstrom's was doing so much better than others in the region. Maybe Arnie was in debt or in trouble with loan sharks like Gerald Jackson. Maybe he over-borrowed to make that grand resort for Isabel and couldn't pay it back, and the same kind of people made examples of his children as the sharks who beat up Gerald and Tommy.

Aware that Sebastian usually went to sleep when everyone else woke up, I typed in the familiar email address anyway.

-Hey, Sebastian, the four girls are safe. Thanks for your help.

He fired back.

-Not a problem. Need anything else?

Did the guy never sleep? I'd hoped he'd say that.

-Since you asked, I'm wondering if you could take a look at Maelstrom Resort's financials.

I was brushing my teeth when my email pinged.

-I've sent attachments so you can see the bank statements and resort's information but the summary is that there's a huge discrepancy between how much the resort loses on a monthly basis and how much he has in the bank. The guy's loaded. Plus, I've located an offshore account but haven't gotten into it yet. I'll have that later today.

That looked intriguing. Most likely Arnie invested wisely years ago, and used that money to keep up the resort, but maybe there was more to the story. I typed,

-Thanks so much, Sebastian. Once again, I owe you.

-Not a problem. Let me know if you want me to dig deeper.

I'd tried to pay Sebastian several times for his help but he always said, "Not a problem." I'd told him my cabin was open to him anytime, whether he needed it for a safe haven or simply as a place to relax.

At 10 a.m. I pulled into Maelstrom's Resort. The only vehicles were the gaudy Maelstrom van, and Pauly's and Dee's cars. No guests were parked at any of the cabins that I could see.

I pushed through the lodge's oversized knotty pine door, rang a bell at the desk, and in a moment Dee appeared from the kitchen, wiping her hands on a towel.

"Hey Dee, I'm sorry to bother, but is Arnie around?"

She looked alarmed. "Oh dear, what happened to your eye? We heard you've been involved in finding those poor girls the Indians were hiding on the reservation. Did one of them hit you?" She looked terrified, as if a marauding band of Ojibwe would surround the lodge any minute brandishing tomahawks.

I involuntarily touched my bandage. "There's nothing connecting any Ojibwe to those girls."

Lips pursed, she said, "They were found on Indian land. I'd say that's a connection."

I could have commented that her own stepson was found hanged on Maelstrom property but that didn't mean she did it, and that I'd found Isabel on mine, but I just left it.

"Is Arnie around?"

"He's in his office, I'll tell him you're here." She hustled up the stairs to the family quarters.

I sat on one of the plush oversized sofas and waited. In a minute she returned wearing her sky-blue down coat, and carrying a tote loaded with a Bible and pamphlets. "He'll be right down. Can I get you coffee before I go to church?" She glanced at her watch.

"I'm fine. Thanks, Dee."

She hitched the tote over her shoulder and the door closed, cutting off her humming rendition of "Onward Christian Soldiers."

I looked up as Arnie and Pauly clattered down the stairs. Arnie spoke over his shoulder. "Get out there and chop some wood for Cabin 6."

Pauly ducked into the kitchen. Arnie marched over to me, head lowered, his lips a tight line. "Didn't you agree not to talk to our family about this anymore? The paper can't possibly be interested in a profile now."

I was slightly nervous. Arnie was unpredictable. "There's no profile. We got sidetracked with the discovery of the girls."

His gaze slid away. "I heard about that. Terrible thing those Indians are doing."

Arnie didn't join me on the sofa, so I stood up. "They think it's an Asian crime ring based in Minneapolis."

Arnie said, "Really? That what Wilcox says?"

"It's not just Wilcox. A task force made up of several different agencies has been investigating it for months."

The kitchen door opened behind us, and Pauly ambled through the lodge rolling up a triangle of pizza." Gotta get my jacket." He jammed the pizza into his mouth, shrugged into a jacket hanging from a peg, pulled ear buds out of a pocket and plugged them into his iPod. Head bobbing, he stepped into the cold, still chewing.

I turned back to Arnie. "So now we're back to following up on Isabel's and Nathan's deaths."

Arnie didn't even try to be a good sport this time. "Did you come here to ask something specific?"

He wasn't going to settle in for a chat, so I got to the point. "I wondered how you reacted to the discovery that Nathan's death was also a homicide. Do you think Isabel and Nathan's murders were connected?"

A vein in Arnie's forehead pulsed, but he kept his cool. "No, I don't think they were connected, and I'm not convinced it wasn't a suicide. You didn't know my son. He was severely depressed, and what do you think my reaction to that news would be? My son and daughter are gone. However it happened, it won't bring them back to me." He pointed to the camera hanging from my neck. "What do you want—a picture a day documenting our family's misery?"

The madder he got, the more Arnie's jowls wobbled. I wanted to talk about the resort, and needed to steer him to that before he tossed me out. Attempting to sound unthreatening, I said, "We thought a story about the new restaurant, and that it was Isabel's pet project, would be a good feature and maybe bring out information that could help."

He wiped a hand over his face. "That's all you want?"

I nodded. "I think people would like to know what your secret is to running such a prosperous resort when so many have closed."

His jaw slackened.

"In fact, the overall tourist trade has slipped more than half what it was three years ago, so I'm assuming your cabins haven't been full either." There'd been no cars when I pulled in.

His smile contradicted the look in his eyes. "Well, now, I believe things are going to turn around, and I'm going to be ready when they do. Is that all?" He guided me toward the door. "I do have work to do."

Short of planting my feet, there was no way to halt my progress to the door. I hurried to ask, "I'm curious how you're financing the new restaurant and all the renovations, you know, in this downturn?"

He laughed, an ugly sound. "You'll ask anything, won't you?"

He grabbed his coat from a peg by the door. "Come with me. You're so interested in my business, I'll show you the restaurant. It's not finished, but it's a beauty. You can take all the pictures you want."

Outside, he pointed to my SUV. "We'd better take your four-wheel drive over there. That road hasn't been plowed."

I guided the SUV through the twisting resort roads. He'd gotten his anger under control, but I didn't trust his sudden attitude change from angry to jovial.

He pointed to an opening in the trees. "Turn down that lane. It leads to the restaurant."

I concentrated on not getting stuck as the SUV churned through a foot of snow to the site. There was no turning back. I'd started this.

The stunning rock and cedar restaurant was set at an angle so the row of windows across three sides offered coveted lake views. The "Isabel's" sign in lights high above the roof would be visible all across the lake.

He unlocked the front door and beckoned for me to follow him. The interior was icy cold and dim.

"Do the lights work, Arnie?" I asked.

"You'll have to imagine how it will look with the tables and chairs," he said.

I wished it were filled with people right now. A gleaming bar, small stage and dance area filled one area, and a massive rock fireplace divided the bar and dining spaces.

Arnie stood at the windows. "We were going to build a dock so guests could tie their boats and walk up to the restaurant. Isabel even planned to have an outside bar and seating right out on the dock. "

I asked, "Are you planning to go ahead with it now?" A look crossed his face that I couldn't read. "Of course, it's going to be exactly the way she would have wanted." He took my elbow. "Come with me. You have to check out the state-of-the-art kitchen."

I hesitated. "I'm freezing, Arnie. If you don't mind, I'd rather get back. It's going to be beautiful, though. I'm sure Isabel would have been pleased."

Too much white showed in his eyes. "I thought you were so interested in it. Come on back. It'll only take another minute." He pulled me toward the kitchen. "You can tell Little all about it. He's welcome to come out and take a look. He'll be impressed."

My senses sharpened and the hairs rose on the back of my neck. Hyper and wild-eyed, funeral Arnie was back. This space was Isabel's pet project.

I slid my elbow from his grasp, but he grabbed my arm and tugged at me. "I paid an architect from L.A. a small fortune to come out here and design this kitchen. You have to get a photo of it. It'll be a scoop."

Who used the word "scoop" these days? "Okay, a quick picture, but Little and Lars are waiting for me. I need to get back."

"Sure, sure."

Even in the dim, windowless kitchen, the brand new stainless steel surfaces gleamed. "I need some light, Arnie." I couldn't see that well with my patch, but I lifted my camera, ready to take a quick photo and get out.

I waited for Arnie to flip the light switch but he didn't. Instead, he opened a stainless steel door and shoved me inside. I stumbled over a step into clammy plastic strips that flapped around my body. A door slammed behind me.

I was alone inside a walk-in freezer.

Chapter 25

I pushed the yellow release knob until my hand hurt. He must have locked it from outside. I threw myself at the door, smacked my hands against it, and screamed. "Let me out!"

And then I realized I wasn't cold. Asking Arnie about his finances must have triggered this insane behavior, but maybe he was only trying to scare me. If the freezer wasn't on, he didn't intend to kill me. My shoulders dropped.

I checked my phone. No signal. I ran my hands along the walls and floor. The flapping things were thick plastic curtain strips just inside the door. I paced, but stopped myself. Was I using too much oxygen?

A whoosh of cold air blew through the vents. "No," I whispered, my earlier panic a rehearsal for the terror now rippling through my body. I curled into a ball and whimpered like a baby.

The temperature dropped fast. I forced myself to breathe slowly; gasping wasn't helping the oxygen level. A dim overhead light had come on when Arnie turned on the freezer, and I could see my prison, empty except for wire racks along each side.

My measured breathing lasted a few seconds, and then I lost all reason and pummeled the door with my fists again. "Arnie, you asshole, let me out of here!"

Mid-yell, the door opened. I stared into the barrel of a gun pointed at my eye.

"Get out here." Arnie grabbed my jacket and pulled me into the kitchen. Pauly stood behind him jiggling from one foot to the other. "Cool," he said.

Arnie snarled at him. "Wipe that stupid look off your face. She might already have Wilcox checking my books, and her brother could be looking for her."

I'd lied to Arnie about Little expecting me.

Stammering, Pauly said, "Why not leave her in the freezer to die and then dump her somewhere?"

"There can't be any evidence she came out here." Arnie pushed me so hard I rammed into the stove. "Sit on the floor." His head jerked toward Pauly. "Tie her up."

Scrawny Pauly was stronger than he looked. He twisted my hands behind me, pulled a rope from his pocket and secured me to a commercial-size range that likely cost as much as a car.

Arnie waved the gun at Pauly. "Now, get inside that freezer and wipe it down."

I sat on the floor with my back against the stove. He seemed calmer than earlier, but I didn't want to invite wild-eyed Arnie back. I kept my tone modulated. "I'm not following what's going on here, Arnie."

That was the wrong thing to say. He towered over me in my much-too-vulnerable position on the floor. I couldn't even try to cover my head with my hands if blows rained down.

But he didn't hit me. He paced between the range and the stainless steel counters, raging and crying. "I planned to go ahead and finish the restaurant and turn this resort into the best one in the county as a memorial to Isabel, but thanks to you, now I can't even have that." He wiped the snot running down his nose with the back of his hand. "It wasn't enough that Huy killed my daughter, now everything that reminds me of Isabel has to be left behind because of your meddling. I have to go back to that godforsaken country that did this to me." He pulled up his shirt sleeve to show his scar-tattoo, looking at me with pure hatred. "In one week, you cost me $40,000, my livelihood and my only link to Isabel."

My mouth dropped open. Arnie was the trafficker Ben hunted. And he thought the man found murdered at the massage parlor in Minneapolis killed his daughter.

Pauly's goateed chin stuck out the freezer door. "You're not going to Vietnam without me, are you? We can hide the girls other places, right?"

Arnie looked like he might explode. "Shut up."

I asked, "Why do you think Huy killed Isabel?"

Arnie slammed his fist on the counter. "That blackmailing weasel killed my little girl so I slit his fucking throat."

The sergeant said Huy's fingers were cut off, he'd been stabbed multiple times and his throat cut. My body shook. Arnie would not let me live. "Why did he try to blackmail you?" I asked, afraid to keep asking questions, and terrified that he'd kill me when I stopped.

His voice hollow, Arnie said, "I got word he was talking to the feds, so I cut him out of the business. He went after my daughter for revenge."

His unpredictable mood swings scared me, but for the moment he seemed not to mind talking. With only a slight tremor in my voice, I asked, "Who sends the girls to you?"

That question broke his trance. His finger wagged back and forth in front of my face. "Nosy, freakin' reporters."

"I'm a photographer."

A sadistic smile played across his face. "You've taken your last picture." He yanked the camera from around my neck, nearly taking my head with it.

I tried to keep my voice steady. "At least tell me how the trafficking works."

He grabbed a chair, turned it around, sat heavily and braced his forearms on the back. "What the hell, I don't mind telling ol' Arnie's story. We can't leave until dark and you won't be repeating it."

I'd been holding my breath, and let it out slowly. I'd bought myself some time. I hoped it was a long story.

Eyes half-closed, Arnie said, "I got started with May at a brothel during the war and I kept her for myself."

Pauly leaned against the freezer door, watching Arnie as if worshiping a god. He straightened up. "I still can't believe Quan's your son. I thought he was just some Vietnamese guy who scored the girls. He must be thirty!"

"You open your mouth one more time and I'm locking *you* in that freezer." Pauly's face retracted into his hoodie.

Curiosity trumped fear, and I asked, "You have a family in Vietnam?"

"By the time I left the Army in '79, May helped me get girls to sell to the soldiers and brothels. We didn't start to transport them to Minneapolis until I came back here and took over the resort—a useful cover for my trafficking business. Paid off the bank and got the place back on its feet. Now it's the best resort on the lake." His voice dropped. "All for my Isabel."

Venom dripped from my voice. "So you recruited Pauly, who lost his own dad and who idolizes you, into this despicable business."

He glanced at Pauly. "The little rat-faced suck-up took right to trafficking. He's so ugly it's the only regular pussy he gets. He should pay me."

Pauly squirmed, his face invisible under his hoodie. Arnie shoved his chair away and bent over me, reeking of bourbon. The zipper of his down jacket caught in my hair. I flinched, expecting a fist. He pulled the new phone from my pocket, and straightened, pulling out the strands of my hair stuck in his zipper. "Ow, take it easy," I said, wishing I could punch him, or at least rub my head.

Arnie looked at his watch, and handed the phone and camera to Pauly. "Take one of the snowmobiles out to the fish house and toss these down the hole. We leave at 2:00 a.m."

Pauly stuffed them into his pocket. "It's not like she could get to them anyway."

"They can locate her through the phone, you idiot. Do like I said."

Pauly shuffled out.

I asked, "Does Dee know about this?" I'd been wiggling my tied hands hoping to loosen the rope, but so far all I'd gotten was a raw spot on my wrist.

"Dee hears no evil, sees no evil, and she's more afraid of me than her buddy Jesus." He pretended to shudder. "I don't have sex with her, but it makes me look better to have a pious wife."

"Do you think Huy killed Nathan, too?" I shifted position and kept twisting and turning my hands, trying to stretch the rope.

Arnie's right eye twitched. "Nathan killed himself."

Did he really believe that? I opened my mouth to ask another question, but Arnie grabbed a dirty rag from the counter and jammed it into my mouth. "Gotta keep you quiet in case snowmobilers are in the area."

The kitchen door shut behind him.

I shook my head to get rid of the thick fog engulfing my brain. I'd suspected Arnie was doing something underhanded, but didn't expect him to be the missing link between Quan and Huy or I'd never have come out here alone. Arnie took the girls to Trung and delivered Hanh to the Shipwreck Bar, his fist smashed into my eye, his boot cracked my rib. I wanted nothing more than to tell Wilcox and Ben, but half-blind, bound, and gagged with a rag full of grout, the odds were against me getting out of this mess before Arnie returned.

My stomach told me it was late afternoon. I twisted my hands and strained at the rope for hours. At some point, my chin dropped forward.

The humming woke me. My eye opened, and an angel who looked like the Michelin Man surrounded by a halo of light floated in front of me.

The glowing angel became Dee in her down coat, illuminated by her flashlight beam. She stood in front of me, a horrified look on her face. Her tote bag with a water bottle sticking out of it was looped over her shoulder. I rocked forward, jutted my chin toward the bottle and grunted.

"You're thirsty." She pulled the rag from my mouth, and poured water down my parched throat. Some missed, sending an icy rivulet sluicing down my neck. I wanted to kiss her rosy cheeks. "I'm so glad to see you, Dee. How did you find me?"

Hands fluttering, she said, "When I got home from church, Arnie told me he was taking Pauly to Minneapolis on business tonight. I didn't want him taking Pauly. They went into Arnie's office, so I listened and Arnie talked about someone being tied up in the restaurant." She clasped her hands together mid-chest as if in prayer. "I thought it might be one of them."

My voice came out in a croak. "You knew about the girls?"

"No! I mean, I saw Pauly taking supplies and asked him. He told me they were helping some girls get to Minneapolis, but that's the first I knew, other than just hearing Arnie talking about the product on the phone." Her gaze dropped to the floor.

"Why didn't you call Wilcox?"

She looked away. "I didn't want anything to happen to Pauly. He said there was a sick girl, and I was going to take her some broth and medicine, but you found them." Now her hands covered her face. "It's all Arnie's fault. He made Pauly do this."

My voice strident, I said, "You have to call Wilcox right now."

She edged toward the door. "I need to go."

"Don't leave me here. They're coming back to kill me." I yanked at my ropes, furious at her. "Dee, please!" My plea echoed in the cavernous kitchen.

She forced a smile. "Oh no, they'd never do that." With her rosy cheeks and short curly hair she looked ready for a sleigh ride with Mr. Claus. "It's in God's hands. Nothing in the Bible says you can't help the ones you love. Pauly's always had it hard. He's Arnie's stepson, but Arnie should have loved all his children alike." She fumbled for a tissue and blew her nose. "All Pauly ever wanted was to be a good son to Arnie."

I wanted to strangle her. "Your boy is in real trouble. How long has he been involved with trafficking?"

She dabbed at her nose with the tissue. "Don't call it that. They were helping the girls to find jobs. I thought it was a positive sign when Arnie showed more interest in my Pauly."

I pleaded. "We have to stop them. Think of all the girls whose lives Arnie has ruined."

She glanced at the door, no doubt fearful of getting caught. "Pauly would do anything for Arnie. Only God should have that power over a person."

Dee attempted to push the cloth back in my mouth, but I made it hard for her by whipping my face back and forth. It didn't take her long to win the skirmish, and I was once again mute.

She hesitated at the door, flushed from fighting with my face. "Jesus understands I have to protect my son."

My frantic guttural sounds made no impact on her. The door closed and Dee's eerie humming rendition of "Onward Christian Soldiers" wafted through the air behind her. That hymn would haunt me forever.

When I heard footsteps coming toward the kitchen, I desperately hoped Dee had come to her senses and called Wilcox. But it was Arnie. At least the waiting was over.

Arnie told Pauly to untie me from the stove and retie my hands in front. I considered that a wonderful development, even though my atrophied muscles shrieked in protest.

Arnie pulled the cloth out of my mouth. "This goes right back in if you cause trouble."

My tongue was thick, but I didn't ask for water. I wasn't sure what the parameters were of my causing trouble. Arnie marched me to my SUV and buckled me into the back seat.

"Where are we going?" My thin voice broadcast fear.

"You're my hostage until I'm safely out of the country. After that, what I did to Huy is nothing compared to what's in store for you." He jabbed his finger in my chest. "I left you for dead at that shack, and the next day you steal those girls from me? Nobody takes from me."

Arnie's laugh chilled me. He poked my chest again. "You must be pretty dumb, blondie. This is the second time ol' Arnie has been one step ahead of you, and this time I'll make sure you die. Right now, you're my insurance to keep Wilcox off my back."

Pauly jumped into the passenger seat, and watched Arnie get behind the wheel. Arnie said, "What are you staring at, boy?" Pauly shrunk closer to the door.

Menace radiated from Arnie, but I taunted him anyway. "I don't get you. You're a decorated war hero. You survived a prisoner of war camp. "

Arnie reared back with a hyena laugh. "I survived by being a fucking informant for eight years." He shrugged out of his jacket and yanked up his shirtsleeve again to reveal the thick scar with the dragon tattooed around it, the red welt part of the dragon's tongue. I thought he was ashamed of it the first time he showed it to me, but he displayed it every chance he got.

He put his jacket back on. "I could either lose an arm and bleed to death an American hero, or get set up in a lucrative business. All I had to do was give them intel, and I still came out of it looking like a hero."

In Little's restaurant, he'd told the story with a different twist. He said he gave them false information. Arnie's treachery probably got Woz's brother killed, and many others.

I was sick of being scared. "You'll rot in hell."

"You're full of shit, blondie. You pretend you want to live in Spirit Lake with your ranger boyfriend, but what you really love is to be in the middle of the gore so you can get your pictures plastered all over the *LA Times* and Internet, and win the big awards. You're no different than me."

"Not true!" I jumped at him to rip the smirk off his face, but the ropes and seatbelt restrained me. My blood thumped through veins too small to carry the pressure. How dare he compare us? All I needed was one chance, and I'd tear him apart. And yet, a small voice inside me wondered if there was truth to Arnie's words.

He put the SUV into gear and drove with the lights out until we reached the highway. A voice on the radio squawked. "Series of storms coming through. Stay off the roads."

We drove for hours, the weather worsening the farther east we went. Snow and trees were all I could see from the back seat. I wanted to ask more questions, but waited. The last thing I needed was a mouth full of dishcloth again, or the butt of his gun bouncing off my head.

I thought Duluth was our destination, but Arnie changed direction and drove north, directly into the bad weather. I hunched forward trying to see through the shrinking windshield space. Arnie concentrated on driving and only spoke once.

235

"Quan won't be able to make it tonight. Afraid of that." It sounded like he spoke to himself.

It took an hour to travel the last ten miles to Grand Marais, a tourist town with a population of about a thousand on the northern tip of Minnesota, twenty minutes from Canada. I expected Arnie to try to get across the border. Maybe he'd untie me or cover me up and hide me in the back, hoping they wouldn't inspect the car closely in a snowstorm. I intended to cause some kind of disturbance to get noticed.

But Arnie turned left onto the Gunflint Trail just off downtown Grand Marais instead of heading toward the border, dashing my small spark of hope. The Gunflint Trail hadn't been plowed yet, and it was even slower going. Outfitters, resorts and homes populated the trail, a well-known entryway to the Boundary Waters lake country.

We eventually turned down a lane and arrived at a ranch-style house no different than hundreds of houses on hundreds of lakes in this area. The SUV's tires spun and stopped half-way up the drive. We were stuck.

"Goddammit, I wanted to park in the garage." Arnie jumped out. "It doesn't matter. By the time they find the car, I'll be in the air." He pocketed the SUV keys.

I looked at my surroundings. The storm was over, and the early dawn light revealed an empty hangar at the edge of the lake. Arnie hauled me out of the car, nearly sending me on my face. Maybe he was taking his frustration at this delay out on me, but I'd had it with Arnie yanking me around.

We waded through calf-high snow to the attached garage. Arnie punched in the key code and the door slid up, screeching from disuse. He herded us inside and the door came back down behind us. Pauly sidled over to a new Arctic Cat parked just inside the double-car garage. He ran his hand over the snowmobile. "Sweet."

I made a mental note that the Cat could be a possible escape route. Even if I could wrestle my car keys from Arnie, the SUV was stuck.

We waited in the cold kitchen while Arnie put on lights and fiddled with the thermostat. He kicked away a rug near the back door, lifted a trapdoor and stepped down a few steps to flip a switch, lighting the room below. I looked down into a space no bigger than eight by eight feet with two sets of bunk beds against opposite walls. A narrow path between allowed enough room to maneuver.

Pauly's eyes were wide. "You keep girls here, too?"

"You think, dumbass? No one knows about this place except Quan and me.

"And me." Pauly's chest puffed out, visibly pleased with his status in the secret life of a sex trafficker.

Arnie gestured for me to go down the steps. I didn't move. His rough hands grabbed me. "I can throw you down, but either way, you're going." With my hands tied, the fall onto cement would break bones. I stepped down, hardly able to contain my fury. If he touched me one more time, I'd kick him just for the satisfaction, no matter what happened next.

He pushed Pauly after me. The trapdoor slammed shut above us and Pauly yelped and banged on the door. "Hey, I'm still down here. Let me out." When Arnie didn't open it, he sat on the steps, his skimpy goatee quivering. "I guess my dad wants me to guard you down here."

I almost felt sorry for the kid.

Chapter 26

A sour odor came from a partially closed door on the far side of the cellar. I glanced inside at the toilet and sink and shut the door. The bunk beds were the only furniture in the space. I sat on one of the lower bunks, hunched forward and studied Pauly. He sat on the top step, listening for Arnie. I needed to turn him into an ally. "You know he doesn't need you. Whatever he has in mind for me is what you'll get, too."

He came down the steps. "Not true."

I tried to sound sympathetic. "He's not taking you. You know too much."

Pauly sank onto the bunk across from me. "Why bring me with him then? Why not just leave me in Spirit Lake?"

"Think about it, Pauly. He couldn't risk you talking."

His face registered alarm. He raced up the steps again, and banged until Arnie yelled through the trapdoor, "Cut it out or I'll come down and slit your throat."

One slow step at a time, Pauly came back down, looking forlorn. "He didn't mean that."

I held my hands out to him. "You can untie me. There isn't even a window to climb out."

He untied the rope, appearing dazed from his new status as prisoner. "He knows I would do anything for him."

That's what Dee said, too. I flexed my aching wrists. "How long have you been involved in Arnie's business?"

He tugged at his chin hair. "Those were the first girls I helped him with. I knew about it, though."

I put my hand on his shoulder and offered an encouraging smile, hoping he'd tell me more. He shrugged it off. "Leave me alone." He lit a cigarette, taking quick, agitated puffs, filling the room with fumes, and climbed to the top step again. With his ear tilted to the trapdoor, he waited like a faithful dog for his master, even though he knew he'd get kicked.

"I don't like closed up spaces," he said.

"You're claustrophobic?"

He shuddered. "He used to put me in the closet when I pissed him off."

"Your mom let him?"

He drew on his cigarette. "She said I should look at the bright side. Better than getting hit." Smoke snorted out of his nose.

"He hit you a lot?" Now I was really feeling sorry him.

He ignored me.

I used the toilet, slurped rusty water from the sink, and sat back down on the bunk. There wasn't even room to pace.

He said, "What if it's true he's leaving and never coming back? Maybe he'll just let us rot down here."

I'd been thinking the same thing. I'd thought I could keep myself safe while searching for Isabel and Nathan's killer. Or did I just want to be near the action—never mind the consequences? Even if an opportunity arose, how could I overpower Arnie and the guy Quan they kept talking about? Would Pauly help me or try again to win favor with Arnie? I knew the answer to that one. I pulled the thin blanket from the bed and wrapped myself in it, out of ideas.

Pauly eventually came down the steps. "I wish I had my laptop. I always write in it before I go to sleep."

"Like a journal?" I asked, not quite keeping surprise out of my tone.

"Yeah, it's not like I have friends at school. I'm always working at the resort. My journal's like having someone to talk to."

What a sad and lonely kid he was. "You can talk to me."

"Yeah, right." Pauly crawled into the bunk across from me, and turned from back to front to his side until he finally slept, whimpering in his dreams. Guilty about the part he played in Arnie's scheme? Or just terrified?

I fished my backup camera out of my inside jacket pocket and photographed the bunks, cement floor, and Pauly squirming on the hard bed. I tried not to think of young girls locked down here over the years, not knowing how much worse things were going to get for them. Shivering in the damp air, I wrapped myself in the blanket again.

Heavy footsteps crisscrossed the ceiling of our underground prison, and my eye snapped open. Murmuring from above probably meant Quan had arrived. Was I about to meet another ruthless killer like Arnie, or a son desperate for his approval like Pauly?

I would not go down without a fight. I leaped out of bed, cried out, and crumpled into a heap. I'd forgotten about my sore ribs.

The trapdoor opened and Arnie yelled, "Get your asses up here."

I stood at the bottom of the steps. "Pauly's asleep. What do you plan to do with us?"

He clomped down, ripped the blanket away from Pauly, grabbed him by one arm and flung him toward the stairs. "Get up there."

Pauly shuffled up the steps.

The deranged madman who hadn't shaved or bathed in too long pinched my chin hard, pulling me toward him. Foul breath like something from the underworld filled my nostrils, and loathing filled my brain. I squeezed the words out. "I need to pee."

"You have one minute." He let go and stomped up the steps.

I splashed my face at the sink, made sure my camera was snug in its inner pocket, ready for whatever came next, and zipped my jacket.

Upstairs, I blinked in the late-afternoon light filtering through a kitchen window. Did we sleep all day? Arnie slammed the trap door shut behind me, and dragged the rug over it with his boot. A man poured water from a teakettle into a cup with a teabag. I assumed it must be Quan. Slender and smaller than Arnie, I could see a resemblance in his face, a fullness that might turn to jowls in midlife.

I stood next to the counter. "Could I have a cup of tea?"

He didn't respond, so I poured myself a cup from a matched set of oatmeal-colored stoneware in the cupboard.

In the living room directly across from the kitchen, Arnie stood watch at a window overlooking the driveway. I could see my stuck SUV under a layer of snow. Pauly sat on the sofa across from Arnie, wheedling. "Dad, it was a joke what you said, right? You put me down there to keep her in line."

Arnie didn't look at his step-son. "Call me Dad again and I'll throw you back down."

Pauly ducked. "Sorry, I forgot. You're taking me with you, right? I mean you brought me here instead of leaving me in Spirit Lake."

"You would have squealed like a little girl the minute Wilcox got hold of you." Arnie came into the kitchen with Pauly trailing behind.

"He could torture me, and I wouldn't say anything, honest."

Arnie watched me drink my tea. "I see you've met Quan, my number one son."

"No!"Pauly sprang at Quan, knocking him to the floor.

I jumped back, sloshing tea.

"What the hell?" Arnie said.

Straddling Quan, Pauly's fists flew, throwing vicious hits to his face and chest, repeating, "I'm the number one son," with each blow.

Quan tried to shield his body, "Arnie, get him off me."

After much too long, Arnie yanked Pauly away by his jacket collar. His chuckle low and nasty, he said, "The weasel's competitive, I see. Who knew you had such a violent streak, kid?"

Quan shook himself off, shooting dark looks at Pauly and Arnie. He blotted his battered face with a kitchen towel. "I'm starting the engine." He slammed the back door so hard the window rattled.

Arnie backhanded Pauly. "You know how to fly a plane? Touch Quan again and I'll kill you now."

Pauly held his flaming cheek. "You don't know what you're saying." He went into the other room and threw himself on the sofa.

I brought the cup to my lips, trying to keep my hand from shaking. "Arnie, what are you going to do with us?"

He pulled a pint of Jack Daniels from his pocked and nearly drained it. "You and the kid are going to disappear in the BW, and ol' Arnie is going to do some disappearing of his own." His face went slack, jowls wobbling. "There's nothing for me here."

Pauly shot up from the sofa with a shocked expression on his face. Arnie didn't notice. He pulled my hands together in front of me, wound the rope around them, knotted it, and pushed me out the back door. "Let's move."

Night came early in the north. It made sense that Arnie would wait until dark to cross into Canada, and knowing that whatever he intended to do would happen at night terrified me even more. He led me to the blue six-seater plane and buckled me in the back, right side seat. I gulped down the fear. "You're really walking away from your resort, this house, everything?"

Arnie stood over me. "I have plenty of money and can always make more. With drugs or weapons it's one score, and you've got to get more product. With sex, the product can be used over and over."

"What about the ones who get sick or die from the abuse?"

He shrugged. "Those we dump."

My mind raced trying to think of something to say that might save our lives. "If you're not coming back, why bother with us? By the time we're found, you'll be across the border."

He stuck his finger in my face. "You need to die for all the shit you caused me. I'll never be able to return to the U.S. I'll have to live the rest of my days with those damn gooks that ruined my life to begin with."

Quan stood behind him, eyes hooded. "Gooks," he said, his voice cold.

Arnie dismissed him with a swipe of his hand. "Get over it. Last I looked, you weren't living on the streets like your mother was when I found her."

Quan's jaw tightened.

Arnie looked around. "Where's the damn kid?" He stood at the plane door and yelled toward the house. "Pauly, get out here."

Pauly didn't appear.

Arnie hurried down the steps. A few minutes later, Arnie ran back onto the plane shouting at Quan. "The fucking idiot took the Cat. I'm going after him."

Pauly used the escape plan I'd hoped to put into action. We hadn't heard the snowmobile above the sound of the plane's engines. He could disappear anywhere on it.

Quan stayed in the cockpit. "We don't have time to chase him. You couldn't follow the sled with that SUV anyway."

Sweating from chasing after Pauly, Arnie slammed his hand against the plane. "He won't dare go to the cops. He'd be thrown in jail. Maybe he's smart enough to stay away from Spirit Lake." He bared filthy teeth. "And if he doesn't, it won't matter. We'll be gone."

Arnie went back one last time and locked the house. When he came on board, he clutched another full bottle of Jack Daniels in his hand.

He buckled into the seat across from me, unscrewed the cap on his bottle, and took a long drink. His sweat, alcohol fumes and foul breath filled the small space. I tried not to gag. He looked over at me, pointed at my bandaged eye and grinned. "Maybe killing's too good for you. I might just take out that other eye and let you wander out there until you freeze."

I turned away, unwilling to let him see how much his comment terrified me. Quan taxied across the lake and we rose into a moonless night. Buffeted by the wind, we cruised low over one frozen lake after another, surrounded by miles of forest, dim shapes barely visible in the darkness.

I couldn't calculate air miles, but it seemed we were airborne less than an hour when Arnie unbuckled from his seat across from me and lurched to the cockpit. I heard loud arguing, the plane dropped, and we taxied to a stop on a lake.

Quan watched, frowning, as Arnie undid my seatbelt and pushed me forward. I planted my feet. With a grunt, he shoved me out the door. Unable to break the fall with my hands, the hit to my ribs hurt so much I might have blacked out for a second.

Arnie followed me down the steps, and I got to my feet before he aimed his boot again.

Quan spoke to him from the doorway. "I thought we were keeping her with us."

"We're in Canada. I only needed her in case Wilcox came after me."

Quan argued in Vietnamese. I wondered if he was uncomfortable with sending a woman to sure death, although he didn't seem to mind selling children into slavery where most died out of the life.

Arnie slid a hunting knife out of a sheath on his belt. "Let's go then."

Quan took a step forward, and pointed at Arnie's knife. "What's that for?"

Arnie whipped his knife around in a slashing motion. "I intend to have a little fun carving her up."

A shiver of fear ran down my spine. I looked around, desperate for a way to escape. Quan jumped to the ground, bypassing the rest of the steps. "I won't have anything to do with that."

Arnie said, "You'll do whatever I tell you to do."

He and Arnie argued again. It escalated into pushing and yelling in English and Vietnamese. Quan said, "I'm through," and tried to walk away, but Arnie caught him in the back with a sloppy right hook, dropping Quan to the ground. "You're through when I say you're through." Arnie's other hand held the knife, but he didn't use it. He'd have no way to leave if he killed Quan.

I took off running toward the woods, about fifteen-hundred feet away, and heard Arnie behind me. "No you don't."

I concentrated on not falling. With hands tied, it took longer than I hoped to reach the trees. I glanced back to see Quan scramble up the plane steps. Arnie spun around and headed back, too late.

The steps retracted, and Quan taxied across the ice. Arnie chased the plane, but he was too far away and too full of Jack

Daniels. The plane lifted. I looked back and faltered, terror turning my body to stone. Quan left us alone in more than a million acres of wilderness. I'd been in a lot of trouble before, but never this bad.

I could barely see Arnie in the dark, but his furious cursing and wheezing alerted me. He was after me again. My feet took over and I stumbled forward to the shoreline. He'd easily track me in the deep snow, so hiding wasn't an option.

I scooped up a fallen branch, about four inches thick, and waited behind a tree. We'd both die out here anyway, but I'd make sure he was first.

Arnie crashed through the brush, only yards away. I could smell his rank body. When he charged past my tree, I stepped out behind him and bashed him in the back of his head with the branch. The hit didn't have much power with my wrists tied, but he fell to the ground, shook like a stunned bear and struggled to his knees.

I'd never win if he got close to me. Arnie'd been swigging Jack Daniels nonstop and didn't look like he'd slept. My hands were tied and I could only see out of one eye, but my legs were strong from all the snowshoeing. I ran back onto the lake to draw him away from the woods. I'd have to wear him out, and for that I needed unobstructed space to move around.

I heard him panting before I saw his dark shape moving toward me on the ice. I let him catch up. "Here I am, Arnie. Let's see how you do when your opponent isn't caught by surprise."

He lunged and swiped. Sensing more than seeing the blade, a strip of silver flashed past my arm. I swerved away from it. Another flash near my face, a glint caught in a sliver of moonlight. I'd forgotten about my blind side, but it was too late now. I danced around Arnie like a matador taunting a bull. I'd let him get close, he'd attack, and I'd jump away. He attacked again and again, and I kept him moving. He flailed wildly, missing the mark. He staggered and went down on one knee, wheezing and dragging in ragged breaths.

"What's the matter, old man? Tired? Can't handle the big girls?" I heard a plane in the distance and glanced skyward.

Arnie rose from his knee and came for me with a madman's laugh. "Quan's back. You're dead."

I leaped away, but a beam of light from the plane flashed across my good eye. Arnie used my distraction to punch me to the ground. He jabbed his knife at my face. I flinched and his knife missed the target, but I felt a sting as it sliced my neck. I lay flat on my back with Arnie spread-eagled over me. He leaned in, the knife's tip glistening red, and cackled. "You're done."

I wasn't done. I drew my legs to my chest and rammed my boots into the soft center between his legs. He howled and fell to the side. I scrambled up and delivered a sideways kick to his head that dropped him all the way to the ground. "This is for all the young lives you're ruined." I raised my boot for another hit, but he wasn't moving.

I stood over him, panting. The monster would not rise again.

The plane's engine rumbled and I could make out faint lights. Quan must have landed. Boots scrunched toward me, moving fast across the ice. I whirled, and struck out with another ferocious kick. The shape jumped away. "Britt, it's me, Ben." He'd dodged my boot just in time. "You're safe." He spoke with gentle command, as if talking a suicide off a ledge.

"Ben?" The blood rushed through my ears deafening me. I couldn't comprehend what just happened, but couldn't stop moving. Now a bright light bathed the scene. A blue plane stood nearby, door open. A bearded man hurried toward us. Woz, not Quan.

Ben flopped Arnie on his back, dragged his arms behind him and cuffed him. Arnie didn't stir. In the short time since I'd knocked him out, icy stalactites hung from his nostrils and slack lips.

Woz grabbed Arnie by the feet and dragged him to the plane. Ben helped wrestle Arnie's dead weight up the steps and into the plane.

In a minute, Ben came back down for me. He guided me up the steps and into a seat. "C'mon, Britt. We need to stop that bleeding." He cut the rope around my wrists and handed me a cloth to hold on my neck. "It's not deep. We'll get you fixed up."

Woz, still getting Arnie secured in his seat, asked, "Britt, why did you kick at Ben?"

My voice sounded robot-like. "Quan has a blue plane, too. Arnie said he was back." I shook my head to clear it. "How did you find us?"

Ben fastened my seatbelt and tucked a thermal blanket around me. "I found your SUV's location through the GPS. Woz met me in Branson, we located your car and started hunting."

"Why Woz?" I asked Ben.

"He knows the area better than anyone and he patrols the border for us, unofficially. We've been looking since early afternoon. We knew you were out here somewhere."

Woz opened a first-aid kit, took the bloody cloth from my hand, and bandaged my neck. "You'll need a few stitches, but this will hold it together."

I asked, "Woz, how did you see us in the dark?"

He said, "The Beaver has a high-powered searchlight. I do day and night search and rescue. We figured Arnie intended to leave by plane through the Gunflint Trail access to the BW. It's a common route for smugglers trying to get to Canada."

"I'm sorry, Woz, I thought you might be one of those smugglers."

"My wife said you were suspicious about the plane." I detected a slight twinkle in his deep-set eyes. "She's not crazy about my side work."

I tried to piece it all together. "Ben, how did you know to look for me?"

"Little was worried about you, so we checked places you might go. Wilcox went to the resort, and Dee acted so squirrely he got suspicious. She's in custody. We'd located Trung and he gave up Arnie, hoping for some leniency. We still don't know all of it, but we had enough to figure out you were in trouble."

"I can't believe you found me out here. I expected to die." My voice wobbled. "Thank you both."

Arnie came to with a shake of his head. They'd put him two seats behind me and to my left. Dried blood stuck to the gray stubble covering his face. I lifted my camera and shot him, repeatedly.

His mouth dragged down at the corners like a clown frown. "Look at me, a regular guy surrounded by a bunch of goddamn heroes. Too many for one poor ol' vet to deal with."

Woz grabbed Arnie's jacket and slammed him against the seat. "Regular guy, Maelstrom? You're the lowest form of human, and I'm going to make sure you're stripped of every medal and commendation you've ever gotten. Everyone will find out what a murdering traitor and scumbag you are."

Arnie gazed at me with his fake affable Arnie face. "I almost got you." I recoiled as if a serpent wrapped itself around me. Ben slapped a band of tape across Arnie's mouth, snapping him back against the seat again.

On his way to the cockpit, Woz stared at me as if not sure what he was looking at. He said to Ben. "Britt hunted the bastard down and beat the hell out of him with one eye and her hands tied. Damn."

Ben sounded tired, and a little bit proud. "She's unstoppable."

Woz climbed into the cockpit, and Ben strapped himself into the seat across from me. The engines rumbled and we were off.

"Arnie said Huy killed Isabel for revenge or blackmail. Do you know anything about that?" I asked Ben.

"I bagged his knife. We'll see if Huy's blood's on it, but it doesn't make sense that Huy killed those kids. They might never have found Isabel, and why fake Nathan's suicide if you're trying to send a message?"

My voice trailed off. "That's what I thought."

He gave me a bottle of water and I gulped it all. He said, "We'll have a lot of questions for Arnie when we get to Branson. Wilcox is going over the Maelstrom van for evidence. Maybe that will lead us closer to Isabel and Nathan's murderer."

In the next minute, shudders like internal earthquakes rocked my body. I reached across the aisle. "What's happening to me? I can't stop shaking."

He covered me with another blanket. "Adrenalin overload. It will get better." He kneeled next to me and cradled my trembling hands in his, spreading warmth through my battered body.

I told him about Pauly being part of it, and that he'd taken the snowmobile. I filled him in on everything, although I don't think I made much sense.

The plane dropped for its landing on Branson Lake, heading for a mass of whirling red, blue and white lights. With a gentle thunk, the Tundra tires Jenna was so proud of hit the ice, and we taxied toward the shoreline where the flashing vehicles waited. On the way down the steps, Ben put his arm around my shoulders and I wrapped mine around his waist. After the adrenalin left, my muscles dissolved into mush. Wilcox and two deputies hauled Arnie from the plane.

"I want to go home to Rock and the guys," I said.

Ben touched my cheek. "Soon." He steered me toward the waiting ambulance where I ended up flat on my back on a stretcher, staring up at the blue and white Beaver. It rose into the air, and I lifted my arm to wave. Woz might have tipped a wing before disappearing into the night sky.

Chapter 27

I stared up at Cranky and Fromm peering down at me as if I were the alien. "Your neck is all stitched up," Dr. Fromm said. "Try to take it easy for a couple of days." He tapped his finger against his chin. "I'm starting to believe in miracles. Ben described what happened to you, but surprisingly, it didn't do additional damage to your eye."

My mouth opened and a ragged whoosh of air escaped. "Thank you, Doctor. Can I go home now?"

"Yes, and if all goes well, the bandage can come off in a couple more days."

I nearly cried with relief.

Cranky leaned in to straighten my blanket. "You can go out and get yourself into more trouble." The duo rolled their eyes at each other on their way out of my room. Their behavior didn't seem very professional to me but I let it go. My eye was okay—all I cared about. I could still do my job.

Ben and Wilcox came in and took up stations on opposite sides of my bed. It was my turn to be cranky. "Why didn't you tell me about Woz, Ben? It would have saved me from wasting everyone's time and making a fool of myself with his family."

Ben glanced away. "Woz's work for us is more effective if no one knows about him."

Wilcox gave me the hard stare. "You had no business going out to Maelstrom's."

"In retrospect, you're right, Sheriff. But at the time, I just wanted a few answers. I didn't think I was doing anything dangerous."

I also wondered if Arnie would ever have been caught if I hadn't inadvertently forced his hand. Everyone bought into his upstanding citizen and decorated war hero ruse, and they weren't even looking at him. But I held my tongue and changed the subject. "Ben told me you talked to Dee."

Wilcox pulled a chair next to my bed, and sat heavily. "That woman, excuse my language, is batshit."

I told them about her visit to the restaurant when I was tied up. "She came to help a child, but found me instead. She left me there, knowing Arnie'd likely kill me. She said God would understand."

"A jury won't," said Ben.

Wilcox worked the brim of his cowboy hat. "She's confessed to Isabel and Nathan's murders, and admitted she watched you drop off Nathan the night he was hanged. She had ambitions for Pauly, and didn't think Nathan should inherit the resort."

I pushed myself up on my elbows. "Do you believe her, Sheriff? Could she have done that on her own?"

"I doubt it. She didn't know any details. Also, we located the match to the white mitten found by Isabel's body. It was at the shack, along with the axe."

"Isabel was at the shack?" I twisted my neck too fast, and my stitches tightened.

He said, "If it's her blood on that axe, we have more to go on. She could have discovered the trafficking and gotten killed for it."

I traced the raised line of stitches with my finger. "What about Pauly? He mentioned keeping an online journal. Maybe you can get access to that for some answers."

Wilcox set his chair back against the wall. "We'll check it out. We have someone watching the resort, but we don't think he's in the area."

Criminals on the FBI's Most Wanted list usually got far away from the crime scene, but I didn't think Pauly was capable of that.

At the door, shoulders drooping as if they held the weight of the world, Wilcox said, "Your pal Tommy is missing along with his dad. Ray's gone to Cloud Lake to see if they've contacted relations up there. I still think he knows more about that shack and Isabel's death than he's letting on. He's my only lead on that, and if he was in on it, he'll pay for it." He warned me to stay away from the murder investigation, and left.

Tommy had a temper and past drug and alcohol problems, but was he capable of murder? He'd saved my life, and yet I was sure he'd shot an arrow at me.

Little had visited me earlier in the day and brought clean clothes. Once he learned Arnie's knife hadn't done serious damage, he called me an idiot and left. I deserved that one. I got out of bed and picked up the pile of clothes from a chair. Ben looked out the window as I pulled on my sweater and jeans. I guess he thought I was modest.

He said, "You'll find this piece of the puzzle interesting. Maelstrom's van with all the advertising was the same light-colored van at the Shipwreck Bar. The Maelstrom ads were peel off decals."

I pulled on my boots and grabbed my jacket from the closet, every muscle in my body sore. "Even if I'd suspected Arnie, I'd never have thought about the two vans being the same." Once again, nothing was as it seemed on this story. Ben waited until I checked out and walked with me to the parking lot where my SUV waited. I didn't know if his being extra kind to me was an improvement or not. Maybe not being annoyed meant he felt nothing for me at all. I touched his arm. "Thanks, you've thought of everything."

He held my gaze for a long moment as if making a decision, but only said, "I've got to get back to the sheriff's."

I wanted to go straight to Spirit Lake to be with the guys and Rock, and sleep forever. But more than that, I wanted to tell the story through my pictures of what Arnie and his gang of bottom feeders had done.

At the bureau, Jason's fingers were flying over his keypad, and Cynthia was working the phone. Ben recovered my camera from Isabel's restaurant with my photos of the "Isabel's" sign and the camera in my jacket pocket had pictures of the cellar at

Arnie's. I downloaded the photos, reliving some of the horror of the past few days as they came up on my screen one by one.

The photos of Arnie in the plane came out decent, even though my hands were shaking when I took them. I got a good shot of his creepy tattoo from our breakfast last week, which seemed like a month ago. I was exhausted, and Cynthia didn't look much better, but our little bureau got another story that would nab the *Strib's* page one.

On the way home, I stopped to purchase yet another phone. I almost bought two, so I could always keep a backup with me the way I did with cameras. But that would be admitting my life was crazy.

Little's blue Jeep wasn't in the driveway in back. I checked the time. Nearly 4:30. Customers would be coming for dinner soon. Rock must have heard my SUV pull in. He bounced out of the garage from his warm spot by the stove and did his happy dance. I would have joined him, but had to be careful of my stitches. Instead, I kneeled and held his warm, furry body against my chest. Being with Rock felt like home and safety, something I sorely needed at the moment.

At the restaurant, Lars hugged me and burst out, "Jayzus, you're crazy."

Lars loved me, but once again, I'd scared my brother and that didn't sit well with Lars. I sat on my stool at the counter. "Where is he?"

Lars set a cup of coffee in front of me. "He took a pan of his wild rice hot dish out to Edgar."

I nodded. "Little likes to listen to Edgar's stories."

"He's cutting it close." Lars frowned. "Do you want something to eat?"

I said yes, but wasn't thrilled at having to rely on Lars' culinary skills. He went to the kitchen and came back a few minutes later. "You make this?" I eyed the turkey sandwich he set in front of me with suspicion.

Lars snapped, "Maybe you don't want it," and slid it away. Teasing him entertained me, but I hadn't eaten since the gruel they served in the hospital. I grabbed it back and took a huge bite. It was mine now.

"I thought so." He held the pot over my cup. "You look tired."

"No more coffee, thanks, I'm going home to bed in a few minutes. What's the latest on Ly and the others?"

His eyes on the door, he told me what happened with the girls while I was tied up with Arnie. "I took Ly and Binh shopping to pick out clothes for Hanh and Kim."

My sandwich wasn't half bad. "Not flannel shirts and suspenders I hope."

Lars slipped his thumbs under his favorite suspenders—tiny walleyes flipping out of the waves—and let them snap back. "You aren't funny. The girls ended up with jeans and sweaters and warm jackets. Also really cute boots."

"Where are they now?" Elbow on the counter, I rested my chin in my cupped hand, barely able to hold my head up.

"Fromm released Hanh and Kim, and we all went to the sheriff's to give their statements. After that, Mr. and Mrs. Vo arrived to deal with paperwork and take them to Duluth."

I gave him a high five. "That's great, Lars."

"Here's the best part. After watching the girls together, the couple said they couldn't separate them." He grinned. "They're keeping them all."

I laughed. "Wow, that's generous, but poor Mr. Vo with all those females under one roof. What if they turn out to be as formidable as Mrs. Vo?"

"Good point." His brow furrowed. "You really should get some rest. You look terrible."

"Thanks, you've downgraded my appearance from tired to terrible in less than five minutes." The idea of sliding under my covers did sound good.

Lars glanced at the door again. "He loses track of time when he's out there." He took the pot off the burner and made the rounds refilling coffees, returned and dropped onto a stool next to me, still watching the door.

I finished my sandwich. "Call him. He wouldn't want to be late for the dinner crowd." Lars was never comfortable on his own at the restaurant.

"I don't like to badger," Lars said.

I took my new phone out.

"No, I will." He pulled out his phone, hit the number, waited, and put it back in his pocket. "He thinks it's rude to interrupt, so sometimes he turns it off when he's with Edgar." He shrugged.

"I'm sure they just got caught up in the storytelling. He'll be here soon." Now I watched the door.

A group of snowmobilers stopped to warm up with coffee and hot chocolate before going home for the day, and Lars hustled to take care of them. Chloe arrived to start her shift, and I stepped into the late afternoon gloom. I knew my brother was too much of a worrier himself to put Lars through this. I called Edgar. He didn't answer either. With his large extended family, someone was always calling to check up on him, so he sometimes unplugged his phone. He said he liked to be where he couldn't be reached, but still.

Little would be back. No reason to get crazy just because Lars didn't like to handle the restaurant alone. Chum would fill in as chef, if needed. Chum was Little's second cook in the summer months, and was always happy to fill in when needed.

I drove to the cabin, dropped off Rock, and thought longingly again of my bed. Then I headed toward the Spirit Lake Loop to Edgar's. Maybe Little slid off the road and was stranded.

A text message pinged just before Edgar's turnoff. I checked it, expecting Little, but Pauly Maelstrom's name appeared at the top. The balloon message said, "Meet me now at Edgar's or your brother is dead. NO COPS."

The car drifted to the shoulder, and stopped. Every part of my being wanted to deny that my worst nightmare was happening. I couldn't think, and my hands trembled too much to drive. I sat frozen until the fear subsided, and rage kicked in. Rage is better than fear, hands down. All pity for Arnie's harsh treatment of Pauly went out the window. A wall of fury settled between my brows. I wanted to kill the twisted freak.

I called Lars and could barely squeeze the words out, knowing how Lars would take the news. "Pauly's holding Little hostage at Edgar's. It's me he wants, though."

"Pauly?" The big man squeaked like a strangled mouse. "I knew something was wrong. I'm going out there."

"No, you can't. And he said no cops, only me, or he'll harm Little. I'm sorry."

Lars sputtered. "We have to call Wilcox."

"I'll call him, but I'm not waiting for them to get there. I think I can talk Pauly out of hurting anyone." I'd hesitated at the word hurting. I couldn't say killing. Little must be alive. Lars mumbled something about closing the restaurant and driving to Edgar's anyway.

I pulled the SUV back on the road and floored it toward Edgar's, slowing at the curves and going flat out on the straight stretches. I hit the sheriff's number.

Wilcox said exactly what I'd expected. "Do not go into that house. It's an order. I'll throw you in jail if you do."

I promised I'd wait, just to get him off the phone. Next, I called Ben. At first he tried to argue when I said I intended to go in.

"Suit yourself." He hung up. That's what Ben always said when he'd washed his hands of whatever foolish thing I was about to do. But this was different. This was Little. There was no way I could wait outside Edgar's house and leave my brother alone in there to deal with that screwed up kid.

Bumping down Edgar's snow-packed road, my mind churned as I tried to figure out how to handle Pauly. Who knew what state he was in after Arnie's betrayal? If Wilcox descended on the place with sirens blaring and guns blazing, I could lose Little. I'd rather lose my own life. I would get there first.

I crested the hill above Edgar's, began the descent too fast and slid down the icy slope. I pulled up next to Little's blue Jeep Wrangler. My throat constricted as I pictured Little bopping through town in the summer with the top and doors off, vegetables from his garden spilling out of baskets as he rounded corners. He always dropped off extra produce at Lakeview Nursing Home, and to the elderly folks who lived outside of town.

I willed myself to think about what needed to be done, and pushed everything else away. A black Audi was parked next to Little's Jeep. I took a quick photo of the license plate with my phone and sent it to Wilcox. He could track Pauly, in case he killed us and got away.

I straightened my shoulders, and strode through the deepening shadows toward Edgar's front door. Curtains and shades were closed on the lower floor windows. The porch light cast an eerie glow in the dusk. Before I could knock, Pauly opened the door and pointed the barrel of a Ruger 9 mm at my chest. His gaze searched the driveway and woods. "Hand me your phone."

I handed it to him, and opened my hands, palms up. "No one's out there. It's just me." Greasy hair hung limp from under his stocking cap, deep circles underscored his eyes. The quivering gun indicated a strung-out kid. He pocketed my phone and pointed with his scraggly chin toward the family room. "Go over by your brother."

Little was sunk down so deep into the corner of the beige sofa, he all but disappeared, but he didn't look hurt. I breathed a sigh of relief. "Are you okay?"

He nodded. The cushions quivered with the vibration from his shaking knees.

I whispered. "Where's Edgar?"

He pointed upstairs. "Pauly locked him in a room up there, but I don't think he's hurt."

Pauly stood near the family room window, peeking through the blinds. Pretending to be composed, I said, "This isn't a good idea, Pauly."

He faced us, legs spread, the gun pointed directly at me. "Killing you is the best idea I ever had. I'll kill your brother first. You'll see what it's like to have someone taken away from you. You screwed everything up from the very beginning, and my life was just getting better."

He'd lost Arnie, and now believed he had nothing more to lose.

Little stood up and cleared his throat. "Are you hungry, Pauly?"

Pauly and I looked at Little. Why was my brother talking about food at a time like this?

Pauly said, "I'm freakin' starving." His wisp of goatee wavered. "There was nothing to eat at the resort. Mom was gone." Pauly's boot smashed into the coffee table and Edgar's cup and magazines bounced to the carpet. Little jumped to the side, wide eyed.

I said, "You were at the resort, Pauly?" I thought Wilcox had someone watching it.

His gun swung toward me again. "Where do you think I got this? I sneaked in from the lake side and they never even saw me."

Little's face was white, but he kept talking about food. "There's some hotdish left. How does that sound?"

Pauly swallowed, and ushered us into the kitchen, Little's element. Often tentative in the outside world, my brother commanded a kitchen like a brigadier general. His voice confident, he pointed at the hotdish sitting on the counter, opened a cupboard, and said, "I'm going to get a plate and put this in the microwave for you."

I sat at the center island across from Pauly while Little punched buttons on the microwave. He opened the refrigerator and brought out a quart of milk, his hand steady as he poured it in a glass. When Pauly's meal was in front of him, Little sat on the stool next to me. We watched Pauly gobble up the hotdish. He held the fork like a shovel with his right hand, while pointing the gun unsteadily at us with his left. He put down his fork and gulped a full glass of milk, still holding the gun on us.

Little pointed to a blueberry pie sitting on the counter. Pauly nodded, and Little cut a huge slice and set it in front of him. He dug in. Little pointed at the milk carton. "You'll need more milk." Pauly lifted his glass and Little filled it full again.

"You make this pie?" Pauly waved his fork at Little. My brother nodded, cut another piece of pie, and slid it onto Pauly's plate. I realized he intended to drug Pauly with food. It worked on me a few times.

Milk dribbled into Pauly's chin hair. "My mom makes okay pie, but this is better. His voice sounded less strident. "You're both still dead, though."

Little drew a quick breath. I asked, "How did you find Little here at Edgar's?"

"Easy. I watched the restaurant. He went to the Post Office and a couple of places, so I waited till he drove out of town." He finished off the milk, burped and settled against the stool back. "It took forever. He talks to everybody." Pauly yawned.

Little's lovely winged eyebrows lifted. "I didn't know he followed me."

I needed to convince Pauly there was a way out without killing us. "Arnie's going to need you now. I know you were a big help as his partner."

He leaped up from his chair, screaming. "Until you came along and took him from me! I wish he'd killed you the first time at the shack."

I'd nearly fallen off my stool when he screamed.

"Scared you, didn't I?" He grinned, his teeth blue from the pie.

I ignored my racing heart, inhaled and let it out slowly. "We're not in a hurry here, right?"

He shrugged and fished a cigarette pack from his pocket. The pack empty, he crumpled it and threw it in the corner. "He'll be sorry for treating me mean when I kill you for him."

Little's body went rigid. With my elbows on the counter, I leaned toward Pauly. "Arnie's behind bars, Pauly. He won't know. Were you at the upstairs window the night I brought Nathan back to the resort?"

"No, we were in Arnie's office."

"So late at night? Why?"

"None a your business."

"Wilcox said your mom confessed to killing Isabel and Nathan."

"She didn't!" He stuck the gun inches from my face. Little recoiled.

I swallowed several times, getting my panic under control. "So what happened?"

Pauly's eyes took on a crazy glint. With a blue grin, he jumped up to act out the scene. "Awright, it was like this. Arnie and I are doing double FaceTime, with Quan on the laptop and Huy on the computer. It's like one in the morning. Huy's mad, and he says, 'You bringing me the girls tomorrow or what?' His nose looks like it's coming right through the screen. 'I've made arrangements,' he says. 'You're slowing me down and I'm losing money.' My dad says, 'I can't get them out yet, too many cops around.' Huy says, 'What shape they in after a week in a fucking shack in ten-below weather?' Dad says, 'They're fine sturdy girls.' Huy says, 'You bring me a damaged product and I'll deduct it from what I owe you.' Dad says, 'You work for me asshole. Do not fuck with me. We had a deal.'"

Pauly thrust his face close to us, and said, "Huy's nose on the screen again, 'The cops have been raiding the massage parlors, asking questions.' Dad yells, 'You keep your fucking mouth shut.' Huy says, 'I'll keep my mouth shut, but maybe I call the shots now. What's to keep me from giving you up? I've got people waiting for those virgins.' My Dad looks like he wants to go right into that computer after Huy, but Quan says, 'I'm backed up here. I have another shipment ready to go. What am I supposed to do, bring them over?' Dad says, 'No! I can't get up to Grand Marais this week to pick them up from you. I told you the cops are swarming everywhere.'"

Pauly looked at Little and me staring at him with our mouths open. He must have liked the attention, because he continued where he'd left off, pacing back and forth in the kitchen, getting more excited as he spoke.

"I turn around and see Nathan in the doorway with his mouth hanging open. He's so wasted he has to lean on the door to stand up. Dad hits the exit buttons, Quan and Huy disappear. We stare at Nathan. He says, 'I won't hide behind the drinking anymore, I'm telling Wilcox.' Dad says, 'You'd ruin me.' Nathan starts to cry and says he has to. It's wrong.' Dad pulls a knife from a drawer and has it against Nathan's neck like in one move, and says, 'Not another word or I'll cut your throat.' The knife is awesome. I want to get one too. 'Nathan says, 'Go ahead.' Dad says, 'You've always been weak, and now you think you can turn on your own father.' He tells me to get package sealing tape from the top desk drawer. He gets it on Nathan's face mid-scream. Dad pulls Nathan's arms behind his back and winds the tape around his wrists. He tells me to back the van up to the side door. No lights."

Pauly patted his shirt for his pack of cigarettes, and I wondered if he'd forgotten we were there. His voice sounded far away, his tone subdued.

"I get the van in position and dad shoves Nathan in, jumps in behind him and tapes his legs together. He tells me to keep the lights off and drive to the last cabin. We pull Nathan out of the van and carry him into the cabin. He's limp at first and then he arches his back and tries to twist away but we get him inside. Dad throws a rope over a beam in the ceiling and makes a noose out of the end of it. I want to learn that too. Dad puts two chairs next to a stool under the noose. We carry him to the middle of the room. I get on one chair and hold on to him but it's not easy. Dad gets up on the other chair and puts the noose over Nathan's head and tightens it. Nathan's eyes bulge and he stops squirming. He doesn't dare move or he'll hang himself. We get down off our chairs and Dad tells me to kick the stool out from under him."

Pauly blinked several times and his voice dropped.

"Nathan's making weird sounds and crying and his eyes are all wide. Dad says, 'I thought you had balls, boy. Do it.' He slaps me so hard I fall over. I get up and kick the stool hard. I'm no weakling. I'd never turn on Arnie. My stomach starts heaving and I puke right on the floor. I didn't know it could take someone so long to die. After he's good and dead, dad takes all the tape off and we wipe off the chairs and put them back. He makes me clean up my mess. It smells so bad, I almost do it again. He grabs a broom and sweeps so our boot prints wouldn't be all over the place. Plus we wore gloves the whole time."

When Pauly finished, he looked at us, startled. He forgot we were listening. I'm sure our faces mirrored absolute horror.

Pauly's chest puffed out. "If Nathan told, it would of shut down the whole operation, and I was just getting into it."

Little exploded. "Nathan was your step-brother. What did he ever do to hurt you?"

His eyes dull, he said, "He didn't deserve to be Arnie's son."

Little had turned green. Swallowing the bile coming up from my own stomach after Pauly's story, I tried another tactic. "Pauly, do you want to do what's best for Arnie?"

"Sure. He's my dad."

Little rose from his stool and gathered Pauly's dishes into a pile. I said, "The best thing you can do to help him is to take care of the resort until he gets out. You're only sixteen. Give yourself up and you might not be tried as an adult. And since you're underage, maybe you'll get therapy or spend time in a youth facility."

He stopped pacing, and nodded. "Everything that happened was an accident, even Isabel."

Little gasped. I wasn't that surprised after what he'd just admitted about Nathan's death. I skipped over the Isabel comment. "And when Arnie gets out of jail, you'll be waiting for him at the resort and he'll be proud of you for taking care of it." Arnie would never get out jail. If Pauly was telling the truth, Arnie masterminded the murder of his own son. "But if you kill us, you'll never be able to help Arnie ever again. They would try you as an adult for kidnapping and premeditated murder."

Pauly blinked several times. Maybe I scared him too much? I needed to mollify him before he slipped over the edge again. "Giving yourself up would be the best for Arnie, don't you agree?"

"I could take care of the resort for him?" Pauly looked sleepy again. I wondered if the combination of letting the story out, and Little's food calmed him.

"Not right away, but it could happen." I patted myself on the back for my brilliant psychological maneuvering.

Edgar's house phone rang and we all jumped. Pauly motioned for us to walk in front of him to the family room where the phone continued to ring. We all looked at the caller ID.

Pauly waved the gun at me, his eyes mean slits. "It's Wilcox. You weren't supposed to tell."

"I swear I didn't. Lars must have gotten worried when he couldn't get Little on his cell."

"Yeah, he left a bunch of messages. Answer it and say everything's okay." He punched the speaker button and set it back on the stand.

I looked at Pauly as I spoke. "Hi Sheriff, this is Britt. What's up?"

"How come Edgar didn't answer his phone? Lars is looking for Little."

"Edgar's in the bathroom. Little and I were about to leave." I hoped he got my hint that our leaving might be permanent.

Wilcox waited a beat. "Look, Pauly, we know you're in there. I have someone here who wants to talk to you."

Dee came on the line, her voice wavering. "Please don't hurt them, sweetie. Give yourself up."

Wilcox spoke again. "Son, we're almost at Edgar's. When we get there, we want you to let those people walk on out, and you need to come out with your hands up. You are in way over your head on this."

Pauly lifted the semi-automatic, aimed, and shot the phone three times.

Chapter 28

Little and I threw our hands up to shield ourselves from flying plastic shards. Pauly aimed the Ruger at me, a sly look on his face. He knew I'd been playing him.

"Arnie would kill me if he ever found out what I did to Isabel." His father-son fantasy slipped away and all hope left his eyes.

Our best chance was to keep him talking until Wilcox arrived. I said, "Isabel found out what you were doing at the shack and you killed her to keep her quiet?"

"She was going to tell Arnie! He'd beat me and she knew it." He waved the gun. "I just wanted to be part of the business like everyone else."

Little and I darted looks at each other. I said, "Everyone? Isabel was involved?"

The gun dropped to his side, and his shoulders slumped. "I'd been watching for a while and sneaked into the shack a couple of times wearing a mask just like she did. Kim treated me nice even with my mask on. I stole barrettes from Isabel and gave them to Kim. Isabel saw her wearing them and knew I'd been there."

I remembered how hard it had been to break that padlock. "How did you get in?"

"They always left the key under the chopping log. No one thought I knew. I just wanted to be one of the family."

Little dropped to the sofa. "Isabel kept the girls locked in the shack?"

"She always helped Arnie when she could. She acted all outlaw, putting on the ski mask and disguising herself when she went out there, like it was a game. She bragged she had the perfect excuse if anyone saw her."

"You mean Tommy?" I asked.

Pauly nodded. "She used everybody. She gave rides to Tommy in case someone saw her turn down that road."

"What happened when she caught you at the shack?" Little asked, sinking lower into the sofa.

Pauly sounded like a petulant child. "I only chased her to scare her."

I pictured the back of Isabel's head, and said, "With the axe."

"We used it for firewood out there. When I caught her I knew nothing would keep her from telling him, so I just bashed her one with it."

Little whispered. "You murderer."

Inches from Little's face, Pauly shrieked. "I'm glad I killed her. Everyone thought she was so great. She treated me like her slave. I hated her, and when she was gone Arnie let me into the business like I always wanted."

We didn't say anything, waiting for the tantrum to end.

Pauly yanked at the blinds and checked out the window again. "I have to kill you and get out of here before Wilcox comes."

I licked my dry lips. "Do you love your mom, Pauly?"

"She's a pain with all the church stuff, but yeah."

I moved away from my brother. If Pauly shot at me, I didn't want Little caught in the middle of it. "She confessed to the murders for you. You're going to leave her behind bars, where she will never see the light of day, or you, again? Think how miserable she'll be."

"Nah, she'll be happy in jail, humming and praying, no cleaning or cooking."

Too much white showed in his eyes. He glanced at the window again. "I gotta go." He aimed. "You ready to die?" His jugular jumped.

Little leaped from the sofa toward me. "No!"

The double crack of a pump action shotgun filled the room. We looked toward the sound at the top of the staircase. A dark figure pointed a 12-gauge at Pauly. It was Edgar! His legs were spread and he let out a battle cry that raised the hair on my neck.

Pauly dropped the Ruger and it skidded across the tiles.

Taller and stronger, I yanked his arm behind him with a vicious twist, shoved him face down to the ground, bent close and whispered, "I killed the last person who tried to harm my brother."

He whimpered. "Don't hurt me."

Not letting up on his arm, my knee in his back, I said, "Little, find something to tie him with."

He ran to the kitchen. Drawers crashed open and closed, cupboard doors banged, and he called out. "All I found is a drawer full of bungee cords."

I yanked Pauly upright and pushed him into the kitchen. "You like to tie people to appliances. See how you like this." We wound the bungees around Pauly and through the handles of the stainless double-door refrigerator.

I stood back to assess our handiwork. The worst he could do was open the doors enough to chill himself or maybe pull the refrigerator down on top of him. I wouldn't mind seeing him squashed.

I unzipped the pocket that held my backup camera, moved to the left until the light and shadow were right, focused on his stringy hair, teeth bared in a blue grimace, bungees crisscrossing every part of his body, and started shooting. My camera was still clicking when the squeal of brakes let us know the sheriff arrived.

I looked out the window as several deputy cars sailed down the hill behind him. Lars's car flew down the hill and onto the ice. Ben's truck pulled up beside the sheriff's. Behind him, the SWAT team vehicle arrived, the back door flew open and four SWAT guys jumped out. I remembered that Pauly had my phone, ran back to the kitchen and took it from his back pocket. I hit Wilcox's cell number and yelled into the phone. "Don't let those guys come in here shooting. Pauly's tied up."

In minutes, every law enforcement officer in the county jammed into Edgar's kitchen—Ben, Wilcox, Ray, and most I couldn't name. A bungee snapped a deputy while he attempted to detach Pauly. "They've got him trussed up like a friggin' Thanksgiving turkey."

I wanted to say that Little was a chef, after all, but held my tongue. The deputies handcuffed Pauly and hauled him out. Only then did I remember Edgar at the top of the stairs.

He was no longer standing there. I flew up the steps three at a time, calling his name. A sound came from the bedroom. "I'm in here."

The 90-plus-year-old man lay on the bed, barely breathing.

I kneeled next to him. "You saved our lives, Edgar."

He wheezed. "He shot my phone."

"I'm going to call for an ambulance, okay?"

He nodded. "Please call Henry, too."

I made the calls. Wilcox had already called the ambulance when they left Branson. Henry said he'd be waiting at the hospital.

The heavy shotgun was propped against the wall. I said, "Edgar, you looked so big and strong at the top of the stairs. How did you do that?"

"I had a little help from my friends." He chuckled and coughed from the effort.

I knew he meant his entourage of ghost ancestors, but I still didn't get how the frail old man managed to appear so formidable.

Medics loaded Edgar into the ambulance. Little broke away from Lars, insisting on riding with Edgar. The door slammed and they took off.

I put my arm around Lars. "You okay, big fellah?"

"Yes, now that I know he's safe." Lars' face was still ashen. "I've never been so scared in my life. I just couldn't lose him."

"I felt the same way." We looked away from each other or we'd both start weeping. He sniffed and said, "Hey, Britt, remember when I said how bad you looked earlier at the restaurant?"

"Yeah."

"You look even worse now." I punched his arm.

He said, "I'd better get back to the restaurant. Chum was just down the street at Olafson's, so he's cooking. "

Dee was sitting in the back seat of the sheriff's car. They'd brought her, hoping she could convince Pauly to come out. To protect her son, the woman looked away while young girls were sold into slavery, and she would have let me die in that kitchen. The deputy in the driver's seat nodded when I asked if I could take a photo. The window slid down.

I raised my camera and caught Dee's circle of pink cheek, staring at nothing, and for once she was not humming. I leaned in. "Dee, do you still believe what you did was right, that God was on your side?"

Her eyes like black holes, she said, "God is dead." Moonlight and flickering lights from the law and emergency vehicles created an eerie glow. My camera clicked, and I stepped away and headed for my car.

Always with me, the ache in my rib hardly registered on my pain meter, but I leaned against the SUV, exhausted. A trickle of blood ran down my neck. The wound hadn't hurt when I threw Pauly to the ground, but it did now.

Ben broke away from Wilcox and came over to me. His jaw tight, he said, "Looks like you'll be visiting Nurse Connie and Dr. Fromm again." He got behind the wheel of my SUV.

Wary, I eased into the passenger side. "Don't start in on me. I couldn't wait. He was going to hurt Little."

His hand smacked the steering wheel. "What's wrong with you? This is the third time you've put yourself in serious danger in a week."

I jumped. "I didn't think of it like that."

Ben put the SUV in low gear and it churned up the hill. He expelled a big breath. "I'm just glad it's over and you're both safe." He didn't talk the rest of the way to Branson. I couldn't think of anything to say either.

Dr. Fromm and Nurse Cranky were busy with Edgar, and I was relieved when an intern re-stitched my neck. Fromm and Cranky were so judgmental.

Little, Henry and Ray were still waiting outside Edgar's hospital room. Just as I walked up, Cranky opened the door and told us he was awake. "You can only see him for a few minutes."

Edgar's color was much better, and he seemed alert. Henry touched his shoulder. "Your ticker acted up again. Too much excitement."

Little stood at the foot of Edgar's bed. "Is there anything you need?"

Iron gray braids stark against the white bedding, the old man grumbled. "Pauly ate all my hotdish." We all laughed, and Little said, "I'll make you chicken wild rice hotdish every week for the rest of your life."

Cranky appeared again and shooed us out of the room with a special tsk in my direction. In the waiting area, I asked Henry how Edgar got out of a locked closet.

"Pauly shoved him in the storeroom where he keeps his hunting rifles. It locks, so the great-grandkids can't get in. He hides a tool to open it from the inside, just in case."

I said, "Henry, you should have seen it. He looked tall and strong, like a mighty warrior."

Always impatient, Ray said, "Of course Edgar appeared taller. He stood at the top of the stairs. Your perspective was off and you saw what you wanted to. Typical white people romanticizing the stereotype. We have enough trouble living in two worlds without you making up ghost stories, and spreading them all over town."

Little said, "We wouldn't."

"Like the supernatural Indian burial grounds myth. I heard someone mention that Maelstrom's Resort was on burial grounds. Did it ever occur to you just about everywhere you walk around here is on Native bones?" Ray stalked away.

Henry said, "Ray sees the poverty, alcoholism and abuse every day as part of his job. It's gotten hard for him to see spirit, too."

Cranky entered the waiting area, her white knee-length uniform a starchy rustle. "Henry, you may see your grandfather, but Dr. Fromm said no other visitors today."

Little and I drove to the sheriff's office to make our formal statements, still puzzling over Edgar with that 12-gauge.

Chapter 29

The next morning I drove to Branson so Dr. Fromm could remove my eye bandage. Underneath it my skin was pasty and shrunken. I blinked in the bright light and cried. I hadn't really believed I'd ever see out of it again.

It felt like I was seeing everything for the first time. Dr. Fromm wasn't an alien but a brilliant and dedicated healer. Nurse Connie, a beautiful angel of mercy.

I even fell in love with the snow on the drive back to Spirit Lake.

The diners at Little's were buzzing about the real Maelstrom family. They'd thought Arnie was a war hero who loved his community, and he'd been their friend. Even Isabel was not the Spirit Lake princess everyone knew. Father and daughter were a heartless and greedy team who held their family captive to an awful secret.

We sat at our usual places—Lars behind the counter, Little on the stool next to me, taking a break after the breakfast rush. The guys already commented on how different I looked with two eyes. Little told me he'd been really worried about my eyesight, and I could see his relief.

The *Strib* lay next to my cup. The paper would run the article as a series, and Jason kept the stories coming. Murders solved, attempted murders averted, townspeople's reactions, and tying it to the statewide trafficking issue. Dee's photo made page one along with Arnie's. Pauly was underage, and they decided not to run his photo with the spread.

Ben's investigation featured heavily in the story. Maps of trafficking routes between Vietnam and Minnesota were included along with statistics on the victims. Trung named others in the ring, and Ben said they were dropping like dominoes.

The photo I'd taken of Ly in the dark shack, holding her sick sister in her arms went viral on YouTube, and Ben said donations to organizations working against trafficking skyrocketed.

Little and Lars were peppering me with questions. Lars put his finger on a sidebar in the paper. "Pauly really did all that Number One Son stuff he wrote in his journal?"

Sipping the orange juice Little poured for me, I said, "It was mostly accurate." Wilcox's investigation uncovered Pauly's online journal. His online name was Number One Son. That's how he began each of his journal entries, beginning years ago. No wonder he'd come unglued when Arnie called Quan his number one son. Pauly's description of killing Isabel and getting rid of her body were as graphic as his retelling of Nathan's murder. He didn't know he'd dumped her on my land. If not for timing and Rock's nose, she might never have been found.

Lars shuddered. "I don't get that whole thing about the shack. The girls thought Isabel and Pauly were the same person?"

A couple sitting at the other end of the counter leaned in our direction, eavesdropping. I said, "Isabel and Pauly were similar height and wore down coats and masks. Isabel never spoke or showed her face, so when Pauly spoke to them after Isabel was dead, they assumed it was the same person." The couple nodded, appreciating the clarification.

Reaching across the counter for a bar towel, Little asked, "What's going to happen to him?" Little lifted my glass and wiped up the drips.

I said, "The courts are working it out. Lawyers are arguing about whether Pauly should be tried as an adult. Ben told me he went to visit Pauly, and he only wanted to talk about Arnie."

271

Little wiped the counter in front of him in a circular motion. "I can't believe Nathan knew about the trafficking."

The part about Nathan still disturbed me the most. "He stayed silent because of his love for Isabel, even though it ripped him apart."

Lars shook his head. "That's sick." The couple at the end of the counter nodded in agreement.

"After Isabel's death Nathan finally had enough and threatened to expose Arnie," I said. "His own father ordered Pauly to hang him."

Lars got up to offer refills to the customers, holding the coffee pot as if too heavy to carry. Little went to the kitchen, speaking over his shoulder. "I can't even talk about this, it's so foul."

Little and Lars didn't want to think about what took place a few miles from where we sat, and I didn't either. No one was happy that Spirit Lake was in the spotlight. Not with that kind of news. I stared out the window. A dark cloud hovered in the distance; another storm was blowing in.

As I grabbed my jacket, Ray called my cell. "I've got someone who has something to say to you."

"Who?" I waited for his answer with one arm in my jacket.

"Tommy wants to apologize."

I told Ray I was at Little's and sat back down. He came in half an hour later with Tommy trailing. I led them to a booth next to the window. Ray, in starched khakis with the tribal police insignia, signaled to Tommy to sit. Head bowed and long hair nearly hiding his face, Tommy slid in. Ray sat next to him.

I looked across the table at Tommy. "I thought you'd be in jail again."

He still didn't look up. I appealed to Ray. "Didn't you guys find out he was dealing to get money for his dad?"

Ray ran his hand over his military short hair. "Not exactly, the guy who supplied meth to dealers on the reservations is in jail in Cloud Lake. He goes by the name Snowy. Tommy was one of his contacts and yes, Tommy contacted him to get meth to sell, but we hauled him in before the deal happened."

Jason and I covered that meth ring bust in Cloud Lake not long ago. I'd gotten photos of the pot-bellied dealer with stringy brown hair being led out of his house in handcuffs. "Snowy snitched on Tommy?" I asked.

Lars held up the coffee pot from his station behind the counter, and caught Ray's eye. Ray nodded to Lars, and turned back to me. "Snowy eventually snitched on everyone to try to get a lighter sentence."

Lars brought three cups of coffee, but didn't stay to chat. He must have picked up on my angry vibe. "Tommy, where did you get the $5,000?" My voice sounded accusing, but I didn't care.

Ray elbowed him. "Go ahead."

Tommy tossed his hair back and finally looked at me, a little bit defiant, but mostly scared. "Isabel gave it to me."

I came out of my seat and grabbed him by his jacket. "You knew about the trafficking? I can't believe what a liar you are. You acted so surprised about the shack."

He ducked as if afraid I'd smack him. "I swear I didn't know about the trafficking. I'd been telling Isabel about my dad and needing money. We passed that pullout where the tracks were, and I said I was going to check for poachers."

I let go of him and sat back down. "Go on."

Tommy swallowed. "She wanted to know if I'd seen anything in that area, but I hadn't. She said if I stayed away from that part of the woods she'd give me the $5,000, but I couldn't ask any questions. I was desperate so I said okay."

"Come on. You didn't figure out she was hiding something bad enough to be worth $5,000 to keep you quiet?"

"I figured she was into something illegal but I never thought about that. I mean, I sold drugs, I got it that she didn't want a lot of questions." His gaze slid away.

"That sounds like a crock to me." I looked over at Ray. "Do you believe him?"

Ray nodded. "It checks out. Isabel made a $5,000 withdrawal from her personal bank account the day after Tommy said they had the conversation."

I leaned into Tommy's face. "That's why you shot the arrow at me? To keep Isabel's secret?"

He put a hand up, ready to protect himself from my blows. "I swear I didn't mean to get that close. You turned right into it. I'm sorry!"

Ray's face looked thunderous. "What are you two talking about? Why would you shoot at Britt? Isabel was already dead, for one thing."

Tommy glanced at the door as if wishing he could make a run for it, but Ray had him boxed in. He looked first at me, then Ray. "I wanted to scare Britt away. I was afraid Wilcox would take the $5,000 back. I'd already told the guys who were after my dad I had the money for them, and was just waiting for a chance to get down to Mille Lacs."

Ray slapped his hand on the counter so hard the people two booths away jumped. "And you were going to sell meth to get the rest. I thought you learned in rehab how bad you were hurting your own people by selling drugs." He held up his hand and ticked off on his fingers the problems it caused. "That stuff is responsible for most of the domestic violence, assaults, burglaries, child abuse and every other problem on the rez."

Tommy's chin came up. "I didn't sell any meth this time."

"But you were planning to, and you could have killed Britt with that arrow." Ray nailed him with the hard law enforcement stare. "Jesus, could you have made any worse decisions?"

Tommy stared out the window, watching sheets of snow blowing across the lake. He didn't have an answer.

My anger at Tommy morphed into disappointment. Maybe not a bad kid, but Ray had it right, he made really bad decisions. I looked over at Ray. "I suppose you'll throw him in jail." After all, he was Sergeant Ray "by the book" Stevens.

He bristled. "It's always about retribution with you white people." He put a hand on Tommy's shoulder. "Tommy was trying to help his father the only way he knew how. We're not condoning that, but we're taking it under consideration. The council is meeting to discuss it. In the meantime, he'll be held in the Cloud Lake tribal jail."

I felt like I'd just been scolded, but relived that Tommy would likely get another chance. "Wilcox is okay with this?"

"We worked it out." Ray sighed. "Unless you're pressing charges. I didn't know about the arrow."

My newly exposed eye drooped with fatigue, and I wanted to go home. "I won't, but Tommy, you need to come back to the rehab center meetings."

He nodded, and said, "I'm sorry I didn't tell them about the shack right away when you dropped me off at the sheriff's. I know it's no excuse, but Isabel getting killed and Wilcox blaming me and my dad in trouble—I couldn't."

"I should have gone in to talk to Wilcox myself," I said, aware that there were a lot of things I should have done differently the past two weeks.

"No, it's on me." He looked at the ceiling.

He still wasn't great at eye contact. "How's everything with your dad now?" I asked.

"I couldn't get the rest of the money for him so he took off. He didn't want me to get back into dealing for him. He said it was better for me not to know where he went."

That was good news, at least for Tommy. "Will you be safe from those loan sharks?"

"I guess I'll be okay."

Ray said, "The Mille Lacs tribal police have cracked down so they've moved on to other casinos. They'll probably be back though." He nodded at Tommy. "You ready to go?"

We all stood up. "Let me know when you're back home," I said to Tommy. "I might have some work for you in Branson helping out with a sick guy at night, if you're interested." Cynthia needed help with her husband and this might be the solution.

"Sure, if I can figure out the transportation."

I thanked Ray for his help in Mille Lacs and said goodbye.

Wishing I could have one more chance to see Ben before making that overdue call to L.A., I headed home, resigned. That wasn't going to happen.

Chapter 30

Marta left multiple calls and emails over the past week, and I was ready to give her my decision. I sat at the round oak table and tapped in her number.

She sounded even more harried than usual. "It's about time you called. I'm tired of getting all my information about you from Cynthia, especially since she only knows what you're doing *after* the fact."

"I'm sorry." I launched into my recent travails, but ringing phones and a loud hum of conversation in the background competed for Marta's attention. "Just tell me your decision."

I told her my conditions.

"Agreed. Can you make a flight today?"

"You're kidding, right?"

"Tomorrow, then. You need to meet with the reporter. You're flying to Jordan in three days to cover that mess in Syria. Oh, and Britt, I'm thrilled to have you back." Her phone clicked off. Marta always wanted everything yesterday.

Jangled by the conversation and Marta's quick hang up, I pulled on my ski jacket and snowshoes and set out with Rock. I pulled my cap low over my forehead against the chill and headed for the southern tip of my property. Rock stayed close, his black and white tail swishing back and forth. Maybe he sensed this would be our last hike together for a long time.

My heart rate spiked when I reached my destination. I stared at the spot where I'd tripped over Isabel's boots. Ben had told me the latest on the Maelstroms. Dee sat in jail and spewed nonstop invectives at God. Satan was her new pal. Arnie was on suicide watch while awaiting trial. When he learned he created the monster who killed his daughter, he slit his tattooed arm. Guards found him before he bled to death.

I'd held out against the freezing temperature long enough on this trek back to where it all began, and turned toward home. What did I expect to find out here, anyway, closure? I thought I'd learned long ago not to be surprised at the way humans treated each other. And my body still felt like a punching bag. Perhaps the battle zone I was headed into would be less dangerous.

Late-afternoon, I went to Little's to tell the guys my decision, but chickened out and looped around the block to Bella's. As always, she sat in her rocker by the window, CNN on the wall-mounted sixty-four-inch television.

Bella pointed her knitting needle at the TV. "I should have been a big shot journalist instead of wasting my talents here."

I dropped into one of the comfortable salon chairs. "You have the best nose for news of anyone I've ever met, Bella."

She pointed the remote to lower the volume. "You should go back to the *LA Times* and do the Middle East trip. That part of the world is never going to be the same—experience of a lifetime."

Bella snubbed me at Isabel's funeral when she heard I might leave. I wondered what caused the change. I'd turned over the rock and revealed the underside of Spirit Lake, and many of the townspeople probably resented me for doing that. I detected something else in Bella's words though, more like a parent who wants her child to achieve an unfulfilled dream.

Violet came into the shop from their residence on the other side of the duplex, brightening when she saw me. "Oh good, let's get to work on you."

"What do you think, ladies?" I lifted my mop of hair. "Is it time to chop this off?"

Bella concentrated on her knitting. "Leave it. It suits you." My jaw dropped. Bella had been after me to cut my hair since I was a teenager.

"It will help hide the scars," said Violet. "Not that they show. Not really."

Violet shampooed, deep-conditioned and trimmed my hair. She waxed my brows. "Tell me if it hurts, hon. Your poor eye still looks sore, but your neck looks better. In fact, I'm just going to put on a dab of makeup to even out your skin tone."

When finished, she held up a hand mirror so I could inspect her work. I touched my hair. It did have a healthier shine. My brows were nicely arched, my skin rosy. I looked like a normal person again. "Thank you, Violet." Before I knew it, she threw her ample arms around me, and I hugged her back.

Bracing myself against the cold, I stepped out of Bella's intending to go to Little's for dinner, but passed it by and went home. I could tell the guys in the morning.

At the cabin, I threw on a flannel shirt Ben left when Gert was alive. It no longer smelled like him, but I hugged myself and pretended it was him. I knew I'd need to tell him, too. I added more wood to the stove and sat with my feet on the warm brick platform. Rock jumped up beside me in the swivel rocker. He'd stay with Little and Lars until I returned. I stroked his fur, lonely already. Near midnight, I went to the kitchen to make chamomile tea. Maybe that would bring the sleep fairy.

I was pouring hot water over my teabag when Rock bounded up from the rocker, barking at the door. I peeked out the window, but the vehicle's headlights blinded me, and I couldn't see who got out of the car.

The late night visitor knocked. I knew there were no immediate threats but waited until Rock's tail wagged, and then opened the door. Ben filled the doorway looking like he was after a suspect. He said, "I saw your light."

I tried to read him, figure out what he wanted, but my heart beat too hard to think.

He squinted. "Are you inviting me in?"

I stood aside, remembering how he'd slammed his hand against the steering wheel at Edgar's, frustrated that I'd gone in to face Pauly alone. My voice small, I asked, "Want tea?"

"No, I don't want tea." He shut the door behind him and I stepped back, but he moved in close and locked eyes with me. "I'm here to tell you I'm over it."

My shoulders drooped. "I know you're over me." He needed to make a midnight call to rub it in?

He hung his jacket on the coat rack. "I meant I'm over trying to stay away from you. You were right. I've been a coward."

I dropped to the sofa, groaning. "I've taken the L.A. job. I leave tomorrow night."

A corner of his mouth twitched. "I didn't ask you to stay."

Another mixed message? I grabbed a photography book from the end table to chuck at him, but didn't get the chance.

He sat next to me, and his lips brushed against my ear. "I love you, and I will be here for you in three months or six or whenever you come back."

I loosened my grip and the book dropped to the floor. "I don't understand. You've been so angry at me."

He took my hands in both of his, pulling me closer to him. "I was mad at you. I wanted to hurt you back, but mostly I just wanted you to disappear. When Marta called, I knew you'd go, and I realized how much you mean to me. I couldn't let you leave without telling you."

My voice flat, I said, "You're going to hate me again."

Ben let go of my hands. "I'm not going to hate you." His thumb tucked my hair behind my ear, and I moved into his touch like a cat, almost purring. He said, "But I hope you'll come back some time."

After so many weeks of Ben ignoring me, the full impact of his hazel eyes on mine, his hands touching me, breathing in his woodsy scent, and his warm body so close to mine overwhelmed me. When I could talk, I said, "I am coming back. I agreed to work for the *Times* as an independent contractor. I can choose my assignments."

He stood, and his voice took on a harder edge. "Of course, Marta knows if the story involves danger and innocent victims, you'd never turn it down."

Attempting to get a grip on my emotions, I said, "It's not Marta's fault. It's me. I don't know why I have to keep doing this work, but I do."

Ben sighed. "Do you ever think it might be about your dad—redemption always out of reach, no matter what you do?"

My chest tight, I said, "I can't think about that right now, but Marta needs me immediately."

His strong arms lifted me to my feet. He kissed me, and said, "I need you immediately, too."

Everything else flew from my mind. We undressed and slid under my comforters. I'd imagined this moment many times. It would be smooth, like all those things we did so well together— pitching a tent, guiding the wires and moving around the periphery letting the tension determine the next step, or paddling a canoe in unison as we glided through the lake or river, and that thrilling rush of pleasure when we navigated rapids and quietly came to rest along the shore.

It wasn't like that, though. Our bodies were taut as fishing lines because this would be the first time and possibly the last time for a long while. It was rowdy and messy and awkward and hungry, and I never wanted it to end.

He sat at the oak table drinking his morning coffee, his dark hair tousled, looking much less dangerous than the night before. Suspect in custody. I'd wanted him for more than a year and been thwarted at every turn. Last night's first lovemaking experience was a double whammy of delayed satisfaction and makeup sex all at once. I was pretty sure I'd pulled some stitches.

He'd flipped my world upside down. I said, "You're making it really hard for me."

His tone was light. "I wanted you to have something to remember, so you'd come back."

Even though my mood didn't match his, I played along. "Sure of yourself, aren't you? Some would say cocky."

He swigged his coffee to cover up how pleased he was with himself. Maybe I overdid the joyful sounds last night, although it was out of my control.

He checked his phone messages, and frowned. "I hate to go, but I've got to get back to work." I watched him stretch and set his cup in the sink. Just a few hours ago, my fingers traveled down his warm back, touching each vertebra, every hollow and rise.

He wandered to the bookcase and picked up my photo of Gert, Ben and me at Winter's resort. "I still miss her," I said.

He set the photo on the shelf. "Every time I walk through that door I expect her to be here."

"Is it too weird that I'm living in her cabin, with Rock?"

He scratched Rock's ears. "It's where you belong. At least part of the time, for now."

I stood close to him and put my arms around his waist. "Don't go yet."

He lifted my hair and kissed my neck below the scar. "I guess I don't have to leave right away." He kissed the spot above my ear where Tommy's arrow pierced my skin. He kissed my eye and I thought if he'd only done that sooner, it would have healed instantly. He kissed my bruised ribs, I groaned, and dragged him back to the bedroom.

Before Ben headed to the Chippewa National Forest, I asked him to give Gert's old Bronco to Tommy so he could help out nights with Cynthia's husband.

I made a quick trip to Branson to tell Cynthia I was leaving. She didn't seem to mind me quitting the bureau on literally no notice. Her mouth curled. "We'll survive." She said she'd go back to using a couple of local photographers on contract. She offered a real smile. "Tommy's help at home will make a huge difference in my energy."

Jason was out on assignment so I called him on my way back to Spirit Lake. I knew he'd liked all the excitement of the past few weeks. He'd gotten lots of kudos for the Maelstrom stories. He said he was sorry I was leaving, but would probably still be at the bureau when I returned. "I'm starting to think my folks were right about being a journalist," he said.

I called Thor and she was slightly miffed that I hadn't stopped to see her, but told me she decided to stay with the sheriff's office for another year. That might also have had an impact on Jason's enthusiasm for the job.

A man of even fewer words than Ben, Woz handed the phone to Jenna when I called to thank him again for rescuing me. Jenna told me that Brody was still sad and confused, but Amber was helping him through it.

My last call was to Ly. She said they were being tutored in English and were all excited about starting school. She said, "This is the American life we imagined."

Unable to avoid it any longer, I pulled into Little's, dreading the upcoming conversation. Little and Lars stood behind the counter. I took a mental picture of them—my tiny brother with eyebrows like golden wings above sapphire blue eyes, and Lars, with his barrel chest and long arms, all the better to protect Little. That's how I would think of them during my absence.

I'd rehearsed my speech on the drive. I sat on my usual stool at the counter and dove in. "Little, every day I watch you research recipes, pore over cookbooks, spend hours preparing wonderful meals for people to gobble up in a few minutes, and then you start all over again. Why?"

He shrugged. "It's what I do. What are you getting at?"

I looked directly at him. "I took the L.A. job. It's what *I* do." I hurried to add. "The job's not full time."

He wiped a spot on the counter. "Tricky." I expected recriminations, tantrums, arguments or even the silent treatment, but Little and Lars remained composed.

"Not full time?" Little came around the counter and sat next to me. Lars sat on my other side. It made me nervous when they did the divide and conquer.

"I'm on contract. I'll be gone three months max." I sipped the hot cocoa in front of me. "I'll always come back to Spirit Lake between assignments. It's my permanent address."

Lars leaned around me and winked at Little. "It works."

Little said, "Only don't shut me out about where you are and what you're doing."

Lars' big head bobbed. "He does get frenetic about your well-being."

"I did that so you wouldn't worry so much, but I promise to keep in touch this time." I pushed my cocoa away. I didn't have an appetite.

Little looked at me, his eyes sad, but proud. "You belong out there doing your crusader thing."

"I'm leaving in a few hours. I know it's short notice, and I'm sorry about that."

His eyebrows lifted. "So soon?"

I ducked my head. I should have told him right away. Sometimes I can be such a juvenile.

He said, "That's okay. I've been thinking about my abandonment issues and I'm ready to move on. Facing down Pauly changed me. I feel like I'm a badass like you now." Little grinned and we did a fist bump.

Lars beamed like a proud papa. "Very good, children. Shall we have a group hug?"

I packed two bags. One held clothes and the other contained my camera equipment and laptop. In less than two hours, I'd closed up the cabin and Rock and I were back at Little's. The restaurant smelled like apple pie.

I dropped my bags at the door. Henry was picking me up in a few minutes. Edgar had an appointment at a Minneapolis hospital that specialized in diabetes treatment, and I was hitching a ride to the airport to catch the redeye. I'd stay with Marta for a day until flying out of the country. Even with a heavy heart, I couldn't deny a spark of anticipation over the assignment.

Lars said Little needed me in the kitchen, code for he didn't want to make a scene in front of the customers. Familiar frown line between his eyes deeper than usual, Little handed me a bag heavy with enough food for a two-day journey. "Remember what you promised, Britt."

"I remember." I knew he'd worry anyway, but I'd contact him as often as possible. We hugged and said goodbye.

Henry pulled up and tooted his horn. I waved from the window and took one last, long look around at the usual crowd—locals lined up at the counter, Chloe ducking in and out of the kitchen, families filling the booths.

Lars walked out with me and tossed my bags in the back seat. He wrapped his big arms around me. "Be safe."

I scratched Rock's ears and told him to take care of the guys, fighting down the lump in my throat. I slid into the back seat, shivering in my thin city boots and black leather jacket, the outfit I'd had on when I came to Spirit Lake a year ago. My zippered down coat hung from a peg in the cabin with Bella's yellow scarf.

Little came outside and the three of them stood under the Little's Café sign. My chest nearly bursting with love, I waved goodbye, clutching the wolf agate in my jeans pocket. I was leaving my pack—an unnatural act—to enter a bloody, war-torn famine and drought-ridden hell hole where I'd take too many dangerous chances. Maybe Ben was right about what compelled me. The black spot on my soul had shrunk a little and I wasn't running away from bad memories this time, but there were always innocent victims like Ly, Hanh, Binh and Kim. Someone had to document their stories.

Henry passed Lars' garage and pulled onto the highway heading south. He glanced at me in the rearview mirror and smiled, his eyes disappearing behind his cheeks. "You'll be back soon."

Edgar dozed for most of the four-hour drive. He woke when we pulled up to the terminal, grinned, and wagged a gnarly finger at me. "Keep your eyes open for the ancestors. I'm sending a dispatch to watch over you."

I said goodbye, hitched my camera bag over my shoulder, and entered the terminal pulling my suitcase behind me. My eyes framed the scene of people arriving and departing. In the distance, the ghostly group melted into the crowd.

Acknowledgments

Special thanks to my dear friend and tireless reader, editor and supporter, Julie Williams; first readers Rae James and Michele Drier; Jennifer Fisher for asking a key question; my talented and wonderful mystery critique group, Pam Giarrizzo, Michele Drier, Mertianna Georgia, and June Gillam; Amherst Artists and Writers workshop leader, copyeditor and all around amazing person, Jan Haag; to my fellow Sisters in Crime, and Gail Baugniet for trading manuscripts; Beth White, proofreader; Karen Phillips, cover artist; cover photographer, Brittany Hedin, and Rob Preece, formatter. To Fred Cotton for his information on small planes—I hope I got it right; Finally, I'd like to thank my husband, Gary Delsohn, for his loving support, and my children, Joseph and Amanda, who inspire me every single day.

About the Author

Linda Townsdin worked for years in communications for nonprofit and corporate organizations, most recently as writer/editor for a national criminal justice consortium. Townsdin's work included editorial and marketing assistance in projects involving cybercrime, tribal justice and other public safety issues. Her short fiction has been published in several anthologies, including the *2013 Capitol Crimes Anthology*. She lives in California with her husband, and wouldn't trade her childhood in Northern Minnesota for anything. http://lindatownsdin.com/

Made in the USA
Monee, IL
09 October 2023

44290809R00166